The Trouble with Evie

Book One
The
Hades
Series

TM WATKINS

2022 eBook / 2025 Paperback

This book is a work of fiction. The names of characters, places and incidents are products of the writer's imagination and are not to be interpreted as real. Any resemblance to persons, living or dead, actual events, locals or organizations is entirely coincidental. With the exception of quotes used in reviews, this book may not be reproduced or used in whole or in part by any means existing without written permission from the author.

Cover Design by Brosedesignz.

www.brosedesignz-bookcovers.com

If you wish to contact the author, please visit: www.tmwatkinsauthor.com

ISBN: 978-1-7637195-3-8

SERIES ORDER

The Trouble with Evie
The Trouble with Hades

CONTENTS

CHAPTER 1

My uncle slowed the vehicle behind the parked car, sighing heavily as he pulled the handbrake on. Ahead of us was the real estate agent, beaming a smarmy smile that held little honesty. The guy was certainly pleasant, fawning all over Brad as if he was going to snap up this amazing deal with whirlwind speed. Little did he know that my uncle had zero interest in the house so long as the structure was sound and it was cheap.

"What number are we up to now?"

"For what? Houses that we've looked at or towns that we've moved to? Both are in double digits."

Brad smiled thinly. His sympathy was lacking, as always.

"Houses that we've looked at."

"This is house number twelve."

"It's certainly more promising than the last one. Come on, let's get this over and done with."

Brad turned off the engine, and the windscreen wipers stopped halfway across the glass. We'd been in Hades for a week, and it hadn't stopped raining. Quite literally. I have not heard a single minute where there hasn't been some form of rain. From a light patter to torrential, it was endless.

"Are you sure you want to live in this town? The name is kind of creepy."

I was expecting the devil to jump out from behind a bush. So far, the only thing that's jumped out at us was a rat. It was in the loading dock at the bed and breakfast we were staying at. Brad had gone down there to collect a delivery, insisting I helped him with the boxes.

"We don't have a choice. Got to go where the boss says, and that's all there is to it."

"Well, you might want to ring your boss and tell him to send umbrellas and raincoats. Maybe a rowboat might be ideal, too."

Brad chuckled as we approached the real estate agent. Like everyone else, this guy assumed that Brad was my father. I looked like Brad. There was no doubt that we were related.

We both had chocolate brown hair and deep green eyes. We were fair-skinned and tall. The only difference, aside from our genders and ages, was that Brad had developed a bit of a potbelly.

Sometimes, Brad would correct a person if they assumed wrong. Sometimes, he didn't bother at all. I guess he only wanted to make sure they didn't think that he was some pervert who was dating a teenager. If they thought that, then they were clearly blind. Brad and I were definitely two peas in a pod.

"Glad you made it, Brad. Did you find the place okay?"

"Yeah, easy as."

He nodded, then turned to me. The artificially whitened teeth stood out in the gleaming smile. I tried not to stare. Tom was a man who liked to keep up his image. I'd only seen him a couple of times for these viewings, but it was obvious that the man had invested a lot of money into the view. Like the fake tan and the pristine suits, the chunky gold ring on his finger, or the fancy watch on his wrist. Tom Garrow was the perfect image of a man who was good at his job and showed it in his appearance.

"What do you think, Evelyn?"

"Well, it's more promising than the last," I muttered. "At least the front door is where it's supposed to be."

The smile faded as he stared at me. He didn't know what to say or how to respond.

"She's joking." Brad interrupted, then stepped between us to cut us off.

As they walked to the footpath, Brad frowned at me. I shrugged. As if I was going to be anything less than honest. The last place did not have a front door, literally. It was sitting on the front lawn, sodden and broken. Inside was completely trashed with graffiti, someone had started a fire in the living room, and there were a lot of used needles and a homemade bong. After seeing the needles, I turned around and sat in the car.

I could deal with bongs, fires, and graffiti, but used needles were dangerous. I wasn't prepared to clean them up, and I didn't think Brad should either. When he asked me what was wrong, I told him exactly what I thought, and unfortunately for him, the real estate agent was right beside him. I didn't care what he thought. It was sheer rudeness to present a house for rent in such a state. If it happened overnight, then I'd say, fair enough, these things happen. But it was evident that the mess or the damage was not new.

From the sidewalk, there were two steps up to the path that cut through the lush green lawn. The front garden didn't have a fence. Instead, a rock wall sat as high as the top step, the garden filled with pretty flowers. Everything looked well-maintained, and I knew that this was not the house for us. I was not a gardener, and Brad never had time to do anything.

He worked for a company in connection with the government. I don't know exactly what they did. It had something to do with technology, phones, and the internet. I'm sure if I was actually interested, he'd tell me. It was a home-based job, something that was not planned and would not remain that way for much longer, not now that I'm almost eighteen. He'd taken this role so that he could raise me. It was his suggestion after my mother's funeral three years ago. I had no idea where my father was. I had never met the man, and neither had Brad.

He wasn't aware of it at the time, but I knew the truth about my mother. She was a prostitute, and it was highly likely that my father was one of her clients. She probably didn't know who my father was either.

Brad was only ten years older than me. He was the late-in-life miracle my grandparents were unaware of until my grandmother started getting horrible stomach pains. One trip to the A&E, and she was pushing his fat head out.

I never knew my grandparents. They died together in a plane crash about a year before I was born.

Initially, Brad and I struggled. I was used to a life where I was usually on my own at night and in school during the day. Essentially, I'd raised myself. I missed my mother, and I still got upset when I thought of her, but it's not like I really knew her. As for Brad, I guess he never expected to have a sullen teenager tossed at him when he was in his mid-twenties. It's not as if he was going out every night, partying with his mates, or bringing women home, but it was still weird, and it took a long time to get past it and become what we are now.

He knew of me, but I'd never met him until the funeral. Brad and my mother rarely saw each other. At least, I think that's how it was. Brad never talks about my mother, and if I bring up something about her, he shrugs. They were not close.

Stepping under the front porch, I looked back at the street. It was pretty. I'll give it that much.

Trees lined the street. Houses were well maintained. I

don't know when anyone in this town was able to tend to their gardens without getting completely drenched, but this place and the houses around it, they were well-maintained.

"Does it ever stop raining?"

The real estate agent had been smiling, now frozen, as he stared at me. I frowned, waiting for him to respond.

"Yes, the forecast says that the weekend should be dry."

Opening the door, the agent started telling Brad about the place. I looked out at the grey sky and wondered how that would clear up by tomorrow.

Entering the house, I was pretty surprised at how spacious it was. The first floor had a lounge room, dining room, kitchen, and guest room. I doubt we would ever have guests stay overnight, so I'm sure Brad will commandeer the space for work.

We'd inspected the three bedrooms upstairs as well as the attic. Apparently, I could have that if I wanted it. The space was certainly large enough to accommodate a bed, maybe a small lounge. It was even wired, so I could have a television, too.

When we'd finished looking at the upper levels, the agent took us down to the basement. It looked as if no one ever came down here, not even to store their junk. The agent found a broom in the closet, testing each wooden step before stepping onto it.

"This place is old," he murmured. "Turn of the last

century, I think. If you're interested in the place, we'll get a builder in to check the stairs."

"It's fine. I can deal with them."

Brad was apparently a handyman now, too. I never knew that. To be fair, I don't think he knew it before today, either. I waited at the top of the stairs, expecting something dire to happen. The house was not creepy or anything terrible like that. It just felt ominous to me.

I don't know why he was volunteering for the job. This place was a rental. It was the owner's job to maintain it to be safe. Thankfully, the real estate agent said they have someone to deal with the issues.

Warily, I walked down the stairs, looking around at the cinder block walls. I thought no one had been down here, but there was something strangely new about the area. Not recently, but perhaps within the last fifty years or so.

Brad and the agent were discussing the pipes and the heating. I ran my hand over the cold blocks, feeling the dust grate against my palm. Something thumped, almost like a dull clunk of a drum. I stopped, waiting to see if it would happen again. It didn't, but the brick warmed under my hand. Moving it to the next brick, I didn't expect it to be warm, too. I kept going, soon finding a cold brick. It was odd. Just one section was warm.

"Is there a hot water pipe behind this wall?"

Hearing their shoes scratch over the dirty floor, I turned to look at my uncle and the agent.

"I wouldn't think so, but anything is possible. Now, what do you think about the place?"

"It's great," Brad offered. "If we can organize it, I'd like to move in as soon as possible. The bed and breakfast is nice but not ideal for the teenager when the pub is so close."

"Of course. I'm sure that we can get things moving quickly."

The two of them walked to the stairs, discussing what needed to be done before we moved in.

"Cleaning," I muttered. "No doubt the person who isn't working yet will be the one assigned to the grand task."

Pulling my hand away, I watched as a crack between the bricks appeared. It was small, but it was there. Brad was already at the top of the stairs. I rushed after him.

"There's a crack in the bricks."

He nodded, seemingly not concerned.

"I'll get the builder in to look at everything." the agent said. "He'll be here looking at the stairs anyway."

Brad watched the agent as he walked through the corridor to the living area of the house.

"We need a place, Evie. I can't keep working in that little hole."

"Yeah, I know."

"It's a good place. Close to the school, the shops."

My derisive stare must have said it all.

"I know, Evie, I do, and I'm sorry. You're going to have to repeat the year to get it finished."

"You know, I'm blaming your boss for this. I don't need to do the year again. I just need to remain in one town for long enough to finish what I've started."

"Well, hopefully, it will be this town. Besides, you know it's better to start from the beginning."

I'd gotten the first month of the school year done when his boss hinted at relocating. Brad asked him to hold out for as long as possible so that I could finish the year out. We'd gotten three-quarters of the way there when the jerk said he couldn't wait any longer, and Brad had to move. As my legal guardian and with no other relative to send me to, Brad had to take me with him.

Brad had stalled as much as he could, but with a deadline looming, he couldn't stay any longer. We had to move.

So, this was us, moving to the little town called Hades. Apparently, it was named after the town founder, Reginald Hades. I looked at the map and thought it was Hades, as in Hell, but that was not the case. His name was pronounced Hah-dess, and that's how everyone in this place said the town name. I didn't believe it. I think that we really are in Hell.

CHAPTER 2

Brad gave me an uneasy smile as we walked through the corridor. It was the same as every other school that I'd been to. Bland white walls lined with dull green lockers. Doors and notice boards broke up the monotonous path with the occasional water fountain.

The stench of this place was all too familiar to me. I disliked school. If he'd asked me what I wanted, rather than telling me what the right thing to do was, I would have gladly told Brad that I was happiest out of places like these. I'd rather get a job and start earning money.

He knew that I didn't want to be here. I'd complained enough. We discussed it, argued, and reached a rational agreement that leaned toward his demands rather than mine. I had to accept it and move on.

Still, I protested all that I could.

Brad's argument was simple. No certificate of completion, no job. Apparently, it was necessary in this crazy world. So, I had no choice, and I had to get this done. My only consolation was that his employer had given him a written guarantee that he would not ask Brad to move to a new location within this school year.

That was one of my biggest issues. I was repeating the year. Things that I already knew, I had to sit through again. Brad said that I might learn something new, but I doubted it.

Brad had given his employer a hard time about moving, stating that I was almost there and then he would not need to be tied to one town anymore. Once I was out of school, we could go anywhere, anytime. So, his boss agreed to let us remain in this town until the year was done. All I had to do was pass.

Pushing the door open, Brad waited as I walked into the administration office. The woman behind the counter looked at us with a smile and a friendly greeting. It was the same old situation, just a different location and different people.

"This is Evelyn Newton. I'm her uncle, Brad. We've got an enrolment meeting at one pm."

"Of course," the woman said with a chirpy eagerness that was sickening. "Have you got the transfer and enrollment documents?"

Brad fumbled through his folder, searching for the papers he'd completed last night. After three years of doing this, I would have thought he'd be used to the mountain of paperwork that came with being a guardian for a child. Yet here he was, pulling out random pieces of paper.

The woman smiled, glancing at me like I'd be able to help him. With a huff, I pulled the folder out of his hands and put it on the counter. The request for the file transfer was on top. She accepted it and turned to the fax machine.

"Who uses a fax machine?" I whispered. "Wouldn't it be easier to scan and email?"

Brad shrugged.

"Looks done to me. You're too technical."

I scoffed at him.

That was a ridiculous statement.

I was not technical at all. I didn't even have a mobile phone.

When the woman returned, I held out the enrolment form and the payment details form. Yes, this was a private school and the only one in this dumb town. That was another complaint that Brad had for his employer. All the towns we have been to have had a variety of choices. I was always enrolled in a government-owned school, which meant that it was free.

Brad was yet to hear back about that one. I think he secretly hoped for a little financial assistance from his employer. It was a long shot but one that I thought was worth it. After all, he was given money to move our things around this country. Why shouldn't he be compensated for something beyond his control?

The woman took the paperwork and disappeared

through a door after telling us she would advise the new enrolment officer that we were there. Brad and I were left to twiddle our thumbs like a pair of clueless fools.

I looked around the small room, noting that we were not alone. A teen boy sat on a chair in the corner of the room.

It appeared that he was waiting to be picked up. His bag was at his feet, flopped to the floor with the top zipper open. Books were ready to spill out of the bag, but I don't think the guy cared.

His head lifted, and when his eyes connected with mine, I frowned. The door next to the desk opened and distracted me. When I turned back, the kid was still looking at me, but it was different now. I could have sworn his eyes were purple.

"Brad, Evelyn, welcome. I'm Maria, the enrolment officer. Please, come this way, and we'll have a little chat."

Maria turned back to the doorway, and I looked at Brad.

"What?" he whispered.

"That kid had purple eyes."

Brad looked at me like I was crazy.

"They would be blue if anything. How can you see that well? He's at the far end of the room."

"It's a small room, and clearly, you need to get your eyes checked."

My grumbled whispers were over now that we had entered Maria's office. She smiled and gestured to the chairs in front of her desk.

"So, you're new to Hades. What brings you to our lovely little town?"

"Work," Brad offered. "I travel because of my job, and it was necessary to come here. My employer has a government contract for the mobile communications network."

Maria's eyes brightened as she listened. Most didn't care to hear what Brad had to say. Just get us in, fill out the paperwork, and throw me into a classroom.

"How interesting. Must be difficult to be so unsettled."

"I'm used to it, but it's been hard for Evie."

Maria's attention turned to me, offering a sympathetic smile.

"Well, hopefully, you'll be able to complete this year with us."

"She will. I have assurances that I will not be asked to move before Evie has completed her schooling."

"I guess that means Hades will get a few mobile phone towers. We've always had poor reception."

The conversation continued, and Brad was lapping up the attention. I noted the lack of bling on her fingers. Either she was unmarried or not into rings. It was highly likely that the attention-starved freak beside me had also noticed that.

I tuned out, letting my mind wander as I stared at the bland white cinder block walls. Behind Maria's desk was a bookshelf stacked with colorful folders and a few trinkets that looked like they'd been made by a kid. Maybe they were from her kids. Perhaps they came from someone in this school that she was close to. I didn't know nor care to find out, merely floating through the thoughts until my uncle stopped flirting with her.

His phone started ringing. I snapped back to the room and the conversation, turning from the idyllic view of the garden outside the window. It was far more interesting than the bland wall, drawing me in with ease.

Maria offered her usual warm smile while my uncle fumbled to switch it off.

"Sorry," he murmured.

"It's alright, Brad. I'm surprised it was actually working, to be honest. Usually, this office is a dead spot for all mobile phones. Anyway, everything seems to be in order, so I think we're done here. Evie's files from her last school will be here soon, which is the only thing we're waiting for. In the meantime, we'll formulate a timetable for the term, and it will be ready for her Monday morning. Evie, if you come into the office, Jane will have it ready for you."

"Sure."

Maria stood and walked to the door, guiding us back to the reception area. The guy with purple eyes was gone, which I found rather annoying. I wanted to see if I was right. Were they just a rich blue, and I was seeing the impossible, or had I really seen the loveliest shade of purple? As we walked through the reception area, I wondered if he was wearing contacts. That would make a lot more sense.

Once he finished his over-the-top goodbye, Brad urged me through the main door like he thought the place was on fire.

"What is wrong with you?" I snapped.

"I have no idea, but that woman just had a really creepy vibe to her."

I stopped, feeling the harsh glare of the sun beating down on me. I didn't care at the moment, too stunned by what Brad had said.

"Wait," I drawled out. "You weren't flirting with her?"

Brad spluttered with shock.

"Seriously? No way in hell. I was trying to get through a painful situation. Did she strike you as odd?"

"Good Lord, Bradley. When did you become so forgetful? I have said for the past week that this place is odd. Did you see the guy's purple eyes?"

"No."

"I thought he might have been wearing contacts."

"Maybe. It seems a bit odd to wear colored contacts to school, don't you think?"

"Like I said, this whole town is odd. It's odd with a capital peculiar."

Brad frowned as he shook his head, unable to hide his amusement.

"Sounds like the perfect town for you, Evie."

"Said the mayor of Weirdsville."

"Come on, let's get out of here. So glad that I don't have to return to this place every weekday for the next year."

"Excluding holidays," I said, jabbing his ribs with my elbow.

"Oh, I don't know. Maybe you could benefit from entering the summer lesson cramming sessions they're holding in the gym."

I sneered as Brad held out the flyer. Surely, he wasn't being serious.

"Pass," I said dryly.

Briskly, we walked to the car. Brad had the engine on before returning the call he'd discarded in the meeting. It was the real estate agent.

"At this point in time, I'd like to reiterate my reluctance to remain in this town," I grumbled as I adjusted the air conditioning vent.

Hades, the town that had not stopped raining in the week that we had been here and right up until we walked into the building half an hour ago, had stopped raining.

There were no clouds in the sky, not even a hint that it had been relentless for a week. The ground was dry. It was a bright and sunny summer day. Odd and peculiar did not cover this place. There was definitely something weird going on in this town.

"Yeah, I know. A part of me wants to join you in that reluctance, but you know how this works. If I don't work, if I leave the town I'm assigned to, I lose my job. When that happens, we'll be on the street by the week's end."

"You need to start a savings plan. I'm sick of this rubbish. Freaky town with freaky people. Why can't they send us somewhere normal?"

"We had normal Evie, and this place is normal. It's just a few weird things and people."

He stopped talking. I looked at Brad as he held his phone to his ear. A smile appeared.

"Hi, it's Brad Newton. I missed a call."

Seconds passed, and the smile on his face increased. I sighed as I turned to look out the window. We'd gotten the place. Knowing Brad, he would sign a twelve-month lease to ensure his boss complied with the promise to keep us here. As much as his employer paid for us to move between locations, I knew that they did not like to pay for us to break the lease.

That meant that we were definitely staying in Hades for the next year. It was not something that I wanted. I actually hoped that his boss would say something and we'd be on the road again. As much as I hated moving and traveling, I think that I hated this town more.

It was going to be a really long year.

CHAPTER 3

Brad sighed as he dumped the box on the floor. It was the last of the things that we had with us in the bed and breakfast. Today was the day that the removal company was bringing our furniture. It was nice to be settled or at least on the path to becoming settled.

The thought of spending a year in this house and this town made me think about Brad's apartment we'd left behind when we began this journey. Brad always said that we'd return to it one day, but he never elaborated on when that would be.

We'd taken the essentials and the sentimental items but left behind the unnecessary things. It seemed odd to leave them behind, but Brad's boss wanted him in the next town by a specific date. So, we packed what we could into the bags that we could find and left.

I knew that Brad would have been given a lot of warnings about leaving to go on the road, but like always, Brad would have flaked on it. He did it constantly. We would have to find a hotel to stay in when arriving in the new town because Brad didn't book ahead. Nothing was ever planned, and there were times when it drove me crazy.

"So when exactly is your boss planning on making you return to the office?"

Brad dropped his bag and looked at me. I wanted to say that he didn't understand the question, but that didn't seem right.

"In a few months," he murmured. "Probably sometime after the year is out."

"Good."

I didn't miss Brad's poky apartment, but the town he lived in was far better than this place.

"I guess we'll sell everything that there are doubles of, right?"

Brad shrugged, more interested in shuffling things around the room.

"Because we are going home after we're done here, right Brad?"

"Sure."

My eyes narrowed. He was murmuring, a sign that Brad was trying to avoid the conversation.

"Has your boss said something?"

"No, Evie."

Moving to the open door, Brad stood on the threshold and sighed.

"I'm glad the rain stopped."

"Yeah, it's great."

He was changing the subject, which meant that there was something he wasn't telling me. It was guaranteed that his boss was already planning the next move. Either that or he wanted to set up a permanent base here. Yes, that would be it. We'd never be able to leave, and that's why Brad was avoiding the subject.

"We're being made to stay here, aren't we?"

"Nothing has been said. I don't know why you're making a big deal out of this."

"Because it feels like you're hiding something."

"Evie," he chided.

I rolled my eyes and lifted my legs onto the bay window seat I was sitting on.

"My job is not going to make us stay here. You've got to make the best of the situation. I don't like moving all the time, but the positive thing is that I get to visit lots of great towns and meet new people. What positives can you find?"

He sat beside my feet, shooting a bright and happy smile at me.

"How about new friends?"

"Sure."

I wanted to say that I'd tried to make friends in the past, but I now saw it as a waste of time. At the first school that I was in after moving in with Brad, I made a lot of friends. It broke my heart to say goodbye. We'd promised to write to each other, which we did for a few months. Then, after a while, the emails stopped.

School after school, I left a trail of sadness and diminishing contact. By the time I was getting close to my seventeenth birthday, I'd given up. Brad suggested that we do something fun for it. I told him not to bother because I didn't know anyone that would want to turn up. He seemed a little puzzled by the statement and pushed me for information. Once I'd relented, he then urged me into socialization groups. It was one of many failures. So, with those events in mind, I decided I would not make friends.

By the time this year was up, I would be eighteen and could remain here if I wanted, but there was something strangely familiar about Brad. It had only been three years, but we'd created a bond. It was odd, but it was us. We were family, and we were all that we had in this world. I will not remain in this town without him, and that is why I will not make any friends. In a year, we will not be living here, and I do not want the disappointment of saying goodbye yet again.

At least, I hope that we will not be here after a year. There was something strange about Brad's mannerisms when discussing the subject that made me think this move was permanent.

I heard the brakes squealing long before the truck appeared at the end of the driveway. One of the drivers got out to assess it, and Brad was on his feet and out the door at record speed. After a quick conversation, Brad turned back and began to climb the driveway. I don't think they wanted to carry the furniture up the steep slope, but getting that truck up the driveway while avoiding the large trees would not be easy.

They were determined. Clearly, destroying a few branches was better than lugging the furniture up the driveway. Brad narrowed his eyes at me.

"Don't," he grumbled. "They'd be blocking the street if they stayed out there. This is for the best."

"Sure."

Brad helped me move the boxes to one corner. We didn't have a lot of furniture, just a few essential pieces that followed us from town to town.

I hated packing. I despised my life being in a box for several weeks while we moved, then tried to find a place. There was no plan, no searching the internet to find a home before we arrived in the town. Brad was not the kind of guy to dive into a situation like that. I think that the lack of information and timelines from his employer made him like this.

"Try to get the washing machine and dryer off first. If we can get it set up, I can put our bedsheets in and have them ready for tonight."

"Good idea. Let's hope they packed the truck the way the storage shed had been."

Brad sauntered out of the house while I searched for the box with our linen in it. We had a set each, and I'd stuffed the linen into the box at the last minute. I usually tried to wash everything so it would be clean, but we ran out of time, and Brad's boss was getting antsy at every minute we were delayed.

The worn-out boxes were all labeled from the first town we moved from. They were far better than the bags we used when leaving Brad's apartment. We kept the boxes, knowing they would be used again. To make life less complicated, I used them for the same items. The linen was in the box marked *last minute,* which meant that it was all the stuff that I'd crammed into the box on moving day.

Dumping the linen onto the bay window seat, I looked out the window and saw Brad talking to the driver. It was a three-man team. The other two were starting to unload the truck. Brad didn't seem overly impressed, turning back to the house with a heavy frown.

Something was wrong. I walked to the door to meet him as he stepped up the few steps to the front porch.

"Why aren't they bringing that stuff into the house?"

"They're refusing because there is some local legend that says this place is haunted. No wonder we got it so cheap."

Stepping past Brad, I walked to the men who stopped when I approached.

"Haunted, as in how exactly?"

"The original owner disappeared. No trace of him was ever found. He didn't have any family, so the fate of this place fell to the town founder, who decided that the place would be rented until the body turned up. The first tenants complained that the house wailed. They moved out after one night. Since then, it's been a long list of people who treat this place like it's an unfurnished hotel."

The last of our stuff was put onto the driveway, and one of the men pulled one side of the doors shut.

"We expect you will call tomorrow to come and collect your stuff, but we don't work on Sundays."

With a firm nod, he returned to the front of the truck as the other door was shut and locked. The other worker looked at me, giving a vague smile before following his co-worker to the front of the truck.

"You could at least take it to the living room," I yelled.

They ignored me. They also started the engine and drove down the driveway without so much as thanks for the business.

"Do you want to know something crazy?" Brad asked as he stopped beside me.

"Sure. Why not?"

It would only add to the rest of this craziness.

"They were supposed to collect payment."

"Pfft. *If* you decide to pay them when they call, only pay half because they've only done half a job."

We turned and looked at the house. It was pretty, a little old, and the chances of it being haunted were high.

"Okay, you start with the smaller stuff while I get the washing machine into the basement."

"How are you going to do that? Those jerks didn't leave the trolley for you."

"Good point. How about I go to the hardware and see what they've got? I'll even buy lunch while I'm out."

"Great. Something fattening, thanks."

Brad chuckled. He was searching his pockets when the real estate agent turned up. A pickup truck stopped behind him, and both men got out of their vehicles.

"Hello, Brad and Evie," the agent said with an eager smile.

It was far too ghastly for my liking.

"This is Ryan, our handyman. You don't mind if he takes a look at the stairs and that crack?"

"Sure. Can you help me get the washing machine and dryer down there as well?"

Ryan gave him a nod.

"Once I check that the stairs will take the weight."

"Then go right ahead."

The agent and the handyman wandered into the house. Brad turned with a smug smile.

"Looks like I saved a few bucks."

"Yeah, but what about my greasy lunch?"

"Alright, how about dinner? We can work for a few hours and get this stuff inside. Then we'll explore the town and see what's available."

"Yeah, sure. Sounds great."

It was lucky that I'd grabbed some fruit on the way out of the bed and breakfast this morning.

We'd been here a week, and so far, we hadn't ventured beyond the bed and breakfast and a few shops on the same street. Our time was either spent searching for a place or being stuck in that room while Brad worked.

When everything was inside, I helped Brad lift the washing machine and the dryer to the front porch so that if it rained, they'd be undercover. It was still sunny, but now there were clouds in the sky. The seconds were ticking before Hades returned to the doom and gloom that had been our first week here.

Brad ventured down to the basement. I sat at the top of the stairs and listened to them discuss the crack. It had gotten bigger since yesterday, and Ryan was concerned that moisture might be the issue. Ryan then suggested that he underpinned the area in case there was subsidence. He'd have to investigate it further, and while he did that, Ryan wanted the owners to authorize rectification works.

"The movers said this place doesn't have owners."

The three men turned and looked at me.

"Technically, the owner is long dead, regardless of what happened to him. At the time, the council decided to wait for relatives to appear and claim ownership, but that has not happened. So, its fate was voted by the townsfolk. Now, it is owned by the Heritage Trust. Hopefully, they won't drag out the approval process."

Tom shrugged, giving me a vague smile that showed the false hope he held. It made me grateful that the stairs were alright because it was obvious that nothing happened quickly in this town. As for the wall, it was hard to say. Maybe they might rush it through, and perhaps I'd wake to find my bed had crashed through the floor and landed in the living room, too.

CHAPTER 4

Brad and Tom were upstairs discussing things that were not interesting at all. I took a pile of washing and went to the basement.

After I loaded it and set it going, I turned to the stairs. The crack was large, and a hole had appeared. It was small, but it was enough to cause problems. Pressing my hand to the wall, I could still feel the warmth. The area on either side of the heat was brutally cold. It was a space no larger than me but at least a head taller.

"You shouldn't go near the wall, kid."

Ryan walked down the stairs with his toolbox in hand. I gave a disinterested shrug and stepped back.

"How come it's so warm in one spot?"

He looked at me like I was weird.

"There's no heat to it."

"Yes, there is. Right here."

After showing him one of the spots, Ryan put his

hand on the brick and shook his head.

"Cold. Are you sure you're feeling okay?"

"I guess not," I murmured. "Do you think this place is haunted?"

"No. Your uncle told me about the removalists leaving you high and dry. Don't worry about those fools."

He looked up at the top of the stairs.

"Sounds like your uncle is calling you."

"He is?"

With a frown, I turned to the stairs. I could not hear Brad calling me.

Searching for him, I found Brad and Tom in the backyard, looking at the forest. At the edge of it, the trees were sparse, and I could see for some distance into the woods. I don't know how deep the forest went. All I knew was that Brad would lose his mind if I said I wanted to explore it.

"Hey, were you calling me?"

Brad shook his head, then flicked his head at a long line of dark trees.

"You know what I'm thinking, right?"

"Yes. You want me to find you some wild mushrooms."

"No. Try again."

The real estate agent was amused.

"Right, okay. Firewood for that awesome fireplace. I've got you covered."

"The trees are part of the forest, which is protected. You cannot remove wood from it without permission, which we will not be getting. Firewood can be bought from the hardware. I hope that you are listening to me, Evelyn, because you are not to go into the forest. Is that clear?"

"As clear as the sky is blue."

Brad looked up and saw the ominous clouds had returned. With a heavy frown and a soft growl, Brad narrowed his eyes at me.

"Yes, I won't go in there. Sheesh, you're so paranoid."

"That's because I know how great your sense of direction is."

"I got us lost one time."

Leaving Brad to continue his discussion with Tom about the crack, I returned to the house and, in particular, the basement. Ryan was still down there doing something that clearly required him to be alone. I might have been fooled into leaving the basement, but I was not blind to what he wanted.

The door was left open, hooked onto the latch to stop it from slamming shut. I quietly tiptoed to the door and listened, hearing nothing. Peering around the corner, I could see Ryan's legs. He was next to the wall, but the toolbox was shut.

That was curious.

The scent of something odd filtered up the stairs. My nose twitched, unable to detect what Ryan was spraying.

Hearing Brad and Tom approach, I stepped back and pretended to be looking for something in a nearby box. They were being so noisy that I knew that Ryan would hear them.

Following them to the basement, I noted that the toolbox was now open, and Ryan had a meter reader out, pressed to the wall.

"Well, I don't think there's a water leak. It's highly likely that the ground has just shifted with the recent rain. I might come back in a week to check on it. Once the ground has dried, we can fix the wall. How does that sound?"

"Wonderful," Tom said with his patented cheery smile.

I gave Brad a look that the other two could not see. He frowned, and then when Tom turned, Brad gave a smile. As they discussed the weather, the three of them wandered up the stairs.

My eyes narrowed as my lips twisted derisively. The handyman had done something, and I knew that the crack in the wall had nothing to do with the rain or moving earth.

Sitting on the dryer was the box of storm supplies. In

it was a torch. Flicking it on, I moved back to the wall.

"Evie," Brad called out.

With a huff, I flicked off the torch and left it on the stairs. Brad was a pest, and it was like he knew when I was up to no good.

Brad was at the front door talking to Ryan when I emerged from the basement. Tom was not here anymore. I don't know if that was a good thing or a bad thing.

"Ryan was just telling me about the original owner of the house."

"He was a bad person," Ryan murmured. "Not surprising that he went missing. He was probably taken out by someone who was annoyed at something he did. Back then, they were known for instant corporal punishment. The worse the crime, the bigger the vigilante mob. If it was a minor crime, I'm sure they would have buried him somewhere and made a notation. The fact that there is no evidence means he was a monster."

"How interesting."

Brad frowned at me. He knew the tone of my voice was insincere. After three years of being in each other's pockets, the man knew me well.

"Not many in these parts will talk about things like that. They like to live in an oblivious world, but I don't. My girls know the truth about this town, and you'd be wise to listen to me as well. Be careful, don't stay out late at night, don't go wandering around by yourself."

Ryan turned to Brad. The frown was heavier than it had been for me.

"You might want to raise her to be independent, and that's great. We all want them to find their own feet, but in this town, we drive our kids to school."

"Gee, you make it sound like you've got a pervert on every street corner," I said, perhaps a little too enthusiastically.

"Wouldn't know about them, just the rules that my old man passed to me and that I passed to my girls. If you don't want to listen, then that ain't my fault. I'll see you both in a week."

And with that grumbling, the man walked out of the house.

Ryan was an odd person, a little gruff, but seemed to have a genuine nature to his persona. That is if I didn't see him doing something highly peculiar in the basement. Brad closed the door and turned to me.

"He sprayed something in the basement."

"Yeah, deodorizer. The room stank of dampness. I just hope he's right about it. I don't want to move again, not when we just got here."

I nodded and turned away, only to have Brad grab my arm and pull me back.

"You know what we're going to discuss, right?"

"Yeah, you're going to lay down the law about going to school, wandering around the town. All this after a little scaremongering from a guy that was doing something shifty in the basement."

Brad rolled his eyes, letting go of my elbow.

"He was not doing something shifty. Rules,"

I scoffed and picked up the kitchen box, hoping he'd get the hint. He did not.

"I will drive you to and from school. If you want to go out with friends, you'll need to notify me where you will be going and, for how long, what time I need to pick you up."

"The friends that I won't make, you mean?"

"Evie," he snapped. "Be serious. We both got odd feelings at the school. This town clearly has some serious weirdness going on, so I want you to do the right thing here. I know that you're almost an adult, and you probably want to get out into the world, hang out with friends, get a boyfriend or girlfriend, whatever,"

Brad shifted uncomfortably, probably remembering the awkward conversation he'd had after I'd come home from school and told him that I'd walked in on the headmaster and one of the teachers having sex in a classroom. He'd flustered a little and said that it was wrong to do that in a school where getting caught was highly likely, considering I'd walked in on them and that he'd be having words with them the next day.

He'd said that love is love, even if it was in the wrong place and wrong time. I smiled and said nothing. Then he asked if I needed a little context, to which I replied that my mother was a prostitute, so I probably knew more than he did. Brad nodded, looking a little sheepish.

"I get it. You want to ensure I'm safe because you love me, and you'd feel bad if something bad happened."

"I just want to do the year here and then get the hell out of this place. Okay?"

I nodded as I opened the box and began unloading the contents into the drawers.

"What if you're made to stay longer?"

"I don't know. I guess we'll figure that out when we get there. You never know. We might come to love the place."

"Doubt it," I cooed as he walked away.

It took all of Saturday afternoon to get the boxes unpacked. In between the boxes, I had to help Brad get the beds upstairs. We had ensemble beds, so that meant that there were no frames to be put together, just a base and mattress. Life on the road and moving constantly meant we had become smart with our purchases.

Pulling the linen out of the dryer, I picked up the basket and moved to the stairs. I could still smell whatever it was that Ryan had sprayed. Curiously, nothing was dribbling down the wall. He must have been incredibly careful, inserting the nozzle into the tiny gap.

Turning to the step, I saw the flashlight that I'd left there earlier. There was too much to do tonight, and I was too tired. Besides, Brad offered takeaway for dinner, and I was not going to pass on that.

Climbing the stairs, I put the basket down and closed the door. Interestingly, there was a large slide bolt for the door. I shifted it across and wondered why it was necessary.

Brad was in his room when I reached the next level. I'd taken one of the bedrooms on this level rather than the attic. It was a bright and airy space, but the first few nights in a new home, I preferred to be close to him. I wasn't scared. I just didn't like to be too far away.

Dumping Brad's linen on the bed, I wandered out of his room and into mine. I quickly made the bed and then took the towels into the bathroom.

The house was in good order. I'd seen some horrid places over the years, and the longer they were let sit without someone living in them, the worse they became. This place was old but looked new. Nothing needed to be cleaned, though I suspect that it was cleaned regularly with the hope that they'd be able to get tenants in and pay money.

"Are we done?" Brad said.

"Absolutely. Let's get greasy."

With a chuckle, we walked down the stairs. Brad grabbed the keys, and after checking the windows and doors were locked, we were out of there.

Driving through the town center of Hades was definitely not the highlight of my evening. We have been to small towns before, we were used to shops being shut as soon as the sun hit the horizon, but this was ridiculous. Hades was large enough to warrant having restaurants open. Even a few takeaway shops would be alright.

Street after street, we searched for something and found nothing. Even the grocery store was shut.

"Well, I was going to suggest buying a roast chicken and bread rolls, but I guess that's not happening."

"Do we have any food?"

"No. How about we see if the bed and breakfast will cook a meal for us?"

"Sounds great."

Because the nearest town was several hours away, and my stomach would not take that kind of wait.

CHAPTER 5

Waking to a new day, I smiled despite the annoyance at being stuck in this town. It was Sunday, and that meant that I could use Brad's computer to play games.

Pouncing down the stairs, I inhaled the delicious scent of pancakes. The lovely couple at the bed and breakfast were more than happy to feed us last night and even sent us away with a breakfast basket. They searched and found a brochure that used to be given out to new residents. It had the opening hours, which were standard for all businesses.

Our window for grocery shopping was small, and once breakfast was over, Brad was going to do the shopping.

"Parcel arrived for you this morning."

Sliding up to the breakfast bar, I pulled the package closer to me. It was wrapped in brown paper and twine, seemingly soft on top with a hard chunkiness to the bottom.

"From who?"

"The school. Apparently, it's enough to get you through the doors tomorrow. You'll need to see the lady at reception about your sports uniform."

"They cannot be serious. I am not doing sports."

"I get the feeling that you're not going to get a lot of choices."

Huffing loudly, I pulled the twine and opened the package. The uniform was simple. A white shirt with sleeves to the elbow, matched with a deep blue skirt that went to the knees. White socks and that chunkiness were the black shoes. All of the sizes were correct, which made me a little uneasy.

"Did they ask you for my sizes?"

"No, and if they did, I wouldn't know what to tell them."

"Then they are definitely weird."

Brad flipped the pancake onto the plate, making a two-stack of fluffy yumminess. He then turned to put it in front of me. The package of creepiness was pushed aside for the plate of deliciousness. I had to use the syrup sparingly as there was nothing else on offer. It was better than nothing, which was the alternative.

One of Brad's pancakes was already cooking. He had two frypans going. The man clearly liked to do the dishes. When he returned to the stove, the second pancake was slopped into the frypan. I had to give him credit. It was undoubtedly an excellent way to get pancakes onto the plates in an efficient time.

We didn't have a dining table. Life was spent with a meal in front of the television, not the greatest, but it was how we did things. It suited us, and to be perfectly honest, it was a complete improvement on what life used to be like with my mother. She *might* have made dinner before leaving for the street corner. If she did, there was a limit on what she did for me. I don't recall a time when we had dinner together.

Breakfast was often spent with me in front of the television, watching the morning cartoons, and then being yelled at for making too much noise. She was trying to sleep, and I was a nuisance. Lunch was the only meal that we spent together, and that was just the weekends. That is if she didn't decide to hit the street for a little early afternoon trade.

One would think that with all the time she spent on the street, we would have been rolling in money. I have no idea what she did with it. Food was always in the cupboard, but it was always a generic brand, and what was in there was limited.

So, moving in with Brad had been a bit of a shock. Having him around all the time was just as bad and took some time to get used to. I could have said that I was used to being alone, and I might have done that quite regularly, but it was always done with a lot of hesitation. I wanted Brad to be at home with me. I wanted company. A parental figure that guided me through life rather than leaving me alone for hours.

She was not a good mother, but that didn't mean I loved her any less or didn't miss her. I still cried, wishing she was here even if my life had improved infinitely. She was taken from me. I used to fall asleep every night expecting to wake up to the sound of the cops knocking on the door. I never believed it would happen. But it did.

Moving the parcel aside, Brad slid up onto the stool and ate his breakfast. Between us was the meal plan for the next week, including lunches for me, just in case they didn't have a cafeteria like the other schools.

"Well?"

"It works."

We finished our stack of pancakes in silence, looking at the week of meals. Brad liked to try and cook, even if he was mediocre at it. He'd had many successes and a few failures.

I didn't mind. I'd happily take the good and the bad any day.

After breakfast, I stacked the dishes while Brad prepared the shopping list.

"You might want to wash that before you wear it. And because I cooked breakfast, you get to clean up. Have fun."

With a merciless chuckle, the jerk left me to wash up. Before I did that, I took the uniform and made sure it fitted. Unfortunately, it was a perfect fit, which did not help the situation. After redressing, I took the clothes to the basement and put them into the wash. They went in together. My aim was that the blue would leak dye and stain the white shirt and socks. Therefore, I will not be able to wear them tomorrow.

Smiling, I turned and left the washing machine to do my dark bidding.

The dishes were done, and I got half an hour of game time before the washing machine started to beep at me. With a skip in my step, I made my way down to the basement. Disappointment soon found me. The damned skirt must have been colorfast.

"How rude," I muttered.

Dumping them in the dryer, I said a silent prayer that the lint filter would catch on fire. Then I retracted that because the whole place would probably burn down.

Returning to the game, I lost track of time until Brad returned home. Pausing it, I ambled out to the car and helped him bring in the groceries.

"Sounds like your clothes are done."

"Yeah,"

"The clothes didn't discolor?"

"No." I grumped.

Brad chuckled, making my frustration worse.

It was warm in the basement because I'd forgotten to open the vent. Pulling the clothes out of the dryer, I thought I heard something thump. Warily, I stood, lifting the basket up with me.

"Brad?"

His heavy boots thumped overhead, making his way to the door.

"What's up?"

"I think I heard something."

He walked down the stairs and looked at me and around the area. It wasn't a large area, enough to fit the appliances and a table if I wanted to fold the clothes down here. I wouldn't. It was too stuffy for my liking.

"There's probably a rat in the wall. I wonder if I can get a pest exterminator out on a Sunday."

Brad turned to the stairs, muttering about Sunday rates. I wouldn't worry about that. I'd be more concerned that the sleepy town of Hades wouldn't trade on a Sunday at all. It was surprising that he was able to get groceries.

His heavy boots thumped up the stairs as I drew closer. My heart was racing as I looked at the crack that had grown overnight.

"Please don't call the exterminator." the wall whispered.

I screamed, dropped the basket, and ran up the stairs.

Brad ran down the corridor, fear in his eyes after hearing my blood-curdling scream. Before I could get a word out, Brad gripped my shoulders, searching for whatever it was that had me sobbing hysterically.

"What's wrong? You're not bleeding anywhere."

"There is something in the wall."

"Yeah, I know, the rat."

"No," I quivered, pressing my back to the wall.

Escape was not that far away.

"Something that spoke."

"Yeah, good one."

Brad laughed but stopped when he saw the horror on my face.

"I'm serious. It said, please don't call the exterminator."

"Well, at least it was polite."

His attempt at a joke was met with nothing but tears and snot bubbles.

"Fine," Brad said with a heavy sigh and a roll of his head. "Let's think about this rationally, shall we?"

I nodded, though I didn't want to discuss it. I wanted to get out of here. To go back to our last home. It was a new build. There was no chance of there being someone in the wall.

"The wall has been up since this house was built. If someone was trapped between it and the land, they would be very dead or very hungry."

"It could be a camera and a speaker."

"Why would they ask us not to call the exterminator?

This doesn't make any sense, Evie."

Brad sighed heavily, leaning on the wall beside me.

"Look, I know it's rough being moved around all the time, but this is the best I could do while I had to look after you."

"Geez, I'm not incapable. You could go back to your office job."

"The woman from child services made things very clear to me, Evie. I had to take complete responsibility and ensure that you did not take a path,"

"What? Did she say that prostitution was bad and that my mother was a selfish person?"

"Prostitution is illegal, and your mother was selfish. She never reached out to me. I would have helped her wherever possible. How many school days did you miss because she passed out from drug use?"

I shrugged. Was I worried about her? Absolutely.

"Did she ever thank you for it or try to clean herself up? No. What did she do, Evie?"

"Punish me," I whispered.

"The woman from child services saw the bruises. There was one thick file on the two of you. Because of that, I've had them breathing down my neck for the past three years. They barely accept all these moves but understand because I had my employer submit a letter that said I was either in the office, on the road, or out of a job. Look, my point here is that you've got one more year. Once you've finished high school, you can go off to college or university or get a job. I can go back to my office job, and we can go home. So, can we get through this year? It's a nice house, right?"

Again, I shrugged.

"I swear, I heard a voice. Am I a liar?"

"No, but,"

"What, Brad? What could you possibly offer to make me think I'd misheard it?"

He stared for a moment, unable to answer me. Then he turned and walked to the basement door.

"Don't go down there," I begged desperately, tugging on his arm.

"Evie, I'm going to see what's going on. This isn't some horror film that has a creepy guy in the wall. The crack is barely big enough to get a screwdriver into it."

The crazy man continued down the stairs. I remained at the top because I did not want to go down there.

"Hello?"

Nothing.

Brad knocked on the cinder block wall.

"Anyone trapped in there?"

Still nothing.

Brad looked at me, giving me a vague shrug. Leaning down, he picked up the clothes and put them back into the basket, then walked up the stairs. Once he was through, Brad put the basket on the lounge and gave me an uneasy smile.

"I don't know what to say, Evie. I believe you when you say you heard something, but there were no sounds when I was down there. Maybe someone said something into the ducting. You could have a prankster sitting outside the house whispering into the pipes."

And I'd just given them a great show. Well, that was just perfect. I'm sure it was some jock that would be telling everyone Monday morning, and by the time I got to school, I'd be the laughingstock of the entire place.

Starting school in a new town was the worst. Not only did I have to make a good impression, but I had to navigate corridors and rooms and try not to annoy anyone by getting in their face or taking their seat. Don't look at a guy for too long. His girlfriend could be watching, and I'd make an instant enemy. Add to that the rest of the female population of the school wouldn't trust me because I'd be labeled a boyfriend thief.

"Because you know that the vent is right next to the fence line. Anyone could jump it and have a big laugh at our expense."

"Sure."

Happy with his efforts at dousing the fire, Brad returned to his task. Find an exterminator. Looking through the basket, I realized he'd left one of the socks downstairs. I couldn't wear any old socks. They had HHS on the sides.

Huffing, I turned and looked at Brad.

"You left a sock downstairs."

"And you are more than capable. There is nothing down there."

"Fine, but if something jumps out and kills me, I will haunt you for the rest of your life."

"I have no doubt that you will," he muttered. "Did you know that there is only one pest controller in this damned town, and his website is atrocious? Can't find any information."

I rolled my eyes, leaving Brad to his annoyed mumblings.

Gripping the rail, I slowly eased my way down the stairs while staring at the crack in the bricks. I was certain my legs would give out at any moment. They wobbled and felt like jelly. My heart was pounding so hard that I could feel it easily. The heavy thrum pulsed hard as the anxiety rose.

"Hello?" I whispered.

Nothing came, and I picked up my sock.

"You scared the life out of me, no one person who is not hiding behind the crack in the wall."

"I'm sorry."

CHAPTER 6

I gasped and stepped back. Wincing as the handrail smacked into my lower back, I squeaked with shock.

"Please don't scream again. I didn't mean to frighten you."

All that I could do was stare. The wall was talking to me.

I was going insane. I'd lost my mind.

There was no one in there. It was not possible.

Maybe there was a hidden path to another place. A tunnel or a door, perhaps. Maybe this was a drug house that people used to move between houses to avoid attention. The wall was not new, but I wasn't a builder, so I couldn't be sure about its actual age.

"Am I really a no-one person?"

"I guess not. This is not real, is it?"

"It is."

His voice was soft and husky, filled with amusement.

I didn't try to be funny, but clearly, I was.

"Are you behind the wall?"

"I am."

"Is there a way out?"

"No."

Warily, I moved from the rail digging into my back, and stepped forward.

"That's not possible. You would be dead unless the wall has only just been put up. How long have you been there?"

"Far too long, and it is possible when you're not human."

I snorted a huff, rolling my eyes with pure amusement.

"Yeah, sure. Good one. You can stop with the jokes. I know you're at the vent whispering this rubbish to me."

"Evie, is that your name?"

"Yeah,"

I couldn't get any more hesitant if I tried.

"What year is it?"

"Twenty, twenty-two."

"Then I have been incarcerated in this tomb for over sixty years. This is not a joke. I am Niko Corbin, and I am a vampire."

"I do not believe you. Prove that you're stuck behind that wall."

At this point, I realized that I was a complete idiot. If there really was someone behind that wall, I was inviting them to prove it. I didn't believe in vampires or anything paranormal, so I didn't think that this Niko guy would be able to show himself, but damn, I really was asking for trouble.

The hole was small, but it was enough. Something poked through the gap, and I stared. It was the tip of material, possibly a handkerchief.

As I reached out for it, my hand was shaking. Slowly, it pulled through the gap. I unraveled the piece of material to see that it was, in fact, a handkerchief, and it had NC embroidered into one corner.

"This can't be real," I whispered. "How are you alive?"

"Vampires can go for a long time without feeding if they enter into a deep sleep. I can go on for many more years provided you and your uncle leave, and I am not disturbed anymore."

"Don't you want to get out of there?"

"Of course, but unless you're going to break the wall, it won't happen."

Pressing my hand to the warm bricks, I now understood why they were like this.

"Are you trying to crack the wall open?"

"Naturally. I am hungry."

"Do you plan on killing us?"

Niko chuckled.

"Would you like me to make an exception for you and your uncle?"

"Absolutely."

"Then it is done, that is, of course, once I am out of here. Before that, any agreement is pointless as I am quite harmless in my current state."

"What did you do to get put in there?"

"Annoyed the wrong people. Now, how are we going to get me out of here? I heard the mumbled words from the builder fellow. He seemed to think that repair was unnecessary, but I'm sure that attitude will change once your uncle has seen the broken wall."

"We don't have any tools that I could use. Even if I get something, he's going to hear me, and Brad is always home."

"Then we shall endeavor to do it as quietly as we can with the tools that you have. This is not part of the original structure. They created the false wall to trap me."

It was odd to think about it, but this madness made me wonder why they didn't kill him. Wouldn't it be easier than all this?

"Yeah," I drawled out slowly. "I guess I could get something to scrape the mortar out. It will take a while, though. Can you cope with that?"

"No," Niko admitted. "And I would not ask you to bring anything to me. Asking you to provide victims would be wrong of me."

"And I would not get it for you either. This might be a small town, but that doesn't make things any easier. You said that you annoyed the wrong people. Are they going to be upset that you're getting out? Cuz, I assume that they're still alive too."

"It is highly likely," Niko murmured. "And yes, they will be upset. I'm certain they will find me and voice their displeasure at seeing me again. Perhaps this time, I will be more prepared for their plans."

Sitting on the bottom step of the stairs, I leaned against the post and looked at the crack in the wall that contained a vampire. That was something that I never thought was possible. The fact that I didn't think vampires were real was enough. Someone, some living creature was behind an almost inescapable wall.

Niko wanted to escape. He wanted me to help him get out. That meant that I was unleashing a monster upon this town. Sure, Niko said he wasn't the only one, but did I really want to add another one? Could I trust him when he said he would not hurt Brad or me?

I had nothing. Not a single answer. All that I knew was that I would help him get out of that entrapment.

It wasn't his only issue. This modern world was not made for vampires.

"You're going to just hate this era."

"How so?"

"Oh, lots of things. Cops are super smart. They have a lot of ways of catching murderers, which you are one because vampires are completely fictional to the entire world. I'm also assuming that because you've been in there for over sixty years, you don't have valid identification. That's going to be a bit of an issue for you."

"This is why we have familiars."

"I thought they were cats for witches."

Niko chuckled, and crazily, I was smiling too.

"Familiars can take on a few shapes, and humans are one of them. They are trusted to tend to tasks for their master, ensure that the vampire remains hidden, and assist them wherever necessary throughout the course of their service. For their efforts, they are protected from their master and other vampires and assured life when others are not granted such liberties. I have not had a familiar in such a long time."

"So, I'd be like your familiar?"

"If that is what you desire."

"What about Brad?"

"We only have one familiar. However, I can extend the vampire master and familiar protection to him as well. That is, once I'm out of here and obtain the necessary items to offer such things."

"Okay, I'm going to get something to start digging you out. While I'm doing that, we can discuss what you did and how we're going to trust each other."

"I look forward to it."

Getting up from the stairs, I quickly ascended them and then peeked around the corner. Brad was setting up his office in the guest quarters. Slipping through the house, I found a knife and a spoon, the only options I had at the moment. This was going to take forever.

The sigh that escaped displayed my sheer frustration. I knew the task ahead of me would consume my entire day and probably most of my night. How patient was Niko? Thinking about it, I turned back and grabbed a second spoon and knife so that he could work on the mortar as well. That might cut the time down.

As I tiptoed through the corridor, I could hear Brad cursing at the internet. Given the issues we've had since arriving, I found it surprising that Hades actually had the internet.

When I reached the bottom of the stairs, I saw a bit of dust push through the crack.

"Hard at work, I see."

"It is what I've been doing since you woke me."

"I woke you?"

"Yes. I'm sure you're wondering why, but I don't know."

"There have been other tenants in this place. Did they

wake you?"

"No."

Well, that was curious. It made me wonder if he was going to crack some corny line like we were soulmates destined to be together for eternity. Oh, I would swoon at the thought of becoming a vampire just to be with my new lover. Blech.

I tucked the spoons and one knife into my pocket, then used the remaining butter knife to start scratching at the mortar below the largest part of the crack. Getting the tools to Niko was ideal, and the sooner I could do it, the sooner he could start digging himself out.

"So, we have to trust each other, right?"

"Absolutely. We both have goals, and I'm sure that you're eager to know that freeing me will not end in your death. Or your uncle. I also wish to know that I will not die because of the two of you."

"Then we'd need to include Brad in this conversation."

"For the time being, it would be wise to keep him out of this. Too many beating hearts will heighten my hunger, and I will grow irritable. Even in the limited time when the two of you are down here, it is difficult. Keep the times to a bare minimum if you can."

"Sure."

Right, don't come down here with Brad. If Brad comes down while I'm down here, try to leave without making it obvious.

"So, we've agreed that we won't kill each other. You'll go out and find your victim elsewhere, right?"

"Absolutely. A wise vampire never feeds in his home."

"Who did you irritate to get yourself here?"

"A vampire became annoyed that I was alive. He decided that in order to rule the vampires in this town effectively, I needed to be in here."

"How come he didn't kill you?"

"I don't know."

Niko's tone was low, almost sounding despondent.

I'd scratched at the mortar for some time, not realizing how much of a dent I was making.

"Evelyn."

Pulling the knife away, I leaned down and looked into the crack.

"Yeah?"

"I can see a lot more now. You are doing well."

"Uh, thanks."

"No, it is I who should thank you. No one has ever shown me such trust and devotion. You know that as a vampire, I could end your life, yet you still work to free me. I will forever be in your debt, and know that I will never hurt you."

"Okay. Uh, ditto, I guess."

Niko chuckled.

The hole that I'd created was enough to poke the knife through. Together, we worked at the hole until it was large enough to get the spoon in. He poked his finger through.

It was so pale. It was nearly white. I suppose being locked up in pure darkness for sixty years would cause that. Could vampires go out in the sun?

"What are you doing?"

"It is a trade for a pinkie promise."

"What are you, five?"

"Evelyn," he chided. "You should not mock the value of a physical agreement."

"Is this like a gentleman's handshake? Because they mean nothing these days."

"Really?"

Niko sounded genuinely surprised by that. Being locked up like this was not nice, but exposing him to this new world was going to be hell for him.

"However, that doesn't mean it's completely dead."

Reaching out, I pressed my index finger to his. It was an odd way to make a pinkie promise that was really supposed to be a handshake of agreement.

The cold permeated through my skin. I held back the

shiver, but it wasn't easy.

"We agree to do what is in the best interest of each other and for your uncle. We shall not attempt nor succeed in killing each other, and we shall never engage the services of another to do it for us. We will protect our coven with our life and do everything we can to maintain the integrity of this bond. In life and in death, we are bound to the master and familiar code."

His finger tilted enough that the nail pressed into the skin. It was like a needle piercing through the skin. I hissed, pulling it free.

"What the hell, Niko?"

"Necessary."

His finger curled tighter, scratching the skin. It was lucky that his nails were so long. Otherwise, he wouldn't have been able to reach it.

"Please return your finger."

"We're doing a blood pact?"

"We are."

Despite the hesitation I was feeling, I returned my finger to his and pressed it against the flesh. Slowly, the finger retracted back into the cavity, taking a long drag along the skin.

I noted that there was a lot of my blood pooling in the underside of his nail.

"Seriously?"

"You have no idea the pain I am in. This will sustain me for a few hours."

"Would you like a raw piece of meat or something?"

"Dead meat is not the answer, I'm afraid."

"Right, pumping blood?"

Niko made a noise that sounded like an agreement laced with feeding on my blood.

"Won't that make you crave my blood?"

"No. You are perfectly safe. If you are ever inclined, please feel free to offer. I can feed without death, and the blood of a familiar is always treasured."

"I think you need to focus on getting out of there before you worry about things like that."

And with that, we returned to the task. Hearing Brad moving around upstairs was a little unnerving. I didn't want him coming down here and asking what I was doing. He would not believe me.

"How come you didn't say anything to Brad when he came down here?"

"At that point, I was not certain as to the person I faced and the values that he held. It would be ideal that my current state is kept quiet, and announcing it to the world is not ideal. With you, it was vastly different. I think I know why, but I cannot be certain until I am out of here. As for your uncle, we can tell him if you so desire, but I need to ensure that he will keep my secret for a little while longer. At least until I return to this world, see what I'm faced with, and then formulate a plan."

"The builder will be coming back."

"I'm sure he will."

It sounded ominous. I didn't think much of Ryan, but I hoped Niko didn't kill him.

CHAPTER 7

I'd worked on my side of the wall for as long as I could in between, keeping Brad at a distance. He'd called me to see if I wanted lunch made, to which I agreed.

Brad didn't say a single thing about why I was in the basement after being hysterical earlier today. I was grateful for that. I didn't need to try and explain my way out of that particular nightmare.

Returning to the basement after lunch was easy. Brad was distracted with getting his office set up before tomorrow. He had to clock on at nine am, and if he didn't, his pay would be docked. It was one of those little rules that came with working from home.

So, I continued to scrape at the mortar until dinner time. Brad bought frozen pizzas, so all he had to do was remove the packaging and put it in the oven. The man was a legend.

After dinner, I quietly returned to my duty. Curiously, there was a lot of dust on the floor. Stopping in front of the wall, I could see that Niko had done quite a lot.

"Evelyn, carefully pull the block out."

Slowly, the cinder block began to move forward. When it was pushed out enough, I jiggled it out of the wall. Setting the block aside, I lowered to see Niko.

The space was cramped. I don't think he had a lot of area to move in.

"Hey there, did you need a little help?"

Niko jostled, moving his body lower so that he could see me. The pale face smiled, and the sharp teeth glistened in the light.

"More than a little."

"Do you think this is enough, or do you need another brick?"

"It will be a squeeze, but I will manage. The question is, what to do beyond that?"

"Well, maybe you might want to go out and find that victim who definitely does not live in this house."

Niko smiled at me again. Filled with amusement and affection.

"My dear Evelyn, we have an agreement, and I am a man of his word. I will protect you until there is nothing left in me. I promise you of that."

"And I promise you. Now, are you going out?"

"It would be wise. While I am gone, you will need to find somewhere for me to rest during the daylight hours and ensure that your uncle does not find me."

"The attic. I think he's scared of it."

"It is just a room."

I shrugged, stepping back. Niko moved into position. First out was his head, then the broad shoulders were crammed in tight at an angle. His frame was narrow, but those shoulders proved to be a problem.

"Are you sure about this? We could pull another brick out."

"It will take too long. I will get there, do not fret for me."

After about half an hour, Niko was in a better position. I gripped his arms and pulled as hard as I could manage. My feet were pressed hard against the wall, trying to drag him out. Then he popped out as if he had some force behind him.

I felt winded as my back hit the floor. To make it worse, I had a damp and dusty vampire lying on my body between my legs.

Niko lifted up onto his hands, then his arms gave out. His body fell back to mine.

"Muscle atrophy," he whispered. "I cannot move."

"Can you heal yourself?"

"It will take time, far too long considering the issues."

"So, you need to feed."

"That is correct."

"You said that you can feed and not kill, right?"

"I know what you offer, Evelyn. Are you certain this is the path you wish to take?"

"Well, you are kind of lying on me. Brad comes down here and sees this, and he's going to get super angry because I'm only seventeen. Besides, we said that we'd do what was in the best interest of each other, and I wouldn't be a very good familiar if I let my master die, would I?"

Niko smiled at me.

Rolling Niko onto the floor, I sat up next to him and held out my arm. Niko tried to lift his arms, but they wouldn't stay up. So, I held my wrist to his mouth. When the fangs pierced the skin, I winced. It was not nice at all, not that I thought it would be.

Niko was quite tall, dressed in a suit that seemed rather fancy. I didn't know much about men's fashion from sixty years ago, so I could only assume that he'd kept up with the times to blend in. Damp and dusty was not the rage at the moment, so the outfit would have to go.

Temporarily, he'd have to borrow from Brad. It was lucky that they were roughly the same size as each other. Brad was a little rounder in the midsection. He liked his doughnuts far too much.

Color began to return to Niko, now flushed with a soft pink tone that seemed to fit well with the dark brown hair and sharp green eyes. To me, he looked as if he was in his thirties, but that was not possible.

"How old are you?"

Niko pulled his fangs out of my wrist. His tongue slid along the weeping wounds, stopping the blood flow.

"Quite old. I am uncertain of how many there are, but I am considered to be an elder vampire."

His eyes lowered as a grim look crossed his face.

"At least, I used to be. Take this as your first lesson, my young familiar. Be wary of those around you, and do not trust anyone."

"Did you trust the wrong person?"

"I did."

Niko sat up, looking a little woozy at first.

"Do you need to have a proper feed?"

"I think that is necessary. However, I don't think that I have the strength to walk any great distance."

"Okay, familiar to the rescue. Come on."

Wrapping his arm around my neck, I lifted Niko onto his feet. He wobbled, reaching for the wall.

"How's that?"

"Getting better. You're not really considering taking me to a victim, are you?"

"Look, I get it. Vampires feed to live, so someone has to die. People die all the time, and we kill our own constantly. We're no better. At least you kill because you're sustaining your own life. Humans kill others for the thrill of it. So, yeah, I am. What are the rules?"

"Don't get caught."

Niko and I looked at each other. Slowly, a smile emerged between us and quickly turned into a giggle. Who would have thought that I'd be friends with a vampire?

We slipped out of the house without Brad realizing, then went in search of the perfect victim. Niko did not have any preferences when it came to what they looked like or their gender. The only stipulation that he had was that they were alone and an adult.

We found a man living in a small house not far from where we lived. He was selected because I suggested that Niko needed to update his clothing. While Niko sustained his life, I packed a bag of clothes and accessories, then found a wash basket to load bed linen into.

Rather than staying and listening to it, I continued to search for things that would be useful for Niko. The man had a camp bed in his garage, so I dragged that out and set it aside with the other items. I also found his stash of money.

Acutely aware of what would happen once the body was found, I wore a pair of gardening gloves that I'd found in someone's garden. Niko could do as he pleased, there were no records of him but me, well, that was a sad tale that came from the life I'd lived with my mother.

Yep, I had a record.

Because I was a child, they did nothing aside from recording my details in the system, and that included my fingerprints. I have no idea why they did it. Maybe they assumed that I would steal again and would need the information. Perhaps they were just jerks. Either way, I had to be careful.

The deed was done, and Niko could walk on his own. I could see that there was a fair amount of lethargy that had remained. He would stop and take a few seconds before starting to walk again.

"I've got school tomorrow."

Niko nodded.

"I will be fine in the attic."

Slipping into the house, I searched for Brad. He was in the office, muttering about something. With a flick of my hand, I urged Niko to hurry up. His steps were quiet on the creaky wood floors. Brad was clearly too invested in whatever he was doing to notice.

"Goodnight, Evelyn. Rest well."

"You too."

Quietly, I closed the door to the attic, hoping that Brad wouldn't find some newfound gusto and brave his fears.

After showering, I fell into bed. It had been a strenuous day, and when I woke feeling drained, I wondered how I'd cope with starting a new school. Dressing quickly, I packed my bag and put it near the door. I had to check on a friend.

Tiptoeing up the stairs to the attic, I listened to the sounds of Niko rustling the linen as he sat up.

"Niko," I whispered.

"Evelyn, you are leaving for school?"

"Yeah. Will you be alright while I'm gone?"

"Yes. I have fed, and now it is time to recover. By this afternoon, I shall be reinvigorated and ready for another conversation with you. I am eager to hear how your first day at the new school goes. Be ready for it."

I chuckled.

"Sure thing. I'll see you later. Enjoy your sleep."

"Oh, I will. Goodbye, Evelyn. Have a great day."

Rushing as quietly as I could, I began to wonder if Brad had noticed my peculiar behavior. When I found him in the kitchen putting the bowl of cereal on the counter, I knew he was completely oblivious.

"Ready for a great first day?"

"Nope."

Brad smiled, rolling his eyes.

"Come on, Evie. One more year, and you're done. Just buckle down, and you'll be out of there before you know it."

"Sure."

We ate breakfast in silence.

My thoughts remained on going to school. First-day nerves were always a stomach churner. I was surprised that it actually managed to stay put.

"Okay, let's get this done."

Brad grinned as he took the plate. It was surprising that he wasn't cleaning them straight away. I looked at the clock and realized why. We were behind schedule. Because he had to clock on at nine, Brad said that he was going to boot me out the door and then rush back home. He added that I'd be a lucky girl if he actually stopped to let me out.

Lifting the bag over my shoulder, I followed Brad out of the house. As I walked to the car, I wondered what he would say if I told him about Niko. I didn't want him to be kept in the dark about it. I will have to discuss this with Niko this afternoon. If Brad went up to the attic and found him, things might get ugly.

Would Brad be brave enough to walk up those stairs? There was nothing to say that he wouldn't.

When he climbed into the driver's seat, I looked at him as I pulled the seatbelt over my body.

"Hey, I left your birthday present in the attic, so no going up there, okay?"

Brad frowned with a crazy smile on his face.

"What is so big that you can't hide it in your room?"

I shrugged.

"You know that I wouldn't go into your room, but sure, I won't go up there. I wasn't planning on it anyway. You know that attics give me the creeps. I heard something moving up there, probably a rat. You didn't leave food up there, did you?"

"No."

"Good. Might be nothing left if you did."

Brad pulled into the street, slowing behind a long line of cars that were dropping kids off. Next to us on the sidewalk was a group of giggling girls walking toward the school. Brad huffed a soft laugh, then turned his smirk back to the road ahead.

"They look like your type."

"Go to hell," I grumbled. "Oh, that's right. We're already there."

"No, I'm just in another town. You're the one in hell. Have fun."

The car jerked to a stop. Brad looked at me with his cheesy smile that, while begging for forgiveness, also didn't want it.

"Yeah, thanks."

"See you at three. If your schedule changes, let me know."

"With what? You haven't replaced my phone."

"You could try getting a job."

Rolling my eyes, I closed the door and stepped onto

the sidewalk. The giggling girls drew closer, looking at me with their haughty smiles. Nothing was said as they passed, then they let out their condescending giggles.

The sooner I was out of this place, the better.

CHAPTER 8

Niko was sitting in a single-seat lounge chair when I walked up the stairs to the attic. He was reading a book. Next to the lounge was a pile of magazines and more books. Brad said nothing about coming up here, no mention of the mysterious rat. Just a quick *how was your day and keep it clean, thanks.* My answer was borderline.

Reaching the top of the stairs, I was greeted with a smile.

"Good afternoon, Evelyn. You will be pleased to know that I have spent my day alone. No visitors."

"Great. Where did you get those?"

"Well, this morning after you left, I timed how long it took for your uncle to return so that I knew how much time I had in the afternoon when he left to collect you. Then, I formulated a short list of the things that I needed to bring me up to speed. You stated that I would not like this era, and I wanted to know the exact details, especially about the intelligence of law enforcement."

He flicked his fingers at the closed book on his lap,

then lifted it to show it to me.

"I know this is a work of fiction, but it seemed to be quite factual in the information, so I believe it was an ideal selection."

The book was crime fiction, and I had no idea if it was well-researched or if it was complete rubbish. Niko lifted a magazine, then smiled.

"It was a curious read. I'll give it that much. I have not had much interest in this type of literature in the past, but it has certainly been enlightening."

"And not based on fact. That's a trash mag, and I would not take any of that on board if I were you."

"Duly noted, though I figured as much. Some of it did seem a tad preposterous. I have a question about magazines. The fellow had a couple that I left behind because I found them rather inappropriate, but I don't really know how to put this,"

"There were lots of naked women in the magazines?"

"Yes. How did you know?"

"For a pale vampire that's been trapped behind a wall for sixty years, you can really change color when you're embarrassed."

"Well, I didn't know how appropriate it was, but curiosity killed the cat, as they say. What is society's view on these magazines?"

I shrugged.

"Depends on who you ask. Me, I don't care. Brad doesn't care, provided he doesn't find a picture of me in one of those magazines or me finding his stash. Which for the record, I don't know if he has one, and I don't intend on searching either. As for the rest of the world, there are some that will be highly offended. Some will say that it's objectifying women. Some that don't care either way and some that love them."

"I see. Do these women get paid for the images?"

"I believe so."

Niko frowned as he thought about it.

"You're going to be entering a whole new world of indecency. Sex is everywhere on the internet. There are actual websites dedicated to videos."

Bewilderment filled Niko's face as he looked at me.

"You are not serious, are you?"

"I am. I tell you this because one day, I'm going to teach you how to use the internet, and soon after, you'll be proficient in using it. It's a dark road that you will stumble into, and before you know it, you'll be looking at things that you never thought possible."

I could see the objection on his face. With a smirk and a shake of my head, I silenced Niko.

"Yeah, you think that now, but trust me, it just takes one little moment where you become curious, and next thing, you're locking doors to drop your pants."

"I would not," he grumbled.

"We'll see."

Niko's eyes narrowed, and for a second, I thought he would say something in response. Instead, his lips tightened into a smirk.

"We shall agree to disagree. Now, sit and tell me about school."

I sat on the other seat, finding it rather comfortable.

"Where did these come from?"

"I returned to our friend. He was most giving."

"Duh, the man's dead, Niko."

"True."

I frowned as I looked around the room.

"You sure did bring a lot back in the short time Brad was away."

Niko shrugged, making me wonder if Brad had taken a detour or two.

"Half an hour at best. Now, your day."

"Boring. Deflating. Demoralizing. I dislike school with a passion. Everyone looks at the new kid like they are diseased. This is going to be the longest year of my life. I've already got homework. How rude is that? My first day, and they lump it on me like I should know what they've taught in the previous lessons."

Unzipping my bag, I pulled out the notebook and crossed my legs on the seat.

"Would it bother you to start your familiar training today as well?"

"Nah, it's cool. You can talk while I'm doing this. It won't take long."

Niko nodded, putting the magazine onto the pile next to his chair.

"We shall begin with the finer details of a vampire. A vampire can go out in the sun, but we pretend we cannot. We prefer to hunt at night because we know the world will see less of what happens. We are not restricted to any particular feeding regime and will do what is necessary to avoid attention. Usually, we associate in covens. A coven, as you would expect, has a leader. It also has a sub-leader who is usually the partner of the leader. Some leaders will form a small group of those who he or she deems worthy of being associated with a title of high rank and will discuss matters of importance with them. They hold no power but can be persuasive and influence the leader's decision regarding those important matters. They are often referred to as a council, but that is not the correct word that the vampires from Europe would like to see used. As they have a council that oversees all manner of things, they deem the word to be too confusing, and a generalized use would risk an association that would be incorrect. They have suggested that names such as committee, panel, or delegation should be used."

"Were you in a coven?"

"I was. We will get to my sad tale another day. Today,

you are learning about vampires so that you can identify them. Hades used to have many vampires, and I can only assume that is still the case. In the coming days, I'm sure that we will be able to figure out a rough population count."

"Is that necessary?"

"Absolutely."

Niko leaned forward, resting his elbows on his legs. The frown he offered was heavy and firm.

"Be warned, Evelyn. Not all vampires are like me. In fact, once you've met another vampire, you might consider me to be quite restrained. If a vampire crosses your path when they are hungry, you will be in trouble. It may not be ideal for me, but if they start to attack, tell them you are my familiar, and that will be enough to stop them. It is prohibited for a vampire to attack a familiar, regardless of who they belong to."

"Why wouldn't it be ideal for you?"

"Because once you mention my name, they will realize that I am not where I should be, and then, they will come here searching for me. Once that happens, they will do all that they can to kill me because they will reason that their last attempt at keeping me out of this town was not enough. When I am dead, your association with me will be at an end, and you will no longer be protected. Neither will your uncle. The vampire will kill you as punishment for setting me free, and they will kill your uncle for the fun of it. I say this to ensure that you understand what you face. Mention my name to save your life, then return here with haste. Be ready to run because it will be extremely necessary."

That was a little more than I needed to hear. Say the name to escape the vampire, but be prepared for a whole lot more vampires to come here and kill me. Such a lovely time to be alive.

"Now, onto a lighter subject. Tell me what this thing is that this strange-looking woman is holding."

"That's a cellphone. I'd show you mine, but it broke, and Brad hasn't replaced it yet. I could show you his, but then he'd want to know what I was up to."

"I see. This outfit that she is wearing. Is that normal?"

"Well, kind of. It's not unusual, but she's famous, so that outfit is probably by a designer, which makes it incredibly expensive."

"So, she paid a lot of money to wear that?"

The tone he used made me chuckle.

"It's possible. Sometimes designers will give them things for free so that their product is seen on the celebrity."

"And this?"

Niko flicked through the pages, finding a picture of a famous couple who were basically slobbering all over each other.

"Is this acceptable behavior?"

"Well, that can depend on who you ask. It's not

something I'd do in public, but I'm not offended by the image."

"I see," he muttered.

"It's a different world now."

"I believe you."

He looked up at me and grinned.

"Though, I must say that it is rather intriguing to see life outside of Hades."

"How the other half live, right?"

"Yes."

Niko continued to study the magazine while I returned to my homework. He tried not to interrupt me, but on occasion, he'd ask about an image, and I'd answer as best as I could. Being polite while informative about the modern world was not always easy. If it was Brad, I wouldn't worry about what I said, but there was a deeper level of decorum that Niko had, and I think that a lot of things would be offensive to him. So, I was mindful of how I explained things. It would not be easy, considering I'd lived a rather colorful life.

CHAPTER 9

The words of Niko's warning lingered in my head as I weaved my way through the corridor at school. When he said that to me last night, I never thought I would realize it was the truth so soon after.

My locker was in the new section. I had the first one in a long row of a wing that had just been built. I was also the *only* person to have a locker in this section. Because it was at the end of the corridor, I was still close to the main thoroughfare where the other lockers were. I was a part of their world, but not really because no one ever turned the lights on. This section was not in use yet, so they didn't think it was necessary.

So, I had to use my locker in the dark. I guess the staff just assumed that, like every other kid in this place, I would have a phone with a flashlight. Ordinarily, I would. My last phone broke, and Brad was yet to obtain a new one for me. The life of an unemployed minor sucked.

But, back to the tale at hand. Me, stuffing my books from my morning lessons into the locker, in the dark.

Mean girls in the corridor, far too close to my locker, giggling and whispering. You get the picture, right? You can see what's going to happen. I hear more than I should. They don't know I'm here. I'm as quiet as a mouse because I know that I'm about to hear something that's worth the effort of hiding.

"Daddy said the master is not happy."

Intriguing. My ears perked up.

"Jeez, Audrey, why does your father associate with those weirdos?"

"Because he said it's worth it."

"They are not going to give him immortality. They won't give it to anyone. You're either born into it, or you are their food."

"I think he's trying to get a closer association that will protect us. Dad got all the real estate contracts, and the competition was eliminated because of this guy wanting to know what was going on in all the houses in this place."

I wonder who her father was.

"That's never going to happen."

"Why is the master not happy, Audrey?"

"I dunno. Dad went to a job on the east side of the town. He said something about a crack in the basement wall."

My eyes widened, and my breath hitched. As I desperately tried to listen, my heart began to thunder so hard it was pounding heavily in my head.

"When Dad told him there was a crack in the wall and the address, he said the guy went off his tree at the underlings around him. Dad said he nearly wet his pants."

The girls giggled. Lockers slammed, and I heard the laughter fade. Quietly, I pulled all of the books out of the locker. I knew I would not be able to concentrate, and the afternoon would be a complete write-off. Stuffing everything back into my bag, I edged closer to the corner of the wall, hoping the girls weren't just a few steps down the corridor. They weren't.

So, I hightailed it down to the office.

The woman behind the counter looked up over the counter when I walked through the doorway.

"Evelyn, is everything okay?"

"No, I don't feel well. Can you please call my uncle and ask him to come and get me?"

"Of course, dear. Go through that door there to the sick bay. Lay on the bed, and I'll give him a call."

Brad wasn't going to believe a single moment of this unless I did the unthinkable. I'd embarrass him, and then he'd stop asking questions, and he'd leave me alone.

I laid on the bed, wondering how many germs were on it. How long did a germ live for? I could hear the soft murmur coming through the wall, the conversation that would be short and filled with disbelief.

Within ten minutes, the door was opened, and Brad was frowning at me.

"Are you lying?" he hissed softly as he leaned down to pick up my bag.

"Women's problems. You know how much pain it causes."

"Believe it or not, Evelyn," he whispered. "I know when you're on. You eat all the damned sweet food that you can lay your hands on, robbing me of my doughnuts."

I followed him out of the sick room, through the office, where he gave the woman a begrudging smile and goodbye, then out of the school. We were in the car before he said anything.

"You have also eaten sugar packets in a desperate attempt to get the sugar hit. I know what you are like and what you need, and the good uncle I am, I buy extra sweet things for you to eat. I also hide my doughnuts."

Brad backed out of the parking spot and began to drive through the car park. Momentarily, he glanced at me, and the slight anger softened.

"Come on, Evie, we had a deal. Just one year, and you're done. Why can't you do that? What's going on?"

"I just need time to adjust. We've been here a week. You know, the last place I had a whole month to roam around, get to know the locals. I knew what the score was before I walked into that place."

"Alright, you want time to adjust. We can deal with that. I want your grades to be reasonable, and if you do that for me, then we can chill it for a few days here and there. Okay?"

"Sure."

Once I deal with the vampire problem.

Niko was asleep when I walked up the stairs to the attic. Brad was in the backyard. He'd lamented that we now had to buy a lawnmower or pay someone to mow the lawns. He was trying to figure out what was the cheapest and if he could make his employer pay for it. Brad's reasoning was that he would have picked an apartment like the last place we lived in, except Hades didn't have any. It was houses with land, lots of lawns to mow, and gardens to maintain.

"Evelyn," Niko said sleepily. "You're home early."

"Yeah, I faked being sick to make Brad come and get me."

"Then something is wrong. Sit and tell me what you have learned that troubles you."

Even though he was clearly tired, Niko rose from his camp bed and moved to our chairs. When he was settled, he waited for me to join him and then offered a reassuring smile.

"Okay, so, I was at my locker, and I heard the mean girls talking."

"Mean girls? Were they horrible to you?"

"No, it's a term that people use to describe girl bullies. They're usually a part of a clique and target, well, people like me."

Niko opened his mouth, no doubt to offer something enriching like I was beautiful, and they were jealous. I raised my hand to stop him, avoiding the dramatic rolling of my eyes.

"Don't go there."

"Don't go where?"

I stared, wondering how long it would take to bring him up to speed on the current phrases and trends.

"It doesn't matter. One of the girls is the builder's daughter. She was talking about what happened after he left here."

"He is a vampire?"

"No, I think he's like a wannabe familiar, but all he's gotten is a little monopolization thanks to the local vampire leader."

"I see," Niko murmured, frowning slightly.

"The girl said that her father told her that the master was not happy. He told the master he was at a job on the east side of town with a crack in the basement wall. The master went off his tree at the underlings around him. I'm assuming she meant the followers?"

Niko nodded wordlessly. The frown was still the

same, but Niko sighed as he stretched back into his seat.

"This was to be expected, though I did not think that the source of the issue would be right before me. Had I known that there was an agent of the leader in this house, I would have taken another path in the past twenty-four hours. Regardless, it is done, and it cannot be changed. All we can do is prepare for the future. With that thought in mind, I want to give you something."

Reaching under the pillow, Niko pulled a pendant necklace out. As he stood, Niko gestured to me to do the same. With a twirl of his fingers, I turned and waited for him to put it on me.

"Wear it always. This is a sign of our alliance. It will show those who cross your path that you and I are one. United as master and familiar."

I turned to Niko, running my fingers over the cold metal. There wasn't much time to see it, but I knew the stone inside the filigree frame was green. I could assume it was jade, but I had no idea because I never bothered to learn what stones were. My life was lacking in money, so pretty gems and necklaces were always beyond my reach.

Niko gripped the edges of my shoulder, looking at me with a warm smile.

"Those who know nothing of this world, they will be oblivious and think that it is just a necklace. Those mean girls, they won't understand. Some may try to take it from you, but it will burn their skin. Only a familiar can wear it after their master has gifted it to them. This will protect you from the other vampires, Evelyn. If they cause problems, ensure it is easily seen, and it will be enough to send them away."

"They're coming for you, aren't they?" I whispered.

"It's okay, my dear child. They can come after me again and again. I will always fight them. Now, we should discuss lore and protections in more depth."

We sat back down. I took a quick glance at the pendant. It kind of looked like those jade ornaments sold at the market stalls. The stone was flat, marked as if something had once sat on the center of the pendant.

"There is little that we can do in preparation for the inevitable. I have not seen a witch in several hundred years, and I doubt they exist now. At least the kind of witch I would require if I were to utilize black magic. Of course, that is dangerous. If we ever venture down that path, we will discuss it again, as it can corrupt the soul. It would have to be a dire situation for me to consider that. Aside from dark magic, we can try the standard weapons, but that only drags out the melee."

"So, how do you kill a vampire? I'm assuming that the standard folklore is wrong."

"Generally, yes. Aversion to sunlight is a created lie, a stake to the heart is lacking in information, garlic is gross, but that is a personal opinion, and holy water depends on the source. We've already covered the sunlight, so we'll go to the stake. Yes, it is an issue, but we can self-heal quite well. To make it effective, the stake has to remain in the body, and the head must be removed. Many forget the latter, thinking that the former is enough. That is another one of those created lies. You will find that many of these folklores are altered to suit our own needs."

Yeah, that made sense. Create a lie, and if slayers or townsfolk toting torches and pitchforks ever became a problem, they'd be doing a terrible job at trying to get rid of their vampire problem.

"We cannot consume food, but if someone were to hold out garlic, it would mean nothing to us. Cram it down our throat, sure, that's a problem as it would be for anyone. And holy water. The standard priest who preaches to his flock once a week is hardly a problem for the likes of my kind. Those found in the suburban church are churned out with information about how to keep the parishioners in his church. How to rake in the donations and ensure that everyone believes in the Almighty, but they are not taught how to deal with real evil."

"Do you consider yourself evil?"

"I take lives. I kill humans, Evelyn. I have no remorse for what I do, and I never will. I will not stop, and there is nothing that anyone can say to alter that."

"You don't seem evil to me."

"Thank you for that. They say that beauty is in the eye of the beholder. I suppose it could be applied to this as well. As for using holy water against a vampire, it needs to come from higher up in the chain. The higher, the better."

"Can you enter holy ground?"

"Vampires are not limited to any place. We do not need permission to enter a home. We can frolic through the holiest of grounds if we desire. You will find that particular lore came from a vampire that had set up a home in an old church and lured people in with the false belief that it would be enough to save them from him."

Charming.

CHAPTER 10

I was tired. Walking through the corridors at school, it felt like I bumped into every single person in the entire building. Of course, I knew it wasn't the case. If it were, I'd have Audrey Hartley glaring at me, snapping her fork tongue with acidic words of hate.

Scrubbing my eyes, I yawned and turned to my lonesome corridor of darkness. Only I wasn't alone. It was the purple-eyed boy, and it looked like he was waiting for me.

His eyes were definitely purple. There was no mistaking them for blue.

"They're coming for you," he said softly.

"Who are?"

"Who are what?"

I gasped, turning around to see Audrey behind me. The other girls were not with her. I'd managed to avoid all of them until now.

"I was,"

Turning back, the boy was gone.

"Nothing," I murmured.

The wise me said to be wary of looking like a lunatic by asking if she'd seen the guy with purple eyes that had disappeared into thin air. This place was clearly more than just a boring town.

"You're Evelyn, right?"

"Yeah, everyone calls me Evie."

Except for Niko, but I couldn't exactly say that.

Audrey smiled as if it was beneath her to offer the gesture to me. Almost like she was being forced into this by a certain master or a father desperate for attention from the very same master.

"I'm Audrey. You're new to Hades."

"Yeah, arrived just over a week ago."

Gritting that forced smile, Audrey clutched her books to her chest as if they were the only thing that could save her. She was picture-perfect, looking like she'd spent a long time deciding on the right cashmere sweater to match the school skirt. It wasn't the school's official jumper, yet it seemed as if no one cared.

The blond curls were artfully placed on either side of her neck, with pink barrettes clipped to the side. Everything was coordinated. Being this close to someone who was the complete opposite must be incredibly difficult.

"Well, that's good, I guess. So, I heard you're living on

the east side."

In the house with a crack in the basement wall? Why yes, Audrey, you are right.

"Yeah, we found a cute house the other day."

"You know it's haunted, don't you?"

"That's what the removalists said, but the builder that fixed the wall said it was rubbish. I wonder who is telling the truth."

I pretended that I was shocked when I gasped.

"Maybe it was the builder. After all, he's working for the real estate, and if we leave because of it, then the real estate will have to pay to move us into another house. They didn't tell us it was haunted. Isn't that illegal?"

"Well, I don't,"

"Gosh, Audrey, maybe the builder was being paid off to keep us there."

"No, I don't think,"

"You are so right. I'm glad that you brought this to my attention. My uncle is not going to be happy at all. If we have to move because of it,"

I shook my head, putting my hands on my hips.

"He'll be so behind in his work. Then there will be a delay in getting better coverage in this area."

"Coverage?"

Audrey's frown deepened.

"Yeah, my uncle works for a company with a government contract for the communications towers. We move around so that he can do the pre-setup works before they start the digging and building. I guess a few more months without cell phone coverage won't matter much."

Her eyes widened. Like everyone in this town, she had the little rectangle permanently attached to her hand, and like everyone else, she complained that the reception was awful. I know because it's all I have ever heard. Brad will be labeled as a hero, I'm sure of it.

"You know, I think it's fine. There's no such thing as ghosts, right?"

"Yeah, I know."

Her smile seemed less of an effort now. In fact, she seemed to shift with restrained excitement.

"So, we're getting better coverage in this town?"

"Well, this is the beginning. My uncle will scope out a few good places, discuss them with his boss, and approach the necessary people. It's all preliminary at the moment. You'd be surprised at how many people protest at having a tower near them. They want great coverage, but they don't want the towers. Can't have one without the other."

Audrey was nearly frothing at the mouth. I think that if I said that she could apply to have the tower in her yard, she'd believe me and happily skip off home to start the process.

"Yeah, it's a bummer but necessary."

When I looked at Audrey, I could see someone who, despite her best intentions, would reveal the game far too early if left to her own devices. The question I had was if she went home and told her father of this conversation, would he pick up on it, or would he be oblivious as well? It could go either way, so it was best to keep the questions limited and mixed.

"How long have you lived in Hades?"

"All my life," she said, beaming her smile. "I just love the place. It's so pretty."

"That's cool."

It wasn't. Boring was a better choice of word.

"What's the place like? It seems pretty laid back."

"Oh yeah," she said. I noted a distinct hesitation in her tone.

"The builder was acting like there are some freaky people in this town. I'm not allowed to walk to or from school. Crazy, right?"

Audrey stared at me.

"Yeah," she said softly, slowly drawing out the word.

"Do your parents let you walk around with your friends?"

"Only in a group. We leave from one house together."

So, her father is besties with the head honcho vampire, and he still can't trust them not to attack his kid. That was interesting.

Niko was right when he said that I'd see that he was different from the others. We'd been in the same room as each other many times for several hours as well. He'd fed from me, and I wasn't dead. We slept in the same house as each other. Yes, it would seem Niko was vastly different from the other vampires in this town. It certainly explained a lot.

"Well, I have to go. My uncle will be waiting for me, and if I'm late, then no towers, right?"

Audrey smiled, though I could see a lot of hesitation on her face.

"Yeah, I guess."

Turning the corner, I moved quickly to avoid Audrey catching up to me. I didn't want to encourage her in any way.

Brad frowned at me as I opened the door.

"Sorry. The local wildlife cornered me."

"Uh-huh."

As soon as the door was shut, Brad pulled out of the parking space. He didn't speed, but I watched him push it to the limit on every street.

When we got home, Brad returned to his office, grunting something about dinner. My concerns were elsewhere, so I didn't hear him.

Niko was waiting for me and listened to everything that happened, then took a few minutes to think about the information. There was a studious look on his face.

"I think,"

"Yeah?"

"I think I like the way that you find the facts without alerting those around you as to what you're up to."

I sighed, rolling my eyes.

"Thank you, Niko. You are, as always, a gentleman. It's not the time for it, though."

"Would you rather I was rude?"

"No, but,"

"But nothing, Evelyn. We have a symbiotic relationship, and I wish to keep things pleasant. I also appreciate the efforts that you go to without any prompting on my part. It shows me that not only do you care, but you strive to be an ideal familiar. You make me realize that my choice in you was extremely wise."

"Okay, sorry."

Setting the book aside, Niko crossed his legs and thought about it some more. I was on edge. I needed to know what was going to happen, what he thought they'd do.

"I saw the guy with purple eyes again."

Niko stopped thinking and gave me a stern look.

"What do you mean again?"

"Didn't I tell you?"

"No. Tell me about both times, please."

"The first time was at the enrolment interview. He was sitting in the reception area, bag at his feet. He looked at me but didn't say anything. This morning, he was waiting for me when I turned the corner to my locker. He said *they're coming for you*, as in me. I tried to ask him what he meant, but Audrey turned up, and the guy was gone. Who or what is he?"

Niko sighed, getting up from the seat. He crossed the room to look out the dormer window. It was a view of the forest, and Niko liked the view. He said he used to spend a lot of time up here when this house officially belonged to him. Now, he considered himself a houseguest and nothing more. It was not his house. It hadn't been that way for a long time.

"Nephilim, a creation of an unholy union between a fallen angel and a demon. There are only a few in existence, as it is rare for an angel to become fallen and even rarer for them to associate with a demon. The creation grows rapidly, becoming an adult in an unfathomable time. When they reach the end of the growth cycle, they are seen to be complete. They do not always appear as a young person. Because they are both angel and demon, they can alter their appearance, and move quickly and without being seen. It is beyond comprehension what they can do, and I find it surprising that one is here. Did your uncle see him the other day?"

I nodded, which seemed to surprise Niko.

"That would be because the Nephilim wanted that and no other reason. They only show themselves to people of their choosing. It is curious. Though, I think it is not worth taking seriously at the moment. What is more intriguing is his determination to find you and deliver his message. I don't see this being about the vampires. Once you are no longer associated with me, they will have no interest in you other than feeding. I can lure them away from you by pre-empting their attack and leaving the house. No, this is something else entirely. Who? Who would come for you, Evelyn?"

I shrugged.

"No idea."

Niko's eyes narrowed as he turned to look at me.

"We have company," Niko said softly.

His eyes shifted to the staircase. I stood and moved to see Brad at the bottom of the stairs. He looked a little angry.

Turning back to Niko, I shrugged.

"I guess it's time."

"So be it."

I quickly walked down the stairs. Brad stepped back.

"Did you bring a guy home?"

"Uh, not quite. This is going to be really hard for you to accept, so I want you to calm down and come up to the attic."

"No on both counts."

"I did not invite him into the house, Brad. He was already living here. Come up to the attic, please."

Not waiting for his response, I turned and walked back up the stairs. Niko was sitting in his seat again. I guess this was his attempt at being less threatening.

Brad warily walked up the stairs. He looked at the man who, while looking human, didn't really appear to be correct.

"Okay, we'll start with introductions. This is my uncle Brad."

Niko nodded his head with a subdued smile. Hiding those fangs for now.

"Brad, this is Niko Corbin. He is the original owner of this house. He was behind the wall in the basement, and he is a vampire."

Slowly, Brad turned and looked at me.

"Have you lost your mind?"

"Bradley, please sit, and we can get to know each other as Evelyn and I have done over the past few days."

"You kept this from me?"

"Well, you wouldn't believe me when I said the wall spoke to me, so what do you expect me to do when I find out it's because we've got a vampire trapped in our house?"

Brad huffed indignantly, then lumped himself into the chair.

"Okay, regale me with this nonsense."

"I was trapped behind that wall for sixty years, punishment for daring to be alive when another vampire had delusions of grandeur. This is the sad tale that we were yet to get to, Evelyn. Hades is actually Corbin territory. My second in charge decided that he wanted several things, and one of them was to rule. He demanded that I hand over the territory to him. I would not do it, so he put me behind the wall. No doubt he claimed that I am dead and that I gave the rule to him."

"Do you know why he didn't kill you?"

"Yes," Niko whispered. "I mean not to lie to you, Evelyn, but it is something that I find troubling to think about. He could not kill me as it would not work, not when I had a child who could take over the leadership. All covens are ruled by a family member. When no one comes forward to take the claim after death, then the second in charge is given the posting."

"Where's your child?"

Niko shrugged, sadly looking away.

"I sent the child and my wife away for safety reasons, and I have not seen them since."

CHAPTER 11

Brad was pacing the living room floor. He insisted that we move downstairs because even though the attic was bright and airy, it was still creepy.

Was he angry? No, I think he was more confused than anything.

"So, let me get this straight. They can't kill you because if they do, the rule of this town will pass to your child, the kid that you've not seen in over sixty years."

"Seventy,"

"Yeah, okay. Seventy."

Brad was about to roll his eyes but stopped when I frowned at him. It was not the time for it.

"And because Ryan saw the crack in the wall downstairs, he'll go and tell the vampire that you're breaking free."

"He's already told him. I overheard his daughter telling her friends. Audrey said that the vampire went off his tree about it."

"Which means that he's not happy and will be considering the next move. I anticipate that he will either send someone here to confirm the details or present himself to take me down once and for all. I cannot predict which one as I have not been around him in a long time. The state of his mind could be healthy or could be quite mad."

Brad looked at me and, in particular, the necklace. The arm stretched out as the glare hardened, pointing to the pendant.

"What's that all about?"

"Evelyn and I have formed an agreement that benefits both of us and, in turn, you. She is my familiar, and through her, I can extend the familiar protection to you. If a vampire threatens your life, mention my name, and all issues will fade away."

"You mean the vampires that want you dead."

"Yes, the very same. There is a code that they will adhere to regardless of any issues that they may have with a vampire. It is against our law to attack a familiar."

"And when you're dead?"

"I don't plan on dying, but if the unthinkable happened, then I would suggest that you tighten your laces and run."

I shouldn't have smiled, but I did. I also shouldn't have giggled, but I did that too. Brad frowned at me. I stopped, pursing my lips in a vain attempt to stop laughing.

"So, what else am I missing out on? You pretending you were sick just to get out of school yesterday, the purple-eyed boy, those Nephilim things?"

"I freaked out yesterday and panicked. Today was just as distressing, and I didn't call you."

Brad huffed, not impressed. I thought it was pretty good, considering that I wanted to run all the way back here and not wait for Brad to turn up and scold me.

"The purple-eyed boy is the Nephilim, and we're still trying to figure that out." Niko offered. "They are the product of a fallen angel and a demon breeding. The fact that it has presented itself to Evelyn twice now is an issue."

Brad's eyes widened as he turned and looked at me.

"Have you ever seen this kid or anyone else like him before coming here?"

Giving Brad a grim look, I shook my head. I would have told him if I'd seen anyone with strange eyes. I would definitely tell him that someone had disappeared in front of me if it happened. The only reason I hadn't told him of today's interaction was that I needed to speak with Niko about it.

"Told you we were in Hell."

"We should have stayed in Gainsport."

"Where you are is of no relevance. The Nephilim will

always find the person they are looking for. As for the vampire problem, this is just one of many, many towns that we are a part of. In fact, many towns had vampires before they had humans."

"Well, yay for them," Brad muttered.

With a heavy sigh, Brad sat in the lounge and frowned heavily. His lips were tight, and his fingers rapped against the armrest. He was thinking, and it wasn't good, going by the look on his face.

"I'll quit work. We can be gone by morning."

"It won't save her."

His fingers stopped, and the frown fell quickly.

"You may not even need to worry. Just because there is a Nephilim hanging around does not mean that there is danger. I know that it said *they are coming for you* to her, but that is no indication of a threat."

"Why would this Nephilim have an interest in Evie?"

Niko turned his head to look at me. Assessing eyes dragged over me, no emotions on his face.

"I have my suspicions that it may have something to do with her father. As we have no way of finding out who he is, we may have to rely on their input into this."

The mind-blowing revelation that my father might be more than just an average human was a little hard to take in. I sat down, staring into nothing.

Did my mother know? Was it obvious? I looked at

Niko, and many aspects of him could be taken as one or the other. He looked human, but he looked wrong. Knowing he was a vampire made sense. All these questions made me wish that my mother was alive so I could ask her. If she was, I wouldn't be here.

Maybe she did know what my father was. What were the chances that she was his familiar? Was that the reason she was always gone at night and sometimes during the day? It certainly fitted the requirements. If that were the case, then maybe she wasn't passed out in bed from drug use. Maybe it was sleeping off a feed.

"Can I ask you something?"

"Always," Niko offered.

"Is it possible that my mother was a familiar for a vampire?"

"Anything is possible. What makes you think that?"

"She was always gone at night, sometimes during the day. I used to think she was high on drugs and sleeping, but I now think that she could have been low on blood after a feed. If she was lethargic, she would be irritable, which could be the reason for her outbursts."

I saw the exchanges that Niko and Brad shared. Niko returned with a vague smile.

"All are valid thoughts, Evelyn. A vampire will feed on a familiar, but usually, it is only if there is no other alternative. To make her lethargic, though, he would have to drink a lot of blood, which would have made your mother disorientated. If that were the case, it would be likely that she would struggle to stand upright, let alone hold the ability to return home. The other thought you must consider is that if this vampire is your father, he would know that you exist and, in that case, you would reside in his home. There is no other alternative to this situation. Vampires keep their families by their side and nothing else. This means that either the vampire in question is not your father, was unaware that you existed, or was too dangerous for you to be around. I do not wish to be presumptuous about the relationship that you had with her, but I heard the conversation that you and Brad had. If she beat you, then I'm inclined to think that she wouldn't care if you were around a dangerous vampire."

"Evie," Brad said softly. "I know you're trying to find something that will make things fit, but I saw your mother's police record. The woman from child services showed it to me so that I would understand because I didn't believe her. No matter how much I said your mother would have asked me for help, she wouldn't hear it. I said that we would meet for lunch. She'd be happy and never ask for a single dollar. The woman replied with the simple statement that I didn't know that you existed. Think about that, Evie. I saw your mother regularly, and she never mentioned you. I did not know you existed until the funeral. When I saw this crying kid in the front row, I looked at her and saw a younger version of my mother. I have no explanation for why she kept you a secret, but she did."

Yeah, I had no idea why she did that, either.

"Perhaps she knew that Evelyn was not completely human. If she displayed peculiar behavior as a child, then it would stand to reason that she would think it was necessary to hide her."

"But I went to school."

"And she also beat you. A broken spirit can do more damage than we see at the surface."

"So, what are we talking about here?" Brad asked. "One of those Nephilim, angel, demon, vampire?"

"There are a few possibilities, and yes, those are all on the table as well."

Brad whistled through his teeth.

"The others?"

"Well, it has been a long time since there has been a witch, but it's possible that they still exist. For a while, there was a shapeshifter problem, but that seemed to stop when the black plague hit Europe."

"Wait, you were alive for the black plague?"

"Unfortunately, yes. If you are wondering, no, it does not kill a vampire, but the blood of the infected was incredibly foul. It is standard practice to leave the healthy alone in such times, which made life rather difficult. This is the reason that my family traveled to this land and claimed Hades as our own. We were one of the first towns to attract humans to it."

"Hang on, they told us that the town founder was Reginald Hades."

Niko held his hands out with a beaming smile.

"So very pleased to meet you. I am Reginald Hades, the town founder of this lovely little place. In a few years, I will, unfortunately, meet with a rather sticky end, but do not fear. Someone will be waiting to take my place. Over and over again until one day, no one will remember what any of the predecessors look like."

"You?" I said dryly.

Niko smiled and nodded his head.

"Yes, me. I picked the place based on the location, near the ocean, with a little bit of flat land for lots of houses and a lovely forest to wander through. With a little land clearing and extremely reasonable purchase prices, they came in their droves, human and vampire. Within a few months, the,"

Niko paused and looked at the front door.

"What's wrong?"

"We have company."

"Good or bad?"

"Bad."

Brad stood and carefully pulled the curtain back, looking out at the front yard.

"I can see about five people, men and women. Walking up the footpath, they'll be here within seconds."

Niko stood, flicking his hand to Brad.

"I am not here. You do not know who I am and do not know that vampires exist. Demand that they leave.

Do not let them into the house. Be forceful, be strong, and no matter what, do not let them see Evelyn."

"Or you," Brad murmured.

Niko smiled with a nod.

My heart was racing as the shadows darkened the glass panels on the door. They were little triangles that were shaped into a half circle, sitting above my head in height. The glass was an odd color yellow, almost mustard.

Carefully and quietly, Brad slid the safety chain over the door. When the person knocked on the door, I jumped. My hand flew to my mouth, holding back the squeak of shock. Looking at Niko, I saw an empty lounge.

Brad rallied himself. With a look of determination on his face, he opened the door.

"Good afternoon. My friends and I are looking for a gentleman who goes by the name of Niko Corbin. Is he free by any chance?"

"No one here by that name."

Brad pushed the door only to stop. I assume that the vampire stopped him. My position behind the door offered no view of what was going on.

"Forgive me, but I'm inclined to think that is incorrect. We have a reliable source that says it was only a matter of time before he was, uh, *free,* if you will, and we'd like to speak with him."

"I think you need to get your hearing checked because I said there is no one here by that name. Please leave."

"Brad, is it?"

He offered nothing but a frown.

"Perhaps we were not clear enough for you. We know that you are harboring Niko, and if you do not provide us with access to him, we will be left with no choice but to report this to our leader. That is something that you do not want as he will not be happy. He will come here personally, and then you and that darling niece of yours will be dead. Is that what you want?"

Brad didn't respond straight away. It was almost like he weighed up the options. I tried to make faces at him, but Brad didn't flinch, just looking at the vampire in front of him.

Would he hand over Niko to save us?

CHAPTER 12

"Perhaps *I* was not clear enough for *you*. Leave now, or I will call the cops."

The vampire chuckled mercilessly. It sent a shiver up my spine. The dark tone of his amusement was another attempt to threaten Brad and, in turn, me. I'm sure he could detect another heartbeat close to him.

"We own this town." the vampire hissed. "Your precious cop is on our master's payroll. I know you are fully aware of what I am and what you are facing. You know the danger that is in front of you, yet you foolishly hide Niko with the belief that he will protect you when our master comes calling. You will regret that, Mister Newton. That little chain will do nothing for you. You best get yourself something worthy to protect her. Otherwise, you will be on the ground dying, listening to her beg you for help. Will he come to her defense? Will he save you before death takes you? I don't think so."

I could see Brad's jaw clench tight. He was struggling to remain strong.

"Until next time."

The shadows slowly faded from the glass panels, Brad watched, and after a few seconds, he closed the door.

He turned and looked at me. Both of us were lost. Brad had just faced off against a vampire that essentially threatened our lives because he would not hand Niko over to them. Someone that he barely knew, Brad protected, and it could be the death of us.

"I hope you know what you're doing here, Evie."

"Me? I know nothing."

"Why are we trusting our lives to this vampire?"

"Because it's the right thing to do."

Brad's eyes shifted to the empty room. Walking quickly, he checked out the area and saw that we were alone.

"Pack your things quickly. We're leaving."

"Niko said that it won't help me."

"That was about the Nephilim thing. These vampires have directly threatened us, whereas that boy just keeps appearing. He's not the threat here. They are."

"You're wrong. He said *they're coming for you.* That sounds like a threat to me. Our best option is here with Niko. We have not been a part of this world. We've got no idea what the right thing to do is, but he does."

Brad gestured to the empty room.

"You mean the vampire that left when danger showed

up."

"He would be somewhere close, don't be so judgmental."

"Why are you so insistent on keeping him safe at the cost of your own life?"

"You did, too."

"No, Evie. I stood my ground to keep them on the other side of the door. Because of that, they will return, and next time, we won't be so lucky. Come on, what's the deal? Are you in love with him?"

"No," I hissed.

I moved to avoid Brad's hard glare, but he shifted back into my space, blocking me from leaving.

"Get out of my way."

"Not until you tell me what's going on."

Brad moved in step with me, getting in my way and generally being annoying.

"Stop it."

"No. You are going to tell me why you are insisting that we stay here with this creature."

The frustration began to set in, overwhelming me to the point that tears were rolling down my cheeks.

"Because I want to, alright?"

"No. It's not alright. You've done nothing but complain about being here, cut school, whined, and done all that you could to drag it down. Now, when I give you the green light to leave, you don't want to. There is only one thing that has changed, and that is the vampire, who I know for a fact won't leave this town either. So, either you tell me what's going on, or I will assume the worst. Given that you are still a minor, I will be packing everything, and we will be leaving. If he's touched you, he'll find a stake in his heart."

"It's not like that."

"Then tell me what it is like."

"I need him."

Brad's frown deepened. His jaw clenched tight again. I wiped the tears away, smiling despite how sad I felt at the moment.

"It's not like that. It just feels like he completes us, you know?"

I got nothing from Brad.

"Almost like I've got two dads. We're like this weird family. I haven't had a normal one, but this felt like it fitted me. Of all the places that we've been to, I've never felt like it was right for us. Niko changed that. I had someone else to talk to, and please don't start about friends. That doesn't work. I've tried and failed so many times. I don't like this town, but he made it less terrible."

"Two dads, huh?"

I nodded, trying not to laugh.

Brad sighed, dragging me in for a hug. They were rare for us. I think that Brad didn't want to invade my space, letting me adjust to the new world that included a man that I barely knew. We were getting there. Slowly but perfectly.

"Alright, Evie. We'll stay and fight with the vampire."

Niko emerged about ten minutes after the conversation. Brad and I were sitting at the breakfast counter, eating the quick dinner that he'd made. It was grilled cheese sandwiches, and they were delicious. I don't know how he did it, but they were always so much better than when I made them.

"Where the hell did you go?" Brad snapped.

"To the other side of the street to watch from a different angle and to remove myself from the house. They would have detected me if I remained, which is why they left so easily. Had I been here, they would have pushed through the door and searched for me. Without me here, they would have resorted to plan b, which was to frighten you into leaving."

"So, what happens now?"

"They will have returned to the leader's house and discussed what they found. With me not being in the house, they will try to figure out where I am. It is unlikely that anyone who has been trapped in pure darkness for so many years will easily go out into the afternoon sun, so they will assume that I am in the forest. They might pre-empt their leaders' thoughts and search the forest before returning, but I doubt it. Most followers lack initiative and do not want to presume what their leader wants, especially one who is known for being so volatile. They will return, though, do not doubt that for a second. The best-case scenario is after eight pm when the humans in this town seem to retreat to their homes. Worst case is anywhere between now and then, which shows that they do not care what the humans see."

"He said that they own this town, cops included."

Niko moved around the kitchen bench, gliding his fingers over the work surface.

"Yes, that is standard. Vampires tend to leave a trail of death, so ensuring that the local law enforcement looks the other way is rather necessary."

Brad picked up the empty plate in front of me, adding it to his own.

"It's going to be a long night. Evie, you better prepare yourself in case we have to flee the house."

Sliding off the stool, I looked at Brad, who was occupied with cleaning the plates. Niko looked between us and offered a vague shrug. Something was off, and I think I knew what.

Moving around to the hall, I leaned against the wall and waited. It didn't take long for Brad to say something.

"She has this ridiculous notion of making you a part of an odd family with us. I hope for her sake that you're not planning on stabbing us in the back when things get ugly."

"I would die for her," Niko whispered. "And you too, if you were wondering. The two of you have accepted me. You let me remain in this house while knowing that I could be your death. You have kept your word by refusing entry to my enemies. You have put yourself and Evelyn in danger, and you are still here. For that, I would show you and Evelyn endless devotion."

"Do you love her?"

"As a father would a child. You are right to be concerned, but you needn't worry. Evelyn reminds me of my daughter. She was a child when I begged her mother to flee. It was a mistake. I know that now."

"They're dead?"

"Unfortunately, yes. I kept her hidden for as long as I could, but the weight of his presence meant that I had to either introduce her to this world or continue to hide her in another location. One held a greater risk than the other, so I went with the best option. I said goodbye to the best things that ever happened to me, and I have spent every day and night since then regretting that decision. To learn of their passing was not easy, and it is why I am so incredibly happy that you are here and not leaving this town. I don't know what will happen, but I do know that running away will not solve our problems."

Quietly, I walked up the corridor to the stairs. My room sat at the front of the house, over the guest room. Dressing for warmth, I tightened my laces and pulled my jacket on. I could feel the cold permeating through the windows. Crossing the room, I thought that if we managed to get any sleep tonight, I'd prefer that it wasn't so frosty in my room.

Looking out the window was a mistake or the best thing I've ever done, depending on how a person looked at the situation. With a gasp, I turned and rushed down the stairs.

Niko and Brad were still in the kitchen, turning to me as I skidded on the wooden floor.

"There's a lot of vampires out on the street."

Niko pulled the curtain back, looking at the forest.

"Empty. Interesting."

"Then run."

"I will not abandon either of you."

"No, but you will lure them away." Brad offered. "Is it better to fight as a group or on your own? We are pretty much useless."

"And I have been trapped behind a wall for sixty years. No part of this is going to work easily. Come with me."

Niko led us to the hall cupboard, opened the doors, and lowered to the floor. With a thump of his fist, one of the wood panels came free. He reached in and dragged out a rifle, handing it to Brad. Next came the bullets.

"Just the one?"

"There is only one of me. However, the cavity is full

of bullets."

Niko handed another box of bullets. Our pockets were full of them now. I zipped my pockets shut, hoping they wouldn't make too much noise if I had to be quiet.

"What's the plan?"

"Approach, let them speak their mind, and then shoot anyone that takes a step closer."

"Will this work?" I asked. "I thought that their head had to be removed."

"Unfortunately, it is only a temporary measure, but it is enough to show that you are a threat and that you will do everything you can to stop them. Regardless, a bullet wound does pose a problem in the immediate future. They would lose a lot of blood, which is a dangerous situation for a vampire. Any that are shot would need to retreat to somewhere safe, remove the bullet, and then feed to ensure continuing health. They would do this at their own dwelling as it is common to pass out because of the blood loss."

"So, you're saying shoot all of them, so they have to run away?"

Niko offered a devilish smile.

"Sounds truly perfect."

CHAPTER 13

The vampires remained on the street for a few minutes, then one emerged from the group. Niko grimaced.

"It has been a long time since I saw that face."

Pushing him out of the way, I looked at the vampire that was determined to destroy Niko. Letting go of the curtain, I turned to Niko.

"Run."

"I will do no such thing."

"I am asking you to do what is necessary. We need you alive. I don't understand why the Nephilim are coming for me, or how to deal with these vampires. I need you to be here with us."

My voice was low, raw, and filled with hurt. I didn't want to lose him as well. For a few years, I'd spent this life with Brad, trying to avoid the thoughts of how one wrong decision could alter our lives forever. I didn't want to lose him, and now that I had Niko, I was just as worried.

"Niko," the vampire called out. "We know that you're in there. Come out and play, old friend."

Niko sighed.

"I am only putting you in danger if I stay."

"Go into the woods," Brad muttered. "We'll let them in, and I will show them the basement. I put the brick back. It looks like the wall is still formed enough to keep you in there."

"They won't believe you."

"It doesn't matter," I said with a grin. "There's a lock on the door on the outside. Get them in there and lock the door."

"They will break it down. I would advise against inviting them into the house, but if you do, then certainly utilize whatever locks and barricades that you can find."

"And you?"

Niko shrugged at Brad. There was a desperate need to keep the three of us together, but the closer we got to the breaking point, I could see that separating was ideal.

"Is there somewhere to wait until they leave?"

"There are many places."

"Then go. We'll find you when they leave."

The door shuddered when something heavy hit it. Already, a crack appeared, splintering the wood.

"Come on," Niko whispered, taking my hand.

We rushed to the back door, quietly slipping through it. Brad pulled his jacket on. The air was so cold that we could see our breath. This place was extreme with its weather.

Crossing the yard, we delved into the forest. We'd made it in a matter of seconds. I turned back to see vampires appearing on each side of the house. They went straight for the back door. Their numbers were few as they had fanned out. I could see one side of the house. Some of the vampires remained there to wait in case we emerged from a window.

"As quiet as you can," Niko whispered.

That was not easy. I'm sure my teeth chattering was louder than the twigs snapping under my boots.

Delving deep into the forest I was not supposed to go near, we walked through the light undergrowth. Through the spindly grey trees that were starting to lose their leaves.

Underneath my foot was a loud crack. My body tightened. I turned to see the vampires turn to look at the forest.

"They're in the forest," one yelled.

"Run!" Niko whispered.

I never thought that I was any good at sports and definitely not running. In fact, I thought that I looked rather odd when I ran. So, I avoided it at all costs. It was no surprise that even after a few seconds, I was out of breath.

What was surprising was how fast the vampires caught up with us. I almost ran into one, gasping as I looked up. His fangs glistened in the moonlight, grinning at me with a dark malevolence.

The strands of black hair fell into his eyes, and his skin was not as pale as I expected it to be. The myths of vampires were clearly wrong, lies created to hide the truth of what really walked among us.

"Hello, my pretty." he snarled.

Grabbing me, I waited for the inevitable that never eventuated. The bulking creature lifted me from the ground, holding me as if I were a floppy doll in his hands. I wasn't heavy, but raising me without even a hint of exertion was unexpected.

He was smiling harder as he opened his mouth. The fangs lowered to sharp points, tapering into a fine point. I gasped, wondering why Niko's fangs weren't that sharp. Was this a different kind of vampire, or was Niko trying to avoid scaring me?

The vampire looked at the pendant. His eyes widened, and the fangs shrank. He hissed, then pushed me away. I fell to the ground, wincing at the pain that reverberated through me.

"Ow," I groaned, rubbing my wrist.

It hurt, likely to be sprained. I could move my fingers, so that was a good sign. Also, nothing was broken, no skin tears, no bleeding. Just a little pain.

Glancing around me, I realized that I was alone.

Thankfully, the vampire was gone, as were the rest of them. The problem was that Brad and Niko were gone as well.

"Brad? Niko?" I called out.

Nothing.

Fearing the worst, I got up from the ground and began to search for them. No matter which way I turned, I saw no sign of where they might be. I couldn't even locate the house anymore.

Searching the forest was no easy task. When Brad said not to go in here, I knew and fully understood why. Becoming lost was a mere step in the wrong direction.

I thought that I heard something. When I stopped, I tried to listen harder, if that was possible. It sounded like the wind whipped past me rapidly, but I knew it wasn't the wind. The wind did not snicker.

A thought crossed my mind that these vampires that were whipping past me were trying to lead me to another place. Perhaps the wrong direction, perhaps away from Brad and Niko. They wanted to separate us, let us get lost in the woods, and then we'd be prime pickings for them.

But I was not attacked. The vampire had me in his hands. I was seconds away from his fangs, yet one look at the pendant, and he backed away with fear. What did it mean?

Touching the cool stone, I thought about it and how Niko gave it to me. We were bonded together, so did that mean that it could lead me to him? I hoped it was the case.

Closing my eyes, I lifted my foot and stepped forward. It probably made me look like a complete fool, but I held hope that this would work.

My hearing became more acute as I listened to every footstep I took. Leaves crunched under my shoes, twigs snapped, and the wind whispered its taunt.

I ignored it all and continued to let my feet take me to wherever they landed. Hopefully, it wouldn't be face-first into the dirt.

Hearing a groan, I opened my eyes and searched the area. Ahead of me, I could see a group of vampires. When I stepped closer, they took off. With sniggers rising into the air, the vampires whipped through the trees and left one behind.

Niko was on the ground, gripping his stomach.

I rushed to him, lowering to my knees. He lifted his hand to reveal that blood coated his palm. The shirt had a great gaping wound, much like his stomach. Blood soaked the once white shirt, staining it with the horror of what they had done to him.

"What do you need? I'll find a victim. Bring them here."

Niko smiled, shaking his head.

"My dear Evelyn, thank you for the offer, but it will not be sufficient. They created a wound that cannot be fixed, which was intentional."

"No," I said, tears welling. "You can't do this."

"I'm afraid there's not much of a choice."

"But we need you. You're not allowed to die."

"Again, not much of a choice. Now, help me sit up against the tree. There is much to discuss before the wounds take me away."

Wiping the tears, I wrapped his arm around my neck and shifted his body to the nearest tree. Then I sat down to face him.

It appeared to take a lot of effort now that his energy was depleting, but Niko reached into that little pocket again and pulled something out. Flicking his fingers, Niko urged me forward.

Pieces of the same metal as the frame around the stone were clicked into place. I looked down at it when Niko leaned back. They were what was missing from the pendant. Two diagonal lines with a C between them.

"Without the bars, it is the pendant of a familiar. With the bars, it is the pendant of a leader. I have a confession, Evelyn, and I hope you will not be upset at me, but I gave that pendant to you because I suspected that you were more than ordinary. You asked why the previous tenants were unable to wake me. It was because they had no connection. But you woke me, didn't you? It wasn't just you. Brad woke me as well. Only the blood of my kin can do this. I don't know how, but somewhere along the way, my daughter must have aged enough to create a child. You, Evelyn, are a Corbin by blood. That necklace, only a Corbin can wear it. Perhaps this is why you feel so close to me. You know your own kin. You know what feels like home."

I sobbed. Wiping the tears away was pointless, but I did it. It was hard to see through the tears. It was hard to breathe when it hurt so much.

"In the house, you will find things. Search the walls and floors. I hid everything that was vital. To claim the Corbin family line as your own, all you need to do is show them the necklace. However, times have changed, and if you need paperwork, it will be in the house. There will be more items in the house. You will find a box that has pieces of jewelry in it. All of these pieces have the insignia, like that pendant. Brad will be able to find something to wear from the box. He is a good man, Evelyn. You would be wise to make him your second in command."

"Shouldn't the rule go to him? He's older."

"But passing the rule goes in order of birth. Your mother was older. Therefore, it passes to you first. Make him your second in charge, it is a noble position, and it is one that relies heavily on trust."

"But we're not vampires."

"Are you sure about that? You are my family, and I am a vampire. Just because the line has humanity in it does not make you any less of a vampire. Members of our family have died, but that does not mean that they died of natural causes. Think about each and every one of them and tell me that Drakkus did not have a hand in their death."

"Drakkus?"

"The enemy. Be wary of him and do not trust him for even a minute. He will try to charm you, but it will only be for his gain, and in time, it will be your turn to be walled behind bricks. Do not make the same mistakes as me, Evelyn."

Reaching out, I took Niko's hand, gripping it firmly.

"Why can't I save you? What did they do to you?"

He gestured to the blade that was on the other side of his body.

"Do you remember our talk about what myths are correct? Well, it would seem that Drakkus had a vial of holy water delivered straight from the Vatican. The holiest of holy, nothing is greater than when the pope blesses the water. We are evil, Evelyn. The sinners go to Hell, but for us, we are the path they walk on. Not worthy of Heaven or Hell, we endure eternity watching others find peace or damnation. It is torture."

Niko winced, still gripping his side as if he thought that the contents of his body would fall out.

"Now, your father. I don't know who he is, but I can sense that there is definitely something unnatural about you. The fact that the Nephilim are hanging around adds merit to that thought. Be wary of the Nephilim. They are not our friends. They may deliver a message and leave. They might come to deliver more than just a message."

A branch snapped behind us. Hesitantly, I turned to see who it was.

CHAPTER 14

Brad stepped forward, lowering to Niko as he pulled the hand away.

"Damn it, that doesn't look good."

"I'm afraid that you are right with that assessment. I'd like to offer a final gratitude to both of you. It has been a wonderful few days, and you might see it as terrible, but I don't. In you two, I can see that my beloved daughter survived longer than I thought she had."

Brad frowned, looking rather confused.

"You have shown me that there is goodness in this world that I thought was gone. Keep yourselves safe, and remember what I said. Search the past, search the house. Take back this town for the Corbin family and trust no one but each other."

Niko smiled, reaching out. The bloodied finger traced over my cheek.

"You look so much like her."

His firm grip faltered. I could feel the life fading as

his hand slipped from mine.

"This is not fair," I whispered, full of hurt.

"Life is rarely fair."

Brad sat on the ground beside me, giving my shoulder a gentle nudge. He smiled gently when I looked at him.

"You wanna make them pay?"

"Absolutely."

"So, what's this thing about his daughter?"

"We're related to him, apparently. It's why I can wear this."

Brad looked at the necklace.

"Yeah, I wouldn't go announcing that too loudly at the moment. I think they're still out there."

Helping me off the ground, we looked at Niko's lifeless body.

"We should bury him."

"We should, but we don't have time for that. There's a cave nearby. It will do for the time being, which will save him from the sun. Tomorrow, I'll find somewhere to dig a hole. You take his legs. It will be lighter."

We moved into position, ready to lift Niko. He didn't look heavy, but neither of us was fit, so this was going to take a lot of effort.

"Going somewhere?"

Brad gasped, dropping Niko's body. Glancing over my shoulder, I looked at the figure and knew it was Drakkus.

"He's dead. You've got what you wanted, so just go away."

Drakkus chuckled. Every part of it grated against me, anger boiling as I looked at what he'd done to Niko. He was such a nice person, and the creature behind me, he was a monster. I was sick of bullies, and that's what he clearly was.

Picking up the rifle that Brad had left on the ground, I stood and pointed it at Drakkus. He smiled mercilessly.

"Little girl, put the gun down and let the big boys talk."

Pressing the trigger, I watched as his body lifted into the air and thumped to the ground. The end of the gun pushed me back, but I dug my feet into the ground. It wasn't much help, though.

"Nope. Hades is Corbin territory, and I am the leader, as placed by the true leader of this town. You've officially been placed on notice. Each and every one of you have got until sunset tomorrow to leave this town. Otherwise, I'm coming for all of you."

Discarding the shell, I unzipped my pocket and put another bullet into the chamber.

"Who is next?"

They all gasped as I swung the rifle around. Within

seconds, they were gone. Drakkus groaned as he sat up, then looked at the wound.

"You shot me."

"Yeah, and I'm going to do it again. This time, I'm going to give you a warning by counting to three. Three."

Pressing the trigger again, I shot the vampire. His body jerked and thumped to the ground. I gladly accepted the pushback from the rifle. I'd even take the bruising that was likely to appear. All were a mark of my strength.

"You stole something from me, and I will never forgive you for it. If there is even an ounce of strength in you, I would suggest that you run. I will hunt you, and I will kill you because I will make you pay for what you did to Niko."

"This isn't over." he hissed, struggling to his feet.

"The words of a villain who has lost the battle."

Unloading the chamber again, Drakkus watched in horror as I pulled another bullet from my pocket. He turned to run. I lifted the rifle, wondering how good my aim was at a distance. Brad's hand pressed to my shoulder.

"Enough. We do not shoot in the back. Only cowards do that."

"He will come for us again if I don't kill him."

"I'm sure he will, but we do what is right. Face our enemy in their death so that their last memory is seeing the supremacy on our face."

I looked at Brad.

"This is a new side of you. Dark, twisted. I think I like it."

Brad rolled his eyes, scoffing.

"Yeah, great. This is what happens when a vampire enters our life. I was a good boy before *he* turned up."

"But he was a good influence on me," I said softly. "Despite the bad things that we did."

"I do not want to know. Give me that."

Brad took the rifle from me, ensuring that it was safe to be slung over his back. With the strap tightened so the rifle wouldn't move, we leaned down to pick up Niko.

It would not be an easy path, but I would walk it with Brad. Together, we'd bury a friend that we barely knew and mourn his loss alone. There would be no great fanfare, no masses to mourn his passing. Just two long-lost relatives saying goodbye to someone who cared.

Yet again, I'd lost a friend, a family member, and someone that meant a lot to me.

The cave was small, but Brad said that it was enough to put Niko in until tomorrow afternoon. He'd come out here, as he'd said, dig a hole, and then move Niko's body once he was sure that the sun wouldn't burn his body to a crisp. I was going to tell him that Niko could walk in the light but refrained from it at the moment. It was sweet that even after he was gone, Brad was doing all that he could to be respectful of his body.

Brad went into the cave first, dragging Niko's body into it. When he emerged, we pulled the bushes over it to keep the sun out. Over the top of the hole, I scratched RIP into the rock face.

"This will be enough. We don't need to disturb his body anymore."

"Are you sure about that? Don't you want a grave to visit?"

"I can come here to see him."

"Well, if you're sure about it."

I nodded, wrapping my arms around his waist. For a moment, we stood there in silence, saying goodbye to someone who shouldn't be dead.

"I'll make a dedicated path that will lead me here, so there's no chance of getting lost. How's that?"

"That's a good idea."

We began to walk back to the house. I don't know why, but it seemed so much easier now. Maybe the vampires were making my mind fuddled. Was that possible? Surely, Niko would have warned me if that were the case.

"What now?"

"Now?" Brad asked, sounding full of hope. "Now we figure out what to do if the vampires don't leave. So, you're the leader, eh?"

"I am. Did you want to be my second in charge?"

"Gee," he said, pretending to scratch his head. "Got a lot on my plate at the moment. You know, work, manage a house, and an unruly teenager."

I elbowed him in the ribs. Brad chuckled as he rubbed the sore spot.

"Sure. I'll be by your side to tell you that you're a terrible leader and that you're making poor decisions."

I knew he was joking, but it would be funny if he did that. I'm sure he could lighten a tense moment with some poorly timed remark.

"I don't want this, you know," I admitted ruefully. "I'd rather Niko was here."

"This is life, Evie. We can't predict any part of it, and it sucks when these things happen. When your grandparents died, I had a girlfriend at the time who said that I was so lucky to be given a large inheritance. I said that I'd rather they were alive and that no amount of money would ever make it easier."

"Did you dump her gold-digging skank ass?"

"Sure did."

We looked at each other, then laughed. That was until I realized that my mother would have been given half of the estate. I guess that went to a drug dealer.

When we reached the edge of the forest, Brad and I stopped. There was not a sign of anything untoward going on or that anything bad had happened. Just a house that waited for our return. The houses on either side appeared to have residents who were still awake. Lights were on, and shadows moved over the curtains.

"How are we going to prove that we are Niko's descendants?"

"By finding the documents in the house. We will trace our family history, and we will prove that this house belongs to his family, not the heritage trust."

"Do you think that the vampires are members of the trust?"

"No doubt," I returned. "They wanted to lure family members out with the offer of this house as an inheritance. Well, he's got a family. I'm not prepared to take any of their nonsense. Niko said something that made me wonder about the vampires in this town. He basically suggested that our family was murdered. Do you know how my mother died?"

Brad shrugged uneasily.

"The coroner ruled it as a drug overdose. You know, I have spent the last three years wondering why I wasn't good enough for your mother, why she decided to keep me out of her life, and yours as well. This revelation makes me think that she knew more than what she let on. Maybe there was a reason that she kept us separate."

"To protect us?"

"Maybe to protect you. My life was erratic. I was always going out and doing stuff. I'd stay at girlfriends' houses. I'd party with friends and stay at their house or a hotel. Being at home happened, but not often. I now wonder if that saved my life. This job, moving around all the time, maybe it's what has kept us alive as well."

"That's possible."

I bet that if we researched every single family member between Niko and us, we'd find suspicious circumstances. My mother could have been drugged. My grandparents' plane might have had a deliberate malfunction. Maybe my great-grandparents died in a way that was far from ordinary. How far back would we go before we reached Niko?

"What are you going to do about your father?"

I shrugged as we crossed the lawn.

"I don't know where to begin with that. With no information and no one to ask, I'm left without direction. I guess I just have to accept that I will never know who he is."

"Well, maybe a clue might present itself in the future, and it will help you edge a little closer. In the meantime, I still want that promise out of you."

Looking at him curiously, I frowned.

"What promise?"

"School. You are to pass this year. Buckle down, get it done, and then you're free. No one wants a leader that hasn't finished high school."

"I'm sure they won't care."

Brad frowned at me as he opened the door.

"Yes, fine. I will do my best. Of course, if vampires threaten my life again, you can't expect me not to deal with it. Then there's the whole leader of a vampire family thing. I'm sure that's going to take up a lot of my time."

He shook his head, unimpressed. Deep down, I'm sure he knew that I would always try, but I liked to lace my days with humor and sarcasm.

The house was empty, not a hint that a vampire had been in here. Brad inspected the front door while I pushed the back door shut. As I turned, I looked over the kitchen counter and saw the purple-eyed boy again.

I gasped with fright, clutching my chest as my heart pounded heavily. The teen boy stared at me. Dressed in a plain blue suit, he looked approachable despite the lingering sensation floating around him that he was the exact opposite.

"They are coming for you."

CHAPTER 15

It was a new day and another attempt at being a normal teenager. The idea that anything about me or this town was normal was becoming a joke.

The world seemed so much crueler now that I'd lost another person that was important to me. Yet again, I was left with one person to stand beside me in this life. I looked at my uncle with fear in my eyes.

"It's going to be okay, Evie. You've got this."

I nodded, even if I didn't believe him. I had nothing.

"Those kids out there, they don't know about what happened. They're oblivious."

As if life could get any worse, Audrey and her friends walked past the car. They were laughing and chatting, more absorbed in their own lives rather than the world around them.

I blamed her father for Niko's passing. If he'd kept his mouth shut, Niko would still be here, and I would still have my friend and confidant.

"Sure," I murmured.

"Hey, I know it's ahead of schedule, but I thought that you might appreciate it. After all, you keep dropping enough hints."

Brad held out a box with a red bow on it. Pulling the ribbons, I lifted the lid and smiled. It was a new phone.

"Thanks. How much did your boss spend on this?"

"I am offended."

Brad pretended to be deeply hurt by the statement, but the smile was a giveaway. His cheeks lifted as the smile grew.

"Fine, I got it for free. Don't complain. You got the phone that you wanted."

"Oh, I'm not complaining, but you will do better for my real birthday, right?"

"Sure, I guess I can get him to supply a case for it."

I chuckled and pulled the phone out of the box, ignoring the bell that was sounding.

"It's good to go. I even charged it for you. My number is loaded, as well as the real estate if you need to call them. Don't know why you would, but it's there just in case. Someone that we know, I guess."

"You are a legend, Bradley."

"I try my best. Now, I heard the bell sounding."

I nodded, but the door wasn't opening.

"You wanted to come back today, Evie. You said you needed to keep your mind active and not dwell on Niko. I know that you've got a lot on your plate at the moment, but you said you were good for this."

"I am,"

Glancing at the clock on the dashboard, I could see why Brad was getting antsy. He had to clock on by nine am, and it was eight forty-five. It was only a five-minute drive, and Hades had virtually no traffic, so there was no issue here. I guess he didn't want to hang around while waiting for me to figure out what I was doing. He was right, though. I wanted to come back. I said that I was good for it. Was I, though?

"This is worse than the first-day jitters. Alright, I'll see you at three."

I opened the door, lifting my bag in the process. With my new phone tucked into my pocket, I closed the car door and began the descent into Hell. Life in high school was always difficult. Being the outcast because of my choices was never on my agenda, but I could see that it would be that way regardless of what I wanted.

As I reached the top of the stairs, I turned back. Brad was still sitting in his car, watching and waiting. He trusted me, but given the current events, he was probably worried that I'd turn around and walk to another location once he'd left. I couldn't do that once I'd walked through the main doors. The teacher on duty would stop me and send me to the office to call him back to collect me. There was no escape from this particular nightmare.

The corridors were full of students. I weaved through them, desperate to avoid their attention. As the new kid, I always attracted far too much of it. This place, though, was different. I was already a blur in the landscape.

The people of Hades were odd. I haven't ventured far in this town, just a few spots on Main Street and home. From what I could see, the people went about their lives without a care in the world. Some knew of the vampires, but most didn't. At least, that's the way that it appeared. Unless I asked every single person in Hades, I'd never know the truth.

All I wanted was to get through each day and have no issues. That was another feeble dream. I should know better than to waste my hope for such things.

Reaching my locker, I opened the door and unloaded the books for my afternoon lessons into it. Checking everything was in order, I closed the locker to see I was not alone. Audrey smiled sweetly at me, and I knew that this was the beginning of a bad day.

Audrey was her usual perky self. Looking extra pretty today with a soft blush across her cheeks, highlighting the gentle curve. She'd donned false eyelashes, and it looked as if she'd just swiped cherry-colored gloss over her lips.

Today's ensemble was not that different from any other day. Only today, there was a string of black pearls around her neck. They were stark against the white cashmere sweater.

I looked at the line of friends, noting that they were

all wearing black pearl necklaces. That was interesting. I'd never seen that before. I would have thought wearing the same thing would be a fashion crime.

As usual, they pushed the school uniform to the limit. It made me wonder how they got away with it.

"Evie," she said in her saccharine sweet tone. "Can we have a moment?"

"Sure," I offered with a disinterested shrug.

Audrey smiled, gripping her books in front of her stomach.

"Great. I just love to chat with people. You like to talk to other people, right?"

I stared at her, wondering what she wanted. The friends behind her, they formed a wall that hid us from the main corridor. I was in my little hovel of darkness, wondering if the janitor would ever turn the light on in this section.

The smile slipped as a hesitant laugh escaped. Audrey gritted her teeth, forcing a smile to remain.

"Well, I guess you may not know because you're new to Hades, but my dad's got this great job as a builder. He's the only builder in this town, and that's because he's helped someone out. Everything was going great until someone stuck their nose into this town's business, and now his friend is angry. He said that my dad is going to lose his placement if things don't go back to the way that they were. You can help him out, right?"

Lifting my bag over one shoulder, I stepped away from the locker and looked at Audrey with a defiant glare.

"Your father is a snake that sold out an innocent person to a murderer. I wouldn't help him if he was the last person in the world. Did you know what he did, Audrey? Did he tell you what happened? Someone died because of your father. He was the one that stuck his nose into something that didn't concern him. I don't care if his friend is angry. That friend knows where I am, and if he has a problem, then he can come and tell me all about it rather than buying you and your friends off with bits of crappy plastic beads."

Audrey looked offended, her fingers scraping over the black pearls. Then, anger consumed her. She pushed me back into the locker, slamming me into the metal door.

"This is all your fault." she hissed. "My father lost his job because of you."

Pushing back on her, Audrey grabbed my shirt. The first few buttons popped open. Her eyes lowered to the pendant. Since Niko gave it to me, I have worn it constantly. No matter what, it was always close to me, and in turn, Niko would be as well.

The anger fell instantly as Audrey sucked in a sharp breath of air.

The rest of the group moved to look at what had quietened Audrey. An audible gasp surrounded me, and the other girls began to back away. Anger began to fill me as I lifted from the locker door, swelling enough to make them all step back to the main corridor, Audrey included.

"You're a freak," Audrey hissed, then turned to walk away quickly.

I huffed, rolling my eyes. I knew that I was still not alone. Turning around, I saw the Nephilim boy behind me.

There might be a day when he wasn't hanging around like a bad smell. Though I shouldn't wish for such things. The day that the Nephilim boy wasn't here was the day that his kind had arrived to take me down.

"They're coming?"

He stared at me and slowly faded into the darkness.

"You know," I called out to the darkness. "You could be a little more helpful and offer something else."

I got nothing in return.

A little information would be great. A few details about how I could deal with the other Nephilim when they turned up. Maybe there was some kind of lawyer I could hire and defend myself.

Clearly not.

Leaning down, I picked up my bag that I'd dropped.

"Who are you talking to?"

Gasping, I turned to the amused voice at the end of the corridor. It was a guy from my year level.

I don't know his name. He wasn't in any of my classes. I'd seen him around in the couple of days that I'd been to school since arriving in Hades.

"Just my friends in the darkness."

He chuckled, leaning against the wall.

Despite this school being fairly strict on hair color, this guy had streaks of blue through the thick black hair. Short at the back and long at the front, the hair fell into his eyes until he flicked it back over his head, revealing more of the blue. It was a close match to his eyes.

"Sometimes, it's a more interesting conversation. I'm Kannon."

He held out his hand, offering a gorgeous smile as well.

"Evelyn, but everyone calls me Evie."

The smile grew, and I saw that all too familiar sign of what I was facing.

"You're a vampire."

"I am. What gave it away?"

"The fangs. Are you a part of Drakkus's coven?"

Kannon scoffed. The smile lessened as he frowned.

"Not a chance in Hell. There are not many of us, but we do exist. The tale of the forest fight swirled pretty fast, but unfortunately for Niko, not fast enough."

"You knew Niko?"

"Not personally. I am only eighteen."

I frowned. Kannon shrugged with a cheesy smile.

"It's standard practice to hold us back a year so that we appear a little older. Not that anyone in this town is fooled. Drakkus has most of the townsfolk in his pocket, one way or another."

We began to walk through the main corridor. There were fewer people around now.

Lessons were not starting for a few more minutes. We had time, but not a lot.

"As for Niko, my parents told me about him. They thought he'd left to search for his wife and daughter. When they heard that he'd been walled up in the house, they were distraught. No one thought he'd be right under our noses."

I stopped next to the door for my first class, giving Kannon a vague smile.

"This is me. It was nice to meet you."

"You too."

Kannon leaned closer as a girl walked into the classroom. His eyes watched her until the door was shut, and we were alone. Turning back to me, Kannon shot me another one of those dazzling smiles. I'm sure it had all the girls in this school spinning.

"You have allies in this town, Evelyn. Do not give up hope."

He lifted upright again, smirked at me, and then turned to continue down the corridor. I stared, even though I should have been getting into the class.

CHAPTER 16

Sitting in front of what was now a tomb, I began weaving the daisies I'd collected along the way.

"So, Audrey bailed me up this morning. Apparently, her father lost his job because of what happened. I'm guessing that Drakkus is threatening him rather than actually taking his job away. I can't believe he actually thought that Audrey would be able to convince me to hand things over to them. Were they always a bunch of morons?"

Niko didn't answer, not that I expected him to.

"And don't go freaking out and go all overprotective dad on me, but I met a guy today. I haven't told Brad. I know he'll freak out. Jeez, he might try and have the birds and bees conversation again. I reckon I could give him a better education about it. Anyway, the guy is a vampire. He only told me his first name, Kannon, but I did a little digging. He said I have allies in this town, and his family is not a part of Drakkus's coven. Have you heard of the Lothaire family? Any insight that you have would be really great."

Tears slid down my cheeks as I continued to tie the flowers together. One little bunch of flowers for a friend that I'd lost. I'd hoped that he would be a father figure to me, to complete the family that I had with Brad. All that I had was a few days with him. They were pretty good ones. I wanted to cling to them for as long as possible. I knew that with time, the memories would fade. Soon, I'd forget what he sounded like, and eventually, I'd forget what he looked like. I'd be left with a vague memory that I could not focus on without a struggle.

That was a depressing thought.

Tying the ribbon around the bunch, I formed a bow and placed it next to the flowers I'd left for him yesterday.

"I'll see you tomorrow."

Standing, I flicked the leaves and dirt away and began the trek back through the forest.

When I emerged, I stopped and tried not to giggle. Brad had decided that because we were staying in Hades, he'd buy a lawnmower. He was struggling to make it start. The neighbor was leaning on the fence, giving Brad his useful but probably incredibly annoying advice.

Brad tipped his head at me as I passed, and the neighbor waved. I smiled, waved back at him, and delved into the house before he offered me help with something.

Grabbing my bag, I wandered through the house and to my room. I was yet to fully unpack, more interested in fighting off vampires that, despite having no real issue with the people who lived in this house, decided that it was necessary to attack.

I'd spent three years with Brad, and in that time, I had not gained many possessions. Life before that didn't allow for it, my mother was always broke, and I was lucky to have a few items of clothes and food in the cupboard.

Brad, however, was a lot more giving.

If I wanted, I could ask him to take me to the mall to buy things. In the past, we'd done that a couple of times. As for now, that was never going to happen. Hades was a small town that did not have a mall. It shut early on weekdays, and there were barely any shops open on Sundays. This place was dull as dishwater.

Last night, Brad suggested that I gave myself a little pick-me-up and hinted at some décor for my bedroom. I could even go to the hardware with him and pick out some paint, maybe wallpaper, if I found something I liked. Brad had never done any wallpapering before, but he said that if I wanted it, he'd figure it out. I'm sure it will end with Brad covered in glue and wallpaper.

Still, the thought of decorating the room was intriguing. I'm sure Niko wouldn't mind if I painted the walls.

As for decorations, trinkets, and all those other things that people put in their bedrooms, I wasn't so sure about it. I'd given it some thought and couldn't think of anything that I wanted. I had my ensemble bed, a desk, a chair, and a dresser. There wasn't much else that I could add aside from a few useless things.

Looking around the room, I knew what Brad was hinting at. He'd finally found the happy me, not overly impressed but ready to stay in one spot, so he wanted to develop that and make it grow. The only issue was that his employer might want him to return to the office once the school year was over. That would mean that he'd have to quit his job because we were stuck here now.

That is unless I handed the Corbin leadership and ownership of this town to someone else. I knew that Drakkus would gladly take it from me and eagerly show me how to do it. I'm sure he'd even throw us a going away party, stand at the Hades town sign, and wave goodbye.

That was not going to happen. I was not leaving Hades. As for handing the leadership over to someone else, I didn't know how to do that, and I wouldn't do it anyway. It felt wrong to even think of it. Niko had given it to me, entrusting his family's legacy to the last of his kin. I hope that Brad and I did the right thing by him.

Pulling out my books and pencil case, I began the mind-melting homework. It was pointless. All I could think about was Kannon.

I didn't want to make friends, and I definitely did not want a boyfriend. Now that we were staying in Hades, would I change my policy on that? Maybe. I had the opportunity to create something that wouldn't disappear once we left for another town. We were staying, so maybe thinking about Kannon with hope in my heart and mind might not be that bad.

Maybe I could let myself make a friend.

I couldn't help myself when I smiled. Thinking about being more than a friend to Kannon was creating some devilish thoughts inside of me.

The mower started, breaking those thoughts, but I didn't mind. I had to get my homework done, and that would never happen if I had spent the afternoon daydreaming about having a boyfriend.

When Brad finished mowing the lawn, he had a quick shower and then appeared at my door. With a gentle knock, he offered a smile.

"If the door is open, you can come in."

"Yeah, but I don't want to intrude."

"Okay, well, we'll set the rule. Door open, and you're cool. How's that?"

"Great. Did you want to start searching the house?"

This was Niko's suggestion in his dying breath. Search the house. Find the documents, find the valuables that he'd hidden.

I looked at the books in front of me, and I realized that I'd done nothing. Just dreamily staring out the window while thinking about someone. I was an idiot because I had so many other things that were more important than thinking about a boy.

To me, searching for important documents was a brilliant distraction and a better use of my time. Closing my books, I stood and stretched.

"I locked the doors and windows, not that I'm paranoid or anything."

"I would be. They should always be locked anyway. We do not trust anyone."

Searching the house was not going to be easy. I knew Brad would stress over everything because it wasn't our house yet. We were tenants and should not be lifting floor panels or removing walls.

We started where Niko pulled the gun out from under the strip of wood. Brad shone the torch around and pulled out all of the packets of bullets, then searched some more. He poked and prodded, trying to jimmy things open.

Making our way into the living room, Brad huffed and sat in the lounge.

"This will take forever, and I don't think we're going to find anything. I looked in that cupboard when we inspected this place, and I never saw a hint of a hidden panel, yet clearly, there was one."

"Alright, let's think logically. We're looking for important papers, so we'd have to assume that Niko wouldn't want them to be damaged. So, I guess nowhere near a water pipe."

Brad seemed eager when he stood, grabbed the notepad off the kitchen counter, and wrote down *no water pipes*.

"But we won't discount them as an option, just a last resort."

"Unless Niko would expect someone to think like that and put it next to a pipe for that reason."

"Brad!" I groaned.

He shrugged, looking rather smug with himself. Brad stared at me, the pen tapping on the notebook.

"Fine. Open the panel under the sink."

It was a tense few seconds waiting for him to lift the bottom plate. His eyes lit up when the panel shifted and came loose.

"So, I guess starting at the opposite of what we'd think. That makes life so much easier."

"It's in a watertight container."

Setting it aside, Brad searched the rest of the cavity and then stood. The box was placed on the counter, looking rather old. Flicking the locks, Brad lifted the lid to reveal a few jewelry boxes and what looked like a picture book underneath them.

One by one, we went through the items, all pieces that bore the family crest.

"Niko said that there would be something that you could wear. I guess when we have kids, they'll have something as well. We're limited to a few members, though."

"Yeah,"

Brad was distracted by the book. He turned it and showed me a hand-drawn image of a handsome man wearing a fine suit. Underneath it was written suggested daywear for the socialite vampire.

He turned the page, offering another image, this time of suggested clothes to wear when entertaining at night.

"Etiquette. Who would have thought that vampires were so refined?"

"Who would have thought they existed?" I muttered. "And that we're related to them. Do you think that we're vampires?"

"I seriously doubt it."

"Niko didn't."

Brad tossed the book back into the box, then returned the jewelry boxes to the tin. All but one was put back, and Brad kept the tie pin.

"We're going to modernize this family because I am not wearing a cravat. A tie will be more than enough."

"Sure thing."

I couldn't imagine Brad in one, either. At my mother's funeral, he'd dressed in a nice shirt and pants but no tie. I don't think Brad actually owned a tie, to be honest.

Brad pinned it to the top of the pocket on his shirt, giving me a smug smile when he gestured to it.

"Good enough?"

"Probably not for them, but I'm good for whatever. Where are we checking next?"

"The fireplace."

Hmm, fire, another enemy of important items. It was a good call.

Brad walked to the fireplace, then began poking the bricks and tried to jiggle the mantle. The hearth was raised off the floor. Under the slab were bricks that matched the rest of the fireplace. I would have thought that it was the ideal place, a loose brick perhaps, but it wasn't the case.

Pushing against the leg, the whole panel pushed out and revealed that it was a cabinet. Both legs and the header were storage for all sorts of trinkets but, more importantly, papers.

Brad began pulling everything out while I sat on the floor and looked through the documents.

"I'm guessing vampires don't have birth certificates, right?"

I shrugged, looking up at Brad.

"If they don't, how do we prove who Niko was? When his daughter was born, was he listed as the father? Was there even a birth certificate for his daughter?"

"I don't know. This looks like it might be a little bit beyond us."

Brad sat on the floor with the items between us. There were photos and a few receipts, but nothing would help us prove we were related to Niko. There wasn't even a document to prove he existed.

"We need to keep searching."

"It's pointless if we can't connect him to us."

I bit my lip as Brad began to look through the photos. They were old but in great condition.

"I might have met someone."

Brad stopped and looked up at me.

"That sounds like you met a boy, and you've been stressing about telling me all afternoon."

Eyebrows raised, and a wry smile slipped across his face.

"Okay, so yeah, it's a guy. He's also a vampire, and he told me that his family knew Niko. They're not a part of Drakkus's coven. He said that we have allies in this town."

"And he could be lying to you. I'm not trying to stop you from forming friendships of any shape, Evie, but I want you to be aware that Drakkus could use your hormones against you. Remember, Niko said to not trust anyone."

With that statement, Brad filled me with hope because of his easy acceptance and then crushed it completely by pointing out the obvious.

CHAPTER 17

I knew that no matter how hard I tried, I could not avoid Audrey forever. I'd delayed walking into the place and lurked in the shadows. I still got cornered in my little hovel of darkness.

Sighing, I shut my locker and flicked my bag over my shoulder.

Yet again, there was a wall of mean girls blocking the view of the main corridor. They tried to intimidate me, but they had no idea. I've been to schools that were so rough they made this place look like Heaven.

Piercings and tattoos were common, even though they were classed as minors. In my math class, I sat behind a guy with a multi-colored mohawk. Thankfully, he always slept in class, so it was never an issue.

There was a definite class system, but it was not based on money or popularity. They'd meet up after school ended and fight. Whoever was still standing after five minutes would climb the ladder.

I was not interested in it, but ignoring it completely

was not an option. Those who didn't participate always watched. It was the only way to survive in a place that was to blend in with the crowd. Audrey and the cashmere brigade, they'd be cowering in the girls' restroom. They'd harden up or crack.

"You can't change my mind."

"I don't need you to change it. I want you to hand it over. You've got no choice. You must hand it over."

"Says who? I don't recall you being the boss of me or the leader of the vampires. Last time I checked, no one had the right to tell me what to do. Go away and stop harassing me."

"You will regret this. The leader is coming for you."

Defiantly, I glared at Audrey. She tried her damnedest to remain strong, but there were hints of how easily she could crumble.

"He is not the leader. Niko was the true leader, and he passed that to me when he died."

"There is a reason that he was put behind that wall. This town will crumble if you return his family line to the rule."

I stepped forward, steeling myself for anything while hoping there would be nothing.

"My family. I am returning my family to the rule. Stop harassing me, and stop sticking your nose into something that doesn't concern you. This has nothing to do with you."

Moving through their imposing wall, I heard Audrey pushing her friends out of the way.

"You're going to destroy this town."

Sick of her constant attempts, I continued down the corridor. The only difference in my previous efforts to ignore her was this time, I lifted my arm and raised my middle finger to her. I smiled when I heard the shock and horror.

"Now, I like a girl who has attitude."

I stopped, lowering my arm to my side.

Kannon emerged from beside the locker. It was almost too convenient. Standing at the end of a long row, he just happened to be in the right place at the right time. I wasn't buying it.

"Interesting. How come you're here?"

He shrugged, lifting from the metal frame.

"I was just doing a little trolling through the feeds, checking out what's happening on the web. You know how it is."

"Well, not in a while. My last phone broke, and I only just got a new one."

"Really? Do you mind if I check it out?"

I shrugged and handed it to him. Kannon looked at it, offering a boyish smirk when faced with the lock screen.

"Come on, don't you trust me?"

"No."

Taking back my phone, I smiled sweetly.

"But if that was a lame attempt to ring your phone and get my number, then kudos to you for the attempt."

Kannon bit his lip, still giving that gorgeous smile. There was something so stunning but so natural about him. It was incredible to look at.

The hair was styled today, pulling the floppy strands back over his head away from the fair skin. He hadn't shaved. Rough growth spiked through, shadowing along the jaw.

"Guilty as charged."

"What else are you guilty of?"

"I'm guilty of wanting to bring down the system," Kannon whispered. "You don't trust me, and I totally understand and don't blame you. In fact, if I were in your situation, I wouldn't either. You should know that my family are not the only ones. We are few in numbers, but we're prepared to help you fulfill Niko's wishes."

Pulling out a notebook, Kannon wrote his number onto the piece of paper and then handed it to me.

"Call, message, pictures. Whatever, whenever. I'm good for it all. You don't need to stress over how long to wait. I'm cool with it all. Just don't leave me hanging, Evie."

"You've got it bad?"

He nodded. I smiled but remembered Brad's words. It was enough to kill the moment, and Kannon picked up on it.

"Doubts?"

"My uncle said to be wary because Drakkus could use my hormones against me."

Kannon nodded with a grim look on his face. Glancing up the corridor, I saw the mean girls lingering. It looked like they were trying to get the attention of a few of the footballers. Kannon pulled my hand, urging me into the narrow gap between the locker and the water fountain.

"Yeah, he'd do something like that, and I understand what you're saying. Your uncle is pretty wise, Evie. Don't stress over it. You need to be aware of things like that because he will try all angles, and yes, the stunningly gorgeous guy that's totally making an idiot out of himself is a solid gold angle."

I giggled, leaning against the wall as I looked up at Kannon.

"We'll take it easy, and then you can learn that I'm on your side, not the enemy. It was before my time, but my parents told me what life was like before Drakkus took over compared to what it's like now."

"Underground resistance?"

Kannon offered a dark smile as he nodded.

His thumb brushed over my knuckles, reminding me

he was still holding my hand.

"You don't know anything about me."

"That's true. Can I be completely un-politically correct in saying that I was bewitched by the outward view and decided that I wanted to learn about the inward view?"

"I guess."

"How about the more that I talk to you, the better the situation is? Did you know that you have a lovely smile, and when you laugh, the smile grows large enough that these little dimples appear on your cheeks?"

"Good grief," I muttered, feeling the heat rising in my cheeks.

Kannon was enjoying my embarrassment. Still, it was sweet enough for me to smile.

We walked to the main doors, and I was almost knocked over by Audrey. She was determined to get out the door before me, sideswiping me in another effort to drag me down. Yet again, I ignored her.

We stopped at the doorway to see that Audrey and her friends were at the bottom of the stairs. Kannon wrapped his arm around my shoulder, dragging me closer.

"Whatever your game is, we're not interested. You've picked your side, and that's all there is to it."

"You're picking her over your leader?" she hissed.

"He's not my leader, and you're human. It is none of your business what I do."

Audrey looked offended, but Kannon wasn't done.

"Literally, Audrey. It is none of your business. If your family is letting Drakkus tell you what to do, then there is something seriously wrong with you and them. Stand up for yourself and stop letting them walk all over you. And leave Evelyn alone. This is not your fight."

"This is my town. My family is directly involved with Drakkus. He owns this entire town."

"Not for much longer."

Keeping his arm firmly in place, Kannon urged me to walk away. There was a massive smile on my face, feeling rather supreme. Sliding my arm around his waist, I looked up at the vampire who knew how to get into my good books.

"So, this is us now?"

"It can be if you want. Still concerned about my loyalty to you? I could get down on one knee and give my eternal, undying oath, loyalty, whatever you want."

I stared, wide-eyed until Kannon chuckled.

"I shouldn't tease, right?"

"Yeah,"

"Sorry, but you're cute when you go bright red."

Narrowing my eyes, I pursed my lips, and Kannon pulled me in for a hug.

"Come on, you can't be mad at me already. Give it a few weeks. Maybe once you trust me."

"I just need time for this. I'm not used to making friends. Brad's job had him moving all the time, and Niko told me to not trust anyone. Given that his own kind killed him, I can understand why he said it. Now, it causes problems for me."

"Yeah, I know. I've seen them kill their own kind as well. Vampires out of their own group. Can you imagine that? Being loyal to a leader and then having him turn around and order your execution? Audrey's parents will soon figure out that they're barking up the wrong tree. The problem is it could be too late for them, and they will be dead. Drakkus will not stop to get what he wants. If that means he has to kill a few humans, a few loyal followers, then he'll do it."

Kannon shook his head with a heavy frown.

"It's not right. I hope you'll be a better leader than that, Evie."

"Yeah, I would have to have a good reason for it before even considering it."

Kannon and I slowly walked to the footpath. The sun was bright, but he wasn't concerned. We were in the shade soon enough. I liked the sun, but I loved the shade. Maybe that was the almost vampire in me.

"You're not moving anymore, are you?"

"No, I think Brad will finish the year and find something else. I guess it all depends on getting the house. If we own it, then he's more likely to stay."

Kannon nodded thoughtfully, saying nothing.

It wasn't until we were out of the blinding light that I saw we were being watched. I knew who it was, though I did not know his name.

Leaning against the tree so that Kannon could see the man, I casually flicked my head.

"Intel time. Who's the guy with black hair sitting at the café?"

Kannon looked across the street, rolling his eyes with a frustrated huff.

"Andross Drohman. You've had a run-in with him, haven't you?"

"Yeah. What gave that away?"

"The fact that you picked him out from over here rather than the other people around the place. He's the second in charge and a real piece of work. What happened?"

I shrugged and lifted from the tree trunk. Kannon was quick to take my hand, walking beside me along the footpath.

"It was the night that Niko died. We were in the forest, and he grabbed me. I thought I was done for, but he saw the pendant and took off. At that stage, I was Niko's familiar."

"He won't abide by the rules. I've seen him take down

familiars before. This is what you need to understand about Drakkus and his followers, especially the ones he has in the inner circle, like Andross. They play by their own rules, and they don't care about anyone or anything. So long as Drakkus is happy and in charge, it's all they're concerned with. As for that pendant, I'd say it's got more to do with your family rather than you being Niko's familiar."

CHAPTER 18

Audrey was walking along the footpath with her friends, whispering while looking back at us. I found it surprising that she was allowed to walk to and from school after her father said that he never let his daughters walk around by themselves. Like many other things in this town, it did not add up.

Brad was already here, distracted by working on his laptop. The crazy guy couldn't step away from work for even a minute. I'm sure his boss would allow a few minutes to pick me up.

Opening my bag, I pulled a pen out and took Kannon's arm. Writing my number on it, I looked up at him with a smile. There was a group of giggles from ahead of us.

"I think you just dropped a few rungs on the social ladder."

"I'd rather climb your ladder."

"Good grief," I said with a giggle.

"Too corny?"

"Just a little, but still rather cute."

"Good, because I meant it in a non-sexual way, just in case you thought I was hinting. Which, you know, that's totally cool if you want to, but I'm not saying that we have to or anything."

Kannon looked at me, and for the first time, I swear it was like he was the one blushing.

"I'll shut up now."

"You just wanted to point out that you don't care what they think, just what I think?"

"That's the one. So, I earned a little trust?"

I nodded, clicking the lid back on the pen.

"Awesome. I am going to say hello to your uncle."

"Seriously?"

"Yep. Not just because of you but because my parents would expect me to welcome him to our town. He's going to be your second in charge, right?"

"Niko said it would be a good idea."

Brad's gaze lifted as we approached. The laptop was quickly put away, and he got out of the car.

"Evie, you're looking rather happy," he murmured.

Me? Nah, it was clearly his imagination. I shrugged, feeling that burning tingle in my cheeks. Brad chuckled and turned to Kannon with an outstretched hand.

"Brad, uncle, and embarrassing guardian."

"Kannon Lothaire," he said as he shook Brad's hand. "I seem to have the same effect on her as well."

They were all smiles at my expense. I said nothing as I leaned against the car. Audrey and her friends were watching intently.

"When you and Evie are settled, my parents would like to invite both of you over for a meet and greet of all the anti-Drakkus vampires that reside in Hades. We've waited for a long time for a true Corbin to return to this town, and they're eager to help wherever possible. I know that, like Evie, you will have trust issues, but be assured that we are not on his side. You'll understand that when you hear their stories. They will make you realize why we want Evie to rule the vampires in this town."

Brad nodded quietly, a little stunned. Momentarily, he glanced at me.

"Uh, okay. Sounds great."

Kannon nodded, stepping back with a subdued smile.

"I'll see you tomorrow."

"Sure."

Kannon crossed the car park and got into his car. Brad was behind the wheel, watching with narrowed eyes.

"Boys and fast cars," he muttered, then looked at me.

"So, I see that you traded numbers."

"Brad," I hissed.

"I don't care what you do with your life so long as you're aware of the consequences of your actions. You are almost eighteen, and I expect that you will make wise choices. If you want to date him, that's fine. He seems quite pleasant."

"He stuck up for me."

Brad stopped what he was doing and turned to look at me. I gave a slight shrug.

"See the girls leaning on the fence? The one in the center is Audrey, Ryan's daughter. Every chance she gets, she tells me to hand the leadership over to Drakkus."

"Is she a vampire?"

"No."

"Do I need to speak to the school about this? I can get you transferred to another class."

Brad started the engine, pulling out of the park and thankfully taking me away from the view of Audrey. Kannon was already out of the park and on the street. He'd just driven past Andross, who turned his head and watched him. The look on his face was dark.

"That's not going to solve the problem. Audrey never says a thing to me in class. It's always in the corridors before and after school, between lessons."

"Well, how about I get you transferred into ones with

Kannon in them?"

"I think that's going a little overboard. I can deal with her. Also, that guy there, he's a problem."

Brad casually glanced out the window.

"I recognize him. Where have I seen him?"

"The night that Niko died. He grabbed me and almost bit me."

"No," Brad murmured. "I've seen him somewhere else."

His fingers rapped on the steering wheel, frowning as he thought about it. Brad always had an intense look on his face when he was overthinking something.

"Stop trying to figure it out. You'll never remember."

"It's right there. I can see him. Kind of."

"Brad," I chided.

With a sigh, he rolled his eyes.

There was silence in the car until we pulled into the driveway.

"The gardener," Brad said with shock in his tone.

"See? You stopped thinking about it. You should always listen to me and follow my advice."

Brad pulled the handbrake on and shot me a derisive stare.

"You were the one that said that chicken place on the

highway looked like a great place to eat."

"It was."

"I spent the night looking down into the toilet bowl."

"An odd choice of activity for the night."

"Puking my guts up," he grumbled.

Pressing my lips tight with a cheesy smile, I fluttered my lashes and begged for forgiveness. Brad shook his head.

"So, where do you know him from?"

"He came here to give me a quote to keep the lawn and gardens maintained."

"He's trying to get into the house. I wonder if he needs permission or something like that."

"Maybe you should message your new friend."

I nodded and pulled out my phone.

Brad began the search while I messaged Kannon. He said that it was guaranteed that's what Andross would have done. As for gaining entry to the house, there wasn't much that we could do to stop him. It was then that I remembered what Niko had said. Nothing could stop a vampire, not even holy ground.

No protections, no laws. Even if there was a law that could stop a vampire, Andross would go against it anyway. He would do anything to keep Drakkus in the top job. Kannon said the sooner I remembered that, the easier it would be to understand how and why Andross did things.

Nothing would protect us aside from the obvious locks and bars. Even then, that could be dealt with. It would be a deterrent, that was true, but when faced with a desperate vampire that was eager to please his master, we would be better off not bothering.

He also added that time was fading, and we needed to claim the leadership soon. Otherwise, Drakkus would send someone here, and that would be the end of us.

I thought it was surprising that he hadn't turned up already. Maybe shooting him twice had put an end to that for a few days. If that were the case, then Kannon was right. We were running out of time.

While Brad searched the house, I did a little family research from my end of the line. Brad had so kindly left his credit card for me to use. Purchasing birth certificates was not cheap.

I started with my own, then my mother's and Brad's. Then I obtained my grandparents. It was my grandmother where I found solid proof. She was Niko's daughter. Crazily enough, Niko was listed as the father on the document. I searched for a birth certificate for Niko but could not find one.

I opted for email and post. The original birth certificates would be posted, likely to arrive in a few days, but I needed something sooner than that. So, the emailed version was far better. Printing them out, I went in search of Brad.

"We've got the proof. Niko was your grandfather."

Brad was stunned.

"I remember my grandmother, but it's pretty vague. I don't ever recall her talking about my grandfather, and when I asked my parents, they said that she never said a word about it."

"How did she die?"

"Robbery gone wrong, I think. I was pretty young. All I remember was that the funeral was seriously low-key. It was just your grandparents, your mother, me, the priest, and a closed casket. The priest said a few words, and we left. No flowers, no wake, we didn't even wait to see the burial. Now that I think about it, I wonder if there was a reason there was no one there."

He took the birth certificates and looked at them, then passed them back.

"Get the death certificates, too. We may need to prove that they died of vampire-related causes."

Returning to Brad's computer, I searched for the documents while doing a little research. I wanted to know how much information I could get out of the government. Turns out, it was a lot.

An autopsy was done on my mother, a drug overdose. Curiously, the toxins in her body were high. The coroner listed many long-winded names that made no sense to me. I wonder if Brad knew what these were.

My grandparents died in a plane crash, and the

aviation authority did a report and released it for public records. Engine failure. There was also a lot of technical information on this that I did not understand. Still, I printed it out and added it to the pile.

As for my great-grandmother, Niko's partner, she died from wounds from a beating. The police report matched the coroner's report. The house she lived in had been ransacked. They noted that her purse was empty, jewelry was gone, and possibly a lot more items, but they had no real idea as there was no one to ascertain what was there before she died. There was no next of kin listed, which meant that she'd cut ties with her daughter.

Was that for her safety, or did they have a falling out? Given what Brad remembered about the funeral, it was likely that they'd parted ways out of safety. Maybe because she had no memory of her father, my grandmother didn't believe her mother when she said that vampires were real and that her father was one. If she didn't have blood cravings, then it would add to the disbelief.

Brad walked past the door, his arms loaded with a box of stuff.

"Hey, did your mother see your grandmother?"

"I remember visiting her, but it was never in a house. Mom would say that we're going to a park and Grandma will be there. I'd be happy playing on the swings while they sat on the bench."

"Together?"

"Well, yeah. That was the point of it."

"The police report from your grandmother's robbery and death noted that there was no next of kin listed."

Brad frowned, shaking his head.

"No, that's not right. I remember a police officer at our house. I distinctly remember hearing him tell my mother that she'd died from her injuries. My mother cried, and even Dad was upset. This doesn't make any sense."

Giving him the report, Brad read through it and shook his head again.

"This is not," he sat down, sounding winded. "This is fake."

"Someone was hiding our family, Brad. This," I said, shaking the document at him. "Is just another piece of the puzzle, it's one big picture of death, and I'd bet anything that Drakkus was the one ordering these hits. Your grandmother, your parents, my mother, they're all dead."

"What about us?" he whispered.

"Maybe the only reason we survived was that your parents kept you and mom hidden, and in turn, she hid me. Maybe beyond her death, we only survived because we moved so much."

"And now we've settled in one place. How long before the reaper catches us?"

"Drakkus will not be our end. We make bold moves to show him that we mean business."

Pulling out my phone, I asked Kannon if he knew how I would be able to claim ownership of the house. He said yes, and that he'd bring the paperwork over today. Time was running out, and it had to be done as soon as we could manage.

"I will make him pay for everything he's done to our family."

CHAPTER 19

The printer whirred, spitting out the final piece of information that I'd managed to find. We had answers, but unfortunately, we had a lot more questions as well.

I don't know if they will ever be answered. Even if Niko were still alive, I don't know if he'd have the answers for me. I couldn't imagine sending away my partner and child. I knew that he'd done it for their safety, but I couldn't do it. I'd go with them.

Maybe Niko couldn't. Would he draw their attention no matter how far they ran? Was it better to send them off into the world while keeping the vampire's attention on him?

With a heavy sigh, I put the papers in order and stapled the documents together. This was my family in one little stack of papers. Life and death, in paper form.

In this, I saw what Drakkus had done to my family. I could have had a loving family life with my grandparents, uncle, and great-grandparents. I could have had my father in my life. But most of all, I could have had my mother.

Wiping away the tears, I wondered how much of her life was a lie. Maybe she wasn't living it on a street corner. Perhaps I was being hidden just like my great-grandmother was. There was so much that I've discovered since coming to Hades. How much more was there to find?

Collecting the papers, I stood from the desk.

My mood was on a roller coaster because of the information that I'd managed to collect. It dropped as soon as I saw the purple-eyed boy. The more I looked at him, the more I realized he did not look like a teenager. There was something about him that gave him an older appearance. His suit never changed, looking perfect. If only he stopped the whole, my race is coming to kill you thing.

"Before you say a word, I want to know things. Will you tell me if I ask you questions?"

The Nephilim was quiet for a moment, then nodded.

"Why are you here?"

"To deliver a warning. They are coming for you."

"Who are?"

"The Nephilim."

"Who specifically? You?"

"I am just a messenger. They sent me here to ensure that you knew that they were coming."

"Why? Because I'm related to a vampire?"

"Your underlying vampirism is not of their concern. They seek out the damned. They are coming for you, witch."

The boy began to fade.

"Wait!"

I stepped forward, and he stopped fading. Tilting his head, the purple eyes harshly bored into me.

"I cannot and will not bow down to the demands of the damned."

"I'm not a witch."

"You are. Your father is a witch. He put his seed into the line of a vampire family and created you, one of the damned. Your father knowingly created a hybrid half-caste child,"

"Hey," I snapped angrily.

The boy's eyes widened with anger on his face.

"Don't you go using derogatory words in this house. Half-caste is offensive. Apologize for your rude behavior."

His face altered immediately, resolute as he stared at me.

"The Nephilim do not follow the demands of any land-bound creature. Mind your words. You will regret them when my kin appear. They will punish you and your father for your creation. They. Are. Coming."

The Nephilim faded fast before I could ask anything more.

"Why should I be punished for being born? That's rather rude." I muttered.

Sitting in the lounge, I felt defeated. This was not good. If dealing with a psychotic vampire wasn't enough, the world decided to throw biblical creatures at me as well. Was I walking around with a target on my back?

"Everything okay?"

I looked up at Brad, unsure of how to respond.

"The boy was here. Apparently, the Nephilim are coming for me because my father is a witch, and it must be illegal for them to breed with vampires. He got super angry at me."

I didn't help the situation any, stirring the pot just a little. That was normal for me, but not the biblical creature's part. I can now see that life in Hades will never be like any of the other towns Brad and I lived in.

"Your mother was not a vampire. Surely that's enough of an argument?"

"You have vampire blood in your veins. It's enough for them."

Brad gasped, turning around to the dark figure that shadowed our door.

"You two need to learn how to lock doors. This might be a small town, but that does not make it trustworthy."

Brad frowned. I could have sworn he said that he did lock the doors and the windows, too. Maybe he forgot the front door.

Kannon wandered in with a laptop bag slung over one shoulder. Sitting down at the desk, Kannon cleared a space.

"Nephilim, eh? That's certainly a mind-melter."

Pulling his folder out, Kannon continued to arrange things. I stood, looking at the documents that were already half-filled out.

"Though it's not surprising if your father is a witch. I take it that you didn't know that?"

"I never knew who my father was."

Pulling a chair, I sat down beside the desk.

"My mother, if you believe it, which now I don't know what to believe, was a prostitute, and I was always told that my father was one of her clients."

"Sounds like a lie to cover the truth and hide you. If your father was a witch, he would have figured out that your mother had vampire blood in her veins and warned her to keep you hidden. Mostly from him. If the Nephilim connected the three of you, they would have figured it out. What is odd is how they managed to figure it out after all these years. What triggered their interest?"

I shrugged.

"What I also find curious is that it sounds like they know who he is and that he's still alive. Do you want to find him?"

Brad and I exchanged glances. To be honest, I wouldn't want to leave Brad behind after everything that he's done for me. He didn't have to take me in. He could have left me in state care.

"I don't have any thoughts on finding him as a figure in my life, but I don't need him as a carer. Brad's doing a smashing job."

"Gee, thanks," he muttered.

Kannon stopped, leaning on the desk as he moved fractionally closer to me.

"The thing you need to think about is the associations you have once you're named leader officially. Witches are not seen in the greatest of lights, so keep that in mind. It's likely the reason that you never knew him growing up. He would know that you would return to this world eventually. Parting ways was in your best interest."

I nodded, quietly taking in the thoughts that swamped my mind regarding my parents and why things happened.

"So, why do the Nephilim want me dead?"

"I don't know if they want you dead, per se, more like just punished. From what I know and have learned, the Nephilim were given a chance at redemption for the crimes of their parents. You know, that whole cross-breeding thing. Their object in life was to stop cross-breeding with other species. If they fail, they don't get absolution."

"They get it as an entire group?"

"No, there are only a few Nephilim left in the world now. They're assigned their own countries to watch over. They have a certain amount of time to clock over before they're granted a meeting and a chance to redeem themselves. You," Kannon said with a glint in his eyes as he cheekily pointed at me. "Are a smudge on someone's perfect record."

"Well, yay for me," I grumbled.

Kannon began filling out the forms. Flicking through the various documents, I held my mother's coroner's report out to Brad.

"Do any of those things mean something to you?"

"I've seen this, and no. The lady from child services said they're the medical names for the drugs that were found in her system."

"May I?"

Brad shrugged, handing the document to Kannon. He looked through the pages and then handed it back to me.

"Some of them are drugs, some I do not know what they are. One of them is vampire venom. Your mother was either directly injected or bitten, and the vampire raised the level of venom that went into her system. Usually, we release a small amount of toxin to ease the victim's mind and close the wound once we've finished. This level would stop her heart. Your mother was murdered by a vampire."

He handed it back with a sympathetic smile.

"Sorry,"

"It's okay."

"Whoever did it put a lot of drugs in her system to cover the reason for her death. They wanted her to appear as if she was suffering an overdose. I'm only assuming, but perhaps they wanted to avoid an autopsy."

"But one was done anyway."

Kannon smiled gently as he reached out, tilting the paper down.

"Yes, but look at that. What does it say?"

"It says relative requested. Who requested the autopsy?"

We both looked at Brad.

"Don't look at me. Your mother's body was already at the funeral home when the cops called me. Well, the office called me because the cops couldn't find me. I was on the other side of the country for a conference."

Kannon finished the document and turned it for me to sign.

"I'm not eighteen yet."

"Yeah, that's another form for you to sign. It will go to you, but until you turn eighteen, it will be with a guardian watching over it. So, that means that you get to fill out paperwork as well."

"That's all that I do in my life," Brad grumbled.

When everything was done, Kannon told Brad where he could lodge the documents. They also discussed driving lessons because it was on Brad's list of things to do. Teach me how to drive. It was a scary thought.

I thought Brad would get upset at not taking me out for driving lessons, but then I realized that he was probably relieved not to do it.

Before he left, Brad said that he hoped to be back in an hour, and if he was going to be any later than that, he'd message me. I think that was a hint. There would be no socks on door handles. Kannon and I were not at that stage yet.

"How about we go to an empty car park and let you go wild?"

"You don't trust me with your car?"

"Have you ever driven a car before?"

"No,"

Kannon smiled, saying nothing as he opened the passenger door.

"You can drive if you feel confident. I just remember what my first time was like. You know what? It's okay. We can go to the lake. The drive is easy."

He held out the keys. There was a lot of hesitation when I reached out. The confidence was gone. Now, I was worried about hitting something.

Getting in behind the wheel, I looked at Kannon, who was still beaming a smile. He offered wordless support in just one little gesture.

Turning the engine over, I felt my heart pump harder. Anticipation was growing. The car was probably more than I should be driving as a learner, but I would take it easy.

Kannon's hand smoothed over my shoulder, pressing deep into the flesh.

"Relax. Put your foot on the brake, and shift the car into drive."

With one hand gripping the wheel tightly, I reached with my other hand and changed from park to drive.

"Did you check your mirrors?"

Grinning, I shook my head.

"That should probably happen first before putting it into drive."

Adjusting the rear vision mirror, I looked out the back window and saw an empty street.

"Okay, foot off the brake and slowly press the accelerator down. Don't forget to check your side mirror and the blind spot."

Checking the mirrors again, I slowly changed pedals and pressed as gently as I could. When the car began to move, I squeaked, and Kannon chuckled.

"Relax. Press a little harder and move to the intersection. We're going left, so don't forget the indicator. You don't want Larry pulling you over. That's ten minutes of your life that you will never get back."

"One of the cops?"

"The only cop. Good guy but easily bought. Can you guess what Drakkus bought him with?"

"Dunno, maybe a case of crullers?"

Kannon chuckled and shook his head.

"Nuh. Refit of the station, new cruiser, and guaranteed safety for him and the family from the vampires."

"Seriously? I am never going to be able to buy the only cop in this dumb town if that's what I'm going against."

"You won't need to buy him off if Drakkus is dead."

Easier said than done. I liked that Kannon was full of bravado for this future fight, but personally, I wanted to dive under the bed and hide for the next year. Maybe even longer.

I ignored the thoughts about Drakkus and focused on driving.

The further I drove along the road, the easier it felt. My confidence grew, and Kannon was always reassuring, which I think helped infinitely. It was a slow drive to the lake, but neither of us cared. I liked being alone with him and the relaxation that he gave with his hand on me.

Turning into the car park, I picked a prime position at

the front where we could look at the water.

The sun glistened over the surface, making it sparkle. This place was gorgeous.

"Okay, foot on the brake and come to a complete stop. Put the car in park and turn the engine off."

Once it was done, I sat with a smile on my face.

"That went remarkably well. I am impressed."

"You're a great teacher."

Kannon leaned one arm on the center console, giving me that cheeky smirk that made my insides liquid.

"Payment can be made at any time, but to avoid accruing a great debt, your teacher would suggest periodic payments."

"Is that so?"

He nodded, biting his bottom lip. All the while, his gaze was on me. He was irresistible, and I knew that I wanted more. That next step, it was right there, and I was ready to take it.

Leaning on the console with him, I closed in. My heart was racing harder than it did when I started driving this beast of a car.

Our lips pressed softly at first, slowly moving over each other. As we grew accustomed to each other, the embrace deepened. Kannon's hand reached out, gripping the curve of my jaw to urge me closer.

I was a little shocked when the tongue slid past my

lips but restrained myself from showing it. This was all new to me. I didn't know much about kissing, but I did know that this was perfect.

CHAPTER 20

"I could really use your help right about now."

The shrub said nothing as my bundle of flowers fell over. Sighing heavily, I propped it back up again.

"Niko," I whispered sadly.

Wiping away the tears, I sat upright and tried to find something positive to tell him. There wasn't much, and I knew that it would slowly degrade into the negative. We take the good with the bad, like always.

"Kannon took me for my first driving lesson. It was fun once I got past the scariness of it all. You didn't hear it, but we might have taken the next step. We're official. I suppose that's a thing, right?"

It will undoubtedly annoy Audrey to learn that we're dating. I would like to think that she's only trying to upset me, but I had a sneaking suspicion that she was after Kannon as a way into the vampire world. It certainly made sense, considering she was desperate to be included in this nonsense with Drakkus.

"We've made the connection. Brad filed the paperwork today. My fingers are crossed, and I hope yours are too. The Nephilim guy appeared again. He said my dad is a witch, and that's why they're coming for me. I don't understand why they care. I know what Kannon said, and it kind of makes sense, but really, why can't they leave me alone? Am I hurting anyone by being alive? This would be so much easier if you were here to explain it to me."

But he wasn't, which was more crushing than I thought possible.

Hearing a crunch, I knew that Kannon was closing in on me. He'd gone for a walk in the opposite direction and said he'd take a slow walk back here so that I had time with Niko. I think that he was more worried than what Brad was. Brad didn't like that I came in here but let me because he knew where I was and that I wouldn't stay for too long.

I was slowly letting go, not that I wanted to. It had only been a few days with Niko, but there was something wonderful about what we had. It was like there was a sense of understanding that I couldn't find anywhere else in this world. Not with Brad, not with Kannon.

I should be used to death by now. Before my mother died, we lived in the roughest part of the city. Death was as common as the sun. I'd open the curtains of a morning and see a man running down the street, stolen goods in his arms. Seconds later, the cops would be chasing him, and the gunfight would happen. Sometimes, it would be a robbery, and the victim would fight back.

Drug users unable to pay. Drug runners stealing. It was why I wasn't surprised that my mother died. I was used to it and expected it, but in a way, I didn't really expect it.

I think that I knew it would happen. Like a whisper in the back of my mind that would never leave, it reminded me that it was only a matter of time before she left me. I hoped that it was wrong. Unfortunately, it wasn't.

Rising to my feet, I flicked away the leaves and said goodbye to Niko. Kannon was leaning against a tree trunk at the end of the path. Within sight but far enough away to still be respectful.

"Do your parents know where you are?"

Kannon chuckled softly as his arms wrapped around me. Mine was around his waist, hugging him tightly. I was falling hard.

"They do. I got the lecture about behaving myself and being respectful to our new leader. Not sure what they'll say about the rest of the stuff."

Ah, the rest of the stuff. He leaned down and took a kiss, adding to the list of stuff. It was the most that we'd done, but there was a lot of it. We were addicted to each other.

"Come on, Brad will be worried."

I scoffed, rolling my eyes.

"You'll soon learn that it is normal for Brad."

"Still not a good time to be in a place you should not be."

"Everyone fears the woods but never says why. Do you know why?"

"Yep. Witches used to hang out in there, casting spells and stuff. It's a little further into the center, you can't miss it, but you should. Well, maybe not you seeing as you are half-witch anyway. A lot of the kids go out there to make a mess of the place. It's like a big game. There are no witches in this town, but there's some kind of spell that rectifies all the issues. They turn a rock the wrong way, and the next day, it's back in the correct place. Break a branch. It's fixed."

We walked through the forest, hand in hand. Before we reached the edge, Kannon lifted our linked hands, kissing the back of my hand. I smiled, feeling a whole lot of things that had never been inside me before.

Returning to the house, we did homework. It was as thrilling as it sounds, but I suppose it kept Brad happy. He managed to acquire a dining table that was perfect for the two of us to work at.

Life, like always, liked to throw mighty curve balls at me. When I was at my happiest, it reminded me that death was always a step behind me.

Or, in this case, standing behind Kannon.

The Nephilim boy stared at me, and all I could do was wonder how long I had before the rest of them turned up.

"I'm glad you're back," Brad said as he approached. "They had space, so they've set the meeting for today.

The woman said that everything was in order and there shouldn't be any issues, so she offered to get it done."

"So, we're going now?"

He nodded, grabbing the keys off the kitchen counter.

Kannon came with us, pointing things out in the town as we passed them. I was yet to check out Hades. Before Niko's death, I didn't want any part of the town. In the short time of knowing him, the place had improved. Now, though, it felt cold and lifeless.

We entered the meeting room, and I was surprised to see the large turnout, given that it was a spur of the moment thing.

"Who are these people?" I whispered to Kannon.

"A few of those who know everything, some who know nothing, the panel, and my parents."

He gave me a sheepish grin.

"I sent them a message. They wanted to be here for it. You know, support and all that."

I nodded with a vague smile, unsure of what to say, aside from a little gratitude.

In the council meeting room, the Heritage Trust sat in panel formation at the top of the room, facing rows of chairs.

Brad and I walked in when our names were called. The Heritage Trust watched as we approached, and those who were in the seats turned to see who was walking in. The last of the Corbin family.

Kannon smiled at me. In the seats beside him were a couple that I presume were his parents. They offered smiles, I tried to smile, but it probably looked weird. I was nervous.

Brad and I sat in the seats allocated to us. The copies of the submitted documents were safely stowed in his folder, along with other things he thought we might need.

"We are here to review the application for the acceptance of beneficiary of the Corbin Estate by Evelyn Newton, overseen by her legal guardian, Bradley Newton."

The man whacked his gavel. I said nothing but thought it was curious that he had one. I didn't think that this was a courtroom.

"You have provided sufficient evidence of your relationship to Niko Corbin. The death certificates have provided a list of all offspring, which proves that there are no other living beneficiaries. You have also provided a will for Niko Corbin, which states the original beneficiary of his estate is his daughter, or if she has passed before claiming the estate, her next of kin shall be the beneficiary. In ordinary circumstances, we would ask to see the will documents from each of the beneficiaries so that we can see the chain as it passes from one person to the next. However, we find the maintenance of the house to be a strain on the funding we get from the government. It does not cover the house as the government does not see it as a house worthy of heritage listing and claims that our officials were wrong to take it in as a noteworthy place. We have unanimously agreed that passing the house back to the original family is in the Heritage Trust's best interest, and therefore, we approve your application."

With another whack of the gavel, I became a homeowner.

"The transfer documents will be created, lodged, and you will be advised of the change of ownership in due course. There is one notation that we'd like to add to this approval. We will be putting the ownership in both names as we believe that your parents, Bradley, would have given to each of their children equally. Evelyn, you will retain your mother's portion of her inheritance, and Bradley will retain his."

Still just as amazing. I'd happily share the house with Brad for the rest of our lives.

"Thank you," I said.

Brad collected the documents he didn't need. A woman approached with a temporary document that proved we'd been given approval and we were now the legal owners of the house.

"Thanks," he said, adding it to the folder.

"It is our pleasure. We've waited a long time to see the Corbin family return to this town."

The woman smiled at me, and I saw the fangs.

"You have more allies than you realize. Be strong friends. With perseverance, we will win the battle."

She returned to her position behind the panel, and the guards ushered everyone who didn't need to be there out.

"Who was that woman?" I whispered.

"Natalia Eastwell. After Niko disappeared, she got a position on the panel and convinced them to retain the house as a heritage-listed place. She is the only reason Drakkus couldn't get his hands on it. Which, I don't know if he would want the house, maybe just a few things inside it."

"It's not about the possessions. It's about domination."

The man held his hand out with a beaming smile that was so familiar.

"Eddios Lothaire,"

I smiled, feeling somewhat awkward as I shook his hand. Kannon's mother was next.

"My lovely wife, Iralya,"

The woman was all too eager. As I shook her hand, I wondered if she was seconds away from a curtsey. Or, God forbid, a hug.

"It's so lovely to meet you. Kannon has told us a lot about you."

"Mom," he hissed.

I looked at him and saw those blushed cheeks again.

"Oh, it's alright, honey." she cooed.

Brad edged his way behind the vampires, looking at me with a smug smile. Meeting the boyfriend's parents was such a fun time.

"You know what we should do? Celebrate the positive outcome."

Iralya turned to Brad with shock and hope in her eyes.

"Do you guys consume anything other than blood?"

"In small amounts, we can digest a few things."

"Though most often, we regret it. Many choose to avoid it altogether, but I find some items to be quite indulgent. I'll pick up some things, and we'll stop by later. Say, seven?"

"Sounds great."

Kannon smirked at me. Were his parents and my uncle about to have a party and get drunk? Maybe. Would they spend the night and early hours enjoying good company and not notice anything else? Perhaps.

I smiled and said nothing, but my mind was going faster than what I could keep up with.

CHAPTER 21

Brad insisted that our homework was done before we could play computer games. Of course, I said it was too noisy downstairs, so he relented and allowed us to do whatever we wanted. I think he was eager for adult company. Also, Kannon's aunt came with his parents, so there was an underlying setup that Brad was eager to let happen. The man was such a tart, and I was cramping his style.

"You know," Kannon whispered in my ear. "If my aunt marries your uncle, we'll be related."

"Oh my god, stop it."

He chuckled, wrapping his arms tighter around me. We were lying on the hammock that Brad had set up this morning. The front deck was the perfect place for it.

Inside, the raucous laughter erupted louder than it had been.

"I like that they get along," I said softly. "Brad needs some friends. With all this moving, he's lost contact with the ones he had. All because of me."

Kannon shifted.

The whole hammock began to swing. This might not have been a good idea.

"You want to know something? There are always options. No matter what the situation, there is a choice. Brad made this one, he picked this life to make yours better, and you know what? Maybe he was being a bit selfish, as well. You don't know what reasons he had. You can't just assume you were the entire reason for constantly moving."

"It was so that he could have a home-based job."

"To be at home for the teenager who was at school? Really?"

Kannon shifted again, now sitting up with my legs over his. The position was a little risqué. At least, it would be if Kannon didn't have a serious mood going on.

"My mother has a part-time job. She delivers my siblings to school, goes to work, and is at the gate at three pm every afternoon. You say Brad took this alteration to his job because of you, but maybe he wanted a change. If they were prepared to let him work from home, then they would be more than happy to let him alter his hours."

I sat up, gripping Kannon as the hammock shifted and swung.

"He said that the woman from child services had a thick file on my mother and me, which was understandable. She wasn't the greatest of mothers. Why did she insist that he watch me like a hawk? Do you think that she knew more than she should?"

"Probably. You'd be surprised at how many vampires there are and how widespread our knowledge is. If she figured out you were Corbin by blood, she would have done all that she could to hide you."

"But not tell Brad, that's a little odd, don't you think?"

"Sometimes being oblivious is for the best."

"Not if we end up dead because of it."

Kannon looked around at the quiet street, sighing softly.

"I know what you're thinking. It's not right, there were other ways that they could have done things, but sometimes, people do what they think is right at that point in time. We don't have crystal balls. We can't predict the future. Besides, maybe this woman from child services had a little input into Brad's job as well."

"We evaded his reach because of moving."

Kannon nodded.

"She knew who you were, or at least you were a vampire that should remain hidden. You're not the only one that has to hide. There are many vampires who think they should lead a coven."

The cold wind made me shiver, wrapping around me like a frosty veil.

"Let's go inside."

Kannon agreed all too quickly, which made me wonder if there was something or someone out there watching us. It wouldn't surprise me if that were the case.

We walked into the house and locked the front door. As we passed the amused and highly drunk adults, I looked at my uncle.

"House locked?"

He shrugged at me, all too merry for my liking.

"Prime pickings for Drakkus if he turns up tonight," I muttered.

"He's still licking his wounds. Word has it, you're a crack shot." Eddios said cheerfully. "Kannon said that you saw Andross outside the school. That's your gauge. If you see Andross watching, it means that Drakkus is unable to leave the house and has the only vampire he trusts watching the town or his interests."

I nodded, finding the information rather intriguing.

After checking the doors and windows, Kannon and I retreated to my bedroom.

"So, tell me why not every vampire can lead a coven."

"It begins with a vampire being of a certain age. Originally, they were of pure blood, but as the lines diversified, that was no longer a requirement. Currently, to start a coven, a vampire needs to have several hundred years of age clocked. The closer they are to four digits, the better chance they have of greater approval. To be honest, I could start a coven, but it doesn't mean I'll get backing from the other covens or even be able to attract followers. If I started one at my age or at any age below what they deem ideal, another leader could attack. It is done as a show of force. They take down the new vampire, call any followers to them, and declare the newly formed coven dead."

Together, we flicked off our shoes and laid on the bed. Did I mention the door was shut? No sock on the handle, but definitely shut.

"They will accept a created vampire provided they've done the time."

"Like me?"

"Well, you're kind of different."

I sat up with a slight frown.

"How so?"

"You're a half-witch, quarter pureblood vampire, and quarter-human. You're a mixed bag of issues. You'll find vampires like the ones downstairs and your allies in this town. They won't care at all so long as you're a good leader, which you're a Corbin, so it's in your nature. There are the likes of Drakkus and his followers who won't like your leadership, using it as an excuse, but deep down, it's got nothing to do with his real reasons. Then there are the others who won't like that a witch has returned to the town or this country, then add to it that you're also a vampire, and they're going to be left feeling uncertain. You're this new breed of being. Vampire, but you don't drink blood. You can walk in the sun without any issue, something that can be hit and miss for any vampire."

"But I don't have any witch skills."

Kannon sat up, a breath's distance from my lips. He smirked, a wild glint in his eyes.

"That's because you're not eighteen."

I settled back into his arms, staying there for a long time.

When it grew close to ten when Eddios appeared at the doorway to tell Kannon they were going home. We said our goodbyes, and I trudged off to bed, tired from a crazy day.

The house was quiet when I woke in the morning. Brad was sitting at the table, looking like death warmed up. Evidence of last night covered the table except for the small spot that Brad had cleared for his coffee cup.

"Good morning," I said loudly.

Brad winced, and I grinned. Life was just too good.

"How are you feeling?"

"I can hear you, Evie. Stop yelling."

Sitting back, Brad groaned and let his head roll backward. My gaze lowered to his forearm, and the numbers scrawled up it.

"I see you traded numbers."

"Huh?"

Brad perked up, frowning at me until I nodded my head at it.

"Well, I'll be damned," he murmured.

"You just might be if you screw a vampire."

"Evie,"

I smiled sweetly and then walked into the kitchen to make breakfast. Brad had left the milk on the counter. It was sweating from the heat of the morning. Making my cereal quickly, I returned it to the fridge and closed the door. Brad was standing behind it. I gasped when I saw him. He picked up his phone from the kitchen counter.

"Would you not do that," I hissed.

"Payback for the high volume. What's the deal with Kannon?"

I shrugged, watching Brad return to his chair.

"We're a thing. Does it matter?"

"I just want to ensure you won't get hurt."

"Thought you didn't care so long as I was careful."

Brad was not responsive. Just groaning into his coffee while rubbing his temples.

"Brad," I grunted.

He looked up. Brad was the poster boy for reasons not to drink alcohol. If that's how I felt the next day, then I gotta say, it's not winning any popularity contest in my mind.

"I do care, just not right now. The light hurts. Where did my coffee go? Did you drink it all?"

"No, you did. The light hurts because you drank too much, and you're hungover."

Getting up from the table, Brad picked up his mug and staggered into the kitchen.

"So, what's the deal?" he mumbled.

"Kannon?" I said, giving another shrug. "We can't predict the future, but Kannon's, I don't know. It's hard to gauge when I have no one to compare him to."

Brad sighed as he put the mug into the sink.

"Look, the way I see it is that he's one of three things. Legitimately interested, letting his hormones control him or listening to his parents to nab himself a worthy position as the leader's partner."

"He didn't know who I was when he said hello."

His head tilted with a raised eyebrow. That was the wordless sign that my statement may not be entirely correct.

"I don't know, okay?"

Brad turned his head slightly, then gasped as he jumped with fright. I turned to see the Nephilim boy standing behind me.

"And here's my daily doomsayer. You're getting old.

Time to get a new schtick and leave me alone."

The boy said nothing as he lifted his arm and pulled back the sleeve of his jacket to look at his watch. As his eyes lifted, darkness filled his smile. Then he faded away.

"Well, he certainly shut you up."

"Yeah," I said as I sighed. "Clearly, it doesn't matter what Kannon's intentions are when I am dead anyway. Between the Nephilim and Drakkus, I am as good as gone. Maybe I should buy a shirt with a target on it and wear it constantly. There might be less of a wait if I did."

Brad looked at me, smiling, but there was no weight to it. The underlying concern was evident.

"I hope you know what you're doing, Evie."

"And if I don't?"

"Then we're all screwed because, apparently, you're our new leader."

"You're not a vampire. I'm not a vampire. This should not be possible."

"Well, it is, so we just have to deal with it as best we can. I don't know how any of the vampires are going to take this."

"Maybe they might demand that we convert."

Brad shrugged, saying nothing in response.

"Bradley," I said with amusement. "You're awfully quiet on that particular subject. Did someone bite you last night?"

"Don't be ridiculous."

I tiptoed closer and reached out. As I pulled his shirt, the neckline stretched and exposed two little lumps that were surrounded by bruising.

"You tart."

"Evelyn," he grumbled. "Don't stretch my favorite shirt. And I'm not a tart. I'm playing hard to get."

"Doesn't look like you put up much of a fight."

He waved me off as if it didn't matter. To me, it didn't. I just liked to tease.

"I'm ready to go."

Brad looked at me, and I shook my head.

"Good grief, Bradley. You need to lay off the booze."

"I don't think that's the issue. Jess has a healthy appetite. She could have gone all night."

"Wow, I did not think you could cross a line, but there we have it."

"I didn't mean it like that. Jeez, Evie, get your mind out of the gutter. I meant that she could have fed from me all night."

Stuffing the lunch bag into my backpack, I tried to ignore Brad being gross, but it was difficult not to.

"They call it delayed feeding."

Difficult because he would not shut up.

"Apparently, it's a thing. It does not cause death, just lethargy. I'm glad she didn't want anything else."

"Aaaand clearly, I was wrong. You can cross a line and then keep walking. I'm going to school. You can take your floozy ass back to bed."

"I'll drive you."

"You are hungover, possibly still drunk. I'd be a better driver than you at this point in time. I'm walking."

Brad followed me to the door, stopping me before I could open it.

"I don't think that's wise. You heard what Ryan said."

"Ryan is a liar. Audrey walks to and from school every day. I don't know why he said that to us, but it is not true. Besides, it's not that far if I cut through the sports field."

"Alright, but I will be there to pick you up this afternoon."

I nodded, refraining from rolling my eyes. I was almost eighteen, and this is what I had to endure. All because of jerk vampires who won't leave me alone.

CHAPTER 22

Walking to school was not a difficult task. It was a short walk to the end of the street, across a quiet road to a footpath between two houses, down another street, and then along another street that ran parallel to the main street through town. I could have walked to the main street if I wanted to, but I couldn't be bothered, and it was pointless. The back street wasn't as populated, but there were certainly a few people around.

It was cooler this morning, but I didn't mind. The brisk walk was good for me. I was in a good mood, still amused by Brad's hangover and Kannon's affection.

As I reached the end of the back street, I looked down the road and saw Tom walking toward his car. He gave me a cheery wave, which I returned. I guess he was happy to get rid of the house. It must have been difficult for him to find tenants for the house that no one wanted to live in. Niko wasn't haunting it, but the place definitely had a creepy vibe to it.

Crossing the road, I stopped and looked at the trees that lined the sports field. I'd forgotten this part of the trek. Brad would have a fit if he knew. I guess that he'd either forgotten like I had, or maybe he'd never seen it. From the front of the school, the sports field could not be seen. It was entirely possible that he had no idea that there was a forest here.

It wasn't thick. I could see through the trees and beyond them to the school buildings. The problem was that the canopy made the area dark and posed so many risks.

Deciding that it wasn't worth the drama if Brad found out, I opted to go the long way around and walked around the exterior. I'd be late for school, but it was better than what could happen if I ventured into the darkness.

A wave of tension flushed through me. Something was wrong. I could feel it deep in my stomach as it churned with anxiety. Looking over my shoulder, I scanned the forest because I knew that if someone was watching me, they'd be in there.

I jumped when Tom started his car. Nervousness radiated through me as the sound of the car engine grew closer. The car passed me, continuing to the intersection and turning right. I didn't think Tom was the issue. He seemed harmless.

Tom was not an issue for my safety, but he was a distraction.

Cold wind whipped around me, and before I knew it, I was thrown against a tree trunk. Deep in the darkness, I hit the hard wood with a heavy thud and then fell to my knees in the scrub. I winced, groaning at how much it hurt.

I could still feel everything, so I don't think anything was broken. Just a lot of pain and maybe some nasty bruising.

My bag fell off my shoulder, slumping down my arm. As it hit the scrub, I looked at it. I hadn't zipped it all the way, and I knew that my phone would be in the pocket at the top of the bag. Was it worth scrabbling for it? Brad would not make it in time if I was able to call him. Escape was a far better option at the moment. Maybe run and then try to ring Brad.

A twig snapped, and a burst of merciless laughter echoed through the forest. All thoughts of calling my uncle were gone in a second.

"Little girl."

I knew the voice. It was Andross.

If I had thought about this before walking out of the house, I would have been much wiser. Yes, Brad was hungover and should have stayed in bed, but that didn't mean I could walk to school without issue.

I thought like this because it was all that I had ever done. Every morning, I woke to a hungover mother, sleeping off the previous night's efforts. I would get myself ready for school, and I would walk there by myself. There was no help from her, ever.

So naturally, I thought that at almost eighteen, I could walk to school like I had done every day previously.

Living with Brad changed that. He made me catch the school bus. Moving to Hades altered it completely. He was insistent that he drove me every single day.

It felt like I was in a cage, freedom denied, so it was no surprise that I'd jumped at this chance to return to the way I used to be.

Young.

Free.

Independent.

I was a fool to think that I could be any of those things now.

What I should have done was call Kannon and ask him to pick me up. That was the smart thing to do, except I had decided that I was still the girl who lived in the big city, and nothing had changed. It was a place where no one cared about anyone else, and even though crime was normal life, it was still safe for me to walk to school. Moving to a small town should have been even safer.

My legs were shaking as I lifted to my feet. I had no idea where he was, and to make it worse, I knew that he wouldn't willingly show himself. He wanted to play a game of cat and mouse before killing me.

"Show yourself, Andross."

He threw me against the tree again, this time appearing as he did it. I had to say, that was a pretty neat trick. Of course, I wouldn't tell him that.

I groaned, feeling the pain radiate throughout my body. It was a sharp snap against my spine, then blistered a blindingly painful path across my back.

"I do not answer to you, half breed." he hissed. "You are not worthy of being called a vampire. You don't even drink blood."

"I have never called myself a vampire."

"And yet you claim the title of leader for our town. Niko fouled his line by breeding with a human, and look at the result of that action. Your abilities are so diluted that you cannot even make your fangs descend. You are not even fit enough to be used as a breeding vessel."

"As if you'd stand a chance." I scoffed.

Andross growled. His eyes widened as his anger intensified. His hand wrapped around my neck, pushing me against the tree. I gasped, feeling his grip tighten. Struggling for air, I tried to fight Andross off, but it was pointless. He was bigger and stronger than me.

"You should learn to keep your mouth shut, mortal."

As his fangs tapered, I knew that it was fight or die. He was here to take me down, and if I stood here and did nothing, I would be dead. Emotions began to build as I thought about everything that would be left undone. Those that I cared deeply for, Brad and Kannon. I was even growing accustomed to Eddios, Iralya, and Jess. All that I had planned, all my dreams, they would be lost to this vampire.

As the negative thoughts plagued me, I could feel

something swelling inside me. Perhaps it was anger. It could have been sadness. All that I knew was that, in the blink of an eye, everything changed.

My heart pumped hard, going from a fear-induced heavy thump to something that was erratic and fast. I was not pushed against the tree anymore, now standing freely in the thick scrub.

Andross was airborne, thumping into the vegetation a short distance away. His lifeless body burned with a blue flame. I looked down and saw the very same fire had consumed my hands.

I yelped, flicking the flames until they dissipated. Then, the fear hit me. What have I done?

Despite the tears rolling down my cheeks, I managed to extinguish the fire. The body was not as burned as I expected it to be, but Andross was definitely dead.

Hearing a crunch, I looked up and saw the boy again.

"Go away," I snapped. "This is not the time for your rubbish."

"This," he said softly. "Is the day that defines your future. Be prepared, Evelyn. The Nephilim are coming."

He still said it. Even after I said not to, he still gave me that *they are coming* nonsense. At this point in time, I did not care, but I really did wish they'd hurry up.

"How is this possible? I'm not a witch. I'm not eighteen yet."

The boy lowered at the waist with a dark smile on his

face. It was a little disconcerting to see something that sinister on someone that looked so friendly.

"Your mother lied," he whispered. "You are eighteen. Your actual birthday was three days ago."

"What?"

The Nephilim shrugged as he stood upright again.

"I do not know the reason for the lie. I just know the truth. You are no longer a witchling. You are a full witch. Not a very good one, but one nonetheless."

He walked to the end of the body, looking at it as he passed.

"Perhaps I am not the only one that knows the truth. Didn't your uncle give you a gift recently?"

"Three days ago," I whispered. "He wouldn't lie about something like that."

"Sometimes, it is necessary to be oblivious. I am told that humans often hide the truth for various reasons, out of necessity, even because they think it's the right thing to do. It doesn't matter why. You shouldn't even think about it as a problem in your life. You've got bigger issues, and it's not just my kind that are coming for you."

His gaze lowered back to the dead vampire at his feet. In the short distance, I saw Audrey and her friends as they crossed the intersection.

Lowering, I hid in the scrub until they passed. I don't think they would see me, but I wasn't prepared to take the risk. Getting caught with a dead body was the last thing that I needed.

Audrey would see it and roll with it. She'd tell everyone in the school, including the kids that she refused to acknowledge because it would lower her popularity. She would enjoy it, ensuring that every single aspect was told in great detail, leaving nothing out. Even if I could prove it was an accident, I'd be an outcast because of it. More so than usual.

The problem was I had to do something. It was glaringly obvious that this was not a natural death. The body had burn marks, but the ground was not on fire. In fact, the only thing that had happened to the vegetation was that it was crushed.

It looked as if his body had been dumped here, long after he'd burned to death. This was not the best place to dump a body. Though, in this town, it was entirely possible to dump someone at the edge of the forest, and no one would see it.

Fumbling through the plants, I found my bag and rummaged through it. Pulling out my phone, I rang Kannon. My hands were shaking. I was freaking out.

"Do you really trust the vampire?"

"Shut up,"

The Nephilim smirked.

"Shouldn't you be leaving now?"

"Not anymore. You've cast your first spell. Now, my presence is permanent until my replacements arrive."

"Great." I groaned.

That was not what I wanted to hear. I'd asked for it. That old saying, be careful what you wish for, well, I'd just learned that one the hard way.

Kannon finally answered after the second time I called him.

"Evie," he crooned.

"I have done something,"

My voice trembled as the tears emerged. Realization of what was going on had hit me, and I was freaking out.

"You know that thing, the half thing."

"You mean, the after you turn eighteen thing?"

"I am eighteen. I'll explain it later. I don't know what to do."

"Where are you?"

"Opposite the real estate office."

"Be there in five."

It was going to be the longest five minutes in history.

CHAPTER 23

I was a mess. Tucking the phone back into my bag, I zipped it up and waited for Kannon. All the while, the Nephilim stood over the body, watching me with a defiant smile on his face. I was still not used to him or his mockery.

"This will not be the answer that you need."

"I don't know what I need. You're not being helpful here. It was an accident. Don't you know that?"

"Of course I do, but I do not exist in this world. I cannot offer anything to any authoritarian that might come across this and point their accusatory finger at you."

"Then help me deal with this now rather than later before the cops become involved."

The boy huffed a soft laugh.

"From what I have learned of this town, you needn't worry about the police. The only cop working struggles to find his car in the morning, so I would imagine that finding a killer in such odd circumstances would be quite difficult for him. However, as you are already aware, the cop is on the vampire's payroll, so he would mention this, and then you'd have an even bigger problem. Am I making this any easier, half-breed?"

I growled at him through the angry tears. He was not helpful at all.

"No. What am I supposed to do with this?"

"Leave it there. How should I know what the right thing for you is? My goal for today was to ensure that you were aware that my kind are coming for you, which I believe I have completed with much success."

Wiping the tears away, I wondered if handing myself in at the police station would stop the Nephilim. They couldn't kill me if I was in a cell being watched by a camera, could they?

"Your kind is intent on destroying me when none of this is my fault. I didn't ask to be created. I didn't pick my parents."

Something clicked inside my mind.

"Did you kill my mother because of this?"

The Nephilim shook his head.

"We did not. Your presence remained unknown to us until recently. As for her death, I think that you've already drawn an accurate conclusion."

"She was murdered because she was Niko's granddaughter."

"Correct. In fact, I believe that you have sought sufficient revenge for it in Andross's death. Perhaps you'd like to pretend that you knew it was fact when the vampires come to lynch you for killing him."

"Andross killed my mother?"

The boy smiled as he nodded.

"In fact, as Drakkus's lover, he was entrusted to do all of the important work. Andross also killed your grandparents."

"Wait, he was with Drakkus?"

"Correct."

"Oh god," I groaned. "Now he's really going to be upset."

"Evie?"

Perking up, I searched for Kannon and found him at the edge of the trees. He stepped in, warily at first.

"What are you doing in here?"

Then he looked down.

"Oh," he said softly. "That's not good. Did he attack you?"

I nodded as Kannon squatted in front of me.

"And you fought back."

Taking my hands, Kannon turned them over and looked at them. The skin was paler than they used to be.

"The color will return soon enough. You're a newbie at this, so you would have no idea what you're doing."

I nodded, tears still streaming freely. Kannon wiped them away, giving me a sweet smile.

"You know that this is not your fault. You defended yourself when an old and very powerful vampire attacked you. He was stronger than you, and the fact that you've come out unscathed is a miracle."

That amused the Nephilim. I scowled at him.

"Tell the boy it is not a miracle. You are of strong witch blood, and now you are a danger to everyone around you, including him. Tell him to run away fast."

"Evie?"

Tears welled in my eyes.

"Can you see the Nephilim?"

"No, are they here?"

"Just one, the same one as always. He said that it was not a miracle. I have strong witch blood, and I'm a danger to everyone, including you. He said that you should run away."

Kannon wrapped me into his arms.

"I'm not going anywhere. You will learn how to use your powers."

As he held me tight, I looked at the Nephilim boy. His defiant smirk hadn't changed, still taunting me as if he could see the future. At his feet was the evidence that

I was dangerous and a risk to those I cared for.

Kannon suggested the easiest and best option regarding Andross's body. Leave it there.

I was hesitant to go with his plan, but Kannon assured me he'd call his father and let him deal with the body.

They had their own code system where they could talk over the phone and not have to worry about anyone listening to them. It wasn't the government that concerned them. It was Drakkus.

Kannon held my hand as we walked into the school.

"You should have called me."

"I know. I didn't think of it until it was too late."

"Well, it doesn't matter. He would have attacked at another time."

The boy was a couple of steps behind us, always haunting me with his devious smile.

"I'm sick of this place," I murmured wearily.

I'd like to say that there was a bonus that it was sunny now, but the rain had set in. Kannon said that we were officially in the wet season, so it wasn't going anywhere for a long time.

"Everywhere I turn, there's an issue waiting for me."

Kannon said nothing in response, but he knew that I was talking about Audrey. She hadn't approached but offered the standard mocking giggle she gave whenever I was near.

"Audrey needs a big wart on the end of her nose," Kannon murmured in my ear as he hugged me.

I smiled, enjoying his affection more than anything. It ended quickly when Audrey screamed.

Kannon and I turned to see Audrey crying as her friends looked at her with fear on their faces. A crowd began to form, and then the laughter erupted.

"Audrey's got a wart on her nose." a boy yelled out.

"She looks like a witch." his friend added.

Audrey's hysterical sobbing stopped as she looked at me.

"You did this," she screamed.

I stared, unable to figure out if she was right or not. It was entirely possible that she was correct, considering Kannon had only just said it. And, of course, that old chestnut that was hanging around and refusing to leave.

Glancing at the Nephilim, he said nothing, but the defiant smile was still there.

"How is that possible?" Kannon said tersely. "You're looking for excuses wherever you can find them. Evie's got nothing to do with a damned wart on your nose."

"I agree."

Gasps filled the corridor as the crowd turned to the principal behind them.

Until today, I'd only ever seen a picture of him in the office. There wasn't much that was different, almost like the man never changed his appearance. The sandy blonde hair was neatly swept to the side, tanned skin, and the whitest teeth I'd ever seen. It was like he was in competition with Tom to be the most overdone, peculiar person in this place.

If that wasn't crazy enough, he wasn't wearing a tie. In the picture, he wasn't wearing one, either. In every single school that I'd been to, the headmasters were all male, and they always wore a tie. This was not a beachside community, yet this guy was dressed like he was about to strut down the promenade and toss some corny pick-up lines at a few unlucky ladies.

"The bell is about to sound. Everyone should get moving now. Miss Hartley, I would suggest that you refrain from throwing ridiculous accusations around. I'm sure you don't want to leave yourself open for defamation charges. Please go to class."

Audrey scowled, then stomped off. The principal stepped back with a smile on his face as he watched her walk away. Those pearly whites were flashed like a sales pitch.

"Mister Lothaire, are you late for class as well?"

"I'm fine."

The bell sounded, and the principal stepped further back, waiting for Kannon to pass.

"Evelyn," the Nephilim said cautiously. "The man

in front of you will only heighten your issues with my kind."

I casually looked back at the boy, frowning slightly. I wanted more information, but I couldn't exactly say something with the principal watching us. Why would a vain principal of a small town high school be an issue for me or the Nephilim?

"Kannon,"

One of the teachers appeared at a doorway, glowering heavily at him.

"Are you planning on attending class today?"

He nodded reluctantly, then looked at me.

"Later, Evie."

As his hand fell away from mine, I felt a mixture of emotions. I'd never felt the need for protection, but right now, I wanted Kannon to remain.

Cold fingers slipped into mine. My body tightened at the sensation of the Nephilim boy taking my hand. It was soft, almost like touching a puff of smoke.

"He will sense that something is different." the Nephilim offered as his grip tightened.

The principal smiled at me, seemingly casual.

"We have not had the chance to meet yet, Evelyn. I am Principal James Harlwood."

He held out his hand expectantly, and the boy's grip tightened immediately. There was nothing that I could do. I had to be civil. So, I shook his hand and felt a surge of power. The man said nothing. Not even a flinch to say that he'd felt it, too.

"It's been a long time since we have had a newcomer in Hades," Principal Harlwood said as he let go of my hand. "Lots of visitors but no one that actually moves here. It is quite refreshing to see a new face around the place."

Then he turned to the corridor, the same way that I was going, and opposite to his office. I guess he was walking with me, and clearly, I had no choice.

"I understand that your uncle is your legal guardian."

"Yes, sir."

"What happened to your parents, if you don't mind me asking?"

"Only if you're not offended by the answer."

The principal looked at me curiously.

"My mother was a prostitute. I never knew my father and can only assume he was a client. She passed away from a drug overdose three years ago."

"Oh, that is unfortunate. My condolences, Evelyn."

"It's fine. As sad as it was, my life is better now that I'm living with my uncle. He has provided a stable home, and I've been able to attend school regularly. Well, this is me."

Awkwardly, I gestured to the restroom door. The

principal looked at it, then gave a smile. It seemed forced and reluctant.

"Of course. Enjoy your day."

I nodded and quickly moved through the door, trying to avoid looking at him or making it obvious that I was dragging a biblical creature behind me.

Moving to the last stall, I closed the door and peeked through the gap.

"What the hell was that about?"

"The principal is a demon." the boy whispered. "He knows what you are."

Putting the lid of the toilet down, I sat on it and leaned my elbows on my legs.

"Okay, time to lay it out for me. Do me a solid and be my teacher."

"Even if it is pointless?"

"Nothing is pointless. He made a concerted effort to extract me from Kannon so that he could interrogate me without intervention."

The boy smiled at me.

"You noticed."

I nodded.

"Alright, an education into demons as requested. They are known to be solitary creatures in regard to their own species. However, they will frequent places like

Hades, where they can manipulate the townsfolk and not be overwhelmed by a large populace. Many will lay low, living a quiet life while hiding what they really do when no one is looking. They will pick towns where a vampire coven is strong. The purpose of this is that they can feast on the souls of the dead. Towns with vampires have a higher death rate, and the residents of a town with a demon in it tend to be quite oblivious to what's going on. It's a symbiotic relationship that one group is usually unaware exists. So that you're aware, he did see me. I held your hand so that he understood what was going on."

"Is he dangerous?"

The Nephilim smiled at me.

"Absolutely."

CHAPTER 24

The Nephilim boy stood beside my desk for the entire day. No matter what classroom I was in, he was there next to me.

"Aren't you bored?"

"I do not understand the concept of boredom."

Closing my locker, I lifted my bag over my shoulder. A shiver went up my spine, and the hairs on the back of my neck stood on end.

"We are not alone," the boy whispered.

"Demon or vampire?" I murmured.

"Demon."

I rolled my eyes and pulled the other strap onto my arm.

"This is getting ridiculous. Now I've got three creatures that want me dead."

"Oh, the demon doesn't want you dead,"

The Nephilim smiled at me.

"He does, however, wish to utilize your services and harness your ability. You should move away before he materializes."

Taking my hand, the Nephilim led me out of the corridor.

"I don't have any ability."

"Wrong," the Nephilim cooed. "You are the offspring of a powerful witch. The demon senses that and knows that you are young and easily corrupted. He would offer you a deal that would seem quite enticing to you, but be warned that it will benefit him more than you. Best that you keep your affection for the boy out of his sight. The demon will remove all obstacles."

His grip tightened, and the cold permeated through my skin.

"Aside from my kind, that he has no control over. Your vampire enemies, though, he could certainly deal with them if you were to strike the right bargain. I would not recommend it, though."

"Selling my soul?"

"Demons are not the devil, Evelyn. They do not have such powers. What he would take, though, would leave you thinking that you had, in fact, sold your soul. I suppose that your lack of knowledge regarding the subject is understandable. Fear not. I will be here by your side until my kin arrives, so you will be safe from the demon."

"What's my father like?"

The bright purple eyes looked at me, wide and perhaps stunned.

"I do not know. I was assigned to you and have no information or thoughts on your father. What I know about him is what I have found within you. The power that flows through your veins is strong, which is indicative of a powerful lineage. There were a few witches that could be your father. However, they are all dead. What we face is an unknown entity, and he will sense that you have come of age. That can be dangerous."

We'd reached Kannon's classroom, I stopped, and thankfully, he let go of my hand.

"How so?"

"Witches are unpredictable, that is why I said, can be dangerous. I have no idea what would happen, but something tells me that he will not willingly emerge from whatever hole he's hiding in. Once he figures out that he impregnated a vampire, the witch will know what is coming for him. Make no mistake, Evelyn, your father will pick his own life over yours. He will leave you to deal with the Nephilim on your own."

"Aren't you just a ray of sunshine?"

The boy paused, looking up to the ceiling as if he had seen someone or something. His smile was malicious but full of amusement.

"However, in recent moments, I have been advised that perhaps those thoughts may be wrong. The future is now unsettled, and there is no direct path ahead. Only time will tell what will happen now."

"Well, that's just great," I mumbled.

He said nothing in response, which was just as well. Kannon's class emerged. The once quiet corridor was now buzzing with life, and I didn't want to be trying to have a discrete conversation with a being that only I could see.

Kannon sauntered out, giving me a peck on the cheek.

"Still got company?"

"Yeah," I groaned. "It's the least of my problems now. Come on, we need privacy."

Kannon took my hand as we wandered to his locker. I was ignoring the Nephilim, who was trying to get my attention to ensure that I knew his kind was my biggest problem.

"Brad said you can give me another lesson this afternoon."

"Once we're away from this place?"

I nodded with a smile until I remembered that the annoyance was still here and always would be. There would be no misbehavior at the lake or anywhere in between.

"Have you heard from your father?"

"Yes, all fixed."

"You know why I ask that, right?"

Kannon grimly nodded as he held open the passenger door.

"It's only been a short while since you shot him. I would not have expected Drakkus to be out at this hour or at all, to be honest."

"He knows."

"No, he probably expected Andross to return at a certain time and has come here to find him. Now, what did we need privacy for?"

Kannon pressed me to the car, kissing over my jaw. It was hard to enjoy it when the Nephilim stared at us.

"Would you go away?" I hissed.

Kannon's head lifted, looking at where my eyes were directed. The Nephilim remained quiet. Just a plain face that offered nothing.

"He won't leave me now because of this morning."

"Sounds like absolute fun."

"Yeah. The privacy thing," I whispered. "The principal is a demon."

Kannon shifted a step back, putting a small gap between us.

"Seriously?"

"If you believe the Nephilim, yes."

"Oh, I would believe them. They don't know how to lie."

"We do not understand the concept of it and the purpose that it serves." the teen interjected.

"Great, thanks for the info."

When I was seated, Kannon shut the door. For the few seconds I was alone, I looked across the road to the café where I'd seen Andross watching us. Now, we had a replacement observer, and he was ready to unleash a whole new kind of war on me. It was like he knew that I'd killed his partner.

Even though Brad said I could have a driving lesson today, we decided against it. I didn't want to be out having fun when there was a rather large issue that had to be dealt with. Well, my life was nothing but issues, but Andross was at the top of the pile.

Brad was stunned when we told him. Seated at the table with coffee in front of him, I'd suggested putting a little kicker in it because he'd want it once I'd told him about my morning adventure. He didn't get angry, not that I thought he would. The worst I'd seen out of Brad was grumpiness.

Part of his subdued mood was because we were not alone. Not just Kannon but his family and a few whom I was yet to be introduced to. They were sitting in the lounge room while we discussed the issue.

"Did you know that I turned eighteen three days ago?"

Brad stared for a moment, then nodded. I was stunned into silence as I stared at Brad. He opened his mouth and then huffed.

"I don't know why she told me a different date, but when the cops cleared the apartment, and I collected your things, I found a note for me. She told me your real birth date, that I had to keep it a secret, and that we should never stop moving. I had to keep you a secret."

"The caseworker?"

"Just another mindless human that knew nothing. She was more interested in getting you off her books than your welfare. I'm sorry, Evie. I didn't want to keep this from you, but the letter sounded like your mother was scared of something coming to get you. She said I had to keep it a secret, even from you. Your mother wanted you to enjoy your childhood as much as you could."

"That makes no sense. Why did she hit me? Why was I the one she blamed for all her problems?"

Brad had a blank expression on his face as he looked at me. Sadness soon gripped him. He opened his mouth to respond, but nothing came out, just a wordless shaking of his head.

The Nephilim was standing behind Brad, giving me a dark smile. Yeah, I knew what he was thinking. I was a problem. I was the reason she was living a life on the run, taking whatever work she could find, which clearly was something that she didn't like doing.

"What about your job?"

"I had to quit, not long after you moved in. Do you remember when I said I'd just got the okay to work from home?"

I nodded warily.

"They said that there was no opportunity to do anything other than the job that I had. I had to do my job or quit. I accepted it because I thought that you'd be alright. You'd lived an independent life with your mother, so I figured you were used to looking after yourself. Getting to school had never been a problem in the past. I thought that your mother was just being well, you know, the drugs."

Pressing my lips tight with a grim smile, I nodded again. Yeah, Mom and her drugs.

"When I came home that afternoon, I was all set to tell you that life was going to be just like what you were used to, just in a different setting. I'd just walked in the main gate, and I was standing at the entrance looking through the mail when one of the other residents was complaining about some creepy guy hanging around the building asking if there were any new tenants."

Brad looked at me directly. The heaviness of his mood was a little startling.

"New as in young girls. She was going to call the cops. She was adamant that this guy was a pervert looking to abduct someone, and it hit me like a wrecking ball. You were new to the building, and you were young and female. He was looking for you. Your mother's letter and this guy, it put a lot of fear in me. So, I formed a quick plan that had us leaving the next day. I didn't pick anywhere. I didn't tell a soul. Once I had you and our stuff in the car, I sent an email to work telling them that I had to quit, giving them the caseworker lie."

"But all your stuff."

"It was still there until a month ago. The building manager has sold it all and wired the money to my account. We've been living off the inheritance. Between what my parents left your mother and me, it's kept us going and doing exactly as she wanted. She was very specific about the money. It was to be used to move us and to keep you from being found. Never stop, always move, be vigilant."

"What did she know?" I hissed at the Nephilim.

Eddios, who was sitting next to Brad, turned and looked at the empty space, then curiously looked back at me.

"Clearly more than she let on. Having never met your mother, I cannot say what she knew. I also lack the ability to see into the past. You can let your anger consume you if that is what you desire, but your emotions are pointless. Your uncle did what was asked of him. Bear him no ill will, Evelyn."

"The boy?" Brad asked.

"Yes, the Nephilim boy is here permanently because of this morning."

With a heavy sigh, I settled back into the seat.

"I'd like to talk about this later if you don't mind."

Brad nodded silently. It was better that we were alone.

"Will Drakkus believe me if I say it was an accident, that I acted unknowingly and in self-defense?"

"Nope," Eddios said curtly. "Once he figures it out, he's going to start preparations. The only thing that is going for you at the moment is this,"

His index finger tapped on the document from the Heritage Trust. The paperwork had been submitted and accepted. We were the official, legal owners of this house and land.

"In their confirmation that you are legitimate descendants of Niko, Drakkus has to accept that you are the legal leader of the vampires in this town."

"But don't expect him to hand it over," Jess said.

"No, he won't do that. Not in a million years. What you do next will define you as a leader and will set the tone for the future. He will expect that you will be full of bravado, and he will anticipate a confrontation."

"I would expect that, too," I said. "But you sound as if you think I should consider an alternative."

"All I know is that he has seen how you fight, how you stand your ground. He might have only had a few days to learn about you, but I promise that he has had every single one of his followers watching you. His thirst to know the enemy will never be quenched. This is how a leader will win the war. They learn their enemy, so they understand them. They search for their weaknesses, their strengths, and anything that they can use to their advantage. I would suggest that you do the same. Also, you will need to learn how to rule. The vampires that I have brought with us, they will give you useful information. Listen to them, Evelyn. They are here to assist you. They want you as their leader."

"They don't know me."

Eddios smiled.

"My dear, you are a Corbin by blood. They already knew you long before you were born."

CHAPTER 25

I learned that to be the true and only leader of the vampires in Hades, I had to take Drakkus down. As in, kill him. Of course, someone else could do it, but to be seen as a strong leader, it was ideal that I did it. Eddios said it would be difficult for me because I was only eighteen and Drakkus was an old vampire. Essentially, I did not stand a chance.

At that lovely revelation, the rest of the vampires were brought into the conversation. I was told their names, but it would take time for me to learn it. I expected the Nephilim boy to tell me learning their names was pointless and not to bother. He didn't. All he did was stand in the corner of the room like a wooden puppet. Lifeless.

The only way I was going to get through this, defeat Drakkus, and survive was with their help. I was grateful to have so many people willing to assist a complete stranger.

There was something that had been hinted at, but I think that Eddios was reluctant to discuss it when no one knew how to teach me. My witch abilities.

"The Nephilim boy said that my father is a powerful witch."

"That may be so, but that doesn't make this situation any easier."

"I need to learn how to control these powers. Look at what I did. It was over before I knew what was going on. I can't ignore what is inside me."

"She's right, Eddios. If Evelyn doesn't learn how to use her powers, then we're all at risk."

"And who would you have teach her, Jess? The witches have not been seen in decades. Clearly, there's at least one out there, but where is he? Even if we went to the town where she lived, it's not an indication that we would find him. Her mother frequently moved to hide. Was it from him or the vampires? Maybe there's a good reason that Evelyn's birthday was off."

Iralya stepped in, placing a firm hand on her partner's shoulder to settle his growing anger.

"I think we can all agree that we need to think about this logically and, perhaps, in stages. The first recommendation that I have is that security is placed around this house and those who dwell in it. We know that Drakkus will stop at nothing to get what he wants, and he may resort to abducting Bradley to make Evelyn cave to his demands."

There was a unanimous agreement, and Jess wrote it down on her notepad.

"An education in becoming a strong leader and teaching Brad how to be her second in charge as the second point. Evelyn needs to complete her schooling. She needs time to be young. The burden of this leadership shall be eased as much as we can manage. At least until the threat is averted."

"A battle plan must be created," Eddios said abruptly. "All of this is pointless if we cannot defeat Drakkus. We'll all be dead. Is there any literature about witches that we can read to help Evelyn?"

Jess looked up from her book, shrugging at her brother.

"There may be something in the library. I can check when we return."

I realized that I'd never been to Kannon's place. He'd been here several times, in and out, as if he lived here, yet I'd not stepped foot into his house.

After that, I tuned out. I was sick of hearing about battles, plans, and how things were going down the drain. Act now before it's too late.

"The hour grows late," Iralya said as she stood. "Kannon has homework, and I'm sure Evelyn does as well. We are yet to feed. Organize the security and bid our friends good night."

Eddios nodded. I stood, and Iralya smiled as she took my hands.

"Darling child, do not fear him. You are powerful, and that is why Drakkus is so determined to win. He knows that you can beat him. This is your family land. The strength that you have far outweighs Drakkus. We will teach you. We will show you how to be a great leader."

I nodded with a smile, pretending that everything was fine. In reality, I was freaking out. There was no way that they'd get the education done in time. It was only a matter of days before Drakkus appeared, wanting revenge for Andross's death.

I was a goner.

When everyone left, I looked out the window. A vampire sat on one of the deck chairs, watching the street. There would be another one near our back door and two on either side of the house. Every so often, they'd check in with each other, and when dawn came, they'd shift into the shadows of the trees and watch from there.

I didn't want to point out that they were easy targets out there. I'm sure they figured that out for themselves.

"Did you want to discuss the letter?"

I shrugged, lumping myself back onto the lounge.

"What's done is done. You did what she asked. I can't fault you for that. Did grandma ever say anything to you?"

"No, not really. I remember she once said that we were like a fish out of water, struggling to breathe because we were not where we should be, desperate to return. All the while, the cat would be stalking us, waiting to kill us. I didn't understand what she meant by that, and when I asked, she smiled at me and said that she hoped that I wouldn't have the same burden as what she had. Still didn't make any sense," he grumbled. "But it does now. She knew, probably wanted to tell me, but thought that giving me a carefree childhood was far better. Maybe she'd told your mother and saw how it affected her and thought that keeping me oblivious would,"

"Keep you sober?"

Brad nodded, sighing as he rubbed the back of his neck. He sat down and pulled out the letter. It was strangely coherent for my mother. I'm sure she wrote it when she was sober, in one of those moments that I rarely saw.

"It says to remember the conversation that the two of you had at Starbucks on my tenth birthday."

"I always sent a present for you."

"Well, I never saw them."

"Didn't you? I've seen you wearing the necklace I sent. The silver chain with the guardian angel on it."

I stared, remembering the day that I'd come home from school. It was sitting on the kitchen counter with a tag that said my name and nothing else. I didn't recognize the handwriting, and when I asked my mother who it was from, she mumbled something that I couldn't understand and then started snoring.

"Did you ask about it?"

I nodded.

"Well, after that, I had to give clothing as gifts. I assumed that she was just going to leave them somewhere for you, so I only wrapped them, no gift tags or anything."

"Yeah, that's probably what she did. She rarely bought clothing for me, and when she did, it was always around my birthday, so I guess it was really you who bought them for me. So, thanks."

It wasn't easy being raised by someone who didn't care or was too high to realize that her child needed things. I had to rummage through charity bins so that I'd have different clothes to wear to school. Being teased for wearing the same thing over and over again was not fun.

Maybe he knew, maybe he was just being nice, but those clothes that Brad bought for my birthday were the greatest thing ever. At the time, I thought that my mother was being generous, feeling guilty, or had a good night out and earned a lot of money. There would be a pile of clothes sitting on the kitchen counter, and it would be enough to last me for a long time. No doubling up on days, no struggling to get the clothes dried before the next day of school.

I took incredible care of those clothes, knowing it would be another year before I got new ones. When a shirt got a tear in it, I asked my teacher if she could show me how to repair it. She did, and the next day, she had a box waiting for me. It was full of different colored threads, needles, a little pair of scissors, and a needle threader. I cried because it was the nicest thing anyone had ever done for me. And yes, I still had that box. It was another item that I treasured enough to keep in good condition.

"I would have preferred to give them to you, but your mother had rules, and I had to follow them. We discussed it at length, almost like she thought she wouldn't make it. Like she knew there was someone following her."

"Did she ever say anything like that?"

Brad shook his head, sitting in the lounge next to me.

I frowned as I thought about my mother, Brad, and all this nonsense. Something struck me as odd.

"Brad,"

Uneasily, he looked at me. He knew that something had clicked.

"Did you pick this town for a reason?"

He closed his eyes, and a soft sigh escaped before his eyes reopened.

"Your mother said you had to return to Hades before your eighteenth birthday. She suggested doing it at the last minute, to give you as much normalcy as possible. I spoke to Niko about it before his passing. He knew why. I'm sorry, Evie, it's not something I would want for you, and if I'd known, I would have never come here. So, I'll give you the bad news first."

Well, that was not what I wanted to hear.

"The Corbin line is incredibly rare because the

firstborn children are always girls. Niko told me that vampires don't give birth to females, and any female vampires that you see are always turned from humans. Our family, we only ever get one female. That's why I'm here."

"This is the bad news?"

"I'm getting there. Trust me, you're not going to like it. So, back in Niko's day, when he was ruling, Drakkus was his second in charge. When Niko and Beatrice became pregnant, Drakkus overheard them talking about the child being a girl. Later, he stated to Niko that he was the only one worthy of the girl's hand in marriage and demanded that Niko agree to the arrangement."

"But he's gay, isn't he?"

Brad shrugged.

"I have no idea. Maybe he takes whatever he can get. Maybe he's gay but wants someone to have his children. Niko said that his child was born female, something that just doesn't happen in their world. Drakkus does not like humans being turned. Niko said that he called it foul blood. Maybe he saw this child as a solution to his issues. Anyway, Niko said he'd already seen the beginning of the insanity and refused. That's when Drakkus left and formed a faction of vampires who were supposedly unhappy with Niko's rule. When he realized that the child and mother were in danger, Niko sent them away with strict instructions to hide no matter what. To pass on the rules to each generation and never come back to Hades."

"But you said that my mother told you that I had to

come back before I turned eighteen."

Brad nodded grimly.

"That's what your mother deemed as the good news. I don't agree, just so that we're clear. I don't know how she found this ruling out, but she did. It was too late for her, but for you, it was a shot at ending this madness for you and your daughter. If you don't stop him, you could end up as his captive. In the laws of the vampires, it is stated that if one vampire turns against another, a blood war begins. Every descendant of the two vampires has the ability to end the blood war if the two warring vampires won't, but they can only do it at a certain time."

"Before they turn eighteen?"

Brad nodded.

"Did I make it in time?"

"You did. Shooting Drakkus was the opener. I don't know how close you got, but Niko said you had done it."

"When did he say that?"

He shrugged uneasily, looking rather morose.

"After the first shot. He was still alive at that point but finally passed after you shot Drakkus the second time."

"So, I can stop the blood war?"

"You can."

"I just need to kill Drakkus."

"Yes."

Well, that certainly helped clear things up for me. I was still in the same spot, still stuck in this horrible predicament.

CHAPTER 26

Brad suggested that it was ideal that I take a few days off school so that I could learn how to deal with the situation. I don't think it was a good idea, but I had to focus on the issues rather than trying to cram more information into my brain.

I think he was feeling guilty over the lies he told and the secrets he'd kept. We'd talked about it for hours last night, once we got past the blood war. I learned that not only had he been in regular contact with my mother, but when I was younger, he had come around to the apartment. I was too young to remember it, but he said I was a cute kid.

Despite the issues in our final years together, Brad said my mother loved me, and he could see it. When I was a baby, it was easy enough for her to move around, but as the years passed, I grew, and then I started asking questions.

Brad stated that it was not my fault. All children were inquisitive. The problem was that the more questions I asked, the bigger burden I became. My mother saved as much money as she could. Most of her savings were spent on moving and finding places that suited her need to hide. Sometimes, those places were not cheap.

Getting up from the table, I wandered to the lounge and flopped on it. Brad lifted his gaze from the laptop and looked at me.

"Problems?"

"The book just confirms that I need to kill Drakkus. Not just to ensure there are no issues but to be seen as strong and worthy of my placement. You know that at eighteen, I won't have much backing from the other vampires, right?"

"But you've got vampires on your side."

"Yeah, but Kannon said that to get a following, a vampire needs to have serious years clocked. If they don't, they're susceptible to a takedown from another vampire. This is our land by blood, but that doesn't mean anything if I can't get vampires to join my coven. I'm not even a vampire," I groaned.

Brad was no help, just giving me a sympathetic smile.

"Not one part of that book has any help for the would-be leader, who is only a quarter vampire. I am a freak."

"Never thought I'd live to see the day you agreed with me."

Pulling the scatter cushion out from under my back, I threw it at Brad. He raised his arm in time, sending it awry with nothing more than a chuckle.

"Do you think I could get everyone to defer this for a year?"

"I seriously doubt it."

"It's always worth a shot, right?"

"You do as you please. I'm sure it won't hurt your feelings when they laugh at you."

"I just want to get my schoolwork done. Is that too much to ask?"

Clearly, it was. My shadow was never far away, staring at me as if there was nowhere else to look. Pulling another pillow out from under me, I threw it at him. The cushion passed through the boy and hit the wall behind him.

"Can I have like five minutes without you staring at me?"

"No."

"Your friends are certainly taking a long time to get here. Are they building the car or something?"

The Nephilim tilted his head.

"Using a horse and cart? Walking? Come on, I need a timeline here."

"I do not know when they will arrive."

"Well, find out. Give them a call on your supernatural phone."

"I do not have a phone of any kind. They will get here when they get here. There is nothing that I can do to change that. You will just have to be patient."

"Yeah, good luck with that one."

Brad returned to his laptop. Now that he was no longer pretending to work, he was researching websites that Jess suggested. They were the ones that were hidden within the deep, dark web. Accessing them required certain codes, which she had supplied.

I asked Brad what he did all day when he was pretending to work. He said he mostly played computer games, kept the house spotless, and planned our next move. Occasionally, he'd do a little fishing and try to find things that I might find useful. Before coming here, he found nothing. Since coming here, he had Jess's help, so Brad found a lot of things.

"So, if you hook up with Jess, does that mean that she'll have a girl as well?"

"I have no idea."

"Are you going to hook up with Jess?"

"Probably."

"Do you say probably because you're not willing to show emotions, or are you worried that she's not interested?"

Brad slapped the laptop lid down and set it aside, frowning at me as he stood from his seat. The mug was empty, and Evie was being annoying.

"I think it's pretty obvious that she's interested."

"Yeah, I saw the second set of bite marks. You tart."

Rolling his eyes, Brad walked into the kitchen and began making himself another coffee. Beyond the kitchen window, a vampire walked past. I was not accustomed to the security guards, and every time they walked past the windows, I freaked out.

"Are you being obnoxious so I will let you out for a walk?"

"Absolutely."

"The only way that I will agree to that is if you take one of the guards. If you can convince them, then knock yourself out."

Sitting up, I found a new zest for the dull morning. I could go and see Niko, say hello, vent my frustrations, and hopefully, return in a better mood. It was asking a lot, but I was hopeful.

The guards were not impressed with my request. They agreed, but it would be the briefest visit I'd ever had. There and back, leave the collected flowers, a short hello, and nothing else.

I think they were spooked, and it had nothing to do with the current issues.

Still, one of them agreed to come with me to the cave. Another would remain at the halfway point where he could see the house and us, and the remaining two would stand at opposite corners so they could see two sides of the house rather than just one. It was a lot of effort for a few minutes.

Of course, I was extremely grateful and was not taking their effort for granted.

My walk to the cave was brisk, only stopping to pick flowers along the way. I tied them into a bunch and set them next to the others. That's when I noticed that the bushes had been disturbed. Stepping back, I saw footprints that were bigger than mine. They couldn't be Kannon's. He kept his distance.

The guard stepped closer.

"Is everything okay?"

"Someone has been here. Those footprints were not here the last time I was."

"I'm going to take a look. Step away if you don't want to see inside the cave."

I nodded and turned my back to him. Anxiety gripped me as I listened to the bushes rustle. Then came the heavy sigh.

"Master," he murmured softly.

Yep, that was a term I was not used to yet. They all used it, and I did not ask one of them to do so. Kannon said that I had to get used to it. This was my life now that I was the official leader of the vampires for Hades. I was that, but it didn't feel right to me. A vampire leader should be a vampire.

Did I agree with Drakkus? In that respect, yes. I

could not understand the vampire's needs, not when I didn't have the same ones as them. If I had advisors, I'd listen to them and do as they suggested, but it was pointless when the members of my coven were limited to Kannon's family and a few friends they associated with. The vampires in this town who were on my side were few in number.

"The cave is empty."

I turned to him in complete shock.

"Someone stole his body?"

"It looks that way. Come, we mustn't linger in the forest."

Glancing around the forest, I couldn't see a threat, but I knew that one existed. I'm sure that one will always exist.

"Is this the life that I will lead, Marco?"

"We could hope for something different, but that would be wasteful. All that we can do in these hard times is strive to do our best and come out on top. You will learn how to cope."

Well, that was not the answer I was looking for. A *sure, it will end soon, and life will be peachy again*, was closer to where I was aiming. Sadly, it was not to be.

Our pace was quick, weaving through the trees along the path that I'd walked more than I'd wanted. If I had my way, Niko would be here, and I would still be his familiar, not a leader. I wasn't a vampire. Just a quarter of me was.

I found it surprising that the vampires were so willing to accept me as their leader, but then again, it might not be the entire truth. I'd seen a few who came to the house last night, but what percentage of the vampire population in Hades was that? Fifty percent was reasonable, though I would prefer more. Dread skipped through me as dark thoughts whispered that it could be less than that. It could be in the single digits.

"How many vampires are there in Hades?"

"I don't know the accurate figure as many move around. We are not bound to a coven for the rest of our lives and are free to move as we desire. Entry into a coven is relatively easy, so there is no issue for us if we want to move to a new place. My best guess would be in the low one hundreds."

"And how many do you think are loyal to the Corbin line?"

Marco smiled as he looked at me.

"Worried about your leadership?"

"Worried that the other side might have greater numbers."

"Ah, well, that is natural. Drakkus has the ability to lure a vampire in. He is a smooth salesman. Of course, he cannot retain them for long. At least those who are not enamored by him. Many leave the flock, usually leaving the town as well. Sometimes, we can stop them before they pass the border. If we can do that, then we show them that not all are like the monster they flee from.

Marco and I emerged from the forest, seeing a curious sight. At the windows around the dining room and lounge room were vampires. They were looking into the house even though Eddios was there telling them to get away from the windows. When he saw us, Eddios urged us over quickly.

"Come, Evelyn, your uncle wishes to speak with you urgently."

"What's going on? Is everything okay?"

"It is not my place to say, my dear. Good luck."

The door was opened, and I was pushed through it. I was about to tell Brad that someone had tampered with Niko's grave when he stood and looked at me with an uneasy smile. From the other lounge chair, a man stood as well.

The dark figure turned and looked at me, giving me a warm smile.

"Good afternoon, Evelyn. My name is Mardyl Charolais, and I am your father."

CHAPTER 27

At eighteen years of age, I'd had a lot of time to think about my life. What would it have been like if my mother cared enough to look after me and not hurt me? If she would have been different if our circumstances had changed.

The biggest question I had in my life was, what was my father like?

I never thought that I'd get the opportunity to answer that question. My mother never talked about my father, so I was left to assume that he was one of her clients.

When it came time to make Father's Day cards in school, I sat quietly and hoped no one would look at me. I wanted to avoid their attention, to go unnoticed. They'd ask where he was, and because I was embarrassed about what my mother did for a living, I said that he was dead.

I shouldn't have been embarrassed, and for a long time, I wasn't. It happened when I was almost eight. Somehow, one of the older boys at the school found out what she did. Maybe he saw her, perhaps someone told him. I don't know how he found out, but he did.

The teasing was merciless, and the name-calling was horrible. They predicted that I would follow her path, and soon enough, I'd be trading favors for a little bit of cash.

At almost eight, I learned that I had an anger problem. After punching the boy in the stomach, he bent over, which made him low enough for me to give him a bloody nose. Once that happened, we had a ring of kids around us chanting *fight* repeatedly until a teacher intervened.

Then, they called my mother.

She was not happy when she appeared at the school office an hour later. I was given a scowl, which I knew meant I would get yelled at later. Waiting in the reception area was like waiting for the executioner.

It was a haunting memory of my mother and the headmaster when they emerged ten minutes later. His zipper was undone, and the tip of his shirt was poking through it. I knew exactly what had happened because the headmaster was always well-dressed. There was never a button undone or scuff on his polished shoes.

Aside from the fact that I knew how well he dressed, I'd already been given a good talking to in his office before he called my mother. He walked into the room dressed as he always was. I didn't make a habit of looking at crotches. After all, I was only eight. It was the look after their discussion that stood out like a neon light. To see him with a slight imperfection was, well, it was obvious. She'd bought him off with a freebie.

Having her as a mother made for an interesting childhood. As for the other parent, he was a mystery up until today.

After seeing the Nephilim in the kitchen, I was already a bundle of nerves. To make things worse, Niko's body was missing. I'd rushed in here to tell Brad, now faced with my father.

But Niko's missing body, the Nephilim that would not go away, and the vampires that want me dead, they're nothing now. Not when faced with the one person I never thought would appear in my home completely out of the blue.

"Well, isn't that interesting." the Nephilim whispered. "I guess it won't be long before we learn of your fate."

"Does it mean you'll be leaving?" I muttered under my breath.

The boy didn't respond, remaining quiet as Brad walked over to me.

"I know this is probably a really big shock for you, but how about you come over and say hello, at least? Mardyl understands that you will be apprehensive."

That's not the word I'd use.

Brad turned and walked back to the living room. I glanced at the Nephilim boy, who had a haughty smile on his face.

"Enjoy it while it lasts."

"Shut up," I said through gritted teeth.

My smile was fooling no one.

Crossing the room, I sat on the lounge as the man who claimed to be my father returned to his seat.

"Uh,"

"Mard is fine,"

Mard looked at me and hesitantly laughed.

"I know that this is not easy for you, and I'm sure you've got a lot of questions and things to say. All that I ask is that you hear me out so that you understand everything, then you may do what you feel is necessary."

"Sure."

I suppose I could grant him that much. Benevolent was surely my middle name.

"As you probably are already aware, I am a witch. I see you've got your friend as well. Mine has been hanging around for a few days now. You turned eighteen if you were wondering why they're here."

"Why not just end this when I was a kid?"

"They do not have the ability to find a witchling before their eighteenth. They've waited patiently."

The Nephilim boy now had a friend, a guy who looked like he was also in his late teens. Together, they sat on the window seat with smug smiles and supreme attitudes.

Mardyl sighed heavily, sipping the coffee that Brad must have made him.

"I met your mother about twenty years ago. She was struggling with a revelation of a family secret, one I'm sure you know about, seeing as there are a lot of vampires hanging around the house. It took a lot for her to confide in a total stranger, but she sensed that I was not human. Witches tend to find socializing to be incredibly difficult. We have a lot of distrust for the world around us and for those who have survived, remember the past vividly."

His eyes lowered to the liquid in his cup, sadness creeping into his features. By appearances, Mardyl looked as if he was in his mid-thirties, but anything was possible when dealing with the paranormal.

I'd learned that vampires age incredibly slowly. Kannon said that his parents didn't have an exact figure, but they knew that Niko was likely to be edging close to a late three-figure age.

"So, naturally, when I met someone who was just as lost as I was, I found the company quite reassuring. Your mother also found the information about her future to be overwhelming as well. As a Corbin by blood, she was a rare creature. I'm sure you're eager for as much information as I can give, Evelyn, and I'm also certain that the vampires outside know little of the old world. I hope that I can give you the information you need and desire. I know that time is of the essence, so I came here as soon as possible. When my new friend turned up, I knew what had happened. It is unfortunate, but I understand why your mother hid you. I am not upset with her."

"How did you find me?"

"The Nephilim, they speak to each other."

"Quite frequently," the boy added.

The other one, he remained quiet. I wish my pest would remain quiet, too.

"You said my mother was rare."

"You are too, Evelyn. This goes back to a time when born vampires were all that existed. They had no idea how they came about, what their origins were, or even how they would continue. Stepping out into the world, the vampires watched as humanity emerged. They learned how humans procreated and looked at their own lives. They wondered where their opposite was."

"They were all male?"

Mard nodded at Brad.

"They were. Something that you will note as you delve further into the world of vampires is that they are always one gender. If they are born into this life, they are born male. These vampires, they could see how to create another generation, and they figured out how to make babies, but they lacked the other side of the equation. Then, out of nowhere, one of them decides that he would try his luck with a human female rather than creating a vampire out of a human and then breeding with her, which had been the norm for a very long time. Finding a lovely human lady, the vampire does his thing, and nine months later, a pretty little lady pops out. That pretty little lady was your grandmother."

"You're saying that after all those years, not one of them thought to try humans?"

"Oh, they tried, but they always turned the woman into a vampire first. The difference in this situation was the woman Beatrice was not completely human."

Niko's wife wasn't entirely human. Well, he certainly knew how to keep me interested.

"So, what was she?"

"Have you ever heard of a shapeshifter?"

"Yeah, Niko mentioned that they died out at the time of the plague."

"That is what they would have you and the world believe. They actually fled and hid. Their adventure across the world began in England. At that point, they splintered as a group, and now they are spread across the world. Beatrice came from a notable family, not overly wealthy, but they certainly had a good reputation. Not that it would matter today, but back then, it meant a lot."

I sighed heavily as I looked at Brad with weariness on my face. His uncertainty matched mine. Returning to Mard, I had one question at the moment.

"What am I, witch, human, vampire, now shapeshifter?"

"I am a pure-blood witch. That makes you half-witch. Your grandmother was half vampire, half shapeshifter. I believe your grandfather was human, so yes to all of them. Does it matter?"

I gestured to the pair sitting on the window seat.

"Pay no attention to them. If the Nephilim actually cared, your great-grandmother and grandmother would have been destroyed by them. I know for a fact that is not the case. Unfortunately, I am the issue in this scenario. Witches are powerful, and there are some that would rather we were dead as a race."

"Do you know Andross Drohman?" I murmured.

Mardyl looked at me with interest.

"Yes, a vampire I hoped to never see in real life. The stories are bad enough."

"I killed him."

That made him sit up with a smile.

"Did you? May I ask for the details?"

"You want to know if I got my witchiness on?"

Mard nodded, eagerly waiting.

"Well, I did, but don't ask me how I did it because I have no idea."

"All the more reason that we find a path to each other. I know it won't be easy for you, Evelyn, but you must learn to hone your skills. If you don't, then you're a risk to everyone around you. I have acquired the house across the road with the expectation that you will need my help. If you don't want that, then those two will have a lot more to say about your life than mine."

Leaning forward, Mard put an envelope on the table.

"Those are what I have from the time that I had with your mother. I can't say that we had a good relationship or that it was healthy, but I cared deeply for her. She wrote to me a few months after leaving, advising me that she couldn't remain in the town any longer and it was best that we parted ways. Understand that she was wise to make that choice, Evelyn. I wanted her to remain with me, but the vampires are always drawn to the witches. It was only a matter of time before she was found, and it was in her best interest to get as far away from me as possible. Likewise for you, though I suspect that the vampires in this town are already frothing at the mouth."

Brad shifted forward, a curious frown on his face as he set aside the empty cup.

"How so?"

"What do you mean? Did you not understand what I was saying when I said that, as a Corbin, she is a rare creature? You are, too, though I think they're not smart enough to figure it out."

Looking at the confusion on Brad's face, I was of the opinion that we weren't smart enough to figure it out either.

"Okay, lay it out because you've got me stumped," I muttered.

"You two are Corbins. You are vampires, and please, none of that half and quarter nonsense. The blood of all runs through your veins. You are vampires. You just don't feed like ones because of the other beings within you. As for the other vampires and their interest in you, that would be because you two are the only vampires that can create females."

CHAPTER 28

We sat in silence for a few seconds, but the questions plagued my mind.

"Because of the shapeshifter in us?"

"Correct."

"Can we change form?" Brad asked.

"I would assume yes, but I don't know how it is done as I have not seen a shapeshifter in many years. The last time was several hundred years ago, and it was at a distance. He was in human form, and within the blink of an eye, there was a cat in his place. Then he took off. Shapeshifters are notoriously secretive, more than witches. You may find that the ability will come naturally. You may find that education is your only answer. If that is the case, then I don't know how you will learn. Perhaps there are books. You may be lucky enough to find another who will be willing to teach you."

Brad and I exchanged looks, thoroughly confused.

"I don't understand how a species can have only one

gender."

"That is a question that is still being asked to this day. The vampires don't know the answer. Many suspect that there is a female version of their race, but they are elusive or hidden in a country or some other random idea that they pull out of the air."

Mardyl flicked his hand dismissively, looking like he lacked the ability to care about the subject. I did. I wanted to know why there were no female vampires.

Brad stood with his mug in hand, taking Mardyl's when he offered it.

"Another?"

"Please."

"You want something, Evie?"

"Juice, thanks."

With a nod, Brad wandered off. He looked like I felt. Confused. Full of questions but not knowing where to begin.

"You said vampires are after us because we're Corbin, and we can create females. Why is this so important as opposed to another race, like humans or witches?"

"Well, there are many that believe they are diluting the line of the vampires by creating children with turned humans. They won't go near a witch, even if they could find one. With a female vampire, they can create a line that is closer to the original source. Also, the more females they can create, the greater numbers the vampires can attain. Your mother told me a story once, hoping that I'd be able to understand her need to hide. It came from her mother, who, as a child, could not understand why she was taken from her home and her father. Your great-grandmother told your grandmother that there was a bad man who found out that she existed and what she was. He demanded that she was betrothed to him, and your great-grandfather would not allow it."

I sent the child and my wife away for safety reasons, and I have not seen them since.

The words saddened me at the time.

Niko's morose face still haunted me. I wish he was here.

"How come my mother never told me these stories?" Brad asked as he held out Mardyl's mug.

"I suppose she thought that you would not carry the gene and that it only affected the firstborn children. Those who are in the paranormal world understand that this is not the case. Your grandmother could not be blamed for this. She had only been a part of the vampire world for as long as your mother had been alive. Your sister told me the tales from your grandmother and how your grandfather kept them hidden."

Still, it was odd that she didn't warn Brad as well. He could have visited my mother, completely unaware of the world that was watching.

"Why did Andross kill our family?"

"Because that is what Drakkus wants. He is angry because Niko refused to hand his daughter over and decided that if he couldn't have a female to breed with, then no one would. He wants to punish every single Corbin in existence for Niko's decision. It is a war between two men that has resulted in many deaths. One sees the rejection as the right thing to do. The other is a petulant child who can't handle rejection. Such is life."

Setting the mug aside, Mardyl gave me a warm smile.

"I will leave you to discuss all the revelations and what you want for the future. I have to get supplies. This town is quite odd, don't you agree? The entire place shuts down at dusk. Almost as if they know what lurks in the darkness."

He chuckled.

"I will see you both at dusk."

Brad closed the door, turning with a gasp, when he found me behind him.

"Something on your mind, Evie?"

"Niko's grave has been disturbed. Did you bury him?"

"No, you said you wanted him to remain in the cave. What do you mean disturbed?"

"Footprints. Marco checked inside the cave. It's empty."

"Drag marks?"

I frowned, shaking my head.

"No, I don't recall seeing drag marks. Just the footprints."

"And I take it that they're not yours."

"No, too big. The cave was pretty low. Could you stand up inside it?"

Brad shook his head as he began to fill the sink with hot, soapy water. With the flick of a towel in my direction, I was on drying duty.

Leaning against the counter, I groaned and rolled my head around to try and relieve the tension.

"Are the vampires still outside?"

"The guards are. I believe that your followers have left to feed. Eddios suggested that a proper meeting be held. Given the issues, he said that sooner rather than later and brief would be ideal."

"And what am I going to say to these people? Hey, I'm your leader, a kid that you've never met before and only got this role because of a distant relation who is now dead because I freed him from behind the wall where he was trapped."

Pulling the plug, Brad took the kitchen towel from my hands while glowering at me.

"Do not blame yourself for Niko's death. If he thought that it was ideal, he would have left."

Well, that was not entirely true. He had ample opportunity to leave, and he didn't. The question is, how far would Drakkus go to end the last of the Corbin line?

My mother and I lived in a city on the other side of the country, so clearly, distance was not an issue. That meant that no matter how far Niko ran, he would never escape. Staying and fighting was the only option.

"Do you know what I don't get? Why this town is so important to Drakkus. Why can't he go to another town, one that's leaderless?"

"I think you might find that this is about Niko refusing to hand his daughter over."

"Drakkus is a pervert."

"Unlikely. He would have waited. Or maybe he might have let her remain in this house until she was old enough. Now, we need to discuss your father before he returns."

There was so much to be said. So many thoughts swirling through my mind. Yet I knew that none of it mattered. He was an answer to my problems, and I knew that I needed him. If I was going to win the war against Drakkus, it would be done with my father at my side.

"I don't know what to say about that. He has proof, and I'm certain he's my father, but where does the trust begin and end? I need to be assured that he will stand beside me and not stab me in the back. Am I going to get that from him?"

Brad shrugged. That was not the answer that I was looking for. As the only trustworthy adult in my life, I looked to him for answers and guidance.

"Trust has to be earned. There is no easy answer to

this, Evie. Just a long and hard path as the two of you get to know each other. Do you remember what it was like when you first came to live with me?"

"It was hell."

He nodded. A soft smile on his face reminded me of my mother.

"It sure was. We didn't know each other, we had issues, and we were both in a bad place, yet we stand here today as a family. It was not an easy ride, we still have our problems, but we trust each other, right?"

"Yeah."

Brad was right, as always. The problem was that I didn't have time to develop trust in my father. I needed him to be on my side right now.

"I don't know what's going to come about with this guy, I just know what we're facing, and I'm sure you've already thought about it."

"He's our only answer."

"No, we probably have several choices, but he's the best one at the moment."

Brad and I were not alone. I was used to the boy now, he blended into the background, and I have found that I have forgotten that he's in the same room as me on a few occasions now.

"Did you want to add your opinion to this?"

"You would not like my opinion."

"Try us," Brad muttered.

"Alright. As I said to Evelyn previously, he is not trustworthy. No witch is. Vampires aren't much better, but I believe you managed to find one or two that alter that particular perception. The jury is still out on that one. I find it difficult to assess vampires as, like witches, I know they are not to be trusted. At the surface level, it would appear that you have a few, but I wouldn't rely on it. As for the witch, there may be a chance that you can trust your father. However, I believe that he is not what you want in your life. I'm sure that you desire a stable father figure in your life, but I'd suggest that you stick with the one you've got. He's proved his worth to you already, and the other lacks the time to do the same. That would be, of course, if he was actually interested in your well-being."

Lifting from the counter, I frowned as I looked down at the Nephilim.

"I can't trust him?" I hissed. "I lack time, and you're telling me I can't trust the man who claims to be my father or the vampires who say they're on my side. Your kind is coming for me, and the vampires want me dead."

"Not all, in both respects."

The Nephilim glowered at Brad. His lips twitched with a hard line.

"What do you mean by that?"

"I mean that you've had ample opportunity to end Evie's life, and you haven't. You can say it's not your job until the cows come home. It means nothing, really. If your kind were smart, they would have sent one to do the job and be done with it. What is this rubbish? Send one to remain with the target while waiting for the others. Seems like a waste, and it makes me think that you're the liar here."

The Nephilim growled.

"You are wrong, but it is of no consequence to me. In the near future, you will be dead and nothing more than a fleeting memory to me. I will not mourn your passing."

Brad smirked.

"That may be so, but I've seen how you interact with Evie. I think you will miss her."

There was no response. The Nephilim quietly faded out of the room, leaving Brad with a smug smile on his face and me rather confused.

"So, I take it that he will miss me?"

"Evie, he might look like a teenager, but I promise you that the soul inside that body is old. The way that he speaks, it is not like you or me. If it weren't true, he'd refute it and carry on with his jibes and annoying behavior."

"Well, that's great. Another creature that wants to get into my pants. Why can't they just go away?"

Brad rolled his eyes.

"You are not seeing this the way that you should.

Instead of focusing on the obvious, think about the situation and your own problems."

"He's going to start flirting with me?"

"Goodness, Evelyn." he scoffed. "No, he's another potential ally. You may not like it, but using this to your advantage could be necessary."

"The boy is not going to come to my rescue. Don't you want to nurture my inner girl warrior?" I teased.

"No," he grumped. "I want you alive, and if that means that a dashing knight comes riding in on his steed, then so be it."

"Aww, it's so sweet that you care."

Brad ignored me, preferring to continue cleaning the kitchen. As for his suggestion, it was a curious one.

CHAPTER 29

The hammock slowly rocked in the gentle breeze. I looked out to the street and watched the land begin to darken. It was not because of nightfall. The rain was returning.

There was a calm feeling to it but something undeniably heavy and unrelenting. It was like the storm would remain and would not leave, like our first week in this town.

Added to the impending storm was a chill that was like nothing I'd ever felt before. I was snuggled between layers of blankets, yet it was still cold. It was quiet, adding to the ominous feelings floating through me.

Any thought of finding relaxation was shot to pieces when I sat up and looked around.

"Where are you?" I whispered.

The screen door opened. Brad let it slap shut behind him.

"Everything okay?"

"He's not here."

"Who? Your father?"

"No, the boy. Now that I think about it, I haven't seen him since you called him out earlier."

Brad gave a disinterested shrug.

"Maybe he's off crying somewhere."

"Brad," I chided.

He wandered over to the railing, leaning with both hands on the weathered rail.

"This is the calm before the storm."

"I was just thinking that. It's kind of creepy."

"You know, annoying the boy might not have been a good idea."

"Too late to go back on it now."

"I realize that. I'm more worried that he was actually telling the truth, and now those other Nephilim are on their way."

I figured they were going to turn up anyway. As for Brad annoying the boy, it was probably a step too far, but it highlighted something that I was not aware of.

Having a biblical being crushing on me was weird. All thoughts about the Nephilim were put aside. My father had emerged from his house. Having him live across the road was good, I suppose. Hopefully, things will work out so that it doesn't get weird or ugly.

"Are you ready for your lessons?"

"Yeah."

My tone was filled with a heaviness that showed how I lacked interest.

"I know that we lack time, but we have to remember that Mard could be our only answer to defeating Drakkus."

I nodded, a little glum at the thought. A part of me wanted to unleash the girl warrior that was hiding inside of me. Then I remembered what happened to Andross. Perhaps it was best to keep the warrior in her cage.

My father had things in his arms, what looked like rolled-up yoga mats. With a smile, he walked up the steps to the front porch.

"Ready?"

"I'd rather ignore the issues."

Mardyl chuckled, then handed one of the foam rolls to Brad.

"Me too?"

"You're learning how to help Evie center herself in case I'm not around."

As he walked into the house, Brad followed my father but shot me a glare. One that said he really means when I shun him from my life, and he's sent off into the world without a connection to his daughter.

Climbing off the hammock, I walked into the house.

Brad and my father moved the lounges further apart so we could sit in the center of the room.

"Hey, do I have any siblings?"

Mard looked up from where he was rolling out the mat.

"I'd like to say no. But anything is possible."

Well, that certainly made things interesting. Taking my mat, I rolled it out. We faced each other, seated and crossed-legged. I hoped that no one would turn up to start something. It would take ages for the pins and needles to go away.

"So, if I meet a guy, how will I know?"

"The obvious answer is genetic testing. It will give you a definitive answer that you will be able to rely on. That is, of course, if you can wait. There is another answer, one that will come to you when you have refined your skills. It is called cognitive connection. In most instances, witches will know who they are related to and do not need this skill. However, in cases like you where you have a father who has lived a full life,"

Brad hummed a soft laugh. Yep, it was certainly an interesting way of putting it.

"It can be something that is necessary. When you walked through the door earlier, I knew you were my daughter for two reasons. One, the Nephilim led me here, and two, I felt the connection."

Distracted, I glanced around the room and noted that

Mardyl's Nephilim was not around either.

"Hey, where's your Nephilim?"

Mardyl frowned as he glanced around the room.

"Renuge?" he called out.

I frowned.

"What are you doing?"

"Calling for him. Is your Nephilim missing, too?"

"I guess. He hasn't shown himself since this morning. We thought it was because Brad called him out on having a thing for me. How come you're calling out that renuge?"

"That's his name. Your Nephilim didn't tell you his name?"

I shook my head, then glanced at Brad. He offered a sympathetic smile. Yes, I should have asked. Maybe then he wouldn't have been such a jerk. Renuge was pretty laid back. It made me think it was because my father had formed an amicable relationship with him. Unlike me and whatever his name was.

"I didn't think they had names."

"They do, and as for him having a thing for you, that is normal. They've been ordered into a life of celibacy because of what they are and the fact that no one above them wants there to be any more of them or anything worse that may be produced. Don't take that the wrong way. The biblical ones love all creatures regardless of what ailments they may or may not have. The Nephilim are strong, they are dangerous, and they are not always the happiest of creatures. Their life is bound to so many rules. They are punished because they were created, yet they know it's not their fault. Their parents are the ones that performed the unholy act, and their union resulted in a creature that should not be. Much like someone else, really. Perhaps our friends have gone off to reason with their overseers."

Yeah, and pigs will fly, too.

I soon learned that the Nephilim's name was Anzide. How did I find that out? He returned, and I asked him, then apologized for not asking sooner. Anzide shrugged as if he didn't care, looking away with disinterest.

Renuge had also returned, looking bored as he sat on the window seat. I was curious as to why they both left and returned together. Anzide's purple eyes lifted with amusement.

"We sought answers. They are coming."

"Oh, that old chestnut. I thought you'd come up with a new line or something. Got a timeframe now?"

"No. However, we were told it was imminent. Perhaps you'd like to return the blood flow to your feet."

Mard perked up, frowning heavily.

"They're here?"

"I lack the understanding of time. All we were told was that we should return to our assignments as they would be over soon enough. To be elsewhere when they come for you is foolish. We are eager to see how easily you will barter for your own life."

My father growled, lunging for Anzide.

"You're wrong," he hissed.

Anzide chuckled mercilessly as he pulled himself free of my father's grip, flicking the lapels of his jacket straight again.

"You know that we talk to each other. We trade the information we have collected so that our masters can formulate the best plan of attack. Does that make sense?"

I thought that he was talking to Mard, but Anzide was looking at me.

"What?" I said, confused.

"Remember what I said, Evelyn. He will hand you over to my masters to save his own skin."

"That's a lie," Mard snapped.

"I do not know the concept of a lie. I speak from gathered information."

Anzide held out his hand, waiting for me to take it.

"Come, return the blood to your limbs before it is too late."

I was surprised at how strong Anzide was when I took his hand and stood upright. My feet tingled with the pricking sensation. His grip tightened, and momentarily, his eyes narrowed.

"Renuge,"

I wanted to gasp, hearing my father's voice in my head. Anzide held my hand tight as he stared at me.

"I can do this. I can give them what they want."

"They want you to be punished."

"Come on, just lead me to her."

A tear emerged, slowly sliding down my cheek.

"More," I whispered.

"It's enough."

"I want more," I yelled.

Anzide was startled at first but then relented.

"Evie?" Brad murmured.

I held up my hand, stopping him.

"Come on, Anzide," I said softly, squeezing his hand. "Give me what I want. Prove it if you think you're right."

Anzide shook his head.

"It's too late. They're here."

My heart rate kicked up, painfully beating inside of me.

I turned to look at the window, and even though Renuge was in the way, I could see the sky darken even more than it had been. It looked as if someone covered this house with a thick blanket that blocked the light.

"It is time, Anzide," Renuge said firmly. "Escort the girl outside."

He pushed Mardyl, earning an angry flick that sent his enforcing hand away. Anzide held back, watching as Renuge walked behind Mardyl.

"He has had all day to teach you basic spells. It wouldn't save you, but at least you'd go out with a bang, yet here you stand, completely clueless about how powerful you really are. You think I mock you or him, which is true, but it is only because you do not harness your true potential. I cannot offer you much, but I can offer you this. Let your emotions take control. It is what I have learned in my observations of you when you attacked Andross."

Anzide's head turned to Brad.

"And you stay inside. You are of no benefit to the conversation, and you endanger your life by being out there. Not just my kind but Evelyn, too. The Nephilim will walk away unscathed, but you may not."

Brad opened his mouth, frowning and ready to say something, but I stopped him.

"He's right. I don't want to come out at the other end and find that I killed you like I did Andross. Just do what he says, okay?"

Brad huffed but nodded. He moved to the window seat and then opened the window.

"Is this good enough?" he grumbled at Anzide.

"Provided she doesn't cast any spells that harness the wind, yes."

With that all too familiar smug smile on his face, Anzide tugged on my hand.

"Come, Evelyn. You would not want to keep them waiting."

Taking a deep breath, I let Anzide guide me out of the house. I would walk bravely to this. I would not cower. My legs were shaking, and my heart was racing hard. I didn't want to be here, but I knew there was little choice. No matter how far I ran, they would always find me.

Three tall Nephilim stood on the grass section to the right of us. Anzide led me to the section on the left where Mardyl and Renuge were already waiting. The battle line had been drawn, and it was the garden path between us.

"Anzide," I whispered.

He looked at me.

"Help me. I'm just like you. I shouldn't be punished for another person's actions."

"I have helped you. I told you what you needed to do. Let those emotions take over. Let the fear consume you. You can't barter your life when your father has already cut a deal with Renuge."

"Was I supposed to cut a deal with you?"

"You had nothing to offer. Nothing you would offer. It didn't take me long to figure out that you wouldn't hand your father over to us."

"You said that you were just a messenger."

"In the beginning, I was. His arrival in this town altered my mission. I told you that he would hand you over to save his own life. This is what he is doing. All that you have is to fight with your power."

My body felt heavy as we finally stopped in place. My father was next to me, Renuge on the other side.

"Tell me he's lying."

"Nephilim do not lie," Renuge said tersely. "Whatever has been said is the truth."

I looked up at my father with tears in my eyes. He'd sold me out, and I was going to die.

CHAPTER 30

The three tall Nephilim stood facing us. The one in the center stared at me.

"Begin the proceedings," he said in a terse tone.

To his left, the Nephilim unfurled a scroll.

"Charges laid against Mardyl Charolais, Patricia Newton, and Evelyn Newton."

I frowned.

"Hold up,"

The Nephilim stopped, and all three of them looked at me.

"Who is Patricia Newton?"

"Your mother."

"Uh, no. My mother's name was Nancy."

"It does not matter. You are a half-breed. Your mother is inconsequential."

"I beg your pardon!" I snapped. "My mother does matter, and she is definitely not inconsequential. How dare you speak about her like that. *Who* is Patricia Newton?"

The three of them offered nothing, and I turned to Anzide, the only one that I could trust would give me a straight and honest answer.

"Do you know who she is?"

"No."

"My mother's name was Nancy. Ask Brad."

He turned his head to the house, flicking his fingers at the window. Seconds later, Brad emerged.

"State your sister's full name, please."

"Nancy Clare Newton."

"Perhaps it was a false name. We know that the Corbin line liked to hide themselves."

Brad shook his head.

"I've got all her papers. She never took a false name. Even Evelyn's birth certificate is registered as her legal name. I have no idea who Patricia is."

Turning to my father, I raised my eyebrows with the hope that he'd be honest. It was a long shot.

"So?"

"Her name was Patricia."

"Hang on a sec,"

Brad scampered back into the house, returning with the envelope that I'd not been able to look at. Pulling out the photos, Brad was shaking his head.

"This is not my sister. You've got the wrong person."

He tossed the envelope at Mardyl's feet, and the pictures of an unknown woman spilled out over the grass.

"You said that you could tell that she was your daughter," Brad snapped loudly. "How did you know so much about Nancy and Evie?"

Mardyl looked at Brad, then let out a reluctant sigh.

"Patricia and Nancy used to share a house before Evelyn was born. Patricia took on her surname as an alias for when the cops were looking for her. I knew both of them, though I only had relations with Patricia. They were both pregnant at the same time. I never saw Nancy after that time. Patricia and the child died during labor. When that lot came looking for answers, I said that either woman was possible."

The Nephilim in the center frowned at Mardyl. A soft growl of anger escaped from Brad.

"You said that you had a cognitive connection," Brad said in a rather loud outburst.

Anzide huffed with amusement.

Brad glowered at him.

"Not real?"

"I have not heard of such a thing, though, to be fair, I rarely delve into the land of fantasy."

As Brad lunged at Mardyl, Anzide pulled my hand back. The Nephilim watched as my uncle took his anger out on the man who was not really my father.

"He's going to hurt him."

"I think that in this instance, Mardyl will refrain from using his powers."

"Not what I meant. Brad is seriously angry."

"Then, so be it. That man walked into your house with the intention of using you to pay for his crime."

Pulling my hand free, I felt the anger build inside of me.

"Did you know?"

"We are limited on information. I was told where to be and who to watch. Evelyn Newton. She would be with her uncle Bradley. Mother dead, and the father being watched by another Nephilim. I was told that because of your father, you were a powerful witch, but if he is not your father, then we have an issue. You are clearly *something,* but as to what, we do not know."

"Shapeshifter," I whispered. "My great-grandmother was a shapeshifter. Can a shapeshifter mimic a witch?"

"They can,"

I turned to the one that spoke, the center Nephilim. He and the two that flanked him crossed the line, slowly moving to us. All the while, they ignored Brad and his efforts to make the liar pay.

The one that was clearly the leader looked down at me. Dressed the same, the three wore dark cloaks that covered them from head to toe. All that could be seen were the deathly white faces that quickly ended at the v-neckline of their clothes.

"We detect the lineage to be mixed, worthy of investigation, and the life to be removed as punishment."

"Unacceptable." I snapped.

His head tilted, an eyebrow raised.

"We do not,"

"I know. You do not bow down to the demands of the damned, but I am not damned."

"*You,*" the Nephilim said curtly. "Are most definitely damned. Your line is detected as vampire, shapeshifter, and human. The lines of the creatures are not to mix."

"And where is our warning?"

That stopped his glower.

He glanced at the one to the right of him. The Nephilim offered a shrug of one shoulder.

"What do you mean, child?"

"I mean, and by the way, I'm eighteen, so *not* a child, that there is no warning about who we are supposed to breed with. Until I came to this town, I didn't know vampires existed. Yet if they remained quiet and assumed that I was a vampire too, and we had a one-night stand that resulted in pregnancy, we'd be in trouble. Where. Is. The. Warning."

He said nothing in response.

"The majority of the people in this town have no idea that they've got vampires for neighbors. We go to school with them, yet no one knows. If it wasn't for Anzide warning me, I wouldn't know that my principal is a demon. How do you expect anyone to abide by these unspoken rules when we don't know what is in front of us? I think that you need to take these questions back to whoever it is that makes you do these ridiculous quests and ask them for clarification."

I was on a roll. With my hands on my hips and a defiant attitude flowing, I was set to take them on.

"All you're doing is creating division between the races. You've got no right to tell us what we can or cannot do in our lives or who we can love or be with. You can't even tell us what is expected of us. How is it that you can demand that we pay when we get it wrong? It's terrible that you're being punished for the crimes of your parents, but there is no way in hell that I will be. It's time for you to leave, and don't bother coming back unless you're going to apologize for being rude about my mother."

His mouth opened. I raised my hand to stop him.

"I am not interested. I've got a lot of homework to do, and I've got a coven to run. So, get the hell out of my town."

I stormed into the house but kept going through the back door. I couldn't be anywhere near the Nephilim, even if one of them was a step behind me. When I reached the forest, I inhaled deeply. Then, as I exhaled, I smiled. It was good to be back on the path to Niko again, even if he wasn't in his cave.

"You did well." Anzide offered.

"Thanks, but it's not over, and I have a lot of issues."

"Your true father will present himself in time."

"I'd rather he didn't. It's easier this way. I don't have to grow trust. I can just plod along in my life, and there are no worries."

"You are a fool if you think that life is that easy."

With a grim smile, I shrugged my shoulders. We stopped in front of Niko's cave. The footprints were still here, but I'm sure that once the impending storm starts, they'll wash away.

"Someone took his body. Who would do something like that?"

"There are many who have no morals. It is better to avoid thinking about it."

Sighing heavily, I kept moving along the path.

"Why did he do it?"

"Mardyl? To have a sacrificial lamb, of course. He knew he needed someone to take the heat, and when he realized that the Nephilim had made a mistake, he rolled with it."

I smirked, nudging his shoulder with mine.

"Rolled with it?"

"Did I use the term incorrectly?"

"No, it just seemed a little modern for you. Maybe you've hung around me for too long."

His eyes narrowed as he looked ahead. Slowly, a wry smile crossed his lips.

"How come you're in a teenager's body?"

"They said it would be more assuring to you and allow me easier access. It would also make sense for a teenager to be seen with another of a similar age if there came a time when I had to reveal myself. Would you prefer that I was older?"

"I'd rather that you were not hiding the truth. You keep saying you don't know how to lie, but this façade is a lie."

Anzide looked at me, curiously tilting his head.

"Unless you're like a freakish monster, then you can stay as you are."

"I am not a freakish monster. Here I was thinking that you were a new age, inclusive human, yet you strike me down with your cruel words."

"Ouch, man. Alright, get your freakish on."

Anzide rolled his eyes. Slowly, the body grew upwards and a little outwards. The slender figure began to emerge, muscular beneath the leather pants and tight, long-sleeved black shirt. I did not lean back and look at any particular curve and how fine it might be.

The whole view was insane.

Anzide stood at least a head taller than me. He still had the purple eyes, but his hair was now black and wavy, falling just past his shoulders.

I bit my lip, focusing on the path rather than how I should have kept my mouth shut.

"Well? Am I a monster?"

Yep. A monster that was always going to haunt me.

"Oh yeah, totally."

Anzide chuckled, nudging his shoulder against mine.

"You're not a very good liar."

Stepping forward, Anzide lifted a branch from the path. We'd reached a clearing, one that I was not expecting to find. This was where the witches cast their spells.

"This is not your land, but you can cast as if you are a witch, provided that the shapeshifter in you is channeling one."

"Sounds complicated."

"And too much for a newbie like you."

"Newbie? You really are hanging around me too much."

Silence hit us as we looked at each other. It was one of those awkward moments that always went one of two ways. We would either fluster our way through the following moments, or life would interrupt us. The universe threw us a lifeline. My phone rang.

Pulling it out, I wondered if Kannon knew I was hanging out with Mister October through to December, aka Mister insanely hot. Would he get jealous now that Anzide was in his true form rather than the harmless façade of a teenager? Though, he might have been jealous of the other form as well.

"Hey, Kannon."

"Hey. Dad left in a hurry and said something about Brad calling him. Is everything okay?"

"Yeah, just the Nephilim showdown revealing that my father was really an imposter looking for a sacrificial lamb."

"Damn," he mumbled. "That's pretty low. I'm sorry, Evie."

"It's okay. I'm just going to get through this year and then deal with the issues. I don't think I'm a witch. Probably just a shapeshifter channeling a witch."

"That's highly possible. You're untrained, so your abilities will be all over the place. Aunt Jess is looking through the library for you. She's made a bit of a stack. I hope you're ready to be bored senseless."

In the background, I heard Jess biting back. Kannon chuckled.

"Anyway, we'll be around tomorrow, provided all is well with your not-a-father."

"Sounds great. Looking forward to it."

As Kannon said goodbye, I felt the weighted stare of Anzide on me.

"Bye," I said softly, then ended the call.

"Why do you look at me like that?"

"Like what?" Anzide asked.

I shrugged, tucking my phone back into my pocket.

"Like any of this is possible."

"Anything is possible in this world, Evelyn. You will learn that soon enough."

We walked back in silence. My senses were heightened, fearing that we were not alone.

I could see the house. I could see the vampire guards roaming back and forth. It made me wonder what the neighbors thought. How did Brad explain people hanging around our house all the time?

Maybe he told them something in between, that they were security because we had issues.

"Can I ask you something?"

"Of course."

"If I was in serious danger and you were the only one around that was on my side, would you help me?"

Anzide smiled deviously.

"You assume that I'm on your side."

"Come on," I grumbled. "I know you are. You like being here."

"But that's the thing, Evelyn. I have to remain as you are still considered an issue until we have finality on the questions you asked."

"So, you don't want to be here?"

Was there a hurt tone to my voice? Perhaps.

"I never said that. Just because I have to stay doesn't mean I don't want to. You should see a physician about your hearing."

We stopped at the edge of the forest, a thin row of trees between us and the expanse of lawn.

"Then you do want to be here."

"Oh, I never said that either."

I grinned, and the façade broke on the figure in front of me. Anzide smiled. It was the first time that I'd ever seen one like this. It was not haughty, mocking, or smug. This was a genuinely happy smile. It was as haunting as the rest of the view, and I began to wonder if it was wise to demand he showed his true form.

CHAPTER 31

A twig snapped in the distance, and we both turned in that direction. It was darkness, pure and unrelenting black, that could hide so many issues. A shiver crept up my spine, fear filling my mind of what might be watching us. What was out there?

"Inside now," Anzide said softly.

Taking my hand, he pulled me across the lawn as I looked back at the forest. I saw the darkness consume the trees as if it was a fog.

"Anzide," I whimpered.

"You asked for protection. Well, you're getting it."

The door was opened, and Anzide looked at the vampires.

"Get inside, or you will die."

They practically pushed me out of the way to get into the house.

"Tell the others to get inside as well. Ensure all the

windows and doors are locked. Perform your protection from within the house for tonight."

They nodded, setting to their tasks quickly. Brad was in the kitchen, quietly watching the situation unfold.

"What is going on, and who the hell are you?"

"Anzide in his true form."

Brad was quietly stunned.

"Those that govern the Nephilim's duties thought the façade of the teenager would be more approachable and engaging."

"Right," he drawled out. "But this is the real you?"

"It is."

"And what's got you two in a spin?"

I pointed through the glass. Brad stepped back to look out the kitchen window.

"All I see is a dark night. Lots of cloud cover, which is expected because it's going to rain in Hades. No surprises there."

"It's not cloud cover or the night. It is the demon."

"Yeah, I was going to ask you about that. I don't recall this ever being discussed. You said that it was your principal?"

I nodded, sitting down at the dining table. Brad and Anzide joined me.

"You can tell him."

Anzide nodded. I had to say, his attitude had improved. That was a bonus, in my opinion.

"Demons are notoriously solitary creatures. They are not supposed to reside in this land, but many find it to be more accommodating that the place where all eternal creatures should reside. How they are in this land is vastly different from what they are usually. They feast upon the souls of the departed and will reside in towns like this one, which has a strong vampire population. From what we have observed of their time in this land, they create a symbiotic relationship that the vampires are often unaware of because they have no idea that the demon is living in the town. The demon keeps the townsfolk oblivious to the high death rate, and in return, it gets lots of lovely souls to feed on. To keep the population up, the demon will cast a lure out occasionally."

"A lure? Like the things they stick on fishing rods?"

Anzide smiled, laughing softly.

"The idea of what you are asking is correct. A demon lure is very simple. The demon will travel to a town. They don't have specific areas assigned to them, but they do like to remain solitary in their control of the town they pick. A demon will whisper into a few people's minds in various locations that traveling to the town would be a great idea. Sometimes they suggest a holiday, sometimes for work. The reasons are always varied to avoid a pattern that will lead to detection. Then, he returns to the town and waits. Visitors come, they might stay, or it might just be a visit. They may die in the town, and they may walk away unscathed. Death is the ultimate goal. If the demon doesn't get what he wants, then he has to cast the lure out again."

"We really are in hell."

"No, no. Hades is not hell, and the demon is not the devil." Anzide offered. "Demons are more common than you think."

"So, do we kill it?"

Anzide shook his head with a determined stare pinned on Brad.

"No. Aside from the fact that you could not do that, it is pointless. He will reappear somewhere else in this town as another figure, and once that happens, you will never find him again. There is also a high chance that this town has more than one demon, even if they don't like to share. You're better off keeping him within your sight so that you know exactly where he is and what he's doing. Keep Evelyn out of his sight as well."

Brad turned to me with a frown.

"Home school."

"We discussed this."

"I am not sending you to that school with a damned demon running the place, breathing down your neck constantly."

"You cannot extract Evelyn. He will know that something is wrong. When that happens, he will alter his form and enter Evelyn's life in another, less obvious way. Keeping Evelyn on a natural path is the only way this will work."

The frown on Brad's face was the heaviest I'd ever seen. There was also a slight bruise under his eye, which I did not see until he turned and the light hit it. I guess Mardyl got a punch in after all.

"This is not open for discussion and definitely not with you."

"I am the only one in this house that knows exactly what Evelyn faces in that creature. If there is anyone that should be included, it is me. You want to keep her safe? It's done by continuing as if there is nothing wrong."

"What does he want?"

Anzide glanced at me, probably remembering the conversation we'd had about Principal Harlwood in the corridor at school.

"At a basic level, a demon would utilize and harness the skills that she has. It doesn't matter if she knows how to use them or not. He will extract what he wants from her. She is powerful, and he sensed that. She is also young, which is ideal for a demon to prey upon as they are usually impressionable and easily swayed."

"Clearly, he doesn't know the real Evelyn," Brad muttered.

I poked my tongue at him, which made Brad smile.

"If he is half as connected as I am, he would have

sensed that Evelyn is more than just an average vampire. We thought she was a witchling, and we have since learned that may not be entirely correct. Your mother had vampire and shapeshifter in her. We know nothing of your father. It could be a witch, or it could be a shapeshifter, as my kin suspect."

Anzide reached out across the table, gently placing his hand over mine, which was balled tight. Brad raised an eyebrow at me.

"If that is the case, then there is less of a chance that they will want you to be terminated. A shapeshifter will be able to detect their own, and it is possible that your father knew your mother was one. They cannot determine the levels, so he would not have known about her being part vampire. Remember that for when they return. You want my help, remember that information. Push them into believing that your father is a shapeshifter."

His hand slid from mine. Anzide turned to look at Brad.

"As for the demon, there is only one solution that will keep Evelyn safe. Permanent protection, which I will give for as long as I can remain here."

Before the conversation worsened, I got up from the table.

"I'm going to lie down for a bit."

Anzide followed me to my room. I don't know what Brad wanted to say about Anzide's offer. I was too tired to care. My body flopped to the bed, and as the world faded, I heard Anzide say that he would ensure that I was safe.

I woke to the sound of the door shutting. Voices and the soft murmur of laughter. Sitting up, I blinked and tried to focus on my room.

It was still a mess, boxes unpacked, stuff everywhere. So far, I'd been too busy with homework and all that other nonsense that was going on. One of them was here, not so much of a nonsense anymore. Now, he was something else, and I don't know what exactly.

"Hey,"

Anzide turned from the window to look at me. He was sitting on the bench seat, not affected by the frostiness coming through the glass. I could see the heat he exuded as the breath escaped his mouth.

"Hey."

"Who is here?"

"The vampires. Did you hear me when I said that I have little trust for them as well?"

I nodded, sitting further back on my bed. Leaning against the wall, I pulled the blankets higher, trying to keep myself warm. The weather in this town was ridiculous.

"I'm sure you don't trust anyone."

Anzide stared, then turned back to the window.

"That's not entirely true."

Anzide's solution for my protection was a little odd, but I was grateful and found it comforting. The problem was that I worried about Brad as well.

"Can I hire the services of a Nephilim?"

Anzide turned to look at me, plain-faced but clearly curious.

"For Brad," I explained.

"Removing all obstacles. You remembered."

A soft smile crossed his features.

"But what of the boy?" he murmured. "I find it curious that you did not ask for him as well."

I was about to say something when Anzide turned to the doorway. Heavy footsteps were running up the stairs.

"Speak of the devil."

Kannon appeared at the doorway, all smiles until he saw that I was not alone.

"Hey," he said cautiously.

He gestured to Anzide, who had returned his gaze back to the window.

"Anzide, the Nephilim. This is his true form."

"Oh."

Warily, he walked into the room, sitting on the end of the bed.

"I thought that you fixed that yesterday."

"Temporarily. They've gone to get answers to a few questions I had for them."

Kannon frowned, quietly accepting but probably not understanding.

"Dad said that Harlwood was in the forest last night. That's creepy."

"Yeah, he was probably watching."

"He would have been watching from the moment he made the connection to you," Anzide said without turning from the window. "You should have heeded my warning."

"It would have been rude."

"And now you pay the price for your civility."

Kannon rolled his eyes. I smiled despite the fact that Anzide was right.

"He would have figured it out regardless." Kannon offered.

"True. However, it would have taken him longer without the physical connection. It could have given Evelyn time to deal with my kin and the monster that is ruling this town."

Brad appeared at the door, flicking his head slightly.

"Dinner is almost done. Hurry up. Jess is waiting."

Kannon stood from the bed, walking to the door. He

turned and looked expectantly at the biblical creature that was still looking out the window.

"Dude, it's polite to let a woman dress in private."

I looked at the clothes that I was wearing, wondering why Kannon thought that I'd be changing them.

"Walls will not stop a demon, *dude*. Shut the door on your way out if you're so worried about privacy."

Kannon was stunned into silence, then looked at me. I shrugged as I walked over to him.

"It's okay. He won't look."

"No, it's not okay, but if you're alright with it, then I guess I am too. See you downstairs."

I nodded, closing the door behind him. Turning, I glared at Anzide.

"Stop being an ass to him."

"He has defined interest in you, and it is not what you desire."

"How would you know what I desire?"

Walking to my cupboard, I pulled out a jumper. It was the only change that needed to happen.

"I know that you desire to be a part of a family. To feel complete. That is why you mourned Niko's passing, why it affected you more than your mother's death. He gave you what you desired. A family unit that was comforting and warm. He nurtured you, he listened, and he valued your life. Just like what your uncle does. Your mother never gave you that, and I suspect that you know that the vampire will not either."

"You can't predict the future."

"No, but I can see more than what is in front of me. The vampires in this town are far from what you want in your life."

"And I suppose that you are, is that right?"

Anzide turned and looked at me, saying nothing.

"Your kind wants to kill me, Anzide. You are wrong about him because you are jealous."

"I know little of that emotion," he murmured.

"Somehow, I don't think that's entirely true. Maybe you just figured out how to lie."

Turning, I stalked to the door. I opened it, but it slammed shut. Darkness encroached my shadow.

"I am not the liar here," Anzide whispered. "I am not the one deceiving you. I said that I know little of that emotion, but that does not mean that I do not know it at all."

Slowly, I turned around, leaning against the wooden door. Anzide wasn't angry, just leaning over me. My heart raced to a heavy tempo as I looked up at him.

"My time in this world has been limited until now. Of course, I know little of these emotions. I am learning them and figuring out my place in this world. What I do know is what I can detect. The boy, his family, and the followers, they are not to be trusted. That is the warning that you are getting from me because you said that you wanted my help to guide you in this world. That is what I am giving you. My perception, what I see, what I can detect. Interpret as you will."

CHAPTER 32

When Brad said that dinner was almost done, I assumed that it was something more than a sandwich. To be fair, it was full of salad and deli meat, but it was not like what he usually prepared.

"Thanks."

"No problem. Sleep well?"

I nodded, not wanting to look up. Anzide was leaning against the wall, looking out the window to the forest. I also didn't want to look up because Kannon was sitting at the table opposite me and clearly unimpressed.

Jess sat beside Kannon, grinning wildly as she held up a book.

"Look what I found last night."

It was a teal-colored book that had nothing written on the cover. Just plain suede.

"It's, uh, pretty."

Jess scoffed, offering a slight frown.

"It's not pretty. It's stunningly beautiful. Touch it. Feel how soft it is."

The book was placed on the table in front of me.

"Do not touch it," Anzide muttered.

Brad turned to look at him. Kannon frowned.

"What's wrong? Is someone at the door?"

Jess's smile had lessened as she looked around the table.

"What are you talking about?"

"Nothing. You know what, guys? I think we should chill on the lessons for a couple of days. Evie's had a rough time today. I think we should call an end to the day."

"Yeah," Jess said hesitantly. "You're probably right. A run-in with a demon is not fun by any means."

She began packing the books back into her bag, then flicked her head at Kannon.

"Come on, bud, I need a lift home."

"Sure. Text you later, Evie."

I nodded, slowly chewing the food in my mouth. He smiled, but I could see that there was a lot of uncertainty.

Brad walked with them to the door. I watched and wondered why Brad was essentially kicking them out.

"Eat your dinner, Evelyn," Anzide said softly. "Everything is fine. You're just tired."

Well, someone has definitely learned how to tell a lie.

Brad sighed heavily and loud enough that I could hear him easily on this side of the large open space.

"You want to explain what that was about?" he snapped at Anzide.

"I can't touch a book, apparently," I answered.

Neither of them was impressed.

Anzide sat at the table, waiting for Brad to return to his seat.

"In my head, he told me to stop you from touching the book and to get rid of them immediately. What the hell is going on?"

"I should have realized it sooner, but I was caught in the mindset that Evelyn was a witch. Do you remember that I said that your lineage was extremely powerful?"

I nodded quietly and with a mouth full of cereal.

"That was correct. I could feel the power, and I still can. They clearly figured it out, or at least think they have. That is why she wanted you to touch the book. I was not visible to them. They did not know why their departure was so abrupt. It was necessary. Otherwise, she would have insisted and continued until you touched the book and then confirmed it. Now, they will retreat and wait until another time."

"Okay, so she doesn't touch the book. What are they trying to confirm? That she's a shapeshifter?"

"No, they would not care if she was one. It is not a beneficial species to them. A phoenix, however, that is a weapon that is incredibly powerful to everyone. Vampire, demon,"

"She's a mythological bird?" Brad interrupted.

Anzide shook his head.

"Do not relate her to what you have seen in books. I require paper and a pen."

"Please," Brad grumped as he stood.

I looked up. Anzide watched Brad as he stalked out of the room. His face was filled with mild amusement as he slowly turned his gaze to me.

"Want to know something fun?"

"Sure."

"If you fornicate with the boy, his life will become a fast-ticking clock. Then one day, not long after the deadly deed, he goes poof and is gone."

I gulped hard as I looked at him. That was a terrible fate.

"How is that fun?"

"Oh, I didn't mean for you."

"You're so horrible to him."

A thought hit me.

"So, if I can't have sex with him, then who?"

"Eternal is the only option if you want your partner to survive."

"How convenient."

"I know," he said smugly.

Brad's heavy footsteps thumped through the corridor.

"Is that why my mother is dead?"

The smile fell away, replaced with a grim twitch in the corner of his mouth and a deep frown.

"Your mother died because of Andross. We discussed this. However, to answer you correctly, yes, she was affected by fornicating with your father. Her life was always going to end."

"So, essentially, he murdered her."

Anzide paused, staring at me with lips parted as he considered what to say.

"He did."

"Great. If you have any knowledge of where he is, keep it to yourself."

Brad slapped the paper and pen on the table and then sat down.

"Okay, smart guy, enlighten us."

Anzide dragged the paper closer, picked up the pen,

and started to write.

"Vampires, witches, shapeshifters are classed as immortals."

He wrote the words down and then drew an arrow to another word, *immortal.* Then he continued with more. All the while, his gaze was down, looking at the words and arrows that formed on the page in front of him.

"It means they do not suffer a natural death but can be killed. They are the original inhabitants of this world. Humanity came later. They are not connected as a species, even if they have many similar features. Mortals are classed as animals, and in this instance, you could even include plants. Mortals are something that dies, like a human. The Eternals are the ones like me, the Nephilim, angels, demons. We do not suffer death in any form and cannot be killed no matter how hard one tries. You, my grumpy oddity, are classed as an immortal because of your mother's line."

"And Evie?"

Anzide wrote *Phoenix* to the side of the groups. Clearly, I was on my own.

"Technically, immortal because of your sister. Then her father threw his genetics into the mix, and together, they created the peculiarity that is an immortal creature that is destined to die and regenerate every hundred years. If you are wondering, there are a few in existence, and they only ever occur when a powerful eternal breeds with another powerful being that is not an eternal. It is likely that the combination of vampire and shapeshifter caused the power to grow in Nancy. However, the deciding factor was definitely your father. If you were to find out who he is, then things will make more sense."

"Is that why Andross burned?"

"It is. You were angry, defending yourself, and you were untrained. That is your father's fault. He should have remained in your life to train you. Of course, he should have stayed away from your mother, but that is something,"

"That we don't need to discuss. I don't want to know a single thing about him. He had sex with my mother, knowing that it would kill her. If you want someone to train me, find someone else. Anyone would be better than him."

Brad left the table, wandering into the kitchen. I watched as he began cleaning the benches and packing away everything that he'd left spread over the counter. It made me wonder if he was trying to hide his thoughts about losing his sister.

Turning back, I was mildly amused by the little doodles Anzide drew around the words. Stick figures with horns or wings. He'd also drawn a stick figure hanging from the gallows with an arrow pointing to it, *the boy* written next to it. Anzide looked up at me, giving a defiant and smug smile. Ignoring him was the only thing I could do.

"Are you absolutely certain that you've got it right this time? You're not going to come up with some other rando creature?"

"Rando?"

"Random."

He smirked, then turned back to the piece of paper in front of him.

"You are definitely a vampire, thanks to Niko's influence. Beatrice gave you shapeshifter abilities. They were both purebloods. Your grandfather, Edward Newton, was human, as was all his family. The phoenix will override everything."

"So, when I get to one hundred, I will combust?"

"That is what usually happens. The phoenix is technically classed as an Eternal but one of those variances like the Nephilim."

"What's their purpose?"

"Originally, they were seen as the keepers of the immortals. They watched over them like the angels watched over the mortals. Now they are just another being that does as they please."

"Will your kind make me pay for what my father did?"

Anzide paused as he looked at me, then sighed.

"Eternals are not supposed to breed. But, they are few in number and have certain desires. They knew the ramifications of entertaining themselves with the immortals or the mortals, so they fornicated with each other. I guess no one thought to tell them that such things lead to things like me. The travesty of it, right? Creating life. How dare they."

I smiled. It was difficult not to find his mockery funny.

"Is there an opposite to them, like the demons?"

"No, thankfully. Originally, it was like a triangle of beings. The two groups of caretakers and the one group who are the collectors."

"You're hiding what Harlwood really wants, aren't you?"

"Yes," he whispered.

"Am I nothing but a piece of meat to all of you?"

"The path to what we want is different, but yes, they all end up in that one place. Avoiding the demon is necessary. Otherwise, your soul will be corrupted, and darkness will consume you to the point that any spark inside of you will be extinguished."

Charming.

Brad frowned as he emerged from the kitchen.

"Going to veg out in front of the computer. The doors are locked, and you're not to let anyone in, okay?"

I nodded.

"Listen to the freak and behave yourself."

Brad turned and walked down the corridor.

"After all that I offer, I am still the freak."

"You turned from a teenager into a man. Though, to be fair, he did say that you were older than what you appeared to be."

"Is that so?"

"Yeah, he said that you didn't speak like a teenager."

"Hmm, I suppose that is correct. Now, we were discussing intentions."

Sighing, I rolled my eyes and got off the chair.

"I get it. I'm a solid gold piece of ass. Let's drop it, shall we?"

Dumping myself onto the lounge, I turned to face the window.

"No, I think that it is imperative that you are aware of the boy."

"You said that I can't. I don't want Kannon to die. I like him too much for that."

"That is your choice, wrong, but still your choice. This needs to be discussed so that you understand why I do not trust them and why you should listen to me."

So, I guess we were doing this anyway. I said drop it, but mister chatterbox wanted to dish the dirt.

"Their original intention would have been to ensure that a union happened so that he could be the leader's partner. Once the first child was born, your time in this world would have ended. As your partner, he would have assumed control until the child was of legal age to lead the coven. Bradley could have stepped in, but they'd make short work of him, too. They might not have had a hand in the treachery that happened in this house, but rest assured, they were fully aware of what happened. They knew where he was."

I looked at Anzide with a frown.

"How do you know this information?"

"Weak minds can be entered on occasion. There are variables to the situation, and I haven't had much of a chance to delve deep. These four vampires are extremely good at hiding the past in their minds. As for their knowledge about Niko, I got that from Jess. Another vampire told her where the original leader was prior to your arrival in Hades. She didn't care because it didn't affect her, and, in her mind, the sole focus is to avoid rousing Drakkus's attention. As for their plans, they will continue. Sadly, the boy has been dragged into their nonsense. I can see that even if he was forced into the situation, he had a genuine interest. Now that they have realized the truth, that interest will be pulled back. Wait and see. They won't risk his life just to get an heir on the non-existent throne."

"They'll just make me abdicate," I murmured. "I can't rule if I can't produce a vampire heir, right?"

The lounge shifted down. I turned my head to see Anzide sitting beside me.

"They won't make you abdicate, but they will use you to defeat Drakkus. Then, they will claim you are not a true vampire and make you hand over the rule. That is not what your great-grandfather would want."

"And what does Anzide want from me?" I whispered.

"To ensure that you reach your potential, to help you through this life and along the dangerous path that is ahead of you."

His hand pressed to the curve of my shoulder, warm and reassuring.

"To get you to the goals that you desire without harm."

CHAPTER 33

Yesterday was thoroughly dull.

I did all my homework, tidied my room, and organized everything. I even did some cleaning. That's why Brad agreed to let me go to school today.

I drove with Brad rather than Kannon. We discussed how I would deal with being at school, the demon principal, and the vampire with questionable motives. Brad recommended that all interactions with Kannon should be pulled back and kept limited. It was easy to say, but in real life, it was going to be incredibly difficult.

Anzide shadowed my every step, unseen by the world around me. No one paid attention to me, oblivious to the point where it felt like I was invisible. Even Audrey didn't turn to make some snide comment or offer a supreme smile.

Turning to my locker, I pressed my head against the cold metal and sighed.

"Why can't they see me?"

"That would be your demon stalker. He's following, focusing, and formulating. They are unaware because he doesn't want them to see what's going to happen. Do not put your books in the locker."

"What about the rest of my stuff in there?"

"It is not important."

Taking a deep breath in, I slowly exhaled and tried to focus. It was not easy.

"I guess this is it, right? I tried, and I failed. Homeschooling for me."

"Sometimes it's for the best. We make our attempts with the hope that they will work, but, in this case, it's not meant to be."

Cool fingers slid over my hand, slowly curving into the palm. Our fingers entwined, I looked at Anzide with a lot of fear floating through me.

"Be brave, Evelyn. He cannot harm you."

The lights overhead flickered, slowly coming to life as the demon emerged from the darkness. It was the first time I'd ever seen beyond this row of lockers. The corridor was longer than I expected it to be, filled with more lockers and doors to classrooms that were never used. It was like they were expecting a surge in numbers, but it never happened. Maybe the demon had cast the lures out to families and was waiting for them to arrive.

"Good morning, Evelyn," Harlwood said in an amused tone. "How are you today?"

"Okay, I guess," I murmured.

Anzide squeezed my hand.

"Actually, I don't feel well. I'm going home."

The demon said nothing, just quietly watching me as I backed out of the corridor. It was lucky that I had the first locker. Otherwise, it would have looked obvious.

"Of course," Harlwood said, taking a few steps forward.

His eyes were pinned to me, the defiant smirk firmly in place.

"But you should stop at the office first. Have Jane call your uncle."

My hand was being pulled back, Anzide tugging it as discreetly as he could.

"It's fine. He won't care."

Harlwood continued to follow me. I wanted to turn around and run, but I was worried about what he would do once my back was turned.

"That may be so, but we have a duty of care to all students. If you don't want him to pick you up, then you must allow the school to notify him that you will be leaving the grounds."

The bell rang, and I nearly jumped out of my skin. All the students and teachers who were in the corridor and completely oblivious to us turned and walked away. Robotic, lifeless.

"Run," Anzide whispered. "He's clearing the room for a reason."

Even though the bell rang and students were moving to their classes, the corridor seemed to be extremely packed. I struggled to weave my way through the crowd. Looking over my shoulder, I saw the principal watching me. Students kept a wide circle around him, moving as if there was a wall that stopped them from getting too close.

"Keep going."

"There are too many."

I did not think that there were this many students in the school. Shoulders hit mine, thumping against me, trying to knock me aside. I knew that this was Harlwood's work, and I knew that he was trying to separate me from Anzide.

"Almost there, push ahead."

His cool grip was tight, refusing to let go despite the determined efforts of the demon.

The doors seemed so far away, appearing as if they moved further back with every step I took. Light flushed as a heavy thumping noise echoed through my head. Blinding white encroached and took away the darkness that was shrouding my mind.

"Evie?"

Blinking, I realized we were outside, and Kannon was walking down the path from where he'd parked his car.

"Are you alright?"

"I'm going home. Harlwood's in there."

He looked at the doors that were slowly swinging shut. I could see the principal standing in an empty corridor, watching me.

"I'll drive."

As Kannon turned his attention back, he saw the one who had clearly remained unseen until now. Kannon's gaze lowered. Our hands were still connected.

"Right, I guess not then. This is it, huh?"

"You know how it is now, immortal," Anzide said tersely.

"Right, the book."

Kannon's eyes narrowed.

"All rather convenient if you ask me."

"This is your doing. Blame only yourself."

Anzide gently nudged me.

"Time to leave before the demon makes another attempt."

I nodded in response but was thoroughly confused.

"Bye," I said softly.

Kannon said nothing as he watched us walk away. I turned back to see him standing in front of the doors, silently observing us.

When we were past the gates, Anzide let go of my hand. We walked along the exterior of the property. The rain had started to fall, gently sprinkling down on us.

"What did you mean by that interaction?"

Anzide looked at me, silently assessing me like he always does.

"When you called the boy to help with the body, he looked at your hands. They were pale from the fire, and he assumed it was because you were a witch, yet they brought the book of the Eternals to your house. Why, Evelyn? Why would they think to do such a thing? No one had even suggested that you were an Eternal before this, and until that moment, it was not even a thought in anyone's mind. Yet, they brought the book, and there is only one person who could have told them the events of that day."

"No," I whispered, sadly shaking my head. "You're wrong. He wouldn't sell me out like that. Maybe they knew from the body."

Anzide looked at me as if I was the one that was wrong.

I didn't want to return to the place where it happened, but Anzide insisted. It was important that I could see the treachery of the vampires in this town. My great-grandfather had suffered by their hand, and I had to learn so that I would not fall victim like he had.

"He assured you that his father had dealt with the body, yet here it lies, waiting to be found by the one vampire that you do not want to find it. I can tell you that there is no way that any mortal or immortal creature could tell exactly what happened, aside from the fact that he burned. They will assume that this is the work of a witch until they can confirm that you are not one."

Anzide turned to me, his hands clasped behind his back and a resolute face offered.

"Tell me something, Evelyn. What difference would it make to your following if you were a witch or an Eternal?"

"I, uh, I don't know."

"It should make no difference to them because if they were loyal to the Corbin line, they would not care either way. You are the leader. That is all that matters. The other side of this is the enemy that haunts your every step. What do you think it would mean to him?"

I shook my head again, giving a shrug because I had no idea.

"A witch can be defeated with another witch, preferably stronger, but even a lesser witch can win with a stroke of luck. A phoenix, on the other hand, they are far more powerful, and it would take nothing for you to obliterate Drakkus, just like you did with mister chargrilled here."

"Gross," I muttered under my breath.

"That may be so, but it highlights the truth. Drakkus wants to know his enemy, and you are number one on his hit list. If he knows the truth, then he will be able to formulate his plans for the future. Left unassessed, you are an unknown entity, and he cannot pin down his life to one path."

The conversation stalled. I felt a dread crawl up my spine.

"Anzide," I whispered. "We're not alone."

Slowly, I turned. At the far end of the forest, closest to the school entry, was Drakkus. He didn't make a move, just his threat given in the one silent position.

"Take it easy," Anzide said quietly. "Walk and put distance between you and him."

"I've seen how fast they can run."

"And he can see me. Trust me, he won't approach you, but he will try to frighten you. Be prepared for it and run if you need to. I will remain at your side for all of it."

I nodded and began to walk away from the body and from Drakkus.

"Time to exit the forest."

We turned, continuing to the edge of the forest. Standing at the edge of the street, I looked around and saw that life carried on as if there wasn't a single peculiar thing going on. Hades was full of the weird and unusual, paranormal and Eternal beings, yet the humans were oblivious because of the demon. He was the one who truly ruled this town.

Tom waved at me, offering his cheery smile.

"Good morning, Evelyn. How's the house going?"

"Great thanks, Tom."

"Have you fixed the crack in the basement yet?"

"Yeah, it's all repaired."

Brad put the brick back, but that was it.

"That's good to hear. Say hi to your uncle for me, won't you?"

"Sure thing."

With another wave, he delved into his shop and left me to carry on with my journey. Glancing at the end of the street, I saw the edge of the forest that held a vampire. He continued to watch wordlessly yet full of hatred.

"Move before he starts something."

We crossed to the other side of the road and then turned down the side street.

"Run, put the distance between you and him."

I wanted to say that there was no point in running. I'd seen how fast the vampires moved, and it would be nothing for Drakkus to catch up to me. Instead, I did what Anzide asked. I ran.

Anzide kept up, merely a figure beside me. Rain began to pour. No longer the light shower. It was heavy. Clouds had formed within seconds, making me think that someone controlled it rather than it being nature.

Running through the hounding rain, I reached the

end of the street and stopped. Street lights had turned on, and at the far end of the road, I could see someone watching me. It was not Drakkus, but I knew he was a vampire.

"Over here." Anzide urged.

Stepping back and out of view, I crossed the road and followed Anzide down a tight gap between two shops. It was barely large enough for them to store their trash cans. Squeezing past them without making a lot of noise was not easy. Thankfully, the lightning and thunder made a lot of noise and covered my efforts.

"Where are we going?"

"Away from the vampires. He's got two associates helping him. There is another that is at the end of the street. We're going to pass him in a minute, so remain as quiet as you can."

Reaching the next street that ran parallel to the one I'd just run down. I peered around the corner and saw the vampire that had remained out of sight. It was obvious that the first one was in full view to herd me toward this one who was hidden.

The problem was that I had to get past him without being seen. If he turned around, I'd be caught. Anzide turned to me, pulling me back into the tight space.

"You're going to that gap over there. Rush to the car, and hide behind it. When I signal, cross the road and hide behind the red car over there. I will tell you when to move again. Run straight to the alley, okay?"

I nodded. Anzide moved out to the center of the road, then flicked his hand. I rushed out over the footpath and hid behind the first car, a blue pickup truck. His hand was up, wordlessly telling me to stop, his gaze firmly on the vampire. With another flick of his hand, Anzide ordered me to rush to the red car across the street.

My heart was racing as I squatted next to the wheel. It was just as painful as my labored breathing and the cramp in my side.

Anzide appeared at the entry to the narrow alley, still watching the vampire. He gave another flick of his hand, and I was up and running again.

With Anzide by my side, we weaved our way through the boxes and trash cans, emerging at the next street. This was where the forest connected to the school, deeper than the narrow strip next to the field but enough to give me protection until I reached the other side. Then I'd be almost home.

It was raining heavily. We were soaked, and it was insanely cold. All I wanted to do right now was curl up in front of the fireplace to warm up.

We stopped. I turned to Anzide and smiled. He frowned slightly when he realized that I was looking at him.

"What?"

"You care."

Lifting to my toes, I pulled his hand down so that

he'd lower just a fraction. It was bold, but that was me. One little peck of gratitude on his cheek.

CHAPTER 34

Trying to be quiet as we walked through the forest was not easy. Every step we took was another beacon that pointed to our location. It was the only choice. Going the other way meant we'd have to walk past Drakkus and his goons again, and I did not want that.

The only consolation I had was that, apparently, vampires had good hearing but not great. To hear us walking through the forest, they'd have to be close. On the street where we'd seen them was not within range. Still, I felt like we needed to be quiet just in case there were more vampires in the forest.

Everything was wet, and there was a low-lying fog that coated the ground like a wispy veil. We couldn't see the ground, but it was there, floating around and creating a heightened sense of unease inside of me. A bird called out a whooping squawk that I'd heard before but made the mood seem ominous in the eerie silence. Anzide held my hand tight, moving us as fast as he dared while always looking around. I think that he was on a higher alert than I was.

I knew we were close to home when I saw the witch's ring. Keeping to the exterior, we continued past it and toward Niko's cave. I wanted to know who had taken his body. I had my suspicions, but for now, it had to wait.

When I saw the fence, I was happy. Getting closer to the house brought a sense of ease, even if we weren't out of the woods yet. Oddly enough, I felt more exposed when I walked across the lawn than when I was in the forest. Maybe it was because I was exposed. Always seen, never missed.

The path to the back door was uneventful. Brad frowned as he watched us walk through the door.

"Okay, so we'll start from the top, shall we? Going to school was clearly a mistake."

"Yeah," I sighed. "Do what you need to get it done here. I'm not going back."

"Already figured that. We'll discuss it at lunch. How about you two get those muddy shoes off? Socks too. Damn it, look at the mess."

Anzide rolled his eyes, flicking off his shoes. I tossed mine to the pile, peeling the wet socks off and leaving them next to my bag. There was mud everywhere, made worse by the water dripping from us. Brad was ushering us away, desperate to stop us from messing up the room. I don't know why he was being so fussy. It's not like the floor couldn't be cleaned. If he didn't want to do it, I'd be happy to clean it up. After all, I'd made the mess.

"Go and warm up before you catch a cold."

With a dejected nod, I turned to the corridor.

"Don't let any vampires into this house," Anzide grumbled at Brad.

"Sure."

As I trudged up the stairs, I thought about going to school now that the demon headmaster had made an obvious move against me. I was done with the place. When I couldn't walk through the corridor by myself, then it was an issue.

Hearing footsteps, I turned to see my silent protection was a step behind me. We were both wet, leaving water everywhere.

Anzide followed me into the bathroom, removing his shirt to wring out over the bathtub. I leaned on the closed door, watching him with a burning curiosity. Well, a lot of things were burning at the moment.

The nicely defined body was too perfect. I guess that's all part of the biblical thing.

"How come you don't just dry yourself?"

"It doesn't work like that. I still have a physical presence. I am bound to certain laws regarding the body and the form, like gravity, for one. I can't fly through the sky, but I can pass through things. It's complicated."

When his hands moved to the top of his pants, I bit my lip, waiting with a smile that could barely be contained. Anzide stopped and turned the top half of his body to look at me. Slowly, my gaze lifted, and I saw how caught I was. He turned completely and then sauntered over like he was the king of the world.

I backed into the wall. Leaning one arm above me, Anzide lowered.

"Do I not grant you privacy?" he whispered.

"Not really. It's kind of perverted how you insist on being in the same room as me."

"I don't look,"

His voice was soft, delicate words breathed out over my lips as he moved closer.

"I'm sure you disobey those physical rules and move your eyes to the back of your head."

Anzide smiled.

"Not possible, but an interesting thought."

For a moment, there was silence. I couldn't help but look at him. There wasn't much else to look at. Just the body that was well formed, tapering down to those narrow hips with the pants that slung low.

"What do you want, Evelyn?"

A lot. More than I should.

"Take what you desire."

His whispered words were pure temptation. As I reached out, I bit my lip, a bad habit that Brad would grumble about if he could see it.

The tips of my fingers traced over the cool flesh, dragging lower. It was tantalizing to touch the skin, watching it move over his body, sinking down to the pants.

Brad knocked on the door, making me jump with fright.

"Hey, Evie,"

"Yeah?"

Anzide moved away, much to my annoyance.

"I thought Anzide might need dry clothes. Does he need something, or can he dry his own clothes?"

"Dry clothes would be ideal."

I frowned, turning around because it sounded like Anzide was on the other side of the door. Anzide and the shirt were gone. I opened the door as Brad turned. Anzide was behind him. He had the shirt back on and looked sopping wet.

"I thought you were,"

Brad frowned heavily.

"Aren't you supposed to protect her all the time?"

"I am. Just getting fresh towels."

"Right,"

It sounded like Brad didn't believe him. Handing over the clothes to me, Brad wandered off without another word said.

Anzide crossed the gap, dumped the towels on the counter, and closed the door. Within seconds, I was pressed to the wall. I was stunned at first, but then reality caught up to me, and I rolled with the moment.

The clothes were dumped on the counter. I don't know if they made it or fell to the floor. I was too wrapped up in the intense kiss. Our lips entwined as the seconds ticked over. His hands moved, slowly pulling my shirt out from the skirt.

Pulling me from the wall, Anzide moved his hands around my body, continuing to tug the material free. Our kiss stilled, eyes pinned to each other. One corner of Anzide's lips curled as his gaze lowered. He began to undo the buttons of my shirt.

The thumping inside of me was fast, excitement spurning on the erratic heart rate.

As Anzide pulled my shirt over my shoulders, he leaned down for another kiss. Chaste but perfect.

I had the auspicious duty of removing the shirt that was far too tight. Already like a second skin on him, the wet material clung to his body. Now, it clung to the side of the bath.

Sitting in the only gap left on the side of the tub, Anzide pulled me closer. Standing between his legs, I looked down at him as he gently kissed my stomach. His hands slid up the back of my thighs, bunching the skirt as he moved. When he reached the waistband, Anzide gripped it and pulled it over my hips.

Wearing nothing but my underwear, I grabbed a towel and wrapped it around me.

Anzide draped the skirt over the side, then stalked over to me.

"Running away so soon?"

"Maybe."

I grinned as my fingers slipped under the waistband, prying open the button of his pants. As I pulled the zipper over the curve, I pressed my lips tight, trying not to smile or giggle.

"Maybe not," Anzide whispered.

He pulled away the towel, tucking it over the rail. The bra and pants were dropped to the floor, soon followed by his shorts. Nerves hit me. I couldn't wait for this moment, but it worried me that it wouldn't be amazing or even great. We were both new to this, both rather clueless. Instinct would take over, but I still worried that it would be as life-affirming as I hoped it would be.

I ignored the thoughts in my head and the nerves that turned my stomach over. My heart was hammering, but that was understandable.

Anzide curved his fingers under my jaw, urging me closer with a soft kiss. Wrapping my arms around his waist, I held him close as the kiss deepened.

The water was wonderfully warm on my cold skin. Anzide's fingers trailed over my arms as we kissed. Backed against the wall, I felt the weight of his body against me. The desperation between us grew. Hands wandered, lips caressed, and words laced with giggles were softly whispered against sensitive skin.

Lifting my legs around his waist, Anzide looked into my eyes as the water rained over us. One whispered word against my lips asked a simple question. *Ready?* I nodded and felt the pressure. With a push, it was done. We were no longer newbies, now somewhere in the land of new lovers.

CHAPTER 35

I woke under the warm blankets, wrapped up in Anzide's arms. I'd fallen asleep even though I didn't feel tired. Maybe the day itself had taken its toll on me.

Demon headmaster attacked. Now ex-boyfriend realized the truth and how we could not be together. Nephilim protector makes a serious move.

His body was warm under the sheets. I snuggled in and savored the moment of peace and quiet.

I didn't know what to expect from my first time, but it was certainly enjoyable. My mother was open about sex. She told me more than she should have and probably not the right things. Still, I'd enjoyed it and was definitely eager for more.

"You sleep deeper when you are relaxed."

He sat up, leaning on one hand as he looked down at me.

"You also look different. Like there is no weight on your shoulders."

"Well, to be fair, my life is not exactly a walk in the park. Imagine losing your mother at fifteen after spending years with her either at work, passed out on the bed, or awake and cursing because you had the audacity to clean the house."

Or worse.

"Then you're tossed at your uncle that you think you've never met before, but it's a lie. In fact, your whole life is a lie. You're made to move because of his job, but that's just your uncle keeping the wishes of your dead mother. You're really some kind of hybrid creature, vampire, shapeshifter, human. A man appears, and pretends to be your father, but he really wants to hand you over to serve as his punishment. Biblical creatures, dangerous creatures. All the while, there's school to be finished. Oh, and don't forget the incorrect birthday, which still has no valid reason as to why.

"And you're an Eternal yourself."

"Ah yes, the missing father and his input into this mess. Do you know where he is?"

Anzide shook his head.

"Good. Don't bother to find out."

"You stated quite clearly that you were not interested. I am not going to waste time doing something that is not pleasing to you."

He lowered, settling against my body.

"I can, however, be pleasing to you in other ways."

"I like the sound of that."

"Evie," Brad bellowed from the bottom of the stairs. "Lunch."

"Or not," Anzide whispered.

We dressed quickly, emerging from my bedroom within a minute.

"Evelyn,"

Anzide stopped me at the top of the stairs.

"It would be wise to avoid telling your uncle to begin with. I'm supposed to be protecting you."

"Not getting into my pants?"

His lips twitched, slowly becoming a smile.

"That would be the one."

"Sure. Probably for the best after what he did to Mardyl."

Brad was protective, perhaps too much. I suppose that he thought that I needed it after everything that I'd been through. It was also possible he was desperate to leave this town just to get me away from Drakkus, but he couldn't.

Turning the corner, I saw an elaborate spread on the table. Salad cut and put into bowls, cheese, spreads, and bread. He'd even set the table for three.

"I have no idea if you can eat, but rather than be rude."

"I can," Anzide said. "But it's often unnecessary. Thank you all the same."

Brad nodded, sitting down. I carefully lowered to the seat, feeling Anzide's presence all over again. It was tender, and I did not want to make it obvious.

"We have a lot to talk about, so how about we start with the obvious, the demon."

"He made a serious move," I grumbled.

"It was a low-grade attack to figure out how Evelyn would cope, if she would react or break down into a mess. He wanted to know what she would do on the low end of what he could throw at her rather than going into a full attack. There were other students around, so I think that would have been a large factor in why he went down this path. He was determined to keep her at the school."

"And what happens now?"

"He will pull back once Evelyn stops attending school. I would suggest that you move quickly on the homeschooling as he could call the authorities on you in an effort to get her to return to the school."

"I don't have to finish this year, you know."

Brad shook his head as he buttered the bread in front of him.

"I've already started the process. You might as well get it done. What else is there?"

"Drakkus made another move."

My knight in shining armor saved me twice today. I wouldn't have even made it out the doors of the school if it weren't for his help.

Brad sighed as he put the butter knife down, glancing between us.

"We need to move." he grumped. "I know you want to honor Niko's memory, but this is ridiculous. We can't trust any of the vampires in this town, can we?"

Anzide shook his head.

"Not even the Lothaires?"

"They are the snake in the grass, waiting for the opportune time to strike. Drakkus is your obvious enemy. He has made it quite clear what his intentions are. The Lothaire family, however, they are the ones that hide what they really want. I would trust Drakkus long before I trusted anyone from that family."

Brad sighed, looking at me with a lot of sympathy. Yes, I liked Kannon. He was a good person, despite the issues that were hiding in the darkness. I would have preferred that he was honest with me, but clearly, I have a sign on my forehead that says dishonesty welcome.

"What about you?"

Anzide stopped piling things onto his sandwich and looked at Brad.

"What about me?" he asked cautiously.

"You know, the Nephilim. What's happening now?"

His eyes darted as the frown deepened, and his head lowered. Slowly, his fingers slid over the edge of the plate.

"The portal is locked," he murmured.

"What?"

Anzide's eyes lifted to me. In them, I could see fear.

"They're coming."

Renuge appeared, looking between Anzide and me. A sly smirk slid over his lips before they opened. I was expecting him to drag us out to the front lawn again, but he didn't. Instead, he pulled a chair out at the other end of the table and sat down.

"Please, continue to enjoy your meal. I can deliver the message while you dine."

I don't know if I could eat at this point in time. It concerned me that they'd do their worst, and I'd be dragged away. Was this my last meal?

"It has been agreed that there is no warning for any immortal or mortal creature about procreation, and as such, all investigations are now finished. The charges against Evelyn Newton have been dropped, and no further allegations regarding this matter shall be brought forward or noted."

"Great," Brad said. "If that's all,"

"No, unfortunately, it's not."

"What now?" he snapped. "You said that it was over."

"It is for that charge. However, the rules for the Eternal are quite clear, and it would seem that someone forgot them."

I looked at Anzide. His gaze lowered to his hands as they lifted. Cuffed like a criminal.

"No," I yelled, standing from the table.

"What's going on?" Brad snapped again.

"The Eternals are not permitted to engage in frivolous activities that can lead to more Nephilim being created."

Brad frowned, still unable to figure it out. Sometimes, it was better to be oblivious.

Renuge stood, and Anzide did as well, but it appeared as if he was dragged out of his seat by an unknown force.

"You won't face charges as Anzide has taken full responsibility already. Sit down before you make it worse for yourself."

"Don't you dare tell me what to do." I hissed.

Renuge said nothing, just a silent smirk that needed to be punched off his face. Anzide trudged behind him, looking back at me.

"Do something, Anzide."

"I did. I saved you from this fate."

The front door swung open, and Renuge walked out as if he actually needed to. I followed them, getting angrier by the second.

"You have no right to do this," I yelled.

Renuge stopped at the top step, looking out at the driveway.

"Friend of yours?"

I looked over at Drakkus and rolled my eyes.

"Go away, loser," I yelled. "I've got way bigger problems than your nonsense."

Drakkus seemed rather affronted that I'd rudely told him to go away. I would have thought after being shot twice, he would have learned that I was not the average woman.

Renuge continued down the stairs, dragging Anzide behind him. Fury filled me because Renuge wasn't listening to me, and that other idiot decided to turn up.

White hot rage crawled up my spine like a thousand spiders rushing to my brain. I screamed as it consumed me, flowing out in one fast ripple that boomed and leveled everything. My head was pounding as the wrath slowly subsided. It was then that I realized that I felt different. There was something wrong.

My hands were flaming blue again. I looked across the charred lawn, the broken bits of wood, and the dead plants, seeing nothing but destruction. Drakkus was on his ass, bewildered as he looked around at the debris. Brad was sitting at the table, staring at me completely stunned because nothing else survived my anger. The rest of the house was blown across the yard, the neighbor's property, and the forest. So much for keeping Niko's house in one piece. I'd just flattened it.

Anzide was still alright, only just sitting up. Renuge, however, he was out cold. Stalking over to him, I picked him up by the lapel of his jacket and slapped his face until he came around.

"Hey," I snapped. "You see what happens when you go against me?"

He struggled with coherence. Dragging him up, I tossed him onto the burned grass.

"Do you see what happens?" I yelled.

Cautiously, he nodded.

"You can go back to wherever the hell it was that you came from, and you can tell whoever the hell it is that thinks they can rule my life and tell them to mind their own damned business. If they come for me, my uncle, Anzide, or anyone else I care about, I am going to hunt them down, and they will not survive. I do not care if you or any of them are Eternal. I will make it my life mission to find a way to kill you and them. Is that clear?"

He nodded, silently stunned. I was not a quiet girl when I was angry. Also, the flames were getting larger. It probably meant that I was getting angrier.

"Good. Remove the cuffs, go home, and tell them to leave us alone."

Metal chinked, and Renuge faded from sight. I turned

to see Anzide getting off the ground, unsteady at first but getting there. The other issue was getting to his feet. With a sigh, I crossed the dead grass.

"Now is a good time, right?"

Drakkus looked down at my flaming hands, casually gesturing to them.

"Do you wish to put the fire out first?"

"No, I may need to use it again. I told you to leave this town."

"You did, but you do not have the authority to do that, despite who you are related to. We have no official documentation stating that Niko passed the rule onto you, so therefore, your claim for the rule is null and void."

He pouted, like mocking me was the thing to do when he'd just witnessed what making me angry does.

"So sad. Now that you've got no home, I expect that it is you who will be leaving this town. It was so nice to know you."

With a mocking laugh, Drakkus turned and walked away. There were a group of vampires waiting at the end of the driveway.

"What right do you have to tell me what to do or where I can live? You are not the ruler of the vampires in this town."

Drakkus stopped, turning to face me.

"We could go back and forth like this for days, my dear Evelyn. What you really need to know is that you've broken one of our biggest rules."

With a flick of his finger, the crowd parted, and Kannon stepped forward. He was dressed in a fine suit, hair neatly styled. His gaze was squarely on me.

When he stopped, Drakkus moved behind him, firmly placing his hands on his shoulders.

"I'd like for you to meet my newest second in charge. After you so callously murdered Andross, I was left in desperate need of a replacement. I found that in this fine creature."

His finger curved over Kannon's jaw, dragging it up to look at him when he reached the chin.

"He offered me something that I could not get elsewhere."

Drakkus smiled at me as he took that final swing. The blow that was a desperate attempt to wound me.

"He gave me answers."

CHAPTER 36

I'd like to say that I was stunned by that, but it was hard to be anything when I was feeling rather emotionless.

After Drakkus enjoyed his moment in the limelight, pointing out that my ex-boyfriend had sold me out and then apparently flipped teams, he gave me an ultimatum. I was the outsider here. I was the one that was on her own. No vampires in this town wanted to associate with me or any Corbin, so, therefore, the rule of the Corbin family was dead. I was to leave town immediately because there was no point in trying to salvage anything when the house was nothing but a pile of rubble.

I watched as they walked down the street, slowly fanning out and dispersing into the shadows. Like he knew that I was watching, Drakkus made a show of his affection for Kannon.

"Well, that was rather unexpected. Did you know he was bi?"

I looked at Brad, who was standing next to me,

watching the figures as they walked down the road.

"No, and I don't care. I'm done with this place. Let's salvage what we can and get the hell out of,"

I rolled my eyes. "Hell."

Brad huffed, then turned to look at the non-existent house.

"You really need to learn how to control your powers."

"I'll say," Anzide grumbled. "I have a lump on the back of my head."

"Shut up, the both of you. What would Niko say if he could see this?"

"Pick up a hammer?"

"Flame thrower," Brad offered.

The two of them laughed. Ignoring them, I returned to the house. The burn marks dragged across the floor, sweeping around the table that was untouched. Nothing burned, nothing askew. I sat down and finished lunch.

"Seriously?" Brad asked as he approached.

"I'm hungry, and we might as well eat. At least then we can decide what's going to happen."

Brad was more interested in finishing his sandwich than the conversation. I'm sure he was itching to find out if his secret stash of doughnuts had survived. I will not be popular if they're burned.

"Okay," Brad sighed heavily. "I'm just going to assume that I know what that was all about and ignore it because I do not want to know."

"Did you need another education?"

"No," he snapped.

"I told you. I know more than necessary about the birds and the bees, thanks to my mother. She was very informative."

"Evie, stop. I said that I do not want to know. Let's just leave it at that and move on to the more obvious issue, where are we going to live?"

"Well, here, obviously."

Brad's face screwed up as he looked at me and gestured.

"You just said that you were done with this town. We're staying now?"

I nodded, mouth stuffed to the brim with the sandwich. I was hungry and wolfing it down fast.

"Where exactly will we be sleeping, Evelyn? You demolished the entire house."

"Not all of it. The basement is still intact."

"And how would you protect yourself from the vampires that want you dead or the demon that is desperate to harness your powers?"

I swallowed the last of my food, wiping my mouth on a napkin.

"To be fair, walls and doors do not stop a demon. It's true that the vampires have physical limitations, but I'm sure if they were determined, they'd get into any place they wanted."

Anzide nodded, much to Brad's frustration. He shook his head and returned to making his sandwich.

"You know, I'm not done with this town."

Brad looked up from his lunch, curiously waiting. Anzide was merely smiling as if he knew me better than I knew myself. That was highly likely.

"Kannon said to me that Drakkus had taken out his own followers,"

He also said that Drakkus would try all angles to get to me, like the guy who was supposedly instantly taken by me. I was a fool, and I fell for it.

"He said that he's seen it. How can I have the rule of this town taken from me for that reason when Drakkus does it all the time?"

"You can't. They killed Niko, yet they fail to remember that."

"Did either of you see them kill Niko?"

We both shook our heads.

"Then, without proof that they've actually killed their own, you've got nothing. You cannot rely on what Kannon has said. Drakkus will argue that Kannon would have said anything to ensure you believed he was on your side."

"Niko was stabbed with a sword that had holy water on it from the Vatican. Who would go to that kind of effort?"

"Someone who wanted to ensure his death was painful. Niko's death is not the path that you're looking for. I can see where you're going, Evelyn. I know what you want, but there will be a different angle."

Brad leaned back, listening to us, silently observing. He smiled at me, earning a frown.

"What?"

"Didn't I say that Drakkus would use your hormones against you?"

"You did. Just like Niko said not to trust anyone."

"Including your own," Anzide mumbled. "It's a sad world, but that's how it is. Some you can trust, and some you can't. You'll never know until it's too late."

After finishing the meal, we began searching through the rubble and cleaning the debris so that we could find as much of our stuff as possible. While we did that, I kept an eye on the surroundings. I didn't want to say anything, but that odd feeling that I got when I unleashed my anger, it hadn't settled. It was like I could feel more than I should, like a connection to something had been created. I don't know what, but I do know that it moved.

Brad had left about five minutes ago to fetch gloves and work boots in case of nails sticking out. It didn't matter that a little nail wouldn't do any damage to us. He said he didn't want to invite the vampires back with the scent of our blood.

The sun filtered in and out of the clouds, making it difficult to search for our things. Anzide was making short work of the planks of wood. Picking them up and tossing them over his head. They'd hit a pile he'd been stacking at the far end of the property. It made me wonder what the neighbors thought. I soon learned he'd created a veil over the property to hide it from them.

"Are you still Nephilim?"

Anzide stopped and looked at me.

"Yes. Just like you're still a mixed bag of goodies."

I huffed with amusement.

"Cute, but not what I meant. Are they going to call you for an assignment or something?"

"No, I've been cut from their world. The price that I pay for my deeds. The price that I pay for loving an Eternal."

I stared with disbelief. Anzide frowned for a moment, slight and short, until he realized what he'd said.

"I don't regret it. Please don't misinterpret what I said."

"So, you don't love me, then?"

He paused, then shrugged.

"I do not fully understand the concept of it, but it came to me after I accepted responsibility for what we did. It was like the wind whispered that the Nephilim should not love another creature. I thought about it and considered the definition of it, *an intense feeling of deep affection.* It made sense, so I guess I accepted that even though I do not fully understand it. It would seem that I am in fact, in love."

Stepping closer, I smiled.

"You sure know how to answer a girl in the most confusing, long-winded way."

"I find it confusing. I find a lot of things confusing. That will change the longer I spend in this world."

"Did you go to another world when you weren't doing their dirty work?"

"It's not another world as such, more like a parallel plane. It's smaller, not much bigger than this town. If I wasn't cut from it, then we could have gone there."

"Sorry, I guess I should have behaved myself."

Anzide leaned forward, kissing me softly.

"Do not be sorry. There were two of us, and I was equally responsible. There are still many places in the portal that we can access."

"Right, so you should have kept it in your pants, then?"

Anzide wrapped his arms around my waist, lifted me off the ground, and twirled me around. I screamed and then giggled. I gripped his shoulders tight, praying he wouldn't lose his balance and fall over.

He stopped, looking up at me. I'd never seen that smile before.

"Do you want me to keep it in my pants?"

"Absolutely not."

Leaning down, I kissed Anzide, wrapping my arms around his neck. He pulled my legs around his waist, the hands sliding under my backside for support. I was wearing jeans, so there was no misbehavior for us. Not that we could, there was no house to give us privacy, and I didn't want Brad returning to find us in the middle of it.

"If you ever want to leave this place," he whispered against my lips. "I can take you and Brad anywhere. I might be cut from their world, but that does not mean I have changed. I know you though,"

My body slid down, and my feet returned to the ground but still wrapped up in Anzide's arms.

"You feel connected to the land. This is the home of your kin. You were destined to be a part of this land. And I know what else you feel connected to."

I tried to hide it, but I'm sure Anzide saw it.

"It moves," he whispered. "You were disconnected until today, but your powers grew, and the links snapped together. Do not be frightened of it, Evelyn. It moves to ensure it survives."

"Niko?" I whispered, tears begging to be released.

"Yes. You said that his body was missing. There were footprints but no drag marks. He did not die that day, but he was badly injured. Putting him in that cave was the best thing you and Brad could have done for him. It might be the only reason he survived."

Scrabbling out of his arms, I looked at the forest.

"I have to find him."

"For what purpose? To let him bask in the sun while helping clean up? Leave him to recuperate in the forest. He will emerge when he is ready."

"But the house,"

Anzide moved around me, blocking the view of the forest.

"He will not care. You and Brad are safe. That is all that a vampire like Niko cares about. He is the kind of vampire that we want in this world. To return him to power, you must let him recover enough to stand up to his enemies. Bringing a frail creature out into the world would just expose him to more danger. They do not know that he is alive. Leave it at that for now. As for the house, we will rebuild."

"That costs money, and the only builder in this town has been bought off by Drakkus."

"Then we shall find a builder from out of town."

"Perhaps I could be of assistance."

I gasped, turning around. Anzide stepped in front of me, blocking me from Harlwood's sight. His hand was already around mine, holding it tight.

"No. We do not need your help." Anzide said firmly. "It was kind of you to offer, but it is unnecessary."

Harlwood scoffed mockingly.

"Come now, we can set aside the pleasantries and get down to the nitty-gritty. I came here because I wanted to lay myself bare, to show the true leader of the vampires in this town that I am on her side, not theirs. They are a mockery of the world of vampires, and I have put up with it because I had little choice. I was here when the Corbin line was in rule. I was the one that suffered the most when he disappeared."

"I find that hard to believe. The Fleming clan has always been voracious in their feeding habits."

"True, but they found themselves a demon of their own, lured it in with an offer the demon could not refuse, and since that day, the demon has fed on everything they gave. I have had nothing but the pitiful offerings of the townsfolk who seem to have extraordinarily long lives. What I offer is not a deal that would have either party suffer or gain needlessly. You can take it or leave it. I will carry on regardless."

Looking around Anzide, I glanced up at Harlwood. He smiled at me, fiendish yet so very welcoming.

"What do you want?"

"To be the only demon in this town. In order to get this, I have to remove the other demon, but they will not leave unless they are no longer being fed by the Fleming clan. As the original demon resident of this town,

I have the final say as to whether this demon stays or leaves, which they will most definitely be leaving. With the Fleming clan gone, the demon will have nothing. All I ask is that I have your assurances that if the demon comes and asks to be your soul feeder, you refuse. If you promise me that, I will remove your vampire enemies as you demand. In return, I will keep the obscuris veil over this town, and the vampires that remain will be able to feed without repercussion. What do you say, Evelyn? Do we have an agreement?"

CHAPTER 37

Harlwood granted us time to consider the offer and to discuss it with Brad when he returned. He offered to return tomorrow at the same time, giving us a full twenty-four hours to consider our options.

While we waited, Anzide and I continued to clean the debris and set aside the possessions that were still in good order. Everything else was put in the pile that was destined to be trash.

Hearing the familiar sound of Brad's car, I strolled over to see the madness he was dragging behind it.

"He's bought a caravan. Is he crazy?"

"I'd say thinking outside the box is closer. The two of you have to sleep somewhere tonight."

We waited next to the driveway as Brad struggled to get the car up the hill.

"That thing is going to give out at any second."

"It certainly sounds like it is struggling."

Brad had a gleaming smile on his face as he passed us, continuing to the back of the property where there was plenty of space. There was also shade to cover it so the caravan didn't get too hot during the day.

Getting out of the car, he gestured with a wide smile.

"Look, one problem solved."

"You're a legend, Bradley. How much did this cost you?"

"Nothing," he said with far too much enthusiasm. "I was in the hardware, and they were looking at me like I had lost the plot, so I said that the house was demolished and we were starting the clean-up. I told them it was a gas explosion. I think they bought it, so if anyone says anything, go with that, okay?"

"Sure."

"Anyway, sitting at the end of the counter was Henry Greene. Have you met him yet?"

I shook my head. I hadn't bothered to delve into this town or the people that live here. Too busy trying to avoid the paranormal creatures in this place. Brad unhitched the caravan, then pulled some bricks out and placed them behind the wheels.

"Nice guy. Said he had a caravan that he'd be happy to give to us, no money needed so long as when we're done with it, we pass on the same charity to the next person."

Brad stabilized the caravan with metal supports, giving the caravan gentle pushes as if he thought that would help. This was a case of the blind leading the blind.

We were useless. I'd never even been inside a caravan.

"I figured that was easily done, so here we are. I know it's not enough to stop the vampires or the demon, but it's a start."

"About that," I murmured.

Opening the door to the caravan, I was hit with a musty wave of air that made me cough.

"We need to discuss it, but damn, maybe air the place out first."

"It was sitting in his shed for a while. I brought cleaning stuff as well."

"Great, more things to do."

I leaned against the kitchen counter. Brad sat at the narrow dining table.

"Harlwood turned up."

Brad glanced at Anzide, who was leaning against the door frame, watching the outside world.

"There's another demon in this town, and apparently, he wants it gone. Drakkus is feeding the demon, so he is missing out on all the souls that die because of the vampires."

"That must make him pretty hungry."

"And desperate," Anzide murmured. "Which is not a

good thing, if you're wondering."

"I figured that. Okay, so what's he offering?"

"'To remove vampires as I demand, and if this demon comes to us and asks to be our soul feeder, we have to refuse. In return, he will keep the veil over the town, which is why no one sees what's really going on, right?"

Anzide looked at me and nodded.

"An obscuris veil is quite common and has no side effects, no issues. It's a plain and boring spell that is chanted once and forgotten about. He can remove it at any time and reinstate it whenever he pleases. The only purpose it has is to keep those within the boundaries of the veil oblivious to everything. They go about their lives with happiness and are completely unaware of the darker side of this life. This town has had a veil over it for a very long time. You saw it, didn't you? That day when we first met, I heard your words that you noticed the peculiarities. You saw it because you were new to the town, and of course, you are immortals, so it doesn't affect you."

"So, what's your opinion on this? Should she accept it?"

Anzide shrugged as he moved to the table, sitting opposite Brad.

"At surface level, his offer is genuine and without complication. You could try to go on your own and take down Drakkus and all those vampires that are following him, but it is a dangerous path that neither of you are equipped for. You might be a vampire and a shapeshifter, but the shell of this body is human. You were raised as a human, and you know nothing of your true ability. As for Evelyn, we only need to look out the door to see the pros and cons of her life. Yes, she is powerful, but she has no control or knowledge."

The wind caught the lace curtain, flicking it up for a brief moment. Neither Brad nor Anzide noticed it. When I looked out the dirty glass, I saw a figure. The shadow turned into the forest, and my heart leaped with happiness. Niko was out there. He was alive.

"Where's the catch here?"

I snapped back to the conversation.

"He's a demon. They are not trustworthy, but they do offer things that are honest and good. They are always out to make their own lives better, so don't think that he's doing you any favors. This is purely for his benefit."

"But if Drakkus and his followers are gone?"

"Then it serves a worthy purpose for Evelyn. You need to figure out who is on his side and who is scared of Drakkus and complying to save their own lives. I suspect that you will have very little in the way of followers when this is over."

"I think that I'll have none."

Anzide shook his head.

"That won't serve Harlwood. If he's offered to specifically remove your enemies, then he knows that there are some who do not fall into this category. He doesn't want all the vampires dead. He just wants the trash to be taken out."

With a heavy sigh, I dumped myself onto the seat next to Anzide, looking through the lace to the forest.

"Niko was out there," I said softly.

"What?"

Brad frowned at me, then turned to the window, pulling the lace back.

"He's dead, right?"

"No," Anzide answered. "Badly wounded, recovering slowly. Give him time, leave him in peace, and keep his presence unknown. Niko will return at the time he feels is right and not a moment before."

Anzide and I continued to scour the mess for anything worth salvaging while Brad cleaned and set up the caravan. There was a shed at the end of the driveway that Brad had said several times that he was going to find the key and open it. He wanted somewhere to store the car during bad weather. Now, he was going to use the bolt cutters to open the padlock.

That was next on his list. For now, he was ensuring the caravan was ready for us tonight.

Brad would constantly flip on his thoughts, making my anxiety about staying here rise considerably. He wanted to keep me safe but knew that Anzide would be rather helpful in that respect. He didn't want me to face any form of confrontation, even though he knew that I'd scraped through reasonably well so far.

And he didn't want me to agree to anything with Harlwood but stated that it was the best option we had at the moment. While Anzide was good for protection, he was of no help regarding the vampire threat. That is, of course, aside from the information which he happened to be full of.

When Brad called us in for the night, I picked up the box of stuff that was getting locked in the shed. Keepsakes that I knew Niko would want. The important stuff, the things that might be necessary, they were stuffed into my bag, which I could grab at any moment if need be.

Looking at the forest, I wondered if he was out there.

"They won't come here tonight," Anzide murmured. "And even if they are that brazen, it won't do them any good. Harlwood's put a temporary protection over the property. I suspect it's a sweetener to make you more compliant, but it's useful nonetheless."

Anzide turned, gripping my shoulders.

"Rest easy tonight."

I paused, sadness finding me quickly as the vision of the forest framed Anzide.

"I want to talk to Niko."

"That's perfectly fair, Evelyn, but we don't know where exactly he is. It's a large forest, and he's hiding. You could go out there and search, but then you're vulnerable to whatever else is out there. He could come here, but then he is exposed. For his safety and yours, be patient. You will be reunited with him again."

"I will?"

As I looked up at Anzide, he nodded, carefully wiping the tears away.

Together, we returned to the caravan that was slightly homelier than when it first arrived. It was old and dated, but it was better than some of the motels we'd stayed in while traveling. That was part of the reason that I had changed my mind about leaving Hades. The house was reasonable, it was structurally sound, and it was not infested with anything.

Well, that was not entirely true, but the point was that I was settled, and there wasn't a single roach or rat to be found. Vampire, yeah, we had one of those, but he was okay.

As for the house, it used to be solid. Now, it was flat.

Brad had bought new linen and washed it at the laundromat after figuring out what we needed. Life was going to be rough for a few days, but I was ready for it. I was not going to complain. Technically, this was my fault. No. It was completely my fault. I had no control over the powers, they had come in fast and heavy, and as a result, the worst had happened.

We were alive. That's all that mattered. We will rebuild, and we will see another day. There were bigger issues that had to be dealt with, issues that needed answers.

CHAPTER 38

When I was done, I sat back, feeling full and happy. My gaze lingered out to the forest. The fog had settled in for the night.

"Do you think he's warm enough?"

"Knowing Niko, he will find a house to invade, feed on the owner, and rest well for the daylight hours. You worry needlessly."

"I care," I muttered curtly.

Brad sighed heavily, giving me the evil glare.

"And I don't? That's low, Evie. If he wanted to be warm, he would have returned to the house. There is a reason that he stayed out there, and you damned well know it. Don't get all snarky about it."

"What if we're wrong?" I whispered. "What if he was sleeping in the attic?"

He was in the middle of wiping the side of the bowl with bread. Brad stopped and looked out the window.

"I haven't heard the mouse in a long time, Evie."

"I'll go," Anzide said as he got up from the table. "Don't unlock the door. I don't need you to open it for me, so don't be fooled."

"You said that there were protections over the property."

"That doesn't mean the demon won't come here anyway. Stay put."

Anzide faded out of the caravan, leaving me alone with Brad. It felt like it had been a really long time since it had just been the two of us. No vampires or Nephilim. No judgmental eyes from the world around us. Brad was always given the stink eye from people who thought he was a pervert chasing a young girl. He'd even had the cops called on him.

Brad was mortified and, since that horrid day, carried the paperwork everywhere with him. It was sad that he had to prove he was related to me. We looked like each other. Seriously, we were so clearly related. I don't know how anyone thought he'd do something like that.

"Tomorrow, I'll organize a builder to come out and quote."

"You are going to have a heart attack. Should I prewarn the hospital now or wait until it happens?"

"You're so funny, Evelyn. What I was aiming for was someone who was possibly on the verge of retirement. I can do the work under his instruction."

I laughed.

"Oh my god, Bradley. When did you lose the plot?"

"At least I'm trying."

I stopped, murmuring my apology.

"Well, smarty-pants, you and lover boy can help. Don't think you're sitting around all day doing nothing."

"I thought that I had schoolwork."

"Late afternoon and night will be more than sufficient. The sooner that house is rebuilt, the happier I will be."

"I've been thinking about what Harlwood offered."

"Me too."

We looked at each other. Brad's eyes darted across the table as he took a deep breath in.

"I don't know, but it seems like a reasonable trade. We can deal with Drakkus and the unwanted vampires, return our family to rule, and we know exactly where the demon is. I didn't know there was another demon in this town, did you?"

I shook my head.

"What about you? What do you think about his offer?"

Before I could answer Brad, Anzide's figure slowly started to form next to the table. His face was grim.

"I couldn't find him. I'm sorry."

I nodded and got up from the table. The hour was late, and tomorrow was going to be a long day. After getting ready for bed, I climbed onto the bunk. Anzide lay on the mattress, leaning on one hand as he looked down at me.

"He will come out when he's ready," Anzide whispered.

"It's not that. I worry that he'll be upset about the house. We've had it for like five minutes, and look at what happened."

Anzide sighed, pulling me closer. Brad began shutting everything down for the night. Five seconds after his head hit the pillow, he was out of it. Brad was making this odd hissing sound that was close to a snore. Whenever he put in a lot of work and was exhausted, he'd be like this.

Anzide and I were nestled into the top bunk. Brad was below. The mattress for the larger bed was outside. In its place were all the things that we didn't want to leave outside.

"We discussed this. He won't care."

"But I care."

"There's nothing that you can do to alter the past. All you can do is ensure that it won't happen again."

Turning to face Anzide, I looked up in the darkness and then settled against his body.

"Can you teach me?"

"I can guide you to the path, but most of this will be learned as you go. The Eternals are not known to write things down or have any form of an education system."

"Who taught you?"

"My parents."

His tone was heavy, no doubt figuring that it wasn't the most ideal answer.

"And they cannot help you either. They have been redeemed."

Sitting up, I felt a sickening dread inside of me.

"Will you be redeemed?"

Anzide chuckled softly.

"You sound as if you want my soul to be damned forever."

"No,"

"But?"

I sighed. My body slumped with defeat.

"You'll leave."

"I know it's terrible, isn't it?"

That was one way of putting it.

"You will be happy to know that because of our efforts, I have been banished, which means that I cannot be redeemed and will walk this earth until there is nothing left of it. You're stuck with me now."

"Well, yay for that," Brad grumped. "If you two are going to spend all night talking, maybe you should do it outside."

Murmuring our apology, Anzide and I settled back into our embrace.

I don't know how long it took for me to fall asleep or when Anzide left the bed, but when I woke in the morning, I was alone.

The metal door was open, but the screen was shut. I could see Brad trying to pull the awning out, and I assumed Anzide was with him out of sight.

Flicking back the sheets, I climbed down to the floor and walked to the door. Anzide was not here, and that's why Brad was struggling.

"Hey, you're up. Come out and give me a hand, please."

"Sure. Just let me get dressed first."

Flicking on my jeans, sneakers, and a shirt, I ventured outside to help Brad untangle himself from the mess he'd made. Pulling the shade free, I clipped it to the pole. Brad had an eager smile on his face, gesturing to the table and chairs.

"Alfresco dining."

"When the bugs aren't biting?"

"Absolutely."

"Where's Anzide?"

Brad flicked his head at the forest, giving me an uneasy smile.

"He's not hopeful but thought it was worth a shot."

"The connection feels thin. Maybe Niko's at the far end of the forest."

"Evie?"

Brad and I looked at each other. The sound of Kannon's voice sent a shiver up my spine.

"You don't have to talk to him," Brad whispered.

"I know, but maybe if I do, there's a chance of altering the path ahead of us."

"Or you could make it worse."

Shrugging, I moved to the end of the caravan and saw Kannon at the fence line in the forest. He looked like his normal self, not the monster he was yesterday.

"Hey," I said, trying not to seem awkward.

"Uh, hey. I just wanted to talk about yesterday, you know, with Drakkus."

"Right," I said softly. "The part where he tried to take away my leadership without authority or the part where you and your family stabbed me in the back?"

He rolled his eyes, looking to the side.

"It's not like that."

"Then what is it like?"

Kannon was struggling, and I could see this for what it really was. Another attempt to make me leave. Drakkus must be getting desperate. Either that or annoyed.

"Let me see if I can figure it out. Your family has always tried to resist joining his clan, holding out with the belief that you can go unnoticed by him if you keep your heads down. I stroll into town, and you think you've got a shot at taking him down, but then you realize that it wasn't working out as your family wanted, and worse than that, because you've associated with me, Drakkus has taken notice. You're in trouble. You know that it's one or the other. Either stand beside him or me. Looking at each of us, you weigh up the options and figure that he's the safer choice because, clearly, I am a lost cause. I don't know anything about being a vampire, technically not one anyway, and my following is extremely limited."

Behind Kannon in the near distance, Anzide was watching. He remained silent and where he was, but I knew that if Kannon tried anything, he'd regret it. The doom on Anzide's face was enough to make me worried about what he'd do.

"But Drakkus, on the other hand, he's got the experience. He's got the backing of a large following. He is this town, right? So, you and your family picked your side. You cut yourself a deal and sold me out to Drakkus by telling him what happened. Did you tell the truth,

Kannon? Did you tell him it was an accident, or did you oversell it to make me look like the bad guy? I asked you for help. You said that your father dealt with it, but you lied. I was there Kannon. I saw the body. Nothing has happened, and you are a liar."

"You didn't tell me you were an Eternal," he snapped.

"And how would I know that?"

"That *thing* that's pining after you should have known. He would have known. He wanted me to die."

Kannon snorted a soft laugh, folding his arms.

"But he got what he wanted. Clearly, I was nothing to you."

"You were everything to me, Kannon. You were the friend that I wanted and needed, but you betrayed me. I trusted you. After everything that you did to help Brad and me, I never thought that what you did yesterday was possible. It just opened my eyes. Now that I know that you didn't hide the body, I realize that you have planned this for a long time. You were playing me right from the beginning. Brad was right, Drakkus used my hormones against me, and I fell for it. Well done, Kannon. I hope you're proud of yourself."

I turned and walked away before he could see the tears. It sucked to be caught up like this, but that's how it was. I'd been warned. I didn't pay attention. It was a hard lesson to learn, but I had to go through it. With a little luck, I'd remember this the next time someone like Kannon entered my life. As for my emotions, I just had to have my moment of sadness and then move on. Hopefully, it will make me stronger, but I doubt it will.

CHAPTER 39

Brad was waiting with a hug, saying nothing but just holding me until I was ready to let go. It took about a minute before I pulled away, wiped the tears, and gave him a sad smile.

"Love hurts, regardless of what the relationship was like."

"I think it hurts more that you were right."

"Yeah, maybe the world's about to end or something."

We entered the caravan. I sat at the table while Brad started making breakfast. Outside, I could see Kannon walking away, Anzide watching from his hidden spot in the forest.

"Do you think that was another attempt to make us leave?"

"I don't know,"

I felt defeated, and the day had barely started. It wasn't even seven in the morning, and I'd had a fight with my ex-boyfriend, now stressing over my life here.

Brad put the tray on the table and started pulling the crockery out. I was loading things, trying to keep myself occupied rather than thinking about Kannon. It was not working, not when I could see Anzide walking toward the fence line, watching Kannon.

"I got the feeling that it was the underlying intention for coming here,"

"But you think he wanted to apologize as well?"

I nodded.

"Then why didn't you let him?"

Brad turned when he got no response. I was frowning heavily at him.

"Humor me and answer the question."

"Because he lied to me about Andross's body. He used it against me and sold me out to Drakkus like I needed to have him angrier at me."

"And you're sure it was him and not Eddios?"

It felt like my heart fell into my stomach.

"Brad," I groaned.

He shrugged and sat at the table in front of me.

"He calls his father and tells him the details. Daddy says, sure, son. Son thinks it's done until trouble hits, and Daddy says that we're doing the unthinkable and we're making sure that as a group, we survive. What is one life against how many they have in their group? Eddios might have had a heart and said we'll give you this information if you agree to let Evelyn and Brad leave the town unharmed. We'll join the clan. We'll behave ourselves, but we have our requirements. As a show of good faith, they hand their son over to be the second in charge to the leader. Maybe that was all they offered. Maybe the rest of it was the sweetener."

"I hate it when you do this," I muttered, getting up from the table.

Rushing through the door, I made my way to the fence where Anzide was still watching Kannon.

"What's wrong?"

"I need a little fact-checking to be done."

"You want the boy to return?"

"If you don't mind."

Anzide disappeared and reappeared in front of Kannon, who stumbled back when Anzide towered over him. Something was said. Kannon turned to look at me, then back to Anzide. All the while, I waited, wringing my fingers with the hope that I'd made this out to be more than it was. Brad might be right. He had a knack for this kind of stuff.

Kannon turned and began to walk back, looking unimpressed. Anzide was no better, walking behind him like a mountain of doom that was ready to explode.

"What now?" Kannon grumped.

"Did you call your father to collect the body?"

He nodded grimly.

"Did he tell you that it had been dealt with?"

Kannon said nothing. Anzide poked him in the back. With a frown that he shot over his shoulder, Kannon turned back to me.

"He did."

"Do you feel betrayed that it didn't happen?"

Angrily, he wiped a tear, nodding in the process.

"Would you like to tell me what's going on, or are you worried about what might happen if you do?"

"You have to leave, but I don't want you to. You have to hand over the rule to him, but you can't, and you shouldn't. He tried to fill my head with all these thoughts about you being an Eternal and how you would have killed me if we progressed and that you should have told me. He said that the Nephilim should have told you what you were, and the only reason he didn't was because he wanted me dead."

Anzide tilted his head, giving me a look of agreement. I frowned at him, and Anzide shrugged as if I should have expected it.

"I had to take Andross's place as payment for not telling him when it happened. We all had to join the clan without complaint and show unwavering loyalty to buy our lives. I resisted him last night. Today, he said I had to walk here and ensure you got the message. He told me the path I had to take. It was in full sun."

I looked down at Kannon's hands. They'd taken the damage when he held them up to hide his face.

"I thought vampires could walk in the sun."

"There are variables. The older the vampire, the greater the power. I'm young, and my skin is weaker than someone like Niko's if that's what you're talking about."

I nodded.

"Drakkus wants a new lover," Kannon whispered.

Another tear followed.

"And your parents think that this is acceptable?" I snapped.

"It's that or die."

Kannon looked up at me. I could see the pain and suffering. How long could he resist before it turned ugly? It was bad enough that he was punished for refusing to entertain Drakkus. If things kept going, it would become something horrible. I could not live with myself knowing that it was going on, and I could have been the one to end it.

"If I leave, will he let you and your family go?"

Anzide stepped forward, ready to say something. I held up my hand, stopping him.

"I want to know the truth, Anzide. I need to know that everything will be okay when Kannon returns."

Anzide was giving me a contemptuous glare as he shook his head. His lips were pressed tight, and his brow was furrowed deep.

"Kannon helped Brad and me claim ownership of this property. He interpreted my mother's autopsy report and confirmed that she was murdered by a vampire. I owe him something, at least."

He was still not impressed.

"But most of all, he was a friend. When I needed it, he was there for me. He stood up to Audrey, he protected me, and he guided me. This has fallen because of Drakkus, so I need to know if you will be safe. Will he release you?"

"He said he will, but Drakkus is not honest. Don't worry about me, Evie. Just be safe. The only way that you will be safe from Drakkus is if you leave."

Kannon stepped back, giving me a sad smile.

"We had fun. It was only a few days, but I'll always remember them. Run Evie. Run before he comes for you, too."

I watched Kannon walk away. He did not turn back and just kept walking. His shoulders were slung low, and his hands were in his pockets.

There was an unmistakable sadness in him that I knew was not a lie. I thought that I could pick a lie, but he'd proved otherwise. Hopefully, I could return to the path of knowing when Kannon was telling me the truth.

I wanted a friendship with him. He was a good person despite the failings of his family. I'm sure he felt hurt and annoyed at his father's actions.

Anzide moved through the fence, watching the sad figure.

"Well, that was a mighty fine performance."

"You think it was another lie?

"He knows I cannot check what is happening in Drakkus's house."

Well, so much for improving my lie detection skills.

Curiously, I looked at Anzide.

"You can't?"

He shook his head, urging me to move back to the caravan. I was hungry, and I could smell the toast that Brad was burning. Hopefully, it won't be black, maybe at that point where it was nice and brown. The butter always melted perfectly when the toast was hot, and the taste of it was divine. My mouth watered at the thought of having toast with butter dripping everywhere.

"No, he must have the demon living in the house."

Damn Anzide for interrupting my food fantasy.

"I tried to get in, but I could feel the demon's presence, which means it's more than the likes of what Harlwood has done here. This is a protection, which means he put it in place and then walked away. Only certain people can pass through it, and it will fade with time. If the demon lives onsite, it is a permanent cover. Anyone can enter the property, but the second they do, the demon knows about it. A permanent cover radiates from the property. I could feel it on the street."

"So, anything is possible?"

"It is."

Brad was fussing over the table, setting everything out in preparation for an alfresco breakfast with the flies. He was shooing them away, making me wonder why he was bothering with it at all.

"We can eat inside if you want. I don't mind."

"I was kind of looking forward to it."

"I know, but until you get screens up, it's kind of pointless."

He shrugged, putting a kitchen towel over the hot toast. Once I'd sat down and picked off the best looking piece of toast, I set out to put far too much butter on it and live out that wild fantasy I'd just had.

As I ate the toast, I thought about what Kannon had said. Whether it was the truth or a lie, Drakkus was still a problem that needed to be dealt with. He wanted us gone, to walk away from this place and the leadership.

I will not do that. Not to Niko. I owed him a lot, and without the house to return to, he could end up in the forest for a long time. He might move on, but I had serious doubts about that. I believe he felt bound to this town and the memory of what he once had when life was perfect.

For him, I had to do the right thing. I had to be

strong and do all I could to ensure that Hades was Corbin territory. That meant that I had to figure out what to do about Drakkus.

Finishing my breakfast, I decided that I would consult someone who had been in this town for as long as Niko had. If there was a chance at understanding what my great-grandfather would want without actually asking him, it might be done with one of the town's oldest residents.

Grabbing the keys, I pulled on my jacket, grabbed my purse, and pushed through the screen door.

"Sorry about the mess. I'll clean up after lunch, okay?"

"Wait. Where are you going?"

"To town. I won't be long."

Walking to the car, I ignored Brad yelling at me that I was not licensed to drive by myself. He gave up by the time I got to the driveway.

"What are you doing?" Anzide said in a dry tone.

"Checking on a few things."

"You can't enter his property."

"Drakkus? I figured that. Besides, I don't know where he lives."

"So then, where are you going?"

"You'll see soon enough."

Within a few minutes of my extremely sketchy driving, I pulled up outside a familiar but much-hated building. Kids laughed and chatted as they made their way into the school. In the distance, I could see the figures of the girls that I loathed.

Taking a deep breath, I got out of the car and stalked into the building before Audrey reached me.

"This is it? You're taking the deal?"

"I want to check on a few things."

"You say that, yet you walk into the demon's domain with a defiance that clearly says you've got a bug up your ass."

I raised an eyebrow at Anzide.

"Bug up my ass?"

"Brad mentioned it, and when questioned, he offered the meaning."

"Right," I drawled out.

Jane looked up as the door swung open, cheerily smiling, until she realized I wasn't stopping.

"Miss Newton!" she called out. "You can't just barge in here without an appointment."

"Sure, I can. Where's Harlwood?"

"Behind you."

I spun around to see the principal standing behind me, just like he said. The demonic smile was full and eager for the next few minutes.

Lifting his hand, Harlwood flicked open the door. Gently, it swung back as if he had complete control over it.

"Come, Miss Newton. Let's discuss how we're going to deal with our problems."

Taking a deep breath, I walked into the demon's office. Would I make a deal? I don't know, but if it meant that I could defeat Drakkus, then I would consider it. If it would be my demise, I guess only time would tell on that one.

CHAPTER 40

I'd walked into an office that belonged to a demon. It was a bold move but not overly unexpected. Technically, I was still a student at this school.

"Please, take a seat." Principal Harlwood said, gesturing to the chairs.

He looked at Anzide, offering a slightly raised eyebrow.

"I assume that your companion is here for guidance and to ensure that I won't harm you."

I said nothing, just giving him a dumbfounded look.

"It's alright, Miss Newton. I am not offended. After all, I am a demon, and you are,"

He smiled, offering that devilishly charming smile.

"Well, you know what you are."

Harlwood sat down, stretching in his seat as it tilted back.

"I can assure you that my interests for the future require you to be alive, so I am *very* inclined to keep you in the best shape possible."

"Is that why you put the protection over my property last night?"

"Those horrid creatures," Harlwood snarled, leaning forward onto the desk. "They would have slaughtered you and your uncle while you slept. The protection that I have placed over the two of you is because I cannot stand that vile thing leading that coven. He is a slimy little pest, and he preys on the students of this school. They should not be fed on nor dragged into that world at such a tender age."

Harlwood paused, calming himself down. When he smiled again, I knew he'd returned to mister charming rather than the monster that had just lashed out.

"Vampires are supposedly well-behaved. They are refined. They are dutiful. Your great-grandfather was an incredibly good man, Miss Newton. I had the pleasure of knowing him for many years, and if I'd known where he was, I would have flattened that house to remove him from it. That was a crime in itself, one that you must be aware of if you are going to approach this situation in the most legal way possible."

"Legal?" I whispered.

The principal nodded firmly, his gaze pinned on me.

"You are the leader. You should do things correctly. Do not base your leadership on anything you have seen from that monster Drakkus. He is not someone that you should learn from. If you want, you should keep in your mind, *what would Niko do?* That is the best guide for you because Niko Corbin was, in all respects, the kind of vampire that the old world would have approved of. If they come here and see this mess, they will wipe out all vampires, and that includes any who are only partially vampires. You, my dear Eternal, won't be affected, but your uncle will be. For his sake, you must clean up this town before the vampires in Europe get wind of what is happening here."

I glanced at Anzide. He gave me a grim nod.

"It's true. They're a bunch of moralistic jerks."

"Great," I sighed. "So, I clean up the town of vampires who don't respect me because I'm not a full vampire."

"They are scared of him. They have seen what he has done to those who question his authority. It is not just Niko that suffered his wrath. There are many who have disappeared over the years. I know where they are because I can detect that. Ashes, if you're wondering. Drakkus has a furnace in a warehouse at the edge of town. He bought the cop off, ensuring he's too busy handing out fines to the knitting brigade for overstaying the parking limits. Drakkus just coasts on by, and that moron pretends that he sees nothing. The bodies are transported out to this place, and then they're never found."

I frowned at the principal.

"Knitting brigade?"

He rolled his eyes, leaning back into the seat.

"This is the drama of my life, Miss Newton. My neighbor is one of them. They're a bunch of old women who congregate in the town hall for a knitting circle. They donate their knitting to the preemie ward at Clarkson Hospital. She whined no end because she'd been in town and parked her car for two hours and five minutes. That stuffed turkey gave her a ticket because she was there for five minutes too long. Can you imagine that? These women take time out of their lives, spend their own money to make tiny beanies for those babies, and that asshole strolls down Main Street every time they're in the building and waits."

A demon that has a heart? It seemed impossible, but there it was.

Harlwood pushed a notepad and pen over the desk.

"Please write what you would like, and I will do the same."

"Don't you worry that someone will hear us?"

"No. I have protections over the room and the building so that Drakkus cannot intercept any calls."

"Is that why the phones never work?"

"It's why the cell towers are always intermittent, yes."

Pulling the notepad off the desk, I rolled my eyes.

"Okay. When he's gone, and I'm the undisputed

leader, you won't need to worry about that. I have better things to do with my days than listening to people on the phone."

"Duly noted."

Looking at the blank piece of paper, I thought about what I wanted for this town. It was simple. I wanted the Corbin line to return to the proper rule of the vampires in this town.

Harlwood held up his notebook.

To be the only demon in Hades.

I showed him my notebook, and the demon nodded.

"Right. Now we have to figure out how we are going to achieve our goal, what we can offer each other, and what we can give in return."

To achieve this, I had to remove Drakkus, and that was basically it. Offering something to Harlwood was the tricky part. Then I remembered that he wants to be the only demon in this town and what he mentioned last night. So, I wrote down that if a demon asks to be the soul feeder for the Corbin clan, I will refuse them to ensure that Harlwood was our only soul feeder. In return for this offer, I wanted Drakkus and the four vampires dead. There were only four out of the five remaining. I'd already killed Andross. They were the vampires that taunted Niko in the forest. They were the ones that killed him.

I could do this for myself, but I had no idea how I'd killed Andross. It was an accident, and I don't want to risk facing off against these vampires and not knowing what to do.

When I was done, I waited for Harlwood. He held out his hand and took the notebook, offering his own for me to read.

I want to be the only demon in Hades. To get this, I will remove the other demon. To ensure that this demon does not approach the true vampire leader of this town and request to be the soul feeder for her clan, I will offer my services and remove the vampires of her choosing. This will benefit me because once the self-appointed vampire leader, Drakkus Fleming is dead, the demon will not have a clan to be attached to.

"Do you know who these other four vampires are?"

I shook my head.

"I cannot assume, Evelyn. I need names or pictures. Other than that, your offer and request are acceptable. What about mine?"

Anzide looked up from the notepad, giving me a soft smile.

"Plain and simple, exactly what this town needs. No Drakkus and only one demon."

"You will note that I have written the vampires of your choosing. I will remove any vampire that you desire, in addition to the ones that you've got rattling around in your head. Just don't go too nuts, okay?"

"Sure,"

"Okay. We'll pick this up again when you've got

names or pictures, yeah?"

"Of course."

Harlwood followed us to the main door. As I turned to say goodbye, I noted that Jane, the receptionist was not at her desk.

"Don't take too long. The protection around you and Brad will remain for as long as I want, but that doesn't mean Drakkus or his goons won't approach you. The sooner we deal with this, the better our lives will become."

"Sure. Hey, I forgot to get my books. Will they still be in my locker?"

"Yes. You are still a student at this school and can return anytime you desire."

"Thanks, but it's a little difficult at the moment."

Harlwood nodded, stepping away from the door. I'm sure he didn't care but probably wanted the true vampire leader walking his corridors for the next few months.

Anzide and I made our way to my dark little hovel, the corridor that was home to my locker and no one else's. I was the new kid. I was given a locker in the new and yet to be used wing of the school. It was right next to the main corridor, but it was dark, and they never turned the lights on.

Fetching everything out of the locker, I shut the door and sighed.

"School was meant to be a way for me to be young

and free," I whispered.

"Having never been in school, I don't know what to say here, but I think you are not missing anything."

Hearing Audrey giggle, I felt my body tighten. She was a horrid human, desperate to do anything that pleased Drakkus.

Anzide put his hand on my shoulder.

"She cannot harm you."

"Audrey," Kannon called out.

Stepping back, I pulled into the darkness.

"Hide me."

"Are you certain?"

"Yes." I hissed.

Audrey stopped at the edge of the two corridors, looking back as Kannon approached. She was all smiles, which was not surprising.

Kannon pressed Audrey to my locker, kissing her hard. It was far more passionate than anything he'd ever given me.

"Bastard," I whispered.

Audrey pushed Kannon away, frowning at the darkness.

"Did you hear something?"

"No," he murmured against her neck.

The hand was moving under her skirt. Kannon had always given the impression that he despised Audrey, yet clearly, it was not the case.

She giggled, trying to push him away. As much as Audrey tried, she wasn't trying that hard. There was nothing new about this. It was obvious they knew each other's bodies and had been physical for a long time.

"Not here."

"I miss you. It's been too long."

"I know. It was killing me to see you with her. Tell me you still love me."

"I do, baby. She meant nothing."

"You say that, but you didn't seem too put out when you had to kiss her."

Kannon sighed as he stepped back, running his fingers through his hair.

"Look, I told you. Drakkus had made a lot of demands, and I had to follow them. He wanted me in that house. Keep Evelyn occupied while my parents searched. Even Jess had her role to play."

"But you didn't find anything."

"I know, and trust me, we're struggling because of it. Now, we'll never get back into that house."

"You will," Audrey said, stepping out from the locker.

She reached out for him, clutching the sleeve of his shirt.

"Your new plan will work. You've just got to push the friend angle. She's dumb enough to believe anything you tell her. Just keep making her think this was all your dad's idea."

"And not mine?"

Audrey bit her lip as she shook her head. A playful smile crossed her face.

"But you didn't mean any of it. You don't like her, right?"

"No, and no. Just what the boss wanted, you know how he is. It will all be over soon."

Audrey pouted, playing with his shirt buttons.

"How soon? Daddy wants answers. He said that you should be doing the right thing by me. We should be getting married."

"Jeez, Audrey, you're not even a vampire yet. Tell Ryan to hit the brakes."

"Well, give him something to work on then."

"I don't know. Drakkus said that once we've got the leadership, he'll put the deal on the table to be signed."

Audrey grinned, kissing Kannon more.

"You'll be the official second in charge?"

"And you'll be a vampire."

Anzide held me tight, his arm across my chest to ensure that I didn't lunge at the lying couple. I wouldn't.

The longer these two kept offering information, the longer I'd stay and listen.

I was of that opinion until Audrey's panties fell to her ankles. Giving Anzide a gentle tap on his arm, I waited for him to get us out of there. I didn't want to be around to watch.

CHAPTER 41

The view of the two liars fornicating against my old locker faded from my sight. Soon, the bright daylight consumed me, blinding me momentarily.

"You can be upset, angry, whatever you want, Evelyn."

We were leaning against the brick wall of the new wing.

The gardens were still pristine. It appeared as if no one had come into this area.

"I don't know what to feel, to be honest. It's a good thing that I know his true value now. I know that what he said this morning was utter rubbish. He doesn't care about me, and I don't think he ever has."

Well, I knew it. It was not a case of, *I think,* anymore. He'd said straight out that he didn't like me. There was a bonus to this little bit of nonsense, though, I had an idea for the future, and it was something that created a lot of amusement in my mind.

Lifting from the wall, I paced a few steps of the pathway while Anzide remained leaning against the wall, being a good listener.

"That though, that was something else. It sounds like it's been going on for a while. Everything makes perfect sense, though. Audrey gives me a hard time, and Kannon sticks up for me and becomes a solid friend. He pushes harder on it and forms a relationship. Niko warned me. He said not to trust anyone. I hate being this stupid."

"You are not stupid," Anzide grumbled.

"But I am, don't you see? I fell for it even though Niko warned me. Even Brad warned me. Jeez, even you said it. Repeatedly too. My hormones got in the way. They took over and controlled everything. Do you know what the worst part of all this is?"

Anzide warily shook his head.

"Kannon was pissed off that I am an Eternal, and if we'd had sex, he would be a dead vampire walking. That means he was prepared to go that far just to get Drakkus what he wants."

"I think you will find that he will benefit just as much as Drakkus will."

"That's hardly the point."

"Oh, I understand, Evelyn, and I wholeheartedly agree that Kannon is a monster. Aren't you glad you can see him for his true worth now?"

I nodded. Anzide held out his hands, pulling me

closer.

"I am glad that you were my first."

"Ditto," he murmured, leaning in for a kiss.

"You never misbehaved with other Nephilim?"

"It was repeatedly told Nephilim were chaste, we were celibate. We were not to engage in any physical activity. I have to say, though, I do think they're missing out."

I giggled, kissing Anzide. With our arms wrapped around each other, we had the moment of our love and affection. It made us stronger, and for me, it repaired the pain in my heart.

Stepping back, I was ready to leave this place, but Anzide held my hand tight.

"Are you sure you're okay?"

I shrugged, thinking about how I felt about this betrayal.

"I am angry. I am hurt. I feel lost. They're playing these horrible games, but they won't win. I've got an advantage up my sleeve now, and I am going to roll with it. I am going to be the bigger person here. I'm not going to be some crying brat that complains that everyone is against her. I will take these photos, I will hand them over, and I will keep the promise that I make to Harlwood. He will help me win this war, and when we're on the other side, I will continue to keep the worthy alliances because, at this moment, he's the best option that I've got. I will reward him for that, and I will ensure that he knows that I appreciate what he's done for me. Unlike other people who in time will learn that they messed with the wrong person."

Giving Anzide's hand a tug, I flicked my head to the footpath.

"Come on, Brad will be worried."

It didn't take long to return to the property. I don't know what to think or feel about it at the moment. The rubble was making life difficult.

"It was a life defining moment,"

Brad looked at me, and I shrugged. Anzide was regaling him with the corridor incident first. He thought it would be more reassuring for Brad if it came from an observer.

They were seated at the dining table, and I was leaning against the counter with my juice.

"And they did it right there in full view of anyone that would pass by?"

I nodded.

"Jeez," he hissed.

"No one passed by. I think everyone was in class."

"Still, a teacher could have walked by. What if they had visitors or parents?"

"I think you're focusing on the wrong part. Are you avoiding the part about Jess?"

Brad shook his head.

"I'm not upset. It was one night, and all she did was bite me. I don't care that she's not really interested. I'm more worried that they had access to the house all night long."

"They didn't find anything. I've got my battle plan for Kannon's new plan, so all you need to worry about is getting that house back up before Niko's ready to emerge."

"But how can I trust anyone now? What if I hire a builder, and they're allowed into this place. Then what? Free access to everything?"

"I can help with that. Find a builder, and I'll check his mind. It's a sketchy process and risky, but it will give you the reassurance that you're looking for."

Brad pulled out a scrap of paper, flattening it on the table. It was a list of names and numbers.

"I rang the first guy, and he said to stop in sometime today before five."

"We can come with you. Evelyn has to do a little reconnaissance work for our new demon friend."

His gaze lifted to me with a heavy frown.

"You're doing this? You're actually going to make a deal with a demon?"

"Agreement."

"Same thing, Evie. You've got the powers. Do a bit

of training with Anzide and kill the vampires yourself. You don't need the demons' help."

"She needs more than a bit. Sit down, and I'll explain the predicament you're in."

Anzide gestured to the seat opposite, next to Brad. I sat down, and Anzide pulled the clean glasses from the counter. They snapped to the table with the juice bottle and a jug of water.

He poured a glass of water and juice, setting the two glasses in front of us.

"We have Niko and Beatrice represented by the water and the fruit juice."

Anzide pulled an empty glass over and filled it with a mixture of water and juice. Then he set the other two glasses aside.

"Your mother, Victoria. The mixture works well, not as well as her parents individually, but still enough. She died young, never reaching her full potential, so we will never truly know how she would have coped."

Anzide tipped half the mixture into a fresh glass, then pushed the cup that represented my grandmother aside. His hand reached out to the counter, and the sugar flew across the small space.

"Edward Newton, your father," he said as he poured the sugar into the cup. "Human, not the same as the others, but still, it works. What you've got here is something that, by appearances, looks okay. Beneath the surface, it's right, but it's wrong. It works, but it doesn't."

There were no cups left. Anzide took the ones that represented Niko, Beatrice, and Victoria and tipped them down the sink, returning with empty glasses. One was set aside, which I knew was me. Two remained, and Anzide poured the odd mixture into each.

"This is you and Nancy. As I said, right but wrong. This mixture works just like your body does. The humanity that is represented by the sugar, it has dissolved. That happened over time, short in this instance, a little longer in your own life."

"The sugar will dissolve in me?"

"No, the humanity in you will dissolve. What remains is unknown. It could be a mixture of the two, or one could dominate over the other. You just have to wait for the sugar to dissolve, my friend."

"Right," Brad said with a heavy sigh.

Half of my mother's cup was poured into mine, and then set aside. Brad was too busy looking at his cup, watching the sugar grains at the bottom.

"You cannot make it go any faster than what the laws of this world dictate," Anzide grumbled.

Brad huffed, then put the glass aside.

In Anzide's hand was my glass, wrapped around it as it sat on the table. His hand reached out, and the bottle of mustard was flung across the room. He turned it over and squeezed it into the glass.

"This is you,"

The yellow slop slid into the liquid.

"Absolutely, one hundred percent, not meant to be mixed with the other liquids in this glass. But, like your mother and your uncle, it looks as if it's okay. The mixture is spreading. It is meshing into its surroundings. It appears to work. Where is the problem here, Evelyn?"

"It's mixed into the other liquids."

He nodded. With a fling of his hand, all but one of the glasses were sent to the sink. The table between us was empty except for the one that represented me.

"You have to wait for the sugar to dissolve, then the three remaining properties within you will duke it out for supremacy. The juice and the water will struggle, and, in the end, they will lose the battle because nothing will beat the mustard. It is powerful, it is strong, but it is nothing until the battle is over. So long as the others remain, it will just be a portion of a mixture."

"So, can she assist the mustard?"

Anzide smiled as he pushed the glass to Brad.

"Please, assist the mustard."

Brad looked at the glass with a deeply confused frown.

"I don't know how. I can't."

"No one can. No one except time."

The cup of the grossly odd mixture was sent to the sink with the other cups.

"This is why she needs help from an external source. Evelyn has to wait for her body to figure out what's going on. She has only just turned eighteen, barely a blip in her Eternal life. She is an adult to humans but an oddity to the Eternals. We are created, we are born, and we age extremely fast. Take me, for instance. My childhood, as humanity calls it, was a week in your timeline. I was born in the early hours of the morning, and by the end of the first day, I was walking and stringing a few words together. I have memories of my mother helping me walk, talking to me, and talking back to her. The next day, I was having full conversations with my parents, running around the house. I even dressed myself. Day three was the beginning of my education in the world of the Nephilim and what was expected of me in this life. Day four, and I was classed as a teenager if compared to this world. I was sent out for work experience with another Nephilim. From there, it progressed until day seven, where I was sent out into the world to do my duty and beg for forgiveness for the crime of my parents daring to love each other."

CHAPTER 42

The builder looked at the pictures with dismay. Anzide remained unseen, pacing the floor behind the man. The greeting and initial discussion were longer than necessary while Anzide checked this guy over. He'd given the all-clear.

There were no thoughts or memories of Drakkus, no knowledge of vampires.

Brad used his phone to take the photos so that he could show this guy the level of destruction and how much we'd done since the incident.

We were getting there slowly. I'd like to put in a solid effort, but the issues that were hanging around were proving to be a problem. Hopefully, making this agreement with Harlwood will give us a little relief.

"You say that it was a gas explosion?"

"Yeah," Brad said softly.

"That's an awful shame. Such a lovely house. Never knew the original owner. Some say he was a bad man, but that doesn't mean the house shouldn't be restored to the way that it was. Better than some modern monstrosity."

The added bonus of Anzide was that he was adding a little acceptance to this. There were no scorch marks, no fire. It looked like the house had exploded, but that's all that there was that was similar.

"Well, it's possible to use some of the wood and bricks. I'd have to inspect them to make sure they're solid. To be honest, you'd be better off ordering brand new. Get a truck in, clear the site, and start fresh."

Brad looked at me, and I shrugged. I was desperate to find Niko and ask what he wanted, but I was told to leave him be. To stay away and let him approach us. It was frustrating, to say the least.

"It will be cheaper too. The amount of time I'd spend searching through the rubble, it would be hours. You could clear the site, pull the nails from the wood, and make neat piles, but I'd still have to go through every single piece to make sure it's viable. This is an old house, it probably had good bones, but that may not be the case now that it's suffered a blow like this."

The builder handed Brad his phone back, then pushed a pen and paper across the desk.

"Tell you what, I'll get the plans for that place. I'll do up two quotes for you. One, exactly as you want. An estimate of time to go through the wood, select the good pieces, and then to rebuild. It will be an open quote because I don't know what you've got out there and what

I won't be able to save. The other quote is to rebuild exactly to the original plans with all new items. That one will not be an open quote because I won't use a single item from the original house. How's that?"

"Sounds great."

"Good, write your details there, and I'll get back to you. Probably about a week, alright?"

"Sure."

Scanning the street, I saw a familiar face across the road. It was one of the women, one of the vampires that taunted us. Pulling out my phone, I discreetly snapped a picture and then looked at the image. It was a fuzzy blur, like a static-filled television screen.

Thinking it was an odd, one-off occurrence, I took another picture. The result was the same. When Brad opened the door, the woman walked away with her friend, and I'd lost the chance.

Anzide looked at the screen, then at the woman who walked away. He turned and waited for the door to swing shut.

"You can't take pictures of them with a phone. Sorry, I should have told you that. Between what Harlwood's doing and the efforts of the demon Drakkus has working for him, they're useless for vampires. You need an older camera, something that is not connected to towers like that one."

He pointed to the horizon where there was a cell tower, small and unassuming from here but monstrously large close-up.

"There's a pawn shop down the street. I'll see you two later. I've got a yard to clean up. Ring me if you're being lazy and want a lift home."

Anzide and I wandered down the street after waiting for Brad to leave. Finding the pawn shop was easy, and as luck would have it, they had an old camera that the man was all too eager to get rid of.

Anzide shot me a smirk as the door clunked shut behind us.

"Was spending a hundred dollars on that ancient piece of technology worth it?"

"Absolutely. Come on, let's take a walking tour of Hades so I can test the camera out."

The camera was hanging from my neck. I trusted the strap, but then, I didn't really. My hand was on it as if I feared the strap would break and this essential tool in my war against my enemies would be lost.

Anzide took the camera bag, lifting it over his shoulder. Hand in hand, we walked down the main street, venturing further than I had in my time in this weird place.

We took a slow path around the streets, stopping by the information outlet to grab a map. Hades was bigger than I thought it was. Though, to be fair, I hadn't ventured far from home or school.

I took photos of flowers, trees, and random people that also included a few vampires. The pictures worked, so we kept going. All images of people would be at a reasonable distance. I also tried to make it appear as if they were in the way of something else that I was taking a picture of. Humans and vampires alike, I kept them all on the memory card so that if a vampire saw me and took the camera from me, they'd think nothing of it. Just a coincidence, that's all.

When we reached the school, Anzide and I crossed the road. Brad was outside the real estate office talking to a woman. Well, to be honest, it looked like he was hitting on her, and she was lapping it up.

"That's some suave moves," Anzide said with a mighty grin. "Maybe we should get some supplies before returning home."

"Like?"

"A tent, earplugs."

I giggled, which made Brad turn. He tipped his head as a greeting.

"Need that lift?"

"Nah, we're cool. You go back to,"

Brad frowned at me.

"Your conversation," I said sweetly.

His eyes narrowed. Fluttering my eyelashes, I moved around my uncle and continued down the path.

"It's sweet, right?"

"Sure," I said as I wrapped my arms around his waist.

"Until you realize that he totally fibbed about what he was really doing. That does not look like he's cleaning the yard."

"Maybe he's searching for helpers."

I rolled my eyes, scoffing. Yeah, that's exactly what Brad was doing. I didn't care. It gave us a moment alone.

We didn't have long, so our footsteps quickened. I think Anzide might have intervened a little.

By the time we reached the caravan, I was out of breath. It didn't bother me, not when I was hungry for a bit of fun.

Our time was limited, but it was perfect. The caravan was our little cramped cavern of love. Rather than risk falling off the top bunk, Anzide pulled the mattress down and put it on the space for the larger bed. Because everything was packed neatly from the back wall, there was still space, but it was limited.

Sweat peppered our skin like little droplets of passion escaping us. Anzide sighed as he settled on my body, the relief of our moment together consuming him.

I stared at the watermarks on the ceiling, smiling because it was the only thing possible at the moment. Wrapped up in how amazing it was to be with someone who cared.

There were differences. I could see them easily now.

Dragging my fingers down his spine for as far as I could reach, I enjoyed the silence of the afternoon. It was nice to have a moment of just us. No demons or vampires, no betrayal or lies. Just love.

Anzide lifted from my body with a wicked smile on his face.

"Two for two and still obsessed with it."

I chuckled.

"And you."

"Good save."

His fingertips dragged over the top of my forehead, pulling the hair back.

"Are you happy?"

"With this? Absolutely. You?"

Anzide nodded, lowering to kiss me softly.

"When I saw you that day, the very first day, I was stunned into silence. When you went through the door, I realized my mistake in the choice of appearance. I was a teenager, but I didn't think it would work. The more you resisted, the more I realized how wrong the choice was. They would not let me change. It added to the foul mood that I found myself in. I knew what was expected of me, but I saw you, and I found something inside myself that I didn't know existed."

"What?"

"Curiosity for love and affection. It grew beyond curiosity and festered into something that was uncontrollable. The boy turned up, making it worse. I could see him for his true worth, but you couldn't, which was frustrating. I knew I'd dug the hole and only had myself to blame for your lack of belief in me. All that I could do was to keep you as safe as I could manage, knowing that danger was always stalking you. Not just the vampires but my own kind. I am the reason they were delayed,"

Anzide had a conspiratorial smile on his face.

"What did you do?"

"Led them astray, false reports. Anything that would delay the inevitable. It was working well until the witch turned up."

"What happened to him?"

Anzide sat up, pulling his pants on.

"The trial was done without proof of a child being born. Mardyl had already admitted to the act and confirmed that a child was created. He was convicted but appealed because he said they forced the confession out of him, and he was under duress. By that stage, the new ruling had come in, so they let him go free. From what I hear, he spent the night celebrating with several vampires. Clearly, he did not learn any lessons from what happened."

Anzide turned, and hungry eyes scraped over me.

"Maybe round two?"

He looked like he was about to say something, but the squealing of brakes ended that. I sat up, looking past Anzide to the kitchen window.

"Is it?"

"Yeah, get dressed."

Anzide quickly pulled his shirt on and then moved the mattress back to the top bunk. I was dressed and doing the once over when I heard the car door shut. Brad's footsteps were heavy, almost like he was trying to make a lot of noise as a warning.

Sitting at the dining table, I took a deep breath and hoped that I did not look as if I'd spent the past half an hour doing wonderful things in this little hot box.

The metal door swung open, and Brad frowned at us.

"How can you stand being in here? Open a window, sheesh."

Then he continued grumping that instead of sitting on our asses, we could be cleaning the yard.

Emerging with the camera, I sat down at the table and began the process of forming the list. I think that I managed to get all of the vampires on my hit list, but I couldn't be certain. One was a little vague.

Brad sat down with his notebook, thumping it to the metal table.

"Well, Hannah gave me a few good places to check out."

"Hannah?"

"The woman that you almost blew my chances with. Next time, behave yourself."

"Always do."

Brad huffed, sounding as if he didn't believe me.

"You keep cramping my style, kid, and you're going to regret it. Loverboy will be so busy that you will forget what he looks like."

"Chill, Bradley. I'm not going to stop you from getting a girlfriend. So, what are these good places that you speak of?"

Brad turned the notebook and showed me. One place was for an industrial bin hire. There was a storage unit place as well as another company that would deliver shipping containers to be used. We could hire security fences if we wanted. She even offered a few names of builders to get more quotes from.

"This is a lot for Anzide to check out. Today took a lot out of him. You shouldn't go nuts on it."

"I wasn't planning on it. I liked the builder. He was pretty straight with what he offered, and, in all honesty, I can't be bothered. I just want the house back, as close as he can manage. How did your list go?"

I shrugged, turning the camera to show him.

"Well, I'm pretty sure I got all of them except this guy I'm a bit unsure about. I know that Harlwood will accept whatever I ask, but I don't want to take out someone that is innocent. I'll keep thinking about it, and hopefully, I'll figure it out."

Behind Brad, I could see the forest. It was like it

called out to me and beckoned me into the warmth of her arms. I don't know why, but I felt at peace when I was there. It was a little scary, and horrible things happened in there, but it still felt like it was a part of me.

"Hey, do you mind if I steal Anzide so I can go for a walk and clear my head?"

Brad rolled his eyes.

"Sure, why not? Today is a complete write-off anyway."

CHAPTER 43

I knew that Niko was not there, but I still returned to the cave. I'm sure Marco has opened his big, fat mouth already and said the cave is empty. Hopefully, they'll think that it was someone else that took the body.

Pressing my hand to the stone, I closed my eyes and lowered my head.

"Come on, Niko, guide me," I whispered.

Memories flashed through my mind, reminding me of that awful night. The vampires that laughed, taunting us. The woman that I'd seen on the other side of the road from the pawn shop, she flashed through first. Then, the others filtered through like a macabre slide show.

"I know that you're probably really mad about the house, and I am so sorry, Niko, but I'm still learning. We're going to rebuild it. Brad's found a builder that will get the original house plans and build from that. It will be the same house but brand new."

My hand slid from the rock as I sat back. Dejected. Lost. Low.

"I know it won't be the house you lived in with your wife and daughter, but I can't change the past. I'm sorry," I whispered. "I hope that in time, you will forgive me."

Wiping the tears away, I put my hand on the cold ground to lift myself up. My mind was fuzzy, and the world started to sway. Anzide was a few steps away, leaning against a tree. He'd kept his distance while keeping an eye on me and the surroundings.

"Let it flow, Evelyn. The mustard is growing stronger. You must let it do what is necessary."

The mustard is growing stronger, my mind whispered.

Has the sugar dissolved yet?

The fuzziness in my mind became thicker. I was on my hands and knees, rasping every breath.

"I can't see."

"Focus, Evelyn. Your body is changing. The mustard is consuming."

"Sugar?"

"Almost gone."

Hearing footsteps, I hoped that it was Anzide and not a threat. I was useless at the moment, unable to see, struggling through my foggy mind. It felt like I was in a rowboat, out on a lake that was surrounded by a thick fog. All I could see were grey clouds and the boat that I was in. It rocked every time I moved. Would I plunge into the murky water if I moved too hard?

"Anzide?"

"I'm here," he said softly.

I felt his touch on my shoulder, and a light appeared in the gloomy sky.

"Go to the light, my love. I am there waiting for you."

There were no oars. I didn't want to put my hands in the water or actually get into it and swim.

"I can't. There's nothing to move the boat."

"Yes, there is. You are there. Use your mind and move the boat. Tell the boat that you want to go to the light."

I did as he suggested, but I did not move.

"Do not be delicate, Evelyn. You are a fighter, a warrior. This woman, she does not take anyone's nonsense. Not the boy, not his human girlfriend, not the vampire that would rob her of everything that she is entitled to. She is powerful and strong. This warrior will stand tall and fight for everything that is right, and she will make her loved ones proud."

"I failed him," I whispered.

"No, Evelyn. You didn't fail, Niko. He is not here to tell you that for himself, but I know he would understand that what happened was an accident. Forgiveness is easily given to those we love. Now, tell that boat to move. Order it. Do it and come to the light. I have something for you."

Focusing on the boat, I got angry and, hopefully,

domineering. The boat shifted in the water, turning slightly towards the light.

"Keep going. You are the boss, Evelyn. You are the one that dictates in this world. Again."

Anzide's tone was more forceful this time. I didn't want this to progress to where he'd be yelling at me. Also, I was on my hands and knees in the dangerous forest. I couldn't see properly, and I felt trapped in this odd world. There was only one way out.

Anger consumed me, muffling Anzide's words about channeling the emotion and using it to steer the boat. It was then that I understood.

The day that I leveled the house, I was angry. The Nephilim were taking Anzide away from me, and the emotion consumed me to the point that I lost connection, and then the worst happened.

"Tell the boat what to do. You are in control. Do not let the boat float aimlessly."

Beneath my hands and knees, I could feel the ground shaking. Anzide's hand on my shoulder became more insistent.

"Focus," he chided sternly.

As I looked at the light, I felt the shaking settle. Slowly, the boat turned to completely face the light, then started to drift.

"Good,"

The clouds began to disperse, and the light grew.

Soon, it was glowing brightly. The boat reached land with a soft thud, sliding up the sand as if someone was there helping it. Warily, I stood and walked to the end of the boat and out into the cold water.

The water lapped at the beach, drawing in and out around my feet. Ahead of me was the light. The sky was no longer cloudy, but it was dark.

"Keep going. You're almost there."

Reaching the top of the embankment, I saw Anzide. He was holding the light. Beside him was an old woman. She was hunched over, gripping a staff while giving me a stink-eye look.

Anzide smiled, urging me over with a flick of his hand.

"You did well."

The woman whacked Anzide on the head with her staff.

"Do not speak with such mockery."

"I believe that she did well." he grumped, rubbing his head.

"But she did not do well. She is Eternal, and she is eighteen. It took far too long."

Anzide's lip curled as he turned to the woman, angrily glaring at her.

"I told you, she didn't know anything until recently."

"No excuse." she snapped. "All Eternals know that

they are different. She was not listening to herself."

Hobbling, the woman turned to walk away.

"We will try again tomorrow."

Anzide flustered, following the woman.

"She doesn't have time."

"Eternals have time. Nephilim do not know how to lie. How is it that you can?"

"It is not a lie. The vampires are coming for her."

"She is Eternal. This is not a problem."

"But her uncle is not. Evelyn cares deeply for him. He is her family."

The woman smacked Anzide on the head again.

"She has others,"

"I know that," he groaned, rubbing his head again. "The great-grandfather is repairing himself in the forest and remaining unseen at the moment, and she does not want to know her father."

The old woman turned to look at me. From under the grey hair that hung loose in her eyes, she shot me another stink-eye look.

"Phoenix should know her creator."

I gasped, and my eyes widened as the forest came back to me.

"Hey, it's okay. You did well."

Anzide pulled me into his arms, holding me tight as I struggled to draw in the air.

"What was that?" I rasped. "Who was that woman?"

"We call her mother, but she is not our mother. She doesn't like the name, and I wouldn't call her that, but that is what the Eternals call her."

Carefully, Anzide lifted me to my feet.

"Easy does it. Going into the portal can be difficult."

"Portal?"

Anzide wrapped his arm around my waist, helping me along the path. Hopefully, I will be better by the time we get out of here. I can only imagine what Brad will think.

"It's like a hub. Mother is usually in this area, as well as a few others. All the areas are connected, and we pass through them to get to other areas."

"Like where you live?"

Anzide smiled.

"Where I used to live, yes. I live here now."

"She wasn't happy, was she?"

"No, you're eighteen, and you have no idea of your powers. Don't take it the wrong way, but they will see you as inferior until you get it right. We'll spend a few hours helping your mind focus, and hopefully, you'll be ready for tomorrow's attempt."

I looked at Anzide, worried because I didn't have time

to be going into portals and come out feeling so deflated.

"Each time will be easier, I promise. This was your first attempt, and you put a lot of effort into getting to land. The more you practice focusing your mind, the easier it will be. In time, you'll learn how to travel from one world to another without going to the gate first."

We stopped at the edge of the forest, looking at Brad, who was still working despite the light fading.

"You should rest. I will help Brad for as long as he wants to work."

"He's going to lose his mind."

"I will explain it to him."

Continuing onto the property, Brad stopped and looked at us. From this distance, I could already see the fear and horror filling his face.

"What's wrong?" he called out as he rushed over.

"Evelyn had her first lesson in going to the portal world. It was an energy-consuming venture. Resting for a few minutes is all that she needs."

Brad helped me to the table and chairs under the cover, easing me into the seat.

"Can't you do this at another time? And why did it happen in the dangerous and unprotected forest?"

"No one can dictate when or where it will happen. It happens, and we have to accept it for what it is. Now that she has made the initial connection, all future visits will happen by choice. It is not ideal, but we can and will perform the visits on the property."

Brad sat down on the chair opposite, glancing at me and then at Anzide as he sat down.

"This is necessary?"

"Absolutely. Otherwise, all the effort you're going to, that house that will go back up again, the houses around us, they will suffer the same as the original house did. The more she denies her dominant creature access to the light, the more the world around her suffers. Speaking of light,"

Anzide trailed off, gesturing to Brad's skin. It was flushed pink, the brightest I'd ever seen.

"I think that being around all these vampires is making your inner vampire surface. Be aware of the thoughts in your mind. If you crave blood, then tell me. We will deal with it rather than ignore it."

"I'm human," Brad whispered.

"You are a mixture of creatures, and the human portion is the weakest of all three. Immortal creatures always dominate over mortal, just as the Eternals dominate over immortal and mortal. You might be human now, but you won't be for much longer. Remember, the sugar will dissolve."

Hunger gnawed. I was feeling a little ravenous at the moment.

"When are you starting dinner?"

"At the same time that you get off your lazy ass and help."

"Hilarious." I grumped. "So much for school work, eh?"

"I have that covered. Look at the bed."

Moving past the bathroom, I pulled back the curtain and saw that Brad had set up a desk. He'd found cushions, a couple of bricks, and a wide plank of wood. The computer had been retrieved and was set up. But the best part of it was the printer was here.

Why was it the best part? Brad had a printer that was one of those multifunction things. I could pull the memory card from the camera, stick it into the port, and print the pictures without connecting to the internet. The less connection I had to the world, the safer my little plan would be.

"So, I guess you're not helping with dinner now?"

"Anzide would love to help you," I murmured, turning on the printer.

"Well, that's just great," Brad grumped. "The biblical creature who has never eaten until he met us."

"It's a great lesson. You'll be an amazing teacher. I have heaps of faith in your ability."

Pulling the curtain across, I hoped Brad got the picture. With a huff, he stomped away. Seconds later, Anzide poked his head through the curtain.

"You know that you should help, right?"

"I've got to get these printed."

Anzide pulled back through the curtain and then pushed it aside. I was given a frown.

"They will wait. You're not going to see Harlwood tonight, and you're certainly not leaving the property. He won't come here looking for them."

Getting up from the bed base, I followed Anzide.

"This kitchen is too small for the two of us."

Brad put the cutting board and knife on the dining table. Anzide smiled as he sat opposite.

"So, you will be my teacher tonight."

"I guess so."

"Did you wash your hands, nose picker?"

"Oh my god, Bradley. You're so crude."

Anzide was smirking at me.

"I do not pick my nose," I muttered.

Brad frowned at me, flicking his head to the bathroom.

"But you have been on an adventure today, so get up and wash your hands."

"Like I wasn't,"

Anzide followed me to the bathroom, washing his

hands and sneaking a kiss.

"Hey, I have a question," I whispered.

"Fire away."

"If we, you know, have kids. Are they going to become an adult in a week like you did?"

Anzide was stunned into silence, and then he frowned.

"I don't know, to be honest. Nephilim age quickly, but clearly, you didn't. Maybe the immortal part of the equation altered the aging process."

He closed in on me, which was half a step in the tiny bathroom. Still, it was kind of hot when he leaned on the counter and got into my space.

"Do you want them?"

"Kind of. I mean, sometime in the future, I guess."

His lips scraped over mine, grinning like a madman.

"Well, if you're unsure about it, we should probably stop having sex," he whispered.

Not only did he suggest preposterous things, but Anzide left the bathroom without kissing me.

"How rude," I muttered.

CHAPTER 44

Whispering woke me. I opened my eyes and listened to Brad and Anzide talking as quietly as they could manage.

When my eyes began to focus, I understood why. Brad was severely sunburned.

"So, I take it that the inner vampire is winning the battle?"

"It appears to be the case," Anzide said.

He held out his hand, helping me off the top bunk.

It was cold this morning, odd considering that it was insanely hot yesterday, but not that surprising considering that this bizarre little town was never consistent with its weather. Pulling on a jumper, I sat at the table and looked at the pink man who was groaning into his coffee.

"What's the plan for this nonsense?"

Anzide sat down beside me, and Brad looked up. It was then that I saw that his face was puffed, looking as if he was having an allergic reaction.

"Jeez, stop drinking the coffee. Clearly, you're progressing to a blood diet."

"I don't want to," he complained.

The cup was full, looking as if Brad had taken one sip. He could barely see out his eyes, just narrow slits in the puffed-up mess.

"He needs blood."

"That's true, but we have a few problems with that. No fangs, no teacher to guide him, daylight, and I would suggest that going out looking like that would not be ideal."

Brad's fingers pushed the mug over the narrow table. It sounded like he was whimpering at the loss.

"You know, when Niko first escaped the wall, he couldn't get up from the ground. He fed on me, and it was enough to get him up and walking. Not completely everything, but I was able to get him to the victim."

"Evie," Brad groaned.

"Look, I know what I know from experience. You don't have fangs, but I can cut a wound and let you drink it. A little bit of blood might be enough to make the swelling go down. Then we can reassess what you need."

"She's right,"

Brad shook his head. Anzide looked at me, I gave him a nod, and he retrieved the utility knife that was in the top drawer.

Taking my arm, Anzide nicked the skin. Brad groaned again, shifting in his seat. It was like he wanted to move but couldn't.

Holding out my arm, I hoped that it would be what he needed.

"You needn't fear hurting Evelyn. She is an Eternal. You cannot kill her or cause injury. This is what you need, and it is the best option at the moment. Take what is offered and do what is necessary."

"Fangs,"

The mumbled word was barely coherent. His lips puffed, and he could barely move.

"Suck the skin. You don't have time for this. It is getting worse. Feed to heal yourself before it becomes uncontrollable."

Brad hesitated. Anzide's anger grew a little as he rose from his seat. Shifting next to Brad, he reached out and took my arm, dragging me closer.

"Feed, I will ensure that she is safe. You have my word."

He nodded, then took my arm. I was now sitting on the table, leaning in an awkward position that was incredibly uncomfortable. Brad had better be grateful.

His lips pressed to the skin, opening to let the blood weep into his mouth. The grip tightened as Brad began to draw the blood out. I looked at Anzide, tilting my head with a frown. Anzide turned to watch closely.

Something sharp dug into the flesh. I winced and tried to pull my arm away. Brad hissed, looking up at me. No longer the puffed-up pink monster, he was a different kind of creature. His bloodshot eyes had changed, now orange instead of the green that all our family had. And I could see them completely.

His skin was pale, no longer pink. Luminous, powdery white skin that was perfect. The scar that sat just under the hairline was gone. His hair, which was always untamed first thing in the morning, had changed. Now, it looked like he'd spent hours in front of the mirror, ensuring the view was perfect.

Everything that I could see had changed.

He was definitely a vampire.

Anzide gently pushed Brad back, giving him a stern look when he tried to resist.

"Bradley, we discussed this. You will listen to me. The feed is over. You mustn't take anymore."

He let go, sitting back in the seat. Blood coated his lips and teeth. The fangs were there, prominent, and they looked incredibly sharp. Of course, I knew how sharp.

"Well, no more sun for you," Anzide said as he inspected the fangs. "Not for many years, I'm afraid. For a few years, you may be able to manage small sections if you are wise and careful."

The top lip was pushed up, and Brad looked at him

with disdain.

Slowly, I slipped back into my seat, and then put pressure on the wound. It was already starting to heal, no longer weeping blood.

"Hungry," Brad grumbled.

"Yeah, me too," I said, taking the coffee.

I'd never drunk it until today, but right now, I needed a pick-me-up.

"Now what?"

Anzide assessed Brad again, then gave me a grim smile.

"He needs a proper feed to return to the more coherent person we're used to. This person is only thinking of one thing, and if we try to ignore it, he'll run off and do something stupid. My concern is that not only would he risk the sun, which is clearly a problem for him at the moment, but he could be seen. If he runs off and does this on his own, he will go to something that seems natural to him. Almost like something that calls to him."

"You mean a person, right?"

Anzide nodded.

"That woman?"

"Yes, she would be his target. Unintentionally, of course. The coherent vampire will always pick something other than their physical desires, and I'm sure the coherent Brad would like this woman alive. So, we help him find someone not on his potential girlfriend list."

"But the sun is an issue."

Brad was like a statue, sitting at the table silently and unmoving. He stared ahead, somewhere to the side of me. It looked like he was dead.

"It is. As for his victim, I think that we are going to have to assist."

Great. Helping another vampire kill a person. I always wanted to be an accomplice to murder. Again.

Because Brad had an aversion to light, we walked through the forest and emerged on the other side. There was a large housing estate, but very few houses were actually built. It was like a certain demon was influencing but not catching his little fishies like he wanted.

Stopping short of the tree line, we looked at the choices. The houses were far apart in certain sections, but in this area, there was a cluster of about ten.

"Too many eyes," Anzide grumbled.

We turned and walked along the tree line.

Brad's movements were robotic. He seemed so lifeless. This was nothing like what I'd gone through with Niko. He was fluid, moving easily. He knew what he wanted and how to get it. I suppose that was experience. Brad was probably struggling.

Reaching the next section, there were three houses. One was visibly empty, and the other two weren't. The closest house had a small family that was leaving. It appeared as if they were going camping.

While the father went and checked the windows on the lower level, the mother ushered the children into the car. The car was packed to the brim, a trailer stacked tight, and the dog was on the back seat barking at them.

"Well, that's a relief," Anzide murmured. "Four sets of eyes, leaving right now."

We watched as the nearest neighbor moved to the fence to see what all the fuss was. Dressed only in a skimpy bikini, she adjusted the outfit and the goods and then waited. She cheerily waved to the father as he emerged from the house. The mother scowled at her partner.

"Ah, the politics of suburbia," I said humorously. "Bet he's porkin' her."

"Porking?"

"Yeah,"

I looked at Anzide with a wicked smirk, then remembered my statue of an uncle was within earshot.

"Sex."

"I see."

His gaze returned to the woman who was now alone. The smile increased, and Anzide glanced back at me. With a flick of his head, Anzide gestured to the view.

The woman was stretched out on the sun lounge, topless and soaking in the rays. I have to say, it was not a bad idea. Get in the rays before the clouds and rain return.

Brad was strained, pulling forward in a desperate attempt to be let free. Anzide held his shirt collar, holding him back. Soft growls began to emerge. I shifted slightly and saw that he was paler than he'd ever been, and his eyes were a luminous orange.

"Are we sure about this?"

"The instincts take over. He will be fine, and if not, I can alter from afar."

"Brad,"

His gaze turned to me. The top lip rippled as he growled.

"Good lord, he's like a rabid dog," I muttered. "Listen to me. Keep it quiet, don't let her scream. And be respectable. Just because the goods are out doesn't mean you get a free feel. Alright?"

His nose twitched as the growl deepened.

"I mean it. Niko would expect that you are a refined and well-behaved vampire. You will not disrespect her."

Even if he was taking her life.

"You've got one chance, and if you screw this up, we're going to make some serious changes that you won't like. You've got freedom, do it properly and respectfully."

Giving Anzide a nod, I held tight and hoped Brad

didn't lash out. He was still for a moment, then took off. I saw nothing but a blur, and seconds later, the woman was pushed off the chair and onto the ground.

There was no sound, not a cry for help, not even a whimper. I stood, silent and stunned. Brad fed without issue.

We knew he was done when he stood and turned around.

"What about the body?"

"We can leave her in this forest. Close to her home, the cop will think that she," Anzide sighed. "Well, we know what the cop will think. He'll tell Drakkus, and then he'll know that there's another vampire in town. The less he knows about what is going on, the better. We clearly can't leave the body too exposed."

Brad was turning pink.

"Get out of the sun," I called out.

He whipped through to the darkness, stopping just short of us. Brad looked, well, normal, I guess. His eyes were slowly returning to green, wickedly glinting as if he was at his happiest at this very moment. Brad looked like he was out of breath. His chest rose and fell in short and sharp movements.

Anzide disappeared, leaving me with Brad.

"Feeling better?"

He nodded.

"What do you think about it?"

"I don't know. There are no thoughts in my mind about it. Just do what is necessary, and that's it. Makes me wonder about Mom and Nancy."

"Maybe they were more shapeshifters than vampires."

"But your mother went out every night. What if she wasn't a prostitute, and the two of you lived off the inheritance? What if she went out every night to feed and ensure she didn't attack you?"

"It's possible, I suppose. Doesn't explain why she was so horrible to me, though."

Brad stepped forward, gripping my shoulders.

"Maybe it does. What if she couldn't feed and had to go without? She would struggle not to attack you. I know how difficult it was to sit across from you when I was hungry. The thoughts in my mind said one thing, but my hunger begged me to do the opposite. Look, I have no idea what the deal was with your mother. When I saw her, she was fine. It was during the day. She didn't turn pink. She ate and drank like a human would and never said anything, but I guess I wouldn't expect her to. Mom never said anything about vampires or shapeshifters."

Maybe she didn't know? Would her mother have told her or kept her in the dark about it?

Anzide reappeared, giving me a grim smile.

"It's done. We're going to have to figure out a plan for

the immediate future. Hades has a lot of residents, and they're all oblivious, but I wonder if some of them aren't as clueless as we think."

"Ryan being one of them," I muttered.

Something clicked inside my mind, and I looked at Brad with a heavy frown.

"Hey, isn't Ryan supposed to be the only builder in this town?"

"According to him, yes, but it's not the case. Ange had a list of builders that I could use."

"Was Henry on that list?"

Brad pulled several pieces of paper out of his back pocket, looking at them.

"Not on Ange's list, but he's on mine that I got from the local paper."

Comparing the two, they were almost the same. Brad's list was the actual trades listing from the paper, and Ryan's business was the largest ad on the page. Ange's list was missing two, and Henry was one of them.

It might mean nothing, but I was dubious.

CHAPTER 45

Brad's movements were much more relaxed now that he'd fed. We walked through the forest, edging along the estate, and passed the cluster of houses. It was there that I felt my heart drop.

In the distance, I could see a group of people, and Kannon was one of them. Audrey wasn't with him, but I saw the woman I'd tried to get a picture of.

"Hey, Anzide, can you zip back and get my camera, please?"

"Sure."

Brad stood next to me, looking at the view of treachery.

"How many in that group?"

"They're all there, the four remaining out of the five and a few extras that are clearly worth taking out."

"Kannon?"

My mind twisted with thoughts of how lovely it

would be to repay his efforts with death, but I had bigger plans.

"I'd rather torture him first," I muttered curtly.

Brad chuckled softly.

The cool wind brushed past us, and Anzide appeared at my other side with the camera in hand.

"Thanks."

Once it was ready to go, I lifted the camera, zoomed in, and took lots of happy snaps. Hopefully, these will be enough for Harlwood. Flicking through the images, I ensured they were all usable and then turned the camera off.

"Let's go. The sooner I get these to Harlwood, the happier I will be."

Leaving the horrid view behind, we trekked through the forest and returned to the caravan. I quickly printed the pictures and then grabbed my things.

"You still can't drive," Brad grumbled.

"Neither can you unless you'd like to look like a cooked lobster all the time. I got to the school on my last attempt. All I need to do is avoid Larry."

"Perhaps it would be wise to note the movements of the town's only cop."

Brad huffed, shaking his head.

"Don't encourage her."

Giving him a doe-eyed look, Brad shook his head.

"Fine, go. Try not to have an accident, please."

Grabbing the keys, I smiled sweetly at him.

"It's all fine. Third time driving, I'm good for this."

"If Larry turns up, I'm telling him that you did not have permission just so that we're clear."

Waving him off, I skipped down the metal steps and onto the grass. Anzide was beside me, looking happier than I'd ever seen.

"What's going on in that mind?"

"Just appreciating everything."

We got into the car, and Anzide watched everything that I did. I knew what he was up to, learning as always.

I was nervous about driving, still new at it, and still unsure of what to do, but there was little choice at the moment. Brad could not drive me. Anzide didn't know how, and it was better that I didn't walk to the school. After my last attempt, I would not make that mistake again.

The drive was slow, I was cautious, and I checked the roads and surroundings constantly. There was traffic, but being a small town, it wasn't a lot.

Once I'd pulled into the car park, I turned off the engine and realized how tense I was. My hands were shaking, and my entire body was tight.

"You did well, Evelyn."

"Thanks."

"We arrived without issue. Be pleased with your efforts."

"Yeah, but what I'm doing is illegal. I've driven twice before this, and I am inexperienced. It's not just illegal. It's highly dangerous."

Anzide gestured to the world beyond the windscreen.

"Life is dangerous. You, however, are vastly different from anyone out there. What you learn in one moment will be retained, and it will thrive within you. Haven't you ever noticed how you just seem to soak in information?"

"No," I said softly.

"But you do, and that's my point. As an Eternal, this is how we learn about the world around us. We experience things, we focus, and we draw them in. This is what I've said to you in the past. I am learning about this world now that I am completely immersed in it. You are doing the same."

We looked at each other. Anzide must have figured it out because he smiled, leaned in, and kissed me softly. I might be able to do this easily, but that doesn't mean I won't freak out because of it. Being full of eagerness was not always a good thing.

When we entered the office, Jane frowned as she looked up at me. Her lips parted to say something, but then Harlwood walked into the office. It was like he knew I was here, which was highly likely considering he was a demon.

"It's alright, Jane. Evie visits us now for social reasons, and I have no issues with her being here or venturing beyond the door without my prior knowledge."

"Of course," she said softly.

Harlwood moved to the door and opened it, offering a smug smile as he looked at me.

"I trust that you come bearing gifts."

"I do. Does that please you?"

"Absolutely."

Taking the pictures, Harlwood flicked through them as he ambled to his desk. His face was plain, offering no hint as to his thoughts or his mood. I was oddly curious, wondering what was going through his mind.

Sitting down, Anzide and I patiently waited. There weren't a lot of pictures to go through, but Harlwood was taking his time and studying each of them quite intensely. Taking a deep breath, he aligned them into a neat stack and then tucked them into the inner pocket of his jacket. Then he smiled at me.

It was a little unnerving, more so when he tilted back in his seat. I don't think he was trying to intimidate me, but that's how it came across.

"I agree with your selection, and it will be done. Do you have a time frame in which you would like the task completed?"

"As soon as you can manage."

"Of course. Any particular vampire first?"

I shook my head. Harlwood was still smiling at me.

"And finally, is there any request for the manner of their death?"

That was certainly a good question, and I wanted to consider it before answering. How horrible could I be? These vampires taunted Niko. They murdered him and stole him from me and this world. This was his land, and they had done all they could to take it from him.

"Nothing, but I request that you are absolutely positive that they are dead, and it meets with whatever is necessary for a vampire to die, *and* I'd like for you to know that these vampires taunted Niko before they murdered him. The blade they stabbed him with was soaked in holy water from the Vatican. Keep that in mind when you take their lives."

Harlwood's eyes lit up with delight, and the smile I thought could not get any creepier increased dramatically.

"Agreed."

With that, our mini-meeting was over. We left Harlwood and returned to the caravan. Now that Harlwood was dealing with my vampire problem, Anzide suggested that I learn how to focus my mind so that going to the portal would be less of a drama the second time around. Mother insisted I reached a certain level before I was even granted an audience with the passage master.

The passage master was the guy who watched over

the movements in, out, and around the portal area. He answered to another guy who watched over the area to ensure it remained structurally sound. If someone like me, who was a complete novice, went into the portal and started wandering around aimlessly, I could hit something. According to Anzide, the portal would tank big time.

So, I had to learn.

Brad was asleep in the caravan, which was now fully air-conditioned thanks to a portable unit that we'd picked up after he sent a message to me saying that he was swimming in his own sweat and that he'd had another shower.

It appeared that Brad was about to become a night owl, which was only natural if he was a vampire. When I looked at him earlier, he seemed like the guy he was a month ago. It was so strange.

"There's no other reason for the sudden change?"

"It's not sudden," Anzide said.

He was desperately trying to make me meditate with him. We were seated under a large tree at the back of the property. It was shaded and quite pleasant. The neighbors could not see us. Anzide had placed several things to block their view.

Cracking an eye open, Anzide huffed. Opening both eyes, he shot me an exasperated look.

"Did the lesson with the sugar mean nothing to you?"

"I just didn't think it would dissolve that quickly."

"Nothing dictates the time, nor does it follow a pattern. It is what it is, nothing more, nothing less."

"But what if he wasn't here?"

"Then he would have figured it out wherever he was when the body settled, as it would have with your mother and grandmother."

Closing his eyes, Anzide rested his hands on his knees, stretching his back as straight as he could manage.

"Stop smiling at me and get on with it."

"Do you think that my mother and grandmother were shifters?"

Slowly, he exhaled, and that serene look on his face was gone.

"It would appear that is the case. However, we will never know unless someone comes forward and offers evidence that contradicts it. Now, would you please do as I ask of you?"

Rolling my eyes, I copied the pose and waited for some form of serenity to find me. It was difficult when I had a lot of thoughts going through my mind.

"You know,"

Anzide groaned loudly, then dramatically flopped backward, landing on the soft grass. His legs kicked out, and his arms fell wide.

I giggled, then moved closer, sitting on his lap.

"I wasn't meditating when it happened."

The silent one looked at me. I smiled and shrugged. Before I knew it, he pulled me down and rolled me onto my back. I shrieked and howled with laughter.

"You are an absolute pest," he muttered from his position above me.

On hands and knees, Anzide looked down at me. The mocking smile said it all. He didn't think that I'd ever be able to concentrate, and therefore, I would not be going back to the portal.

"Do I really need to go to the portal?"

He silently nodded.

"Why?"

Settling onto the grass beside me, Anzide lay on his side, keeping me close.

"Because it has regenerative properties. You are a phoenix. Out of every Eternal being that is here, there, or in the beyond, they are the one creature that absolutely needs to maintain their regeneration levels. If you let them get low at this age, it's not that bad, but once you get closer to the hundred years, you'll need those levels to be at the highest to bring down the change over time. If you don't keep the levels up, it will take longer, and you'll be weaker because of it. That puts you in a lot of danger, and this is not the place to be toying with fate."

"But I'm immortal,"

"Yes, that is true, but what if Brad is seriously hurt

and you are the only one that can help him? What if you could have been in your transition phase for a week, but because you faltered, you take a month, and that extra time just happens to coincide with Brad's issues? You would not be able to help him. In fact, you'd be in a worse state than he would be. Transitional phases are like a deep sleep. You will wake here and there, but the majority of the time is spent in your sleep chamber."

"My bed?"

"No," he said as he shook his head. "Closer to a coffin. So, does this explain the necessity of going to the portal, or will this be another lesson that passes through and does not sink in?"

For a moment, I thought that being a good girl was the best idea, but I decided against it. Being cheeky was much more fun.

"Does what sink in?"

His eyes narrowed as the scowl tightened. Anzide was seconds away from tickling me to death when a woman called out.

"Hello?"

We both sighed, looking across the lawn at the figure walking up the driveway. It was the woman that Brad was talking to at the real estate office.

"What's her name again?"

"Playtime interrupter," I murmured. "Otherwise known as Hannah."

We got up from the grass as she approached. Hannah was all smiles as she crossed the grass, aside from the few times when her heel sank into the ground. Flicking away the pest at my side who was digging his finger into my ribs, I smiled and hoped that I was being pleasant enough for Brad's desperate needs.

"Hi, you must be Evelyn. I'm Hannah."

"Hey," I said, then gestured to the annoying one. "That's Anzide."

Her eyes turned to him, pressing a thin smile.

"Nice to meet you. Is Brad around?"

"He's asleep."

"I'll go wake him," Anzide muttered quietly.

That was curiously odd.

Anzide crossed the lawn quickly and entered the caravan. Looking back at Hannah, I got a smile that was definitely uneasy. Was it because she wanted to date my uncle, or was it something else?

CHAPTER 46

Brad was standing under the shade of the caravan awning as he talked to Hannah. Whatever Anzide had said to him in the caravan had him spooked, but not enough to send her away. In fact, it looked like the complete opposite, which was not amusing to the huffing dragon beside me.

"I think that we can agree that any attempt at entering the portal at the moment would be foolish, so how about we just stop?"

"Fine," he grumped.

"What did you say to Brad?"

"That there's something different about her."

"Vampire?"

Anzide shook his head, then stretched out to lean against the tree trunk.

"No, something else. I can detect the fact that she is not mortal, but there's something blocking me from entering."

"Hmm, like Drakkus's house."

He sat up and looked at me with a stunned expression.

"The demon," he whispered.

We both turned our heads and looked at Brad and his would-be love interest. She was all smiles and giggles, affectionately slapping the air near him.

"Good lord," I muttered. "I don't act like that, do I?"

"Oh yeah, it's a real disgrace."

Anzide was grinning by the time I looked at him. He shrugged with his devious smile shining, then returned to the view.

"It appears that you are like your uncle. You don't listen to me."

He was looking at Brad. The smile was gone, and in its place was a deep frown that showed how unimpressed Anzide was.

"I told him to avoid interacting with her at all costs and definitely not invest time that will lead to anything progressing. That looks as if he has not paid any attention to me."

"Did he understand what you were saying? Because you do tend to talk in riddles."

"Nonsense."

"You are indirect and often confusing. Did you tell him that you detected something abnormal, or did you just say, I've got a bad feeling about this woman?"

The silence said it all. Rather than dwelling on it, I returned to watch my uncle fall victim to a demon. Well, romantically fall victim.

With another smile that seemed as if she was almost gushing at him, Hannah turned and walked out from under the awning. She looked at us and waved. It was like she had no idea what we were. We both returned the wave and watched as she turned to walk down the driveway. Brad remained under the shaded cover, also watching the bewitching blonde.

"Are you sure she's the other demon?"

"No, but I can assure you she's not a vampire."

"Shapeshifter?"

"That is possible. If she is aware of her nature, she will not willingly offer her species. Neither will a witch, and yes, that's another possibility."

"What's more likely?"

"Witch."

Brad looked at us, then flicked his head, urging us into the caravan with him. We stood, crossed the lawn, and entered the caravan. Before I closed the door, I looked down the driveway and saw Hannah getting into her car.

All seemingly normal.

"What's wrong with her?"

"She's not mortal. The exact details are blocked, and that is a worrying detail."

Brad sighed as he sat at the table. Rubbing his eyes, I saw the weariness that was taking its toll on him.

"You should go back to bed."

"I'd like to, but I think sleep will evade me for a while. A routine will happen, I'm sure."

Sitting down, I settled in and waited for Anzide to join us. He was raiding the biscuit jar. I think that out of all of the biscuits that had been in there, he's eaten most of them. With two in hand and one being crammed into his mouth, Anzide joined us at the table. Brad smiled and shook his head.

"We can never escape the sugar cravings."

"That's probably half your battle."

"Ah, yes. My beloved doughnuts, how I shall miss them. So, what's Hannah's deal?"

"One of three choices. Witch, shapeshifter, or the demon we've been looking for."

"We could ask Harlwood. He will know what she is."

I shook my head.

"Can't. He's not available until the information is collected, then he'll notify us of when the first death has happened. He won't even be at school. He said that he was going to take a few personal days to get the job done quickly. I think that he really wants this demon gone, and if we're associating with her, it could prove to be a problem."

"Well then, we really do have a problem because I agreed to a date tonight."

The thought of getting Brad out of the caravan seemed so tantalizing that I was almost ready to say that it was a brilliant idea and then proceed to help him select an outfit to wear. That was not going to happen, much like the date tonight or me having alone time with Anzide.

"But she might not be the demon, right? Don't you know how to detect your own kind?"

"She has it blocked."

"Why would she do that?"

Anzide shrugged. "Probably because she knows about Harlwood. It really does point to her being the demon, you know."

Brad groaned as he slumped back into the seat. His head rolled back against the wood panel behind him.

"I find a nice chick that's,"

"Please don't cross the line again." I interrupted.

His head lifted, and I got a frown.

"I was going to say, intelligent and knows what she wants in her life."

Well, yay for her.

"This is ridiculous. How about we go to every single person in this town and form a database of who I can and cannot date? How's that? We're not upsetting the precious demon, are we?"

Getting up from the table, Brad began unbuttoning his shirt as he turned and walked to the shower.

"Why is this tin can so damned hot?"

"Because you are still in the alteration process. Give it time."

The door was slammed shut, and seconds later, the water started.

"How long will it take?"

"I have no idea."

"Another one of those unknowns?"

Anzide sighed as he nodded. "Yeah, one of those unknowns."

Hearing gravel crunching, Anzide stood from the table and looked out the window.

"It's the builder. Must be the day for visitors."

Thumping on the bathroom door, Anzide told Brad the builder had turned up.

"It looks like he's got some stuff for you. Plans, papers."

Brad opened the door, looking like he'd gone crazy with powder. Hair wet, dressed but still damp and deathly white.

"You look terrible. Are you hungry?"

"I'm fine."

His tone was clipped, pushing past Anzide. Brad opened the door and offered a welcoming smile to Henry.

"Afternoon, Brad," Henry called out.

"Anzide," I whispered, urging him over with a panic that was rising. "He's hungry. This is not good."

"I know, but there isn't a single thing we can do to stop this from happening. All we can do now is make sure Brad knows that we're watching him. Put Brad into the corner, then sit next to him. I'll sit next to Henry, and then if he starts to act weirdly, I will see it."

Getting up from the table, I waited. Anzide moved to the back of the caravan, giving Henry space to sit down.

Henry gave me a warm smile as he tipped his head.

"Afternoon. I was just telling Brad that I managed to get the plans ahead of schedule, ran the figures, and came up with a number. Thought it would be a good idea to run through them and then check what's going on here with the other quote."

"Sure, take a seat."

He sat down, Brad moved, and I stepped in his way, raising an eyebrow at him.

"Not a chance in hell," I whispered. "You know

where you belong."

Brad's lip twitched derisively, but he moved to the other seat and sat down. Now that he was suitably taken down a peg, he was restrained and behaving himself. I sat down next to him, and Anzide moved into place next to Henry.

As Henry talked about the quote, I tried to listen, but there wasn't much point when I was too busy trying to concentrate on Brad. I never expected to be a babysitter for my adult uncle. How long would this last? When would he learn control?

This made me wish that Niko was here to guide us. We had nothing except for Anzide's knowledge that was lacking. It also didn't help that the vampire, the shapeshifter, and the human were still duking out inside him. Clearly, the vampire was the dominant, but was that going to be permanent, or was this only temporary?

There was no point in asking Anzide. I knew that it would be a waste of time. I could search for Niko, ignoring Anzide's words about leaving him to rest and waiting until he emerged of his own choice. The problem was he was the only vampire that I could trust. The other choices were incredibly unwise.

Of course, there was one option, and it might be reasonable, aside from the fact that I know that he'll tell Drakkus. I could talk to Kannon, stating that I was worried for him. Regardless of whether we were here or somewhere else, Brad would still be the same. He would still struggle with these changes.

Maybe it might give us a reprieve. If Kannon thinks that setting Brad loose on the world was a bad idea, he might suggest to someone else that waiting a few weeks would be ideal. It was an interesting thought.

Henry looked up from the papers, glancing between Brad and me. He seemed concerned, looking at Brad more than me. I subtly kicked Anzide under the table.

"If this is a bad time, I can come back."

"It's fine," Brad offered in a tone I'd never heard from him.

It was dark, deeper than it should be.

"You look sick. Have you been to see the doctor? Sharon's a nice lady. It's rough only having one doctor in this place, but she copes rather well."

I watched as Anzide's eyes widened with horror.

"That's a great idea," he murmured, getting out of the seat. "We'll take him there now."

"Sure," Henry said. "We can pick this up when Brad's feeling better."

He slid over the seat, picking up everything except the quote.

"I'll leave this for you to go through. If you have any questions, just give me a call."

Anzide showed Henry to the door while I kept a firm grip on Brad.

"Get out of my way," he hissed under his breath.

"Absolutely not. Behave yourself."

Brad frowned. His hands were balled tightly on the table.

"You know what you've done? You've delayed the process of rebuilding the house. Instead of going through the quote today, we're waiting until you feel better."

My tone was terse as I air quoted *feel better*. He was not ill, and it was frustrating to have such a setback.

"Get yourself together." I snapped.

Getting out of the seat, I turned my back. Perhaps it was a mistake, maybe it was the best thing to ever happen.

In the three years that I've been with Brad, he's never gotten so angry at me that he acted out, which was saying something because, in the beginning, it was not a great time for us.

Feeling my arm pull back, I turned and looked at Brad as he got up from the seat. The ice-cold grip tightened around my wrist as he angrily looked at me. His brow furrowed deep, creasing hard. With the fangs bared, he snarled at me.

"Do not subject me to your vampire nonsense. Go feed Brad and do it so it doesn't come back to bite us on the backside."

Wind brushed over my face as he pushed me against the bathroom door. It was a blur, so fast that it shocked me. Pinned to the door, Brad exposed his fangs more.

"I could drain you," he whispered.

"And I could destroy you." I returned. "However, I choose to remember that you are my family, and I would not harm you like that. I would expect the same in return."

The caravan shifted as Anzide walked up the steps. Brad looked at the door. As Anzide appeared at the doorway, Brad chuckled mercilessly.

"Then perhaps I will destroy the one who is taking you from me."

"Why would you do that to me? Don't I suffer enough waiting for Niko to return? What about everything that Kannon did to me? All the things that are going on right now, and you think that taunting me with that threat is a good idea. That's a low thing to put out there."

Anzide disappeared, reappearing at my side.

"You're missing the obvious," he whispered.

The obvious.

For a moment, I turned from the view of flaming orange eyes that were shining with the same anger that was written all over his face. Anzide's calming features were reassuring but not helpful.

The corner of his lip turned up slightly as he faced Brad.

"We're in this together. I know that this is hard for you to deal with, and you're already struggling with all the other issues that seem to be plaguing you at the moment, but understand that I am not trying to take her from you. She will always be here."

It hit me. I really did miss the obvious.

I'd spent three years clinging to Brad because he was all I had left in this world. Within weeks of arriving in this town, I'd changed. I've grown more independent, and I've gained another person that meant everything to me. I'm sure Brad felt the same about Niko, but he wasn't around for long enough for Brad's emotions to fester into this.

Maybe the underlying vampire traits that were now surfacing were causing issues as well. Regardless, this had to be dealt with.

How? I hugged him.

With my arms wrapped tight around his waist, I rested my head against Brad's chest and held tight. Not just because I wanted to make sure he understood that he was still my world but because I feared the worst.

His body sagged as his arms wrapped around me. A soft sigh escaped, and Brad returned the love.

CHAPTER 47

Anzide frowned at me. I stopped pacing the floor and huffed.

"I can't just wait for it to happen."

"Of course, you can. Harlwood will not want you anywhere near him when he takes down the first vampire."

"I just want to go and look."

"No. Harlwood gave strict instructions for your nocturnal habits. You remain on the property at all times."

"He's right," Brad mumbled. "Vampires feed at night, Drakkus and his followers will be the most active, and they will be searching for you. Don't make that search easy."

Anzide pointed to the seat next to him with a frown still showing. Reluctantly, I sat down.

"There is much to gain for him. Harlwood will ensure that he lives up to his side of the deal,"

"Agreement," I interrupted.

"Yeah, whatever you want to tell yourself."

I looked at Anzide. He shrugged as if he almost agreed with Brad.

"What's the difference? You agreed on it, and you made a deal. It's the same thing, Evie. So long as we keep our side of the deal, there is no issue. I won't see Hannah. I'll totally ghost her."

"Which will be so easy to do in a small town."

Brad frowned at me. Right now, he looked normal. Fed, lucid, and a soft pink color.

"You know what you should do? Wait until I speak to Harlwood. I'll get him to confirm if it's her or not."

"So, she can still come here?"

"No," Anzide said firmly. "If she is the demon, then her presence will linger, and Harlwood will detect it and think that we've gone against the agreement. Keep her away from this property no matter what."

Sighing heavily, Brad turned the quote from Henry to me.

"I can do this, but it will be tight. We will have to live off your inheritance after I pay for this because it will almost wipe out everything I have."

"You don't have to," I murmured. "I'd rather you take it from my money."

"Look, you're not seeing this correctly. I know that

you want to pay for it because you think it was your fault,"

"It was my fault." I interrupted.

"Not entirely. You were unaware of your ability, which can be blamed on your father. Renuge was taking Anzide away, and Drakkus turned up. Those things putting pressure on you were too much, and it's only to be expected that it would erupt as it did. See? Loverboy agrees with me."

Anzide was frowning at Brad.

"I do agree. If you want me to continue supporting your statements, it would be wise to use my given name rather than the taunt that you offer."

"Sure, sure," Brad said as he rolled his eyes. "The point that I'm trying to make is that while you were the one that demolished the house, the entire blame cannot be pinned on you. As for the money, I'm assuming that as the vampire leader, you'll need to be financially fluid. My money is yours, just like yours is mine because we're in this nightmare together, but I think that at some point in the future, there's a line that needs to be drawn into the sand. It will show you as a great leader who is separate from everyone else, including me. You can't be this independent and strong leader if you're getting an allowance from your uncle, can you?"

Feeling rather low, I didn't know what to say. What he said made perfect sense. Drakkus would be loaded, I'm sure of it. We're only assuming, but it was likely that I had to have a bit stowed away as well.

"Look, at the moment, we're pooling our money to get this done. I'll build the house, and you'll pay the bills. When the house is back, and everything is peachy again, we'll revisit this. The remaining money will be split sixty-forty so that you've got a decent amount in the bank. How's that?"

"It's okay, I guess."

"Good. I'm hungry."

"I would advise against going into the forest. Perhaps if you took the car and went into town, it would be safer. Just avoid other vampires and come straight back."

"Can we go with him?"

"No." Anzide grumped.

Anzide looked between us, then let out a frustrated huff.

"I went out to search for Niko again and ended up going past the woman's house. She has a partner who had clearly reported her missing because Larry was there. They haven't found the body, but you can guarantee that Drakkus will know by now. All the vampires that he has control of will be on the lookout for a vampire, but they will already know who it is because of the proximity to this place."

"Will Larry turn up?"

Anzide shook his head.

"It is doubtful. Drakkus wants to show his power, and to let a human cop take down a member of the

Corbin family would be a missed opportunity. That's why you need to be careful out there. Listen to your instincts, and pay attention to your surroundings. Get your feed done, and don't waste time with unimportant things. You managed to harness the skills quite well when you fed on that woman, and I would imagine that nothing has changed."

Brad nodded and got up from the table. Once the jacket was on and the car keys were in his pocket, he was gone.

"Should we be worried that something will happen?"

"Vampires are a remarkable creature, even if they are classed as a newborn. They adapt quickly, which you saw when Brad fed on that woman. He was reluctant when we were here at the table, but that soon passed. Once he knew that it was within him, Brad let the vampire take control. I suspect that all of his humanity has faded. As for the shapeshifter, it is hard to say. There could be something left within him, but it is unlikely."

"Do I need to sleep with one eye open?"

Anzide chuckled.

"Did you need to when Niko lived in the house with you?"

"No, but Brad's a newborn. He's clearly struggling."

"That was because the humanity was dying, and the shapeshifter was fighting with the vampire. It was also because he didn't understand and was hungry. He will learn control, and he will not be hungry provided that he finds a worthy meal."

"And if he doesn't?"

"Then I will watch over him."

I distracted myself by tidying the van, putting things away into their temporary homes, and generally trying to avoid thinking about Brad being alone.

Anzide looked at the clock, giving me a grim smile. It had been an hour.

Brad wasn't here. We hadn't heard a peep out of him, and I was worried. There was a lot of danger out there, and he was a prime target for Drakkus and his followers.

"I can go out and search for him, but I can't guarantee that I will find him. As much as this is a small town, there are a lot of places to hide."

"Yeah, but we're in a really bad situation. Brad's taken too long, and if one of the other vampires has found him, he could be in danger."

With a nod and a heavy sigh, Anzide stood from the table.

"Do not leave this van unless it is on fire. Is that clear?"

"Sure."

Leaning down, Anzide kissed me. It was hard to resist him when he was being so caring. My hand smoothed over the bristly jaw, enjoying the moment of affection. Our time alone together was becoming increasingly less and less, which was annoying. The sooner the house was back to the way that it was, the better.

"I won't be long."

Anzide faded out of the caravan, leaving me alone. It was at that moment that all the bravado left me, and I suddenly wanted him to come back. Rushing to the door, I flicked the lock and silently prayed that if the horrid vampires of this town came calling, it would be enough of a deterrent.

All but the light over the main bed was off. I snuggled into the corner and played games on my phone. There wasn't much else to do. I'd finished my school work, I couldn't travel to the portal without Anzide, and there wasn't a single book in this caravan to read.

Hearing a thump on the door, I jumped with fright. Gritting my teeth together to ensure I remained silent, I carefully sat forward and looked at the thin metal that would not withstand a desperate vampire. Was Harlwood's spell enough to keep Drakkus and his underlings away?

"Evie?" Brad called out.

Sighing heavily, I put my phone down. Getting up from the bed, I walked to the door.

"What took you so long?"

Opening the door, I saw the hungry Brad, who was a menace.

"Brad, did you feed?"

He stepped up onto the first metal step, staring at me.

"No," he murmured.

Warily, I put some distance between us. It was not enough, and I hit the edge of the dining table.

"Why not? Where's Anzide?"

I got no answer, just a vampire that took another step closer. His eyes were turning orange, the skin was pale, and those horrid fangs were tapering thin. He was ready and willing to take whatever he could, and in this case, it was me.

"Don't do this," I whispered. "You need to control the hunger."

"I tried. They all run away. You're the only one that doesn't run off screaming."

"Okay," I said, trying to be reassuring. "You need a few more lessons. Maybe a little guidance from Niko."

Brad huffed like it was beneath him yet funny.

He swooped with such speed that I didn't see it until he had me pinned to the table. I struggled but was not winning the battle. Brad had more to gain from this. At least, I guess that's what he thought. I wanted to fight him off, but it wasn't easy. My life depended on it, yet he was winning. Maybe he was just stronger than me.

"Please," I begged. "You'll regret this when it's over."

The fangs were bared at me. A soft hissing noise echoed as he approached, ready to bite my neck. There was only one solution, and I didn't like it. Only one way out of a dire situation. I kneed him in the groin.

Brad groaned with a mighty wince on his face, buckling over and freeing me.

"Sorry," I called out, rushing to the door. "I really do want cousins someday. I'm sure you'll be fine."

Grabbing the keys, I pulled the door shut and locked it. He was temporarily trapped until he figured out how to unlock the door without the key. It wasn't easy, but it could be done. I hoped it would take him a while to figure it out, but Brad was a smart guy, and of course, he was hungry.

Looking around, I realized that there was no one that could help me. If I ran to the neighbors, I'd put them at risk. I could wait for Anzide to return, but that might take a while. And, of course, I could stay and duke it out with my uncle, hoping to remain unharmed while not doing too much damage to him.

The desperation was clearly taking over.

Brad thumped his body against the door. Angry words were spat out. I stepped back with no idea of what I could do to make this better, to stop the ravenous vampire.

I looked at the forest. It was not an ideal situation. In fact, it was the worst place for me to be right now. As I thought about vampire abilities, I looked around at the yard and then the forest. Brad was insanely fast in open areas, which meant that I stood no chance of outrunning him here. The vampires that taunted Niko, they moved through the forest in short, sharp bursts, which indicated that they couldn't maneuver around objects at fast speeds.

Was I better off in the forest?

The door swung open with a mighty clatter, and one angry vampire stood at the doorway, heaving as if he'd just run a marathon.

Brad began to stalk me, slowly moving closer. Even though I was backing away, he still managed to close the gap with larger strides.

In another blur of movement, Brad knocked me over, pushing me down to the grass. The fangs were out again, and this time, he was wise enough to put weight on my legs. My arms were held out wide, and I could not move.

Tears streamed freely. I looked up to the man who had been my world for the past three years, who had saved me from a life in foster homes, and who had given me so much freedom. For us to be like this, it was beyond wrong.

"Please don't destroy the trust that we've built."

Brad frowned, tilting his head back a fraction. It was like the request had registered in his mind, but he couldn't understand what I'd asked of him. It was enough though. The thoughts in his mind were distracting enough for him to shift his focus elsewhere, so I used them to my advantage.

Knocking him back, I scrambled to my feet. As Brad lifted from the ground, I punched him and ran.

CHAPTER 48

I didn't stop, but I definitely looked back. Not just because I was worried that Brad would come after me but because I was worried that I'd knocked him out. I don't know if that happened. He was on the other side of the caravan. Maybe he was giving up on me and would find another source of blood. I could only hope.

The problem was, I couldn't go back until he was gone. I watched and waited, living in the hope that Anzide would return and find a way to calm Brad down. There was no movement. Brad had not emerged from either side of the caravan.

It was possible that he'd walked to the street and was now on his way to somewhere else. I felt sorry for the victims of vampires but, as always, grateful that it wasn't me. An odd thought occurred to me as I watched the caravan. Brad's speed was incomprehensible. The day that he took down that woman, he had her on the ground and was feeding from her within seconds. She didn't get the chance to scream.

Yet, with me, he was somewhat slower. Was that hesitation? Did he know who I was when his mood altered like that? I hoped it was the case.

Feeling agitated, I walked a few steps to the side to see if I could see Brad. When I saw his shoes, I felt relieved and guilty all at once. Thankfully, he was sitting up, leaning against the caravan wall. At least he was okay and, of course, not stalking me. Was it safe enough to return? I highly doubt it.

Hearing a twig snap behind me, I gasped and turned around. I didn't want to say his name out loud, but I desperately wanted to know if it was Niko. Would he approach me if he saw me? I thought he would, but when no one came forward, I felt upset. He was angry at me. I'd destroyed his house and all those memories of his wife and daughter.

To make it worse, I couldn't feel the connection to him. It made me wonder if he'd severed it out of anger. That was fine. I deserved that. I didn't have any rights to this place or his legacy after what I'd done.

Birds squawked in the distance, taking off into the canopy. I gasped and turned to my left, where the sound had come from.

"Hello?" I said.

My voice was timid, even if I was trying to remain calm.

I couldn't feel my connection to Niko. I was stuck in the dangerous forest until Brad calmed down, and I was definitely not alone.

Was it better to face the hungry vampire or the unknown figure in the forest? It could be Drakkus or one of his followers.

Branches shifted to my right. Whoever it was, they were closing in, and they were surrounding me. I had to return to the property. At least I had Harlwood's protection. It wouldn't stop the ravenous vampire, but it would stop whoever was in the forest.

Turning, I thumped into something hard. In the darkness, I couldn't see who it was, but I knew that I was in serious trouble. They'd crept up behind me, and I hadn't heard a single thing.

I screamed, but the cool hand pressed to my mouth, muffling the sound. Coldness swept over me.

As the figure let go of me, I heard the gentle sounds of water lapping at the shoreline.

"Easy does it, Evie," Anzide said softly.

I gasped a soft cry, wrapping my arms around him. He'd dragged us into the portal.

"Why are you in the forest?"

"Brad was hungry and attacked me."

Anzide grumbled something. I leaned back and looked at him curiously.

"That explains why he saw me and took off. I guess he figured that I'd come looking for him once I found out."

"He needs help. Brad said that they all ran away screaming."

Anzide nodded, then crushed me into his body for another hug.

"Was it him in the forest?"

"No. I don't know who it was, but they didn't attack, so I'm led to believe the options are few in number."

Letting go of me, Anzide took my hand. We were taking a slow walk along the beach.

"Will he be okay?"

Anzide shrugged.

"Like I said, newborn vampires are remarkable. He will cope with what he has to do, but the problem is not what he is but who is out there, ready to take him down. I also monitored the other vampires when I was searching for him. They're all on the other side of town at the moment, so hopefully, that will be enough for him."

I nodded, grateful that he would be okay but still worried. He attacked me, but at the end of the day, he was still my uncle. He was still learning how to be a vampire, and we were stuck in this crazy situation where he had no role model, no guide, and no leader. Brad really needed Niko.

"I couldn't feel the connection to Niko."

Anzide pulled me closer, wrapping his arm around my shoulder.

"It can happen. If he's sleeping after a feed, it might be so deep that the connection goes down. It feels like it's disconnected, but it's not really."

"So, he wouldn't have disconnected it."

"Not possible."

Anzide pulled back to look at me, offering an uneasy smile.

"Did you think that he'd disconnected intentionally?"

I nodded, feeling the sadness all over again.

"You know, I did say that Niko would not be upset at what happened. He is the kind of vampire who has incredible understanding and can see the truth in many things. Even if you'd done it intentionally, there would be some form of forgiveness within him. I know you're feeling a lot of guilt, but you shouldn't."

I stopped walking. Anzide turned and looked at me.

"Something wrong?"

I twitched a smile as my eyes narrowed.

"You've spoken to him. When were you going to tell me?"

Anzide stared, then sighed.

"How did you know?"

"Because you speak as if you've had conversations with him. No one would know what Niko was like unless they met him. What you've just said, it proves it. Only someone who has spoken to Niko would know how wonderful he is. So come on, when were you going to tell me?"

"It is not safe to speak of him being alive. You know this. What if someone was on the outside of the caravan listening to us?"

"But it's true?"

Anzide nodded, pouting at me.

"Am I forgiven?"

"Only because you're doing everything you can to ensure he is a secret."

With a mighty grin, Anzide wrapped his arms around my waist and lifted me off the sand. I howled with laughter, shrieking a little too. When I stopped and looked down at Anzide, I leaned down and kissed him.

Sliding my arms around his neck, I kept him close while enjoying the passionate embrace. It was moments like this one that made life so much better.

Returning to the caravan was done with a lot of trepidation. I feared that Brad hadn't fed and was still desperate to sink his fangs into me. He wasn't the same person that he was a week ago, and that saddened me quite a lot.

Anzide said that Brad had taken off when he returned. It was possible that Brad was still out there. Maybe he'd found a poor, unsuspecting victim to murder.

It was midnight when we returned. The street was quiet, and there were no lights on in the neighbor's houses. It was strange to live in a town that shut down completely like Hades did. Even in the dullest towns Brad and I had ventured to, someone was always awake. But not Hades.

I thought that it was like Hades had a switch, and once it was flicked, everything was off. Although, I seriously doubt that the vampires remained inside at night. They seemed to do as they pleased, regardless of what anyone else might want.

As for Brad, he was near the door to the caravan, snoring. Anzide looked at me with a slight smirk. Flat on his back with arms flailed out, Brad was out of it. And he looked fed.

Anzide nudged Brad's leg with his boot, waiting for him to wake. With a snort, Brad woke up. It looked as if it had been a rough night.

"Your behavior tonight was appalling. I hope now that you've fed, you're aware of the situation that you put your niece in and how it could have easily become dangerous for her. To escape you, she fled into the forest, and there was someone out there. It was not a friend, and I think that my return was the only reason that she is still here."

Holding open the door, Anzide waited for Brad to pass through. They both gave me a grim look. Yep, things were not good.

I was about to enter the caravan when I stopped and looked at Brad as he slumped into the seat at the dining table. He was better than this. No matter what, he was always my protector, yet in this one instance, he'd changed.

Slowly, my gaze turned from the morose figure, who was likely to be internally chastising himself harshly, to the divine creature beside me. Anzide's head tipped slightly, waiting for the insightfulness to spring from me.

"The demon put a spell over him."

He said nothing for a moment, then nodded.

"Good call. That's," Anzide sighed as he leaned on the door frame. "Yeah, it's not impossible. In fact, I'd say that it is highly likely if Hannah is the demon on Drakkus's payroll."

With a flick of his head, Anzide urged me into the caravan. Things wouldn't be great, this conversation was going to be difficult, but it would be okay. We would learn from the events of today and take them onboard, learn from them, and create something better.

Anzide sat opposite Brad while I raided the cupboard for things to eat. I don't know why, but I felt hungry. I felt hungry after going into the portal last time but didn't think much of it because I hadn't eaten in a while anyway.

Remaining at the counter, I snacked on a small packet of biscuits. My orange juice poured, and the scent lingered and made me salivate for a taste. Ignoring the conversation, I tossed the packet of biscuits aside and drank until there was nothing left.

When I was done, I realized that I was being watched.

"Thirsty?"

"Just a little."

Anzide said nothing else in response, just watching me with a plain face.

"So, I think we can agree that you won't go near Hannah again, right?"

"Yeah."

Brad sounded defeated, but there was no anger to be seen. I think the actions of today have soured the mood.

"You can't help it when she's doing things like this," I offered.

That made Brad perk up and look at me. Previously, he'd favored the table with his sadness.

"How so?"

"If Hannah is affecting your mood, altering your hunger, of course, you won't have any control over it. How do we know that she's not putting spells over you?"

Brad shrugged.

"For all we know, she could be making it specific to me. You know, attack Evie and drink her blood."

"Yeah, I guess."

Sitting down next to Anzide, I shifted so that I was facing him.

"What's the range of a demon spell?"

"It can depend on things like wind, interference, and distraction. In a place like this, if she were in the forest and it was quiet like it is now, I'd say the fence line would be enough."

"Would the caravan make any difference?"

"It wouldn't work. She'd have to make direct contact. It means that she's either done it the last time they saw each other, or she's done it when he wasn't aware she was around. It's possible that she changed her form to avoid detection. This means that we can't trust anyone, and now, we're at risk of upsetting Harlwood. If he turns up, Brad cannot go near him until the spell residue has left. He stinks of demons."

I couldn't smell anything different about him, but to be fair, I hardly knew a thing about this world.

"Why can't we just go to Harlwood and tell him what's happening? If we say that we think she's done these things, but we're not certain, surely he could figure it out and tell us."

"If this was just a clear-cut case of being in the wrong place at the wrong time, probably. The issue is that he's entered her space enough to catch her attention. They're dating. It might have ended, but it happened. Am I right, Brad?"

The sheepish gaze lowered to the table as he murmured something.

"Damn, you're nasty," I crooned.

"Please, like you're any different, banging a Nephilim," Brad grumbled. "But in regards to Hannah, no, we haven't."

"Porked it?"

"Evie," Brad hissed.

He was blushing, which was a little amusing. I tried not to tease Brad too often, but sometimes, it was far too easy.

"Which is just as well. Being an immortal, you can't fraternize with an Eternal, and she would know that. Regardless, you still stink of her. She would have known that another demon was making a play for becoming Evie's soul feeder. Her aim would be to enrage the demon enough that he tells Evie to take a hike. Then she can stroll in and offer a little insight into her life, and if things turn bad with Drakkus, she's got another vampire family to move on to. Approaching Harlwood is your only option, but I don't know if it's going to turn out the way that you want it to."

CHAPTER 49

Because Brad could not go out in the sunlight at the moment, Anzide and I went to the grocery store with a long list. Getting in early, we went straight to the meat section and grabbed a lot of varied cuts. This was an alternative blood source that Anzide suggested that Brad used when getting close to feeding time. It wasn't the complete answer, and it wouldn't satisfy Brad at all, but it was enough to stave off hunger for a little while.

With the bottom of the cart loaded, we wandered through the aisles, picking off the things that Brad had suggested on the list and the things we wanted. There might have been too many biscuits.

Turning into the medical aisle, we stopped and stared. Kannon was here. His hand reached out, and he was in the process of taking a packet of condoms from the shelf. His gaze turned to us, and the eyes I'd once dreamily stared into widened.

"Uh, hey. They're not for me."

Of course not. They're for Audrey.

"Jess gets embarrassed."

"Sure," I offered with a sweet smile.

Kannon looked at the cart full of groceries, awkwardly shifting on his feet.

"So, I guess that you're not leaving town."

"We talked about it for a while," I offered. "But Brad's having a few issues at the moment. The shifter in him is making a play for dominance, so it's kind of obvious that there's something wrong."

"Right," he nodded, giving a sympathetic smile. "Not a good look. I guess you guys can't be traveling then."

"Yeah. So, if you could tell that meathead leader of yours to back off, I'd appreciate it a whole lot."

Kannon rolled his eyes.

"Evie," he chided.

I shrugged and pushed the cart around him.

"Just saying it as I see it. Later."

We continued through the aisle. I stopped at the toothpaste and quickly tapped out a message to Brad, just in case he got visitors. If I was going to be making things up, he needed to be on board with the lie.

He responded quickly, which was interesting because I thought he needed sleep. Brad said that he was feeling tired and told us to be quiet when we returned. When the next message followed, I understood why he was awake. Hannah had messaged him as well.

"Hannah wants to go on a date."

"He can't go."

"I'm sure Brad is aware of that. He's asking what to do."

Anzide sighed as he began to push the cart.

"It's hard to say. If he refuses, then she could turn up wanting to know what's going on. I'm assuming that at the beginning of all relationships, it's like ours?"

I looked up at him with a cheeky grin.

"Hot and heavy."

Anzide nodded with a knowing smile.

"So, she'd think something was wrong if he refused to go on a date, right?"

"Yep."

"And she'd turn up to make sure that everything was okay. Alternatively, he could agree to the date and go on it, risking Harlwood's wrath."

"Screwed either way."

Anzide said nothing as we turned into the next aisle. Thankfully, Kannon had fled the shop in haste, leaving us alone to do our shopping in peace.

"How about he agrees to go but then doesn't turn up?"

"She would wait, but then she'd wonder if everything

was okay. The least she would do is call, which I don't think she would do. The risk is far too great because I believe she will want to check on him. Especially if she's cast this spell."

I sighed heavily, wishing for an easy answer when there was nothing.

"What if he ends it completely? Calls her out on being a demon and says that she can't be coming around to the property anymore."

"And if she's not the demon?"

I groaned a frustrated growl.

"You're not making this any easier. Brad wants an answer."

"And we have nothing. The scenario with the least amount of damage is that he refuses to go on the date, and if she turns up, then we'll just have to send her away. I will have to watch Brad closely, but it's a much better solution. We still risk Harlwood finding out, and that will happen. That's a definite, but we can plead that there weren't a whole lot of choices available to us."

With that, I tapped out the message, adding that he should wait until we returned so that Anzide could be there to cut Hannah off at the driveway.

Brad didn't respond. I hoped that he was asleep but feared that he'd received visitors, or rather, one visitor.

Our return back to the caravan was quicker than it should have been. I think Anzide feared the outcome of any messages more than I did.

Warily, Anzide entered the caravan while I waited in the locked car. There was no chance of him getting in unless he had gained super strength that could rip through metal.

Seconds later, Anzide appeared at the door. He wasn't exactly over the moon with happiness, but he wasn't frowning either. I guess Brad was okay.

Opening the door, I got out as Anzide approached.

"Well?"

"Awake, tired, annoyed, hungry. He's going out to feed soon but has agreed to take me for protection. The dilemma is what to do with you."

"I'll go with you."

Anzide nodded and then moved to the back of the car. Unloading the groceries has never been a fun task, but I did it without complaint.

"It seems like the only logical solution, but I don't like it."

"There's not a lot of alternatives available to us. Unless you want to collect Brad's meal for him."

Anzide stopped, looking at me with intrigue.

"You're not seriously considering it, are you? I was joking."

"It would solve the problems I can see happening if you step over the fence line."

Lowering the lid, I sighed heavily.

"Last resort. I don't want victims brought to the property or dumped near it either."

"How about a victim brought to the area? Brad feeds, and I'll take the body away?"

"Not a whole lot better, but I guess there's not much choice."

Anzide nodded. We were in a difficult situation, and I knew that he wanted to keep me within the demon protection as much as possible. The sooner Drakkus was dead, the better.

Anzide was dumping the body when Harlwood turned up. I was not expecting him to arrive so soon after giving him the photos, more so when he said that it would take a few days.

I looked at Brad, who was much calmer now that he'd fed. He sighed and gave me an uneasy smile.

"We didn't know until it was too late. Remember that."

"Yeah. Let's hope that this goes well."

Harlwood smiled as he approached.

"I have news, good and bad."

"Us too."

He nodded, glancing around the makeshift campsite.

"Yes, I can sense the demon. It is unfortunate but not

surprising that they made a play for you. I'm just glad that I got in first."

"You're not mad?"

"Absolutely not. I knew the demon would attempt to become your soul feeder."

He paused, looking at Brad.

"Though I would not expect that."

Harlwood turned to me, his eyes searching for a few seconds before he offered a curious smile.

"And yet, you survive. Perhaps thanks to your Nephilim, hmm?"

"You know that Brad attacked me?"

"I sense there is a spell on Brad if that's what you mean. Yes, I am aware of what the demon has done to him. It is wearing off, if you're wondering. The more feeds he has that are not what the demon wants, the stronger his will against the demon grows."

He turned to face Brad with a stern frown.

"But understand that one forced feed will undo all your hard work. Maintain your strength and fight the spell. You have almost won the battle. Avoiding the demon would be a good idea, too."

Harlwood gave me a questioning look.

"Hannah. She works in the real estate office."

His eyebrows raised in acknowledgment.

"There are better choices for you, Brad. Especially now that the immortal creatures within have dominated over the mortal form. I'd push towards vampirism if it were me. After all, you are a Corbin, and it would help your cause if you had at least one vampire in the family."

Harlwood stopped and looked at the forest with a smile.

"Or more," he whispered. "Good times are ahead of you, my dear. Be patient."

I nodded, knowing exactly what he meant. Niko was growing stronger every day that we were apart.

"In the meantime, the good and the bad. The good news is that I have attended to the lower-rank vampires as you requested. They are, in every sense of the word, dead. It will be some hours before Drakkus realizes, which is just as well because it leads me to the bad part of why I am here."

"Drakkus is not dead."

"No, he is not. I am fully capable of undertaking the task, more so if his precious demon is occupied, which thank you for that. I am sure that your interactions with her enabled the process to move easily and quickly. As for Drakkus, my issue is that I don't think that I should kill him. Trust me when I say I'd dearly love to but correct me if I'm wrong, but isn't this a blood war?"

I sighed, nodding.

"Yes. I have to be the one that kills Drakkus. We're doomed."

Harlwood smiled, and out of all the ones he'd offered, I had to say it looked like the sincerest one I'd ever seen.

"You say that, but look at what you did to the house. Channel your powers correctly, and you could be a formidable foe. I can see with my own eyes how powerful you are. I hear tales of how you do not back down, even when your enemy appears stronger than you."

His eyes shifted to the forest, and I turned to see Anzide returning.

"Good afternoon, Anzide. We were just discussing a few things. I just mentioned that all four of the lower rank requests were attended to but not the leader because I was sure that this began with a blood war."

With pursed lips, Anzide nodded.

"And in light of the fact that I promised to attend to the leader's death on your behalf without remembering about that little piece of the equation, I came to alter the deal with you. In my inability to kill Drakkus, I am falling short on my side of the deal, which I dislike. You have already shown yourselves to be trustworthy by refusing the demon, so I believe it is imperative that I comply equally as fast. You may ask anything of me, and I will provide."

"Fix Niko." I blurted out.

Harlwood looked at me curiously, the smile stalling on his face as he glanced at Brad and Anzide.

"Are you sure about that? You wouldn't prefer that I

fix the house or help you with your lacking skills?"

I shook my head.

"We need him."

Thinking about it, Harlwood was quiet for a few seconds and then nodded.

"Yes, I can see your point. Brad struggles with the changes, you should learn your skills naturally, and of course, the element of surprise with the original leader of Hades would blow Drakkus out of the water. However, just so that you're fully aware, you are still the one who needs to kill Drakkus. You opened the door, and now you need to walk through it. To do that efficiently, I can see that you need more than just your skills."

Harlwood raised his arm and pulled back the sleeve of his jacket. His gaze lowered to his watch. I frowned, wondering what was going on.

"And that should do it."

With happiness showing on his face, Harlwood looked at me.

"I have completed my side of the agreement, and I hope you are pleased with my efforts, Evelyn. I strive for peace in this town, which we have not had in many years. If you will excuse me, I have a demon to find and watch."

I was a tad stunned as I watched Harlwood walk away. I should have asked what he was going on about, but Harlwood had a way about him that made me just a little lost.

With a frustrated huff, I turned and walked into the caravan. It was then that I realized that we were not alone anymore.

Niko smiled at me, holding open his arms. The few steps between us were a blur as I rushed to his welcoming embrace. Niko hugged me as I cried, apologizing for everything.

"Evelyn, my dear, do not apologize for the house. I understand it was an accident, and I'd much prefer my family was alive than an old house to remain standing."

Urging me out from his chest, Niko wiped away the tears.

"You have come so far without me. Why did you think that you needed me now?"

"I've always needed you. We're so lost."

Niko shook his head with a smile.

"My darling, you are not lost. You are exactly where you need to be."

CHAPTER 50

Niko stepped out of the tiny bathroom in a pair of Brad's long pants. As he pulled down the shirt, I saw the stab marks. They were purple and puckered, looking as if they still hurt. Niko gave me a smile.

"A warrior accepts all wounds as a badge of honor."

"Yeah, but they are pretty gruesome."

Niko merely smiled as he sat at the table in front of me. Brad and Anzide were outside, sorting through the rubble and continuing to clear away the mess.

"All of the vampires that inflicted those wounds are dead."

"Yes, I heard whispers about Andross. I would have loved to have seen that happen."

"He was the one that killed our family."

Niko sighed as he looked at the photo of Beatrice and Victoria.

"If I'd known their fate would have been no different, I would not have sent them away."

"But in doing so, you started a path that led to my mother, Brad, and me."

"Everything in this world happens for a reason," he offered. "Even death is sometimes necessary, unfortunately."

Tucking the photo back into the pile of things that had been salvaged, Niko clasped his hands and looked at me. Since his return, which has been a grand total of ten minutes, he's been subdued but in a good mood. He was still happy, but there was something else.

"Are you alright?"

"I am, thank you. It was an interesting feeling to be dragged through the forest by an unknown source while the sensations of repairs wriggled through my body. I am fully repaired, and interestingly, the demon ensured that I did not need to go out and feed tonight. I suspect that he believes that Drakkus will be on the warpath once he realizes what has happened. That was a mighty fine agreement that you made, Evelyn. Be proud of your partnership with James. He has a good heart, despite his nature."

"Thanks. I was a little nervous, but he was completely honest, and Anzide was there as well, so I guess that helped."

"Ah, yes. The Nephilim. That was an interesting turn of events."

Niko had a wicked smile on his face.

"Yeah. Who would have thought that would happen, right?"

"Anyone with eyes in their head and, perhaps, a little knowledge about biblical creatures. They are designed to love all creatures, which is strange considering how harshly they are treated when they act on those feelings."

I said nothing but could feel the heat rising in my cheeks. He was my great-grandfather, and the subject was thoroughly embarrassing.

Niko leaned his head on one hand, assessing me and my flaming cheeks.

"You're an Eternal, Evelyn. There are not many choices for you in this world."

"I know. If it weren't for Andross getting in first, Mom would have died because of one."

"Evelyn, I know that the subject of your father is a touchy one, but the powers that rule over your life will insist that you meet with him. He should be the one that trains you. I'm surprised that they're letting Anzide do it, to be honest."

"Yeah, the woman in the portal said I should know him. He knew what he was doing when he had sex with my mother. He knew that she would die. How can I forgive him for that?"

"I don't see how you could."

Feeling low, I looked out the door and saw Brad as he walked to the pile of wood. He was pushing a cart full of external panels.

It was almost dark outside. I figured they'd spend another hour out there before the mosquitos became too much for them. Then, it was going to get a little crowded in here.

"How am I going to defeat Drakkus?"

"By spending as much time learning from Anzide. Don't worry about the house. It can wait. I'm sure James will allow an extension of time for your education. After all, you're an Eternal. You can pick up anything and learn it much faster than the average human. Focus on the largest issue in your life and take each day as it comes."

Anzide appeared at the door.

"We have company."

"Good or bad?"

"I don't know. Brad said her name is Natalia."

"The woman from the Heritage Trust committee. She's the one that convinced the committee to take your house."

Niko thought about it and shrugged.

"It is not a name that I recall. If she's been a part of the process to keep this land in our name, then it is possible that she is an ally. Still, to be safe, I should hide."

That was a good call. There was no guarantee that her opinion was the same after all this time, and just because she'd petitioned to put the house into the trust's care, it didn't mean that she wanted Niko in power. Her reasons might be completely against Niko. Maybe she'd spent years searching the house while knowing exactly where Niko was.

When he was on the other side of the curtain, I gave Anzide a nod. Then, I began clearing away all of the unnecessary items that were on the table. Until we knew what her story was, I wasn't going to trust her with a single piece of information.

She appeared at the door, smiling at me.

"Hello, Evelyn."

"Uh, hi. Come in."

Brad and Anzide were behind her, neither giving me a single clue about what was going on.

"Take a seat. Sorry, we don't have much else at the moment."

"Yes, I heard, and it is unfortunate but understandable. It doesn't matter. Houses can be rebuilt."

Natalia paused for a moment, looking at me as if I was something rare. She was the rare one here, a vampire going against Drakkus.

"I suppose you're wondering why I'm here."

Yep, I think we're all wondering that.

Natalia was a pretty woman. The long brown hair was neatly pulled into a ponytail that draped over one side. She offered a smile, but I could see that there was a hint of sadness in her deep green eyes.

"I should have identified myself when you appeared at the meeting, but I wasn't sure who I could trust. This town has many who are on both sides of the fence and will happily jump it to ensure that they survive. You've seen it already, haven't you?"

Regretfully, I nodded.

"I'll start with my return to this town. When I arrived, Niko was missing, and Drakkus hadn't been able to get into the house."

"But he put Niko behind the wall, didn't he?"

"I think that he ordered someone else to do it, and they walked away, thinking their leader would be able to enter without issue. There were a few followers who were holding out with the hope that Niko would reappear which became a form of a blockade that stopped him. No one knew where Niko was which I found to be rather dubious. I recently learned that the vampires who put Niko behind the wall were murdered by Drakkus as a punishment for his inability to enter the house. Whispers state that the blockade was strong, ensuring he could not enter. I think that Drakkus, perhaps Andross as well, were the only ones who knew where Niko was. I only recently learned of the truth when it was too late. This time Niko truly was dead and,"

She paused, looking like she had so much regret. The tears welled in her eyes, ready to drip free. She cleared her throat, giving me a grim smile.

"I returned to Hades a few months after the incident and made casual inquiries. What I got were rumors that he'd fled the town in search of his wife and daughter, abandoning the coven. It was plausible and when I could, I ventured to the surrounding towns to search for him. Knowing that Niko would always want this land to remain the coven sanctuary, I formed a plan to ensure it remained that way. I applied for a position on the board and managed to convince them to take the house into their care. It stopped Drakkus because of one little ruling. Until Niko was declared dead and his line was no more, the house could not be sold or removed from the Corbin family. Drakkus has never truly trusted me or even liked me, for that matter. I stopped him from complete control, and the only reason that I survive is because I know how to hide."

Natalia smiled. It was dark, devious, and truly decadent. With the rich red lips pulled tight into the smile, I knew that she was more than what she seemed. A vampire? Perhaps, though, I doubted it.

"So, how do you hide?"

Natalia pressed her lips tight and then let out a soft sigh.

"Okay, but you can't tell anyone the truth. If Drakkus knows it, then he's going to figure out a lot of things."

"Sure. Secrets kept."

It was the strangest thing that I'd ever seen. Before me was a woman who went from being a pretty brunette with deep green eyes to a completely different brunette with those lovely emeralds shining brightly at me. Her face was slender now, her cheekbones a little more defined. The skin was paler, but the rest of Natalia remained the same. I'm sure a lot more changed, but I wasn't about to ask her to prove it.

"You're a shapeshifter posing as a vampire."

"I am, and I bet you're wondering why."

"Yeah, I have to say that I am intrigued."

Anzide was quiet as he leaned against the kitchen counter, but Brad was frowning with narrowed eyes. Natalia looked at him and tilted her head.

"Something wrong?"

"I know you from somewhere."

"Yes," she said with a growing smile. "You do. You might have been a toddler when you last saw me, but you were a bright child."

"Wait, you knew Brad when he was a kid? Did you know my mom as well?"

Natalia nodded, and I felt like I had been winded.

"I'll go back to the beginning so that you can understand things a little better rather than this beating around the bush. My name is not Natalia. It's Beatrice."

"Oh," I said dryly.

"Yes, oh. How did I survive Andross?" she shrugged. "It's a rather awful tale, one that I'm not proud of, but I didn't expect that he'd kill the poor woman. It began not long after my darling Niko sent me away with Victoria. We moved to a town that wasn't that far from here. I couldn't bear to be apart from him, but Niko insisted that Drakkus did not get his hands on Victoria. We remained in the town, hidden and waiting for the day that Niko came to get us. Victoria grew up, fell in love, and married Edward. He was a lovely fellow, so very understanding of our situation, and assured me that he would do everything in his power to protect Victoria and their children."

She wiped a tear away, her hand shaking as she tried to smile. It sucked that one psychotic vampire had destroyed a family like this.

"We parted ways for most of the time. It was a day not long after Bradley was born when I saw Andross. I told Victoria to take the children and run. To get as far away from the town as possible. Andross found the woman that I'd been posing as, assumed it was me, and killed her. I've never been proud of the fact that the woman had to die so that I could live, but if it meant that I could keep this property in our family, then it had to happen. When Andross was gone, and the authorities collected the body, I insisted that they did an autopsy. Then, before they left town, I met up with Victoria one last time. I told her that I was returning to Hades so that I could turn the attention away from her. It was the only way that I could ensure that they'd have a normal life. I gave all the warnings that I could to Victoria and Nancy. I guess you were too young to understand what I was saying."

Natalia smiled as she shrugged.

"So, that's it. That's my secret. I'm your great-grandmother."

Well then, do I have a doozy of a secret to tell you. It's going to knock your socks off.

"When I saw you at the meeting, I knew instantly. I looked at you, and I saw myself."

I guess that was true. Niko did say that I looked like her, though he never specified who *her* was.

"Okay, so we've got a lot of things to get through here, but I've got to know, why now? Why didn't you come here after the meeting?"

"I didn't think that you'd believe me. You were faced with so many liars and vampires trying to pull you in all directions. I didn't want to add to that stress. I should have, though. I should have come here and told you everything that you needed to know about me and the past. I'm sorry, Evelyn. It was wrong to hide from you. I guess the fears of the past will always be strong."

"Well, I killed Andross, so you don't need to worry about him. Will you excuse me for a moment?"

She nodded as I got up from the table. I moved to the curtain, slipping into the small section between the material and the bed. Niko looked up at me, lost and sad.

I sat down, taking his hands into mine.

"She looks like me," I whispered. "So, I guess it's true, right?"

He gave me a vague shrug.

"How will you know if she's truly Beatrice?"

His mouth opened, but nothing came out. I stood, taking his hands with me. Hopefully, I could be the reassurance that he needed.

Moving through the curtain, I wanted to ask one last question before the big reveal.

"How do we know that you're not working for Drakkus?"

"It is a tough question that I will never be able to answer you and expect you to believe me. I am a woman of her word. I have never agreed with anything that Drakkus has done or what he wants. I am not working for Drakkus and never will. As I said, I am not his favorite person because of my actions. It's why Natalia Eastwell has never been pursued to be a part of his coven. Of course, he's frequently tried to kill me, but I outwit him. It's not that hard, to be honest. He's not the brightest spark around."

I felt a poke in my back.

"Okay, that's good. I ask because of the obvious and because of something that may not be obvious."

Brad and Anzide smiled. I couldn't help but join them. For this woman who supposedly was my great-grandmother, it was confusing. She frowned, watching as I pulled back the curtain.

I could feel Niko standing behind me, the shadow that was my lifeline.

Beatrice stared, the frown falling away in an instant, replaced with sadness.

"Niko?" she whispered as the tears began to fall.

I stepped aside for Niko, leaning against the bathroom door as they hugged. It wasn't my parents, it wasn't even my grandparents, but this was something equally as good. Piece by piece, we were getting there. When I saw the teary reunion, I felt the pain in my heart. I had to fix the issues. I had to bring this family back together again.

CHAPTER 51

The caravan tilted as the dancing duo moved out of the way, continuing their little love fest at the other end. I smiled, leaning on the kitchen counter. Watching Niko and Beatrice return to the way that they were was a beautiful thing to be a witness to.

It was nine am, and we'd been up for several hours clearing the debris. We'd taken a break for a few minutes to have something to eat and drink. The day was starting to warm up, but it was agreed that Anzide and I would return to the mess. Brad would sit under the marquee and go through each of the planks of wood, pulling out the nails. I don't know what his plan was, but the wood and the bricks were all sorted into piles.

I looked at Niko and Beatrice and wondered if Brad was planning for a different kind of life. The kind that needed a much larger house. If he found someone, they'd have kids. At some point in the future, Anzide and I would probably take that path, too. There was even a strong chance that Niko and Beatrice might have more. We would be in a house that, while big, was in reality, too small for us as a group.

Beatrice shrieked with a giggle when Niko turned her under his arm. It started to turn a little naughty when she curled back into his arms. I turned away, not wanting to see my great-grandparents kiss. Brad merely rolled his eyes.

"Missing out, eh buddy? Need to get yourself a little vampire action?"

"Not right now, thanks. Aside from the fact that the caravan is not big enough for the five that we clearly have now that good old grandma is back, we have a looming war, and we don't know who is friend or foe."

I had to say, he was right. We'd been stuck in this situation for just a few days, and it wasn't getting any easier. The only reprieve that we had from each other was when we did things outside of the caravan. Brad and Niko would go out to feed, and Anzide and I would go grocery shopping.

"Evie?"

Everyone paused at the sound of someone who could cause a lot of problems. I looked at Niko, the one person in this infernal tin can that had to be kept a secret. He should be dead and I wasn't prepared to tell the world differently just yet.

Stepping out of the caravan with my permanent security guard not far behind, I walked around the side to see Kannon standing at the fence line.

He gave me a vague smile that died just a little when

he saw Anzide.

"Kannon," I said tersely. "Why are you here?"

He shrugged uneasily.

"You look a little stressed. Is something wrong, something you need to tell me?"

"I'm sorry for everything. You know it was not my idea, and I hate that it came between us."

Well, that's not entirely true. I wasn't going to tell Kannon that I'd seen him and my other nemesis, Jess Hartley, screwing against my locker at school. Their lust filled words before the defiling were enough to open my eyes to the truth. I was just grateful that I had Anzide's help to hide from their sight. Otherwise, I would have never known.

"I want you to win. You have no idea what it's like being under his thumb. I want out, I want to walk away, but I can't."

Aww, no turning your girlfriend into a vampire and becoming the second in charge of Drakkus's coven? Such a pity.

With another shrug, Kannon's gaze lowered.

"I just thought I'd say that."

"Okay, well, thanks for that. I guess."

When Kannon wasn't looking, I turned to Anzide, and after giving him a subtle smirk, I flicked my head. He frowned but accepted my silent request to put some grass between us. If I was going to get anything out of Kannon, it would be done without Anzide around.

He began walking along the rear of the caravan, pretending to inspect it while still remaining close to me. It was enough, and Kannon watched for a few seconds before looking at me with hope. I wasn't fooled but pretended to be the same old Evie who didn't know that she stood in front of a liar.

"I want to be friends again. I'm sorry that I got angry about the whole Phoenix thing. It's just that Drakkus said that you should have known and were intentionally trying to hurt me. All of his core group started on me, saying that you were trying to kill me. It was Jess who pointed out that you clearly had no idea."

So, he has a core group and still demands that the eighteen year old becomes his second in charge? That did not make any sense. I think that I needed to pay a visit to the local demon headmaster. Clearly, something had happened, and it made me wonder if he'd removed Hannah, the other demon.

"Well, I'm glad that Jess was using her brains. I'm pretty sure that you could have easily figured out how clueless Brad and I were, considering how much information you offered."

Kannon clearly had a mission here. He said he wanted to be friends again, which I guess he figured entitled him to gain access to the property. With the two newest additions to the contents of the caravan, it wasn't happening. I had to keep Kannon on a leash but not close enough that he thought it was alright to climb over the fence.

A thought entered my mind, and it fitted with my other idea to go and see Harlwood.

"I was thinking about returning to school."

I could see Anzide turn his head and look at me. I wasn't looking at him directly, but I figured he was frowning at me, too.

"But it just seems so hard, you know?"

Kannon nodded, giving me a soft smile. Yeah, I caught you on my web, little boy.

"I can deal with Audrey easily enough, but if Drakkus is causing problems, then Brad's not going to let me go anywhere near the place. What do you reckon my chances are? Can I get a year from him?"

"I, uh, I don't know."

"Well, look at it this way. I can leave today, but I'd have to start at another school, and I don't think that's fair. He started this nonsense. I was minding my own business."

"Yeah. I'll say something if you like."

"I'd appreciate that."

He began to turn away, stopping before he got too far.

"I'm sorry about Niko too. That was wrong what they did to him."

"Actually," Anzide offered as he moved in behind me. "I think you will find that it was illegal. Your leader had the audacity to accuse Evelyn of murdering a vampire, yet he does the same thing. He was a murderer long before Evelyn was even born."

"Yeah, I know."

Anzide stepped forward, giving Kannon a dark smile.

"There is something that you should know about us eternal creatures. We are permitted to take a life if it is necessary to sustain the lives of others around us. No repercussions, so his accusations against Evelyn are completely false. She could have taken Drakkus out without a single problem from the Nephilim, just like how nothing happened after Andross's death. You could have had it all but you picked the wrong team. So, run away, little boy. Run back to your master and tell him what you've seen like the good little lap dog that you are."

When he turned, Anzide winked at me. The grin was merciless, but I knew he'd said it all on purpose. It was not an angry outburst. Every little part of it was intentional.

Returning to his slow walk next to the caravan, Anzide pretended that he was calming down. I could feel the anxiety radiate but not from Anzide. Turning back to Kannon, I found the source.

"You know that it's illegal for a vampire to kill another. If the vampires from Europe turn up and find out what he's done, they're going to take down the entire clan. So, I guess you really did pick the wrong person."

With a shrug, I smiled and began to walk backward. Kannon gave me a pleading look.

"What do you want from me?" he whispered sadly. "I had no choice. I had to follow what my parents said was the right thing to do."

Oh, if only that were the truth.

"I don't know what you should do. If you go against Drakkus, you could end up dead."

"I could be your spy."

But how could I trust you?

"Sure. Pave your way back to me with information. It's a good move, Kannon. If you're careful, Drakkus will never know."

A soft smile filled his face as Kannon stepped back into the long grass. He nodded his acceptance and began to walk away. I watched until Anzide returned to my side.

"Information?" he murmured.

"I'm sure it will be the complete opposite of the truth, but it will be interesting to see what Drakkus wants to be fed to me. In the meantime, I want to visit the local demon to get some other kind of information."

No one thought that it was a good idea to go wandering around so soon after Harlwood had removed the vampires, but they accepted that I did things that were necessary in my mind. It was always ticking over with thoughts about this blood war and how to win it. How to save my family.

Jane looked at me with an uneasy smile as I walked to the door. It opened as if there was a demon behind it. Harlwood smiled, gesturing to the darkness of the corridor to his office.

"To what do I owe the pleasure of this visit?"

"I have some questions and thoughts."

"Then proceed," Harlwood said as he sat down.

Anzide sat on the chair next to me, unimpressed that I was here. Brad wasn't happy either, but at least they agreed that getting the questions answered was a good idea.

"Have you done something to Hannah?"

The demon smiled as he tilted back in his chair. His hands were clasped over the front of his chest.

"Perhaps. Why the concern?"

"Kannon turned up at the property. It was a little unexpected, and it made me wonder if their precious demon was no longer able to interfere."

"You would be correct in that theory. Hannah is no longer a resident of Hades, and I have gone to great lengths to ensure that her sudden departure was expected but hidden from Drakkus to avoid his wrath. I would appreciate it if you could avoid making too many waves regarding her absence."

"Sure. Have you managed to get into his house?"

"Not as yet, but I ensured that Hannah dropped all

protections before she left. You could go for a wander if you desired, though I wouldn't recommend it. I'm sure your uncle would have a fit if he knew, among others," he smirked, tipping his head at Anzide.

"Yeah. I was also going to ask about returning to school."

"You can return any time you like. Drakkus is your only issue, so once he's gone, you're free of the problems. As an Eternal, your learning can be fast-tracked to bring you up to the rest of the year level. So, you could take a couple of weeks to deal with the vampire and then come back when you're ready."

Harlwood narrowed his eyes as his tented index fingers pressed against his lips. It wasn't easy to have a demon assessing me like this.

"You know, I find myself eager to be free of the pestilence. I can't kill him for you, we've established that, but perhaps there is another way to assist you."

"I don't have anything to offer you now. You're the soul feeder for this town."

"I know."

Standing, he walked to the window. From where I sat, I could see the extension and the pretty garden. It made me realize that Harlwood probably saw us the other day when Anzide pulled me through the wall.

"How would you feel if the town grew a little more?"

"I don't know. Do you mean like more human residents?"

"Yes. I haven't cast a lure in a long time."

He turned, his hands clasped behind his back.

"Never saw the point. Not when my feeds were being taken from me. I am hungry, Evelyn. I've waited a long time to have this town back in my arms. I've also watched as it progressed under Niko, then stalled when Drakkus took over. I'm sure it will change in the coming days after his passing but I'd like to give it a little shove. You can think about it and discuss it with your family, but I'd like to modernize Hades. Just a little though. No one wants too many cops to bribe, am I right?"

I chuckled, shaking my head. No, definitely not. Buying Larry's indifference to the vampire's antics was going to be difficult, especially when Drakkus had been so benevolent to him.

"I will stop by tomorrow. There is someone I'd like to say hello to, and I'm sure he's recovered enough for a chat."

As I stood, I nodded.

"I'll let him know."

CHAPTER 52

Anzide opened the door, waiting until I passed. He didn't say anything until we were in the car. Yet again, I was driving without a license. I was much better at it now. It didn't freak me out, and I drove with a lot of confidence.

"So, your thoughts?"

"It's odd. Harlwood's offering to do something that is common for demons. They're always throwing lures out. Modernizing, though, eh," he shrugged. "It has its pros and cons. Come on, let's get going before Drakkus gets out of his seat."

I started the engine and turned to face Anzide.

"I have a question for you."

"Sounds dubious, but go ahead."

"If I drive past Drakkus, will you give him a pressed ham for me?"

"I dread to ask, but what is a pressed ham?"

"Your bare backside pressed against the window."

Anzide smirked, shaking his head.

"No, you nuisance. Get the car moving in the right direction."

"Party pooper."

I drove through the streets, avoiding the cafe where Drakkus was sitting. How he knew that I'd be here was curious, but I suppose that it could be a coincidence. Harlwood did say that he was sick of the vampires in Drakkus's coven preying on the students.

There was one stop that we had to make before returning home. Niko suggested something more than the flimsy efforts Brad had put up to cover himself from the sun. A heavy gust of wind could expose him, and Niko warned that for Brad, it could cause problems. So, we were at the hardware store, searching for a tent or something similar.

There were no tents. It seemed as if the rain riddled town of Hades dampened the minds of the residents to the point where they never wanted to spend time outside. Anzide found a tarpaulin and metal poles. All we needed were a few pegs and some rope. We found the pegs, but our search for the rope stopped abruptly when we saw Eddios and an unknown man.

They were looking at the ropes. Eddios had a basket that had tape in it, as well as other things beneath the rolls that I couldn't make out.

"Stay here," Anzide said softly.

He faded from sight as he moved towards the aisle. Seconds later, Eddios appeared. I couldn't hide. It was too late.

Anzide was a step behind him as Eddios walked closer. There was a lifeless, almost robotic state to the vampire.

"Hello, Evelyn," he said in a dull tone, staring ahead.

He kept walking. Curious, I followed and watched him walk out of the store. Anzide turned back, waggling the rope at me.

"I found rope."

"Cool. What was the deal with Eddios?"

"Oh, that. I entered his mind, which is something that, technically, we're not supposed to do, but after seeing the contents of his basket, I deemed it worthy. Turns out, he was planning on abducting someone. Any thoughts on who the lucky person might have been?"

"Me."

"Yep. Planned on walking into the property when Brad was feeding because, in his mind, he believed that I'd go with him to make sure he was feeding correctly."

"And now?"

"Now he's seen what can happen if he tries anything that stupid. I can give extremely vivid visions to a weak mind, and Eddios was a perfect candidate."

"Do you think that this was an order from Drakkus?"

"No, this was an attempt to buy favor from his leader. Drakkus knows that if he is to legally rule, he has to win the battle. If he found out what Eddios was planning, he'd be angry. So, I don't know, either keep it to yourself or shout it at him as you drive past him at the cafe."

"With the pressed ham, right?"

Anzide chuckled, wrapping his arm around me.

"You just want me to take my pants off."

"Guilty as charged."

Once the items were paid for, we walked out of the shop. Anzide dumped the items into the trunk while I ordered two milkshakes for us to have on the way home.

We reached the car, and before I got in, I saw Jess emerge from a shop on the other side of the road. She stopped and stared. Almost like she knew where Eddios was and what he was getting from the shop.

I said nothing, sucking on the shake as I looked at her. She scuttled away, not acknowledging me, which was fine. I didn't need her to say hello, but I wanted her to know she was on thin ice.

Sliding into the seat, I put my drink aside and sighed heavily. Being a leader was not fun.

"It's going to get better, right?"

"One would hope so, but I doubt it."

We were almost home when I saw the flash of lights in the rear vision mirror and the chirp of the police siren.

"Well, isn't this just a pain in the proverbial backside?" Anzide muttered. "Want me to deal with him?"

"Only if it starts to get out of hand."

"Would that be before or after you're handcuffed and in the backseat of his car?"

"Oh, you'd like to see me in handcuffs, wouldn't you?"

Anzide smirked, saying nothing as he looked out the window.

I turned the engine off and rolled down the window. Then I watched Larry approach.

"What did Harlwood call him?"

"An overfed moron."

Larry leaned down, narrowing his eyes at me.

"Evelyn Newton?"

"Yes,"

"A little bird told me you're driving around this town without a license."

"Mosquito." I interrupted.

Larry frowned at me.

"The birds are not the ones whispering to you, Larry. They're blood-sucking mosquitos, and I'm one of those bug zappers that will take great pleasure in removing all of the nasty mosquitos."

Confusion hit him before he snapped out of it.

"Do you have a license?"

"Nope."

"I'm going to have to ask you to step out of the vehicle, Miss Newton."

"Come on, Larry. You know what the score is here. I'm the leader of Hades, not Drakkus. Pick your side carefully because you don't want to be on the wrong side when the blood war begins. Even something as simple as arresting a leader when you could have just looked the other way will be remembered."

Sweat trickled past his temple, and Larry gulped hard.

"If you want to save face with the faux leader, then perhaps you could say that I produced a license. If he suggests it was fake, then you could always respond that it was a brilliant forgery because it looked so realistic to you. What do you say, Larry? Are you prepared to look the other way?"

"You'll offer a deal?"

"Of course. What do you want?"

"Protection of my family."

"That's it?"

He nodded.

"They're never a target, never followed, never attacked. Every single generation from now until the end of time."

Huh. I guess it was a little more than a simple request.

"Sounds reasonable, but as the years pass, your family will need to be presented to us so that we know who they are. This place will grow, and in time, you and your family will be just another face in the crowd. Define yourselves to survive."

He nodded and lifted upright to walk away.

"And Larry?"

"Yeah?"

"You've been handing out parking fines to ladies that knit beanies for premature babies. Stop that immediately."

"Uh, yeah. Okay."

I watched as he returned to his vehicle and then left.

"God, would you look at that nonsense."

Under a tree was a familiar sight that watched us. Even from this distance, I could tell that Drakkus was not impressed.

"You're good for the ham, right?"

"I am not baring my backside to anyone."

"Fine. Can you hold the wheel while I do it, then?"

Anzide chuckled.

"The way that your mind works is just incredible."

"Yeah," I hummed. "Stay put."

Taking my drink, I pulled out the straw and lid, dumping it into the trash as I passed it. Drakkus looked a little stunned as I approached, glancing around as if he thought something crazy was going on.

"You're never going to win, but nice try."

Pulling out the front of his pants, I upended my milkshake while smiling at him. His nose twitched with anger.

"Little girl," he growled.

I pouted.

"Are you going to tell me that I'm in for a world of pain?"

Stepping back, I fluttered my lashes at him.

"I'm already there. You took Niko from me. You took my family from me. Do you remember what I said to you when you killed Niko?"

Drakkus said nothing.

"Hades is Corbin territory, and I am the leader, as placed by the true leader of this town. You've officially been placed on notice. Each and every one of you have got until sunset tomorrow to leave this town. Otherwise, I'm coming for all of you."

Taking another step back, I smiled as sweetly as I could.

"It still stands. I have the list in my head. I've wiped all but one from it. Be ready for me because I will keep my word."

Turning, I walked away, stopping briefly to dump the cup into the trash.

Anzide was quiet as I got in the car and started it. Drakkus stood silently in his death stare, with sodden pants and milk all over the sidewalk around him.

I could feel my heart racing. The world seemed disconnected as I turned through the streets.

"Evie," Anzide said in a panicked tone. "Pull over."

We'd reached a quieter section of town. Forest lined one side of the road, empty industrial buildings on the other. The car skidded in the gravel. I opened the door, feeling the hot rush slide over me. The sound of Anzide calling out to me was a distant noise as I ran.

I was in the forest, decorating the vegetation with the contents of my stomach.

"Adrenaline," Anzide said as he offered a bottle of water.

"Thanks."

I took a swig, rinsed my mouth, and spat it out.

"Was I mad to do that?"

"Absolutely, but honestly, it was the best thing I've ever seen. The look on his face was complete shock."

Pulling me in for a hug, Anzide and I stood at the

edge of the forest for a few minutes. All I needed was for my mood to settle.

I thought about my life and what I'd said to Drakkus about how he'd taken my family from me. It was the truth but not entirely correct. I had Niko back, and now Beatrice was with us. Brad was coping, and I guess he welcomed the extra company. We'd figure out what to do about the house, maybe even make some improvements now that there were more of us. We were an odd little puzzle, but that was fine. To finish, to put the final pieces into our life, to keep my family safe, I had to do one more thing.

I had to kill Drakkus.

The Trouble with Hades

2

TM WATKINS

With the end of the blood war looming, Evie struggles to cope, knowing that she is untrained and not ready to take on a dangerous vampire. All the while, the secrets of her world continue to accumulate.

Her powers are growing, and she must be taught how to control them. Evie must face the one person she vowed she would never meet—her father.

If meeting her father wasn't bad enough, the powers that rule the portal will be. They're determined to make her fall, strip Evie of her powers, and banish her to the land of the outcasts.

Few are standing in Evie's corner. With help from Hades' resident demon, Evie's coven grows to those who will stand beside her in the war and those who will protect her. All she has to do is get everything right.

Can Evie win the blood war against a powerful vampire and keep the Corbin coven in her family?

FROM THE AUTHOR

Thank you for reading. I hope you enjoyed the book as much as I loved writing it. If you would like to read more, please check out my other books.

Please also consider signing up to my newsletter to be up to date with all future releases.

www.tmwatkinsauthor.com

ABOUT THE AUTHOR

TM Watkins lives in Brisbane, Australia with her family. She spends her days contemplating the next adventure for her characters and her nights writing about them. Her life as an author began on Wattpad and Radish Fiction under the pen name xMishx.

To join the mailing list, please sign up at

www.tmwatkinsauthor.com

www.ingramcontent.com/pod-product-compliance
Lightning Source LLC
La Vergne TN
LVHW050909080826
845145LV00001B/32

* 9 7 8 1 7 6 3 7 1 9 5 3 8 *